MW01126222

UNINTENDED WITNESS

A Novel

BOOK TWO OF THE UNINTENDED SERIES

D.L. Wood

CleanCaptivatingFiction™

UNINTENDED WITNESS
Book Two of the Unintended Series

Unintended Witness is a work of fiction. Names, characters, places and incidents either are the product of the author's imagination or are used fictitiously. Any resemblance to actual persons, living or dead, events or locales is entirely coincidental and beyond the intent of either the author or publisher.

ISBN-13: 978-1-7238-4904-6
Printed by Kindle Direct Publishing, U.S.A.

Published by Silverglass Press
First Edition

D.L. Wood
www.dlwoodonline.com
Huntsville, Alabama

Dedicated to the one who saved me.

ACKNOWLEDGMENTS

These books would not happen without the enthusiastic help of my editorial readers: Barbara and Shaw Gookin, Kimberly Pugh, Judy Wallis, Laura Stratton, Sarah Nuss, Alesia Smith, and Jan McClelland.

Thank you to my mom and dad, Lynn and Bob Plummer, for fact-checking local matters for me and for your advice on the legal aspects of the book. I have been out of the practice of law far too long to be accurate on my own.

Thank you to Chris Olson for his advice about the recording studio.

Thank you to my editor, Chelsea Hahn, for being so excellent and for seeing what no else sees.

Many, many thanks to my friend, Luana Ehrlich, author of the Titus Ray Thrillers, who has been so kind to hold my hand and guide me through this journey of being an author.

And finally, thank you to my husband, Ron, for always being so supportive of me in this writing endeavor and everything else.

ONE

When all else fails, use a bomb, he thought, as thumb and forefinger twisted white and red wires together and pressed them into the small package before him. A slight autumn wind chilled the beads of sweat not caught by the black toboggan pulled low on his forehead. Being seen was a definite worry. As dark as it was at eleven o'clock at night, the nearby lights of Main Street offered just enough illumination to make movement on the construction site detectable if someone happened to look at the right moment, especially with him exposed on the skeletally-framed third story. He was moving as fast as he could, but time was quickly running out and it was making him nervous. He had allotted fifteen minutes for setting the device. Twenty had passed already. Not to mention the five minutes that he already wasted waiting out an unexpected patrol car that had swung by the Starbucks across the street for a quick pick-me-up.

A steady drizzle fell as he continued working, ignoring the ticking clock in his head. Finally, after just a few more adjustments, he made one last twist and it was done. Three strips of silver duct tape secured the device low behind some temporary wooden scaffolding where it wouldn't be seen. Until tomorrow night, when everyone would see it.

Everyone.

TWO

The weak, late afternoon October light filtered through the windows of Chloe McConnaughey's white Honda Civic as it crested another green hill in the heart of the Tennessee Valley. Her heart beat faster with every passing mile as the moment she had been waiting twenty-five years for drew steadily closer.

She was eight years old the last time she saw him. Exactly eight, actually, as it had been her birthday and she was falling asleep with dreams of the day's birthday cake and presents and, unbelievably, a pony ride. It had been the best birthday she and her twin brother, Tate, had ever had. The last good one they would ever have.

He had snuck out in the darkness, sometime after kissing them goodnight and weepily declaring how much he loved them both. She remembered the stout smell of Woodford Reserve that had punctuated his words. At the time, she chalked up his tears to what their mother had called "overindulgence." She had hugged him, kissed his cheek, and rolled over, snuggling the new stuffed unicorn he had bought her as she drifted into la-la land. The delusion hadn't lasted long.

The next morning she padded into the kitchen looking for pancakes, but instead found a whimpering, gin-soaked mother, clutching the remnants of a scrawled letter explaining how her father had run off with a lady that worked in the copy room of his law office. And that was the end. The end of birthdays and of pony rides. The end of pancakes. And eventually, the end of their mother. Tate, too, as it turned out. Though that would take much longer and be infinitely more painful.

Another white fence scrolled by as she rolled closer to Franklin, Tennessee, the quaint town just south of Nashville where her father, Reese McConnaughey, now lived. The unreality of this, of her going to meet him, pummeled her again, and not for the first time, she considered turning the car around. *No*, she thought. *You've decided. Be decided.*

As if on cue, a ringing sounded through the car speakers. Grinning at the caller identification, Chloe pressed a button on her steering wheel.

"Hey you," she said, the weight in her chest lightening.

"Hey beautiful," Jack Bartholomew replied, and she immediately pictured him, mobile phone to his ear, his smile drawn up towards spirited green eyes and a bone structure that reminded her of the guy that played Captain America in the Marvel movies. "You there yet?"

"Nearly." Her eyes flicked to the navigation screen. "Just a mile and a half till I get to his neighborhood."

"How are you doing?" he asked.

"About how you'd expect. Nervous. Apprehensive—"

"Excited?"

She hesitated. "Truthfully? I don't know."

"I'm proud of you."

"Don't be. I haven't done anything yet. I might take his head off once I get there," she groaned.

"You'll do the right thing."

"So how's the shoot?"

"Great. I'd forgotten how much fun this is." Years ago, Jack had leveraged his experience as a Navy SEAL and best-selling author of the true-life military thriller, *Battlezone Zero,* into occasional consulting work for Hollywood—work that often pulled him away from his not-so-star-studded day job as an English professor at Emory. This time he was scheduled to be in Los Angeles for the next three weeks on the set of a movie about a futuristic World War III. It sounded more glamorous than it was, or at least that's what Jack kept telling her. *Easy for him to say,* she thought, as he continued, "Oh, and I met Jude Law today."

"You need to shut up now."

He laughed, and the warmth and wholeness of it enveloped her. It felt like home. "Thought you'd like that."

"How's the leg?"

She heard a discouraged intake of breath on his end. "A six," he answered, "but there was a lot of walking today." Nearly eight months ago he had taken a bullet in that leg while protecting her from killers hunting her because of events her brother, Tate, had set in motion. Jack still hadn't completely recovered and by the end of most days he was limping. They had come up with a short code of one to ten to describe his pain level. Lately it had been hovering around four or five.

"Use the cane, Jack. That's what it's for."

"Yeah, yeah, that's what the doctors keep telling me. I'm fine. I'll double up on the ibuprofen tonight."

"Don't overdo—"

"Not overdoing. Just doing." It was his go-to comment when it came to his leg and a sure sign that he wanted to drop the topic.

"Okay," Chloe replied, taking the cue just as the navigation system announced her turn was in another half mile. "I'm almost at the turn, Jack. I'm going to have to go. Can I call you after?"

"'Course. You'd better. I love you."

She grinned. "I love you, too. Bye."

The second he hung up it was as if a little of the air had been sucked out of the car. They had only been apart two days, but she already missed him. It was strange for her to realize how attached she had become in such a relatively short time. He was her person. As someone who had grown up with trust issues, it was foreign to have anyone finally, and so completely, push past all her barriers. But then again, Jack wasn't just anyone.

She had met him in February, only months before, while on a photojournalism assignment in the Caribbean. It was a chance meeting on a spectacular beach, although, truth be told, Jack later admitted their meeting was more orchestrated than he had initially let on. Less than twenty-four hours after that meeting, Tate's people had come for her, murderously intent on recovering what Tate had stolen from them.

At that point, most reasonable people would have run away from her and never looked back. In general, people don't stick around to help strangers once guns get waved around. But not Jack. He could have left. Should have. Instead he stuck by her, refusing to abandon her, even when she eventually accused him at gunpoint of being part of the conspiracy. She had been wrong, of course, something he still took great delight in teasing her about. A warm smile spread across her lips. He really did love to tease her.

All those months ago, though he barely knew her, Jack had exhibited more selfless and genuine concern for her than anyone in her family ever had. More than her self-consumed mother and her misguided brother. And definitely more than the absentee father she was about to see.

It was that loyalty that got Jack shot and nearly killed, and why they were in a Miami hospital room when her father had finally decided to reach out to her after a quarter-century of silence. Reports of Tate's death and the unraveling of the money-laundering syndicate that was responsible for it had been plastered all over the news and her father had seen it. Learning of his son's death had sent him into a panic, which only escalated when he couldn't track Chloe down either. Desperate, he started bombarding every agency even remotely attached to the situation, until finally making headway with the U.S. Attorney's office in Miami, which had connected him to Chloe.

When they handed her the phone, she hadn't even been able to take his call. It was just too much on top of everything else. Instead she pushed her father to the back of her mind and focused on helping Jack. After a pretty pathetic bit of initial resistance from him, she brought Jack back to her place in Atlanta to help care for him while he recuperated. It had taken all of one week for them both to dismiss any thought of him ever returning home to New York. He gave NYU notice, snagged a teaching position at Emory and found an urban loft off of Peachtree Street just half a mile from Chloe's rental house. He even found a best friend in Jonah, Chloe's golden retriever who, before Jack, had never liked any man she had dated. Chloe had taken that as a very good sign.

The Civic hugged the next turn and was flooded by a piercing orange glare cast by the setting sun. Chloe brought her hand up as a shield, stealing a sideways glance at several dark horses in a distant grassy meadow, dramatically backlit by the glowing hues of the horizon. Wishing she had time to stop and capture the view in a few photographs, she pressed on, making a mental note to come back and try another day.

The truth was that, initially, Chloe had believed that maybe if she ignored her father, Reese might give up and just disappear again. After all, he had erased himself from her life once before. But, instead, the more she ignored him the more he texted and called. Finally, one day, she just caved.

Hardest phone call of my life, Chloe thought. *Well, second hardest. Getting the news about Tate was the first.*

But the phone conversations with Reese proved too emotionally trying, and she insisted on communication by text only. That had actually worked pretty well, keeping some semblance of a protective guard between them which made her feel safer. But even in the texts Reese persisted in asking about meeting in person, something Chloe just couldn't bring herself to do.

Then, after months of keeping Reese at bay, something inexplicably shifted, and meeting him became not just something Reese needed, but something she needed too. She wasn't sure why. Jack said that, unless she faced him, she might always wonder. That something in her needed to confront him in order to truly heal. She didn't know if that was true. Maybe it was simpler than that. Maybe she just needed to stand in front of him and ask whether the office copy lady had been worth it.

Whatever the reason, she didn't feel she could put it off any longer. And so here she was, barreling towards Reese McConnaughey at fifty-five miles per hour with no real idea of what to expect once she got there.

Would she cry? Scream? Stare blankly into the eyes of the man who had discarded her to see if anything with a heart lived inside? Did he have illusions of heartfelt father-daughter bonding or did he just want to say sorry and feel better about himself?

So many things she did not have an answer for. But one thing she did know. She would tell him about Tate. About what Reese's leaving had done to him. She owed her brother that.

"Prepare to turn in 200 feet," the pseudo-human voice of her GPS instructed blandly, as she zipped under the last traffic signal before her turn.

Whatever happened, she was determined to make a good showing and not come apart. No matter what. Pushing down squiggly tendrils of fear, Chloe said a quick prayer and turned into her father's neighborhood.

THREE

It wouldn't be long now. The last of the construction crew had left for the day ten minutes earlier, locking the chain link fence that enclosed the site. The intentional choice of this vantage point made it possible to watch for any stragglers—anyone unexpectedly still on the property. Just to be sure they were all gone, he would wait another fifteen minutes before setting it off. It would be perfect. Enough foot and street traffic to make a scene. A definite statement.

He checked the time once more and the mental countdown began.

* * * * *

The neighborhood where her father lived was an eclectic mishmash of architectural styles. Many of the homes were older, often cottage designs from the 1920s and '30s that had retained their facades, whatever renovations may have occurred inside. A few looked like they had been built in recent decades, probably after the original homes had been torn down. And then there was her father's street, Honeysuckle Court, consisting entirely of brand new construction. These were long, tall structures, occupying the better part of deep, narrow lots that extended down both sides of the dead-end road. These homes were bright and well landscaped with lush, still-green lawns, presumably benefitting from built-in sprinkler systems that had protected them from the months of dry Tennessee summer. An American flag extended from the porch post of more than one house, and yellow mums and lingering impatiens in reds, pinks, and purples welcomed her as she drove past.

At 209 Honeysuckle Court she slowed to a crawl, pulling to the curb in front of the two-story, red and white-peppered brick house with black shutters and an open porch. *My father lives here*, she thought, the notion still surreal. A faint numbness spread through her as she turned off the car and sat there for several minutes, taking it all in. His house boasted a splash of flowers like she had seen in the other beds on the street. *Did he plant those? Or would he have a landscaper?* A black Lexus sat in the driveway. *So he clearly has money. Or at least likes the illusion of it.* What would it have been like to grow up in a house like this instead of the run-down fixer-upper he had left them in? Or the foster home apartment she and Tate had been sent to after that? She looked for other signs of personality, something to indicate what he might be like, but there was nothing unique, really. It looked like every other house on the block. *Wonder what that says about him*, she mused.

"All right, McConnaughey. This is stupid," she told herself, and though she didn't feel any stronger, she grabbed her purse and keys and stepped outside.

The fall air seemed fresh and full of possibilities after several long hours in the car, but as she marched up the short path to the richly stained front door, her legs felt wobbly. Whether from lack of use or anxiety, she didn't know. She pressed the doorbell, which chimed pleasantly, clearly oblivious to the momentous nature of the meeting about to take place. Suddenly she wanted to run. Or stay and punch him. She could probably get one good punch in before he was ready for it. Would that make her feel better? *Stop it,* she told herself, feeling ridiculous. *Stand here. Stand up. Do what you came to do. And let him, and all this baggage, go.*

Several moments passed with no answer. She had texted him an hour ago to let him know she was close. He had texted back that he would be there. She rang the bell again. The three-tone chime echoed away, but still no one answered. *He promised he would be here,* she thought, a tiny banner of anger beginning to unfurl inside. But then, he had made lots of promises, hadn't he? Lots of broken promises.

Heavy, thudding footsteps pounded towards the door from the other side. Her heart jumped as the door flew open.

"Sorry, sorry," Reese McConnaughey sputtered, standing in the doorway, a bit out of breath. "I was upstairs. Didn't hear the bell."

He was tall, though not as tall as Tate had been, with brown hair a bit darker than her loose, tawny curls, sprinkled with a significant amount of gray. His eyes were amber, exactly the same shade as hers. Exactly the same shade that Tate's had been. He wasn't overweight, but carried a bit of heft, like someone who had once worked out regularly, but now was a little fluffy in places. It was a stark contrast to her petite, five-foot-four frame. Catching himself, as if just realizing why he was at the door and who he was opening it for, everything about him seemed to soften.

"Hi, Chloe," he said hesitantly, almost as if afraid of her response.

"Hi, Reese," she replied evenly. She used his first name like a shield, refusing to resort to anything more familiar. She just couldn't.

"You came." He remained there, unmoving, one shoulder still behind the door that filled the space between them. Nervousness emanated from him, his face pinched in uncertainty as he blinked. Concern creased his forehead, along with something like…sadness.

She had not expected that. Not sadness. Not nerves. Cold, aloof, unaffected…she had expected those things. But this emotion…it set her off balance and she found herself almost feeling sorry for him.

Almost.

Fully intending to speak, she started to answer him, but instead only managed to nod. Her voice didn't seem to be working properly.

He spoke up instead. "I can't believe it. You look just like—"

"Don't say my mother."

He pressed his mouth shut to stop himself from finishing the sentence, and they stared at each other for a few moments, both apparently at a loss for how to continue.

She noticed that his face was oval-shaped, like hers, though his complexion was much darker than the fair one she and Tate had inherited from their mother. His face was also worn, lined by time or stress or maybe both. And his eyes seemed tired. From his direction, the strong scent of something woodsy floated out to her on the breeze.

"I don't know how to do this," she admitted.

"You want…you want to come in?" He stepped aside and gestured towards the foyer. She could see walls painted bone white and a high ceiling with a rustic chandelier hanging from its center.

"Could we maybe just stay out here for a minute?" she asked, nodding her head towards two thick-cushioned chairs on the porch.

"Sure," he replied, following her over. As they lowered themselves onto the deep-red upholstery, a loud rumbling, something not quite like thunder, sounded from somewhere in the distance.

She turned her head towards the noise. "What was that?"

"Probably construction. Downtown. So…you found it all right?" he asked, rubbing his hand on his chin nervously.

"Yeah." She swallowed uncomfortably.

"Thanks for coming. I wasn't—"

"It's a work trip. I'm doing an article on the town. So I had to be here anyway. It just worked out." It wasn't a lie. As a photojournalist for the online travel magazine, *Terra Traveler*, it was her job to create compelling articles on desirable travel locales. Franklin was a Civil War town that had morphed into a charming Southern vacation destination and would easily make a great article. She had reasoned that, by making the next few days about something more than just a personal trip down bad memory lane, she would have a built-in reason to have to stay if she started to chicken out. Since her editor, Izzie Morales, was also her best friend, Chloe had not had to work very hard to convince her to let her do the piece.

"Oh. Okay," he fumbled. "Um, and…how are you? And Jack?"

"Good. We're good. He's in California now, on a movie shoot."

"The consultant thing," Reese said, seeming to recall the fact from their prior text conversations.

She sighed. Was this his plan? Small talk? They finally lay eyes on each other for the first time since she was eight, and this was the best he could do? Growing annoyance sent heat rippling across her skin.

His eyes smiled weakly, as he apparently noticed her discomfort. "Sorry. I'm not very good at this." At that moment, his cell vibrated vigorously from the pocket of his tailored khakis, but he ignored it.

"Well, it's been a while," she said, unable to keep the disappointment from her tone.

"I made a mess of things, I know," he said, diving in as the words seemed to come more quickly. "There's so much to say…I don't even know where to start. I've been practicing this for months and I still can't get it right. But, I know I need to start with…I'm sorry."

I'm sorry. Even though he spoke the words with what seemed to be genuine regret, right now they felt like the two most insufficient words in the entire English language. She was about to tell him so when his phone vibrated again.

"Do you need to get that?" she asked him.

"No." He licked his lower lip nervously. "I mean it, Chloe. I'm sorry. For all of it. I wish I could tell you—" A xylophone-like ring tone interrupted him and surprise highlighted the lines on his face.

"Um, I am so sorry, but I actually do have to get this. Just one minute, please," he apologized, pulling the phone out and rising to step a few feet away as he answered.

Chloe could hear his end of the conversation from where she sat. "You okay?" he asked quietly, then paused, listening. His body went rigid. "Stay there. Stay right there," he said in alarm. "I'm coming down there." Whoever was on the other end must have argued the point because his voice rose, his tone commanding. "I'm not kidding. Stay. Right. There. I'll be there in two minutes." He turned back towards Chloe, shoving the phone in his pocket as he backpedaled toward the driveway.

"I'm sorry," he mumbled, moving toward the Lexus. "I have to go. Just…just stay here. I'll be back as soon as I can. Go inside. Make yourself comfortable," he urged, moving to the driver's side door.

"Wait—you're leaving me?" Chloe asked in disbelief.

"I'm sorry," he repeated, his voice panicky as he ripped open the door. "My daughter's just been in an explosion."

FOUR

He has a daughter. Another daughter.

When he had first spoken the words, shock had coursed through her, disabling her from being anything but numb. Part of her had wanted to head right back to I-65 and set a course for home. She could be in her own bed by one or one thirty a.m., pick Jonah up from Izzie in the morning, and forget this ever happened. Who could blame her?

But she hadn't headed back to I-65. Instead, when he had slammed on the brakes before driving away, and asked if she wanted to go with him, she had slipped in the passenger side of his Lexus. She still wasn't sure why.

A daughter, she thought. *A daughter he has somehow neglected to mention.*

Racing well over the thirty-five-miles-per-hour limit, Reese hurtled his car across a small bridge to the next traffic light, headed down Main Street towards the center of town. He pumped the brakes as they met with a line of cars moving increasingly slower, passing old brick buildings that housed quaint shops, including a bookstore, historical society, and a Baskin Robbins. Sirens pierced the air as they finally reached the entrance to the two-lane roundabout encircling the town square, where traffic had slowed to a standstill.

"Come on!" Reese barked at the cars, the first thing either of them had said since leaving the house. Annoyed, he honked his horn uselessly, as a minute ticked by with no movement, leaving them facing the roundabout, but unable to enter it. The town square inside the roundabout consisted of a large, grassy plot with a towering Confederate statue at its center, flanked by Civil War-era cannons in field carriages on each of the square's corners. Looking out across the square, directly opposite of where they were boxed in, Chloe could see the length of Main Street that continued out the other side of the roundabout. A few blocks further down that same road, heavy, black smoke billowed hundreds of feet into the sky.

"This isn't going to work," he snapped, gripping the wheel tightly. "We can't even exit to a side street."

"Reese…was that your daughter on the phone?"

"We—what? Um, yeah," he answered, distracted. "That was her."

"So she's okay?"

"I don't—hey, hold on," he warned just before jerking the wheel hard to the right and pulling the car halfway up onto a small open space on the sidewalk. The rear of the Lexus jutted out into the street, but there was arguably enough room for others to get around, if traffic ever started moving again. Reese yanked the keys out of the ignition and darted out the door.

"Come on!" he yelled, weaving through the traffic, making a beeline for the continuation of Main Street across the square. Chloe raced after him, her numbness ebbing as concern for the girl, mingled with shades of jealousy, grew. Reese had never been this concerned about her. *Never.* But then a pang of shame struck her. The girl was probably scared, and might even be hurt. Visions of a small, elementary-aged girl cowering against a building materialized in Chloe's mind and she turned on the speed to catch up.

But by that time, Reese, already a dozen yards ahead, wasn't that easy to spot and Chloe lost sight of him several times as they ran down the wide sidewalk lining the two blocks that comprised the west portion of Main Street. People packed the way, apparently coming out of the multitude of shops to see what was happening. It was like an obstacle course, trying to avoid crashing full speed into one of the bystanders.

"Reese!" she yelled, but he was barreling towards the towering black cloud without regard to whether she was keeping up. They crossed through another intersection and down another row of shops, including a soap store blowing tiny bubbles over the walk where a distracted mother frantically pushed a stroller right in front of Chloe. She dodged hard to the left to avoid knocking the stroller and the child inside onto the concrete, nearly colliding with an iron lamppost. Regaining her balance, she chased Reese to the end of Main Street, where it fed into a five-street intersection completely blocked by a crowd several rows deep. Every face was taking in the spectacle across the way where a fire blazed on the second and third stories of a partially constructed structure.

More sirens wailed as another fire engine joined an engine and fire truck already parked at the site, their firefighters aggressively deploying equipment in the direction of the building. Crushing jets of water from high-powered hoses attacked the flames and doused the areas of the site not already burning. Multiple police cars lined the streets on either side of the site, their blue and red lights flashing out of sync in a disorienting fashion. Standing on her tiptoes, Chloe swiveled back and forth until she spotted Reese on the street corner across from her in front of a frozen yogurt shop. He was arguing with a teenage girl dressed in black, who was gesturing animatedly with her hands. Chloe pushed through the sardined crowd to get to them. As she drew closer, she could make out bits and pieces of their exchange.

". . . told you I was fine! You didn't have to run up here like a maniac!" the girl was shouting.

"You said you were in an explosion, Emma! What was I supposed—"

"*Was* an explosion. I said there *was an* explosion. Not *in an* explosion, Dad."

Just a few feet from them, Chloe slowed her steps, unsure how to make her presence known, or even if she should. The girl, Emma, looked to be in her mid-teens, with straight, ebony hair that fell to her shoulders and bangs that slanted across her forehead. She had a couple of extra earrings in her left ear and her black skinny jeans were tucked into her dark gray suede boots. She must have noticed Chloe eyeing her, because she paused mid-shout to turn towards Chloe and bark, "Can I help you?"

"Oh," Chloe mumbled, "sorry. I just…I—"

"This is Chloe," Reese announced matter-of-factly.

"Who?" Emma squawked, her face scrunched up in apathy until something clicked for her, and her forehead rose. "Wait. Chloe…" She spoke the name as if trying to remember something. "Not *the* Chloe. Not my long-lost sister, *Chloe*." Her words had a bite to them, sharp edges meant to cut.

"Emma," Reese snapped. "Don't."

Emma spun back to him. "So this is why you told me you needed the house today? You said you had a business meeting you couldn't handle at the office. Has Tyler met her yet?"

"Emma!" Reese said sharply. "Stop—"

"Who's Tyler?" Chloe interrupted.

Emma's eyebrows shot up. "Seriously?" She turned on Reese. "You didn't tell her about *her little brother*?"

A little brother. The fact swept over Chloe like an unexpected wave taking out a surfer. First a sister she didn't know about, and now a brother. Was there anyone else? What other secrets had Reese thought she didn't need to know? Why not tell her about these half-siblings before she came? At least then she could have been prepared. But now…more secrets. More lies.

"McConnaughey!" All three of them turned toward the voice calling from the direction of the construction site, where a balding man in his late fifties or early sixties forcefully shoved his way to them through the crowd. He had leathery, excessively tanned skin and an expensive suit with the shoes to match. A younger, harried-looking man followed him, working to keep up. He was tall and also sported a high-end suit, though he wore his much better. His wavy, loose hair, the color of rich mocha, had clearly been styled to look as if it had just "happened" like that, and was paired with a well-trimmed, slight beard that wasn't much more than a sculpted five o'clock shadow.

"You need to get your client under control!" the balding man barked at Reese, getting right up in his face. He slung his right hand back, pointing in the direction of a couple of police officers closer to the site gathered around a middle-aged man in baggy jeans, with shaggy, brown hair and a full-on beard, holding a cardboard picket sign at his side.

"Mr. Donner—" Reese started.

"That idiot actually did it this time! He bombed my building!" he gesticulated wildly again in the same direction. "I'm at home, two blocks away, when—BOOM!" He threw his arms in the air, miming an explosion. "I get a call from my foreman that my construction project is in flames! Flames! This one," he said, casting the dark-haired man beside him a contemptuous glance, "says he's got it under control, but clearly that's not the case. Three weeks ago Sims trespasses on my site and attacks me—"

"His picketing sign accidentally hit you," the younger, dark-haired man disagreed.

"—and now this," Donner continued. "He's gone too far. Those cops are carting him away. Tonight!"

"Mr. Donner, you need to back off. Now," Reese spoke sternly, and Chloe noticed that at some point he had protectively inserted himself between Emma and Donner. "As soon as I'm done dealing with my daughter—"

Emma's eyes rolled. "I don't need you to deal with me. I told you I'm fine. I was just calling to tell you what happened!"

"I mean it, McConnaughey," growled Donner. "*This* is the kind of client you're representing! You think *this,*" he swiveled to gesture at the burning building, "is good for the town? I want to bring business into it and he wants to *blow it up*! Sims is done!"

"Umm," Chloe interrupted, "look, I think I should go. She's okay," she said, nodding at Emma, "and you clearly have things to do."

"Wait, Chloe, please—" Reese said, taking her arm, but dropping his hand quickly when she glared at him.

"This is ridiculous," growled Donner, and he stormed off towards the picketer, who was still engaged with the officers.

Reese turned his attention to the dark-haired man. "How did you get here?"

He shook his head, his eyes betraying his exasperation. "I'd just left the office and was only a block away when Sims called my cell. For some reason," he said with a slight, sarcastic smirk, thumbing at the building behind him, "he thought they might assume he was the one responsible for this. He was picketing out front again when it blew." He clasped Reese's shoulder. "We'd better get over there. It'll take us both to rein Sims in before he says something stupid." He turned to look in the direction of the picketer, who now seemed to be engaged in a shouting match with Donner.

"Fine," Reese replied in surrender. "But, Chloe," he said, turning imploringly to her, "please, just don't go. Okay? Just head back to the house and I'll meet you there as soon as I can."

"Yeah. Sure," she said dispassionately, backing away from the group.

"Wait, how will you get—"

"I'll call Uber or something. It's fine." She thought he might argue, but instead he nodded, turning to quickly follow after the dark-haired man, already pushing through the throngs of bystanders.

She watched him go and then started walking in the opposite direction. She wasn't going to wait for him at the house. All of this was a sign that her coming here had clearly been a huge mistake. He wasn't ready to reconcile, to own up to his failures. He wasn't even ready to tell her he had other children. *That I've got other siblings,* she thought, a coldness gripping her heart. No. This was over. She would just forget about doing the piece on Franklin, and have Izzie assign it to someone else for another issue.

She was going home.

FIVE

But first, coffee.

Directly across the street from the frozen yogurt place was a Starbucks. Chloe moved towards it slowly, edging her way through the gathered crowd who were standing shoulder-to-shoulder with their cell phones raised, taking video of the fire.

As she opened the door, rich, roasted scents wafted past Chloe, a relief from the heavy, singular smell of acrid smoke outside. The place was nearly empty. The patrons that remained lined the broad front windows, looking out at the fire. Two baristas stood behind the counter chattering excitedly with one another, one gesturing urgently at the burning building.

"You guys still taking orders?" Chloe asked.

The nearest barista nodded, abandoning her conversation with her cohort to take Chloe's order for an Earl Grey Latte. Chloe was turning to find a seat to wait in when she heard her name called from the direction of the door.

"Chloe! Hey Chloe!"

It was Reese's daughter, Emma. Her…sister.

"Hey, it is 'Chloe,' right?" she asked. "Dad told me about you."

Wish I could say the same, Chloe thought. "Yeah. That's right," she replied.

Emma wasn't alone. Two teen boys flanked her sides. The one on her right was tall, red-haired, fair and freckled, dressed in jeans, a ball cap and dark sneakers. The one on her left, wearing khakis and a red button-down, was sepia skinned and a bit shorter and stockier.

"You're not staying," Emma said bluntly.

Chloe sniffed, trying to decide whether to be honest or not. She settled on the truth. "No. I think it's better if I go."

Emma scoffed. "It's him, isn't it? He chased you off already."

"It's complicated," Chloe answered.

"Because he didn't tell you about us."

Chloe hesitated. This girl was smart. "That's part of it."

"Chloe!" sounded from behind her, as the barista placed a logo-emblazoned paper cup on the pick-up corner of the counter.

Chloe stepped back over to claim her drink. "Look, it's just not the right time," she said over her shoulder to Emma, then moved to the counter housing the sugars and cream. She ripped open a packet of cane sugar. "Maybe I'll try again sometime. Just tell him I said goodbye, okay?" she said, smiling sadly at Emma before turning to head out the rear exit.

"I can tell you about him."

Chloe stopped walking, but didn't turn.

"You came all this way," Emma prodded. "Don't you want to know the truth?"

* * * * *

The bomb had done its job well. They were still fighting the flames, with the whole street still watching. Though only twenty minutes had passed since the explosion, more than enough damage had been done. The better part of the third floor was scorched, black burn marks streaking the metal girders. The scaffolding near the blast point was destroyed, the pieces of its support frame shooting off at odd angles and its temporary wood plank flooring either irredeemably charred or completely missing. Partially melted orange construction netting that had been ripped to shreds flapped soundlessly in the wind above the throngs of onlookers.

Maybe now the message will get through, the bomber considered, as yet another fire truck pulled up. *Maybe not,* though, considering the spectacle Donner was making in front of everyone.

If not, that'll leave only one option.

* * * * *

Chloe stared at Emma from across the table that they had commandeered in the front corner of the shop. It faced the street, giving them an up-close view of the chaotic scene outside.

Chloe blew on her latte. The swirls of rising steam told her it would be several minutes before she could sip it without scalding herself. "What exactly do you want to tell me about Reese?"

"What do you want to know?"

It was a loaded question. And her answer now wasn't the same as it would have been a couple of hours ago. "I'm not sure you're the person I should be asking," Chloe replied, "and I'm not sure this is the place." She smiled thinly, casting a quick glance at Emma's friends.

"Don't worry about them," Emma insisted. "They know everything. This is Jacob," she said, gesturing to the red-shirted one, "and this is Trip," she said, gently elbowing the redhead in the arm.

"So you're Emma's sister?" asked Jacob tentatively.

"Half-sister," corrected Trip.

"I guess so," Chloe admitted.

"He," Emma said disdainfully, jerking her head towards Reese in the crowd beyond the window, "didn't even tell her about me. Or Tyler." Reese was still in the thick of it, standing beside the man in baggy jeans wielding the picketing sign as he argued animatedly with Donner.

"You know," Chloe started, nodding in Reese's direction, "he was really worried when he got your call. Practically flew down here." As the words left her lips, she was already asking herself, *Why am I bothering to defend him? Why do I care?*

"Whatever."

Chloe sighed. Apparently, Reese's relationship with his second daughter was just as screwed up as the one she had with him. Or didn't have, rather. As she considered whether she ought to get up right then and go, she watched as the man with the picket sign raised it above the crowd and shook it, causing Donner to explode into another fit. Reese stepped in, apparently trying to talk Donner down. "It looks like Reese has his hands full with that picketer," Chloe commented, as two police officers cleared some space between the arguing men, who continued yelling at each other.

"That's Jacob's dad," Emma explained, her voice a bit softer. Jacob said nothing, but somehow suddenly seemed to take up a little less space.

"Emma's dad is his lawyer," Jacob explained vaguely.

An uncomfortable silence hovered over the group. "Well, I hope he's okay," Chloe said kindly. "He looks pretty upset."

"He's mad about that guy," Emma pointed at Donner, "and the building that just blew up. Before he started building it, Jacob's dad was trying to buy the site, but Donner ended up with it—"

"Stole it out from under Dad, you mean," Jacob muttered.

"Yeah," Emma conceded. "Stole it and built that building. Jacob's dad hasn't taken it well."

"Whoa," interrupted Trip, leaning forward in his chair to get a better look at the firefighters in the cherry picker hosing down the building. "Did you see that? The fire is kicking up again on the second floor!"

"Hey, hold on," Emma said, whipping out her cell and handing it to Chloe. "Can you take our picture before they put it out?" she asked, leaning back and kicking her feet up on the table and putting her arms around the boys, who were on either side. Squeezing in against Emma, the guys leaned back and kicked up their feet like she had.

A wave of discomfort washed over Chloe. Something didn't seem right about snapping a selfie in front of a dangerous fire endangering lives and causing what was probably millions in damages. But she didn't feel she could refuse and keep things amicable. "Okay," she said, raising the cell and counting, "One, two, three," before snapping the photo.

"Thanks," Emma said, reaching for the phone. "Lemme see it first." She examined the shot, then, apparently dissatisfied, shook her head. "Nope. I don't like that. Lean in more guys, and put your feet down. They're blocking too much of me. One more time," she asked, handing the phone back to Chloe as they all sat up, rocked forward and leaned over the table, trying out the different pose. Chloe groaned internally. If this was any indication, Emma appeared to be exactly the kind of selfie-obsessed teenager people believed all teenagers to be.

"Great, thanks," Emma announced after scrutinizing the second photo, then tapping the screen a few times, ostensibly uploading it to her social media accounts.

Chloe changed gears. "So you guys were nearby when the explosion happened?"

They all nodded. "We were headed here, actually," Trip offered. "We were almost to the door when this huge 'boom' went off."

Chloe's gaze drifted back to Reese, who was still talking with Jacob's dad. They must have finished with the police officers, because they had managed to pull him away from the site, and now stood just outside the Starbucks. The dark-haired man, the one who had walked up with Donner, was there too. Chloe nodded in his direction. "Who's that with Reese and Jacob's dad?"

Emma glanced over, and a knowing smile erupted. "You mean Holt?"

"Oh, man," Trip groaned. "Do not get her started."

"Who's Holt?" Chloe asked.

"Holt Adams. I think he looks like McDreamy from Grey's Anatomy. Best hiring decision Dad ever made."

"He works for your dad?"

Emma nodded. "He's an attorney in his office. He's over a lot, meeting with Dad at the house. I don't care, though. Tyler loves him, and as long as he looks like that, it's all good."

"Ugh," said Jacob, rolling his eyes. "Girl, I do not want to hear that."

"You're just jealous," teased Emma.

Chloe zoned out for a second, watching the three men, when suddenly Holt's eyes flashed up to meet hers. He cocked his head, as if intrigued by her attention. Chloe quickly turned back to Emma.

"So," Chloe started, "you said you could tell me the truth about Reese. What truth?"

Part of her felt guilty for talking to Reese's child behind his back and indulging the teen's obvious desire to malign her father. But another part cared more about the information than the guilt. She was curious about what it was like to have Reese McConnaughey around as a father and wasn't sure if or when she would get the chance to ask Emma again.

Emma snorted. "You saw us out there. It's a nightmare," she replied emphatically. "He's a complete pain. Overbearing, doesn't trust me. Not to mention he's always busy with work. The only time he manages to carve out is when he wants to lecture me."

"It could be worse," Chloe said, fighting back shades of bitterness. At least Emma had grown up with a father. However flawed he might be. "He could be gone all the time."

"If only. I wish it was him that had left instead of Mom." Her eyes narrowed. "Did he tell you that she left?" Chloe's blank expression gave her the answer. "Yeah," Emma sniped. "I'm not surprised."

So Reese's wife—Andrea—the mother of Emma and Tyler, the woman Reese had left Chloe's mother for, had left him. Yet another fact Reese had chosen to keep to himself. Had Andrea left him in the same abrupt manner in which Reese had left Chloe, Tate, and her mother? Or was it a slow parting, an increasingly wider separation until she just disappeared altogether? The irony of the contrast between Chloe and her half-sister wasn't lost on her. Chloe had spent her whole life wishing Reese had not left. Emma had apparently spent much of hers wishing he would. But the similarities were also undeniable. They had both been abandoned by one parent, then lost the other: Chloe losing her mom to alcoholism and death and Emma apparently losing Reese to his work.

Emma watched Chloe as she processed. "You know, I can't blame you for wanting to go. If I came all that way and met Dad I'd be disappointed too." She shuffled in her seat, glancing off to the far side of the room before speaking again. "But you know…you haven't met Tyler yet." She paused for a breath. "You really shouldn't leave without meeting him. He's only eight and he'll just die if he finds out he has a sister and didn't get to meet her."

Emma's plea was for her brother, but something in her tone, the way she held herself, suggested that maybe something more was riding on Chloe's answer. There was a hopeful expectancy shimmering somewhere behind her eyes as she waited, a hint that maybe she wanted Chloe to stay for herself, but didn't trust her enough to expose her emotional jugular by asking.

When Chloe didn't object, Emma seemed to sense weakness and pressed. "I've got school tomorrow, but I'm not scheduled to work after so I could show you around and everything. You don't even have to see Dad if you don't want to."

"I don't know," Chloe said hesitantly. She could stay and meet the boy. Only, what if that made it harder? Wasn't it less complicated to just leave now, before she got entangled in this second family drama that Reese had going on?

But something in Emma's eyes pulled at her. It wasn't a physical familiarity. The girl, with her sweeping black hair and vibrant blue eyes, bore no resemblance to Chloe and Tate. But something else, something in her gaze, something in her voice—a longing, maybe—that was something Chloe *did* recognize. An all-too-familiar flicker of hope that maybe, just maybe, you might not be completely alone in this world.

"Hey," said Trip. "Something's happening over there." He was pointing in the direction of the site, where a number of police and firefighters had converged on an area towards the back of the lot. "What are they are looking at?"

A dull buzz spread amongst the patrons in the shop as the activity on the construction site grew a bit more frantic, culminating with a paramedic from a nearby ambulance rushing into the middle of the gathered emergency personnel. Emma and the boys stood, moving to stand against the glass for a better look, at the same time a teenaged boy stuck his head in the front door.

"Hey!" he shouted, his face ripe with macabre excitement. "They found a body! Somebody's dead over there!"

SIX

Chloe crawled between the crisp, white sheets and the fluffy toile duvet, holding the phone between her ear and shoulder. "I swear, Jack, she doesn't want me to go. It's the weirdest thing. It's like she wants me around so she can complain to someone who understands how awful he is." To Chloe's left, a fire flickered merrily in the white brick fireplace of the little second-floor room of the Victorian bed and breakfast just a block off Franklin's town square. Its quaint guest rooms were like something out of a magazine, which they would be after Chloe's article on the town.

"Sounds like a typical teen daughter. Maybe she figures she's found an ally in you."

"Maybe." As she answered, Chloe squirreled further into the bed, nearly getting lost in the down pillows.

"I still can't believe you've got siblings you never knew about."

"I really don't know how to feel about it. On the one hand, I've got this instant family—well, at least in name—and after Tate died, I figured that I was pretty much alone in the world as far as family went. So maybe it's nice to realize I'm actually not. But on the other hand, accepting them feels like I'm betraying Tate. He was my family. For my whole life. Now I'm supposed to just accept these strangers that my father considered more worthy of his devotion than me and Tate? I don't know if I can do it."

"You're doing the right thing by staying. Just take it one day at a time."

"Yeah, I guess," she conceded, rolling over towards the fire. "So how are you?"

"The shoot went well. I had to teach a mega-star who shall remain nameless how to run while holding a rifle. He kept doing this limping thing—at first I thought he thought it looked cool or something, then I realized he was just copying me." Jack laughed, but with a little too much effort behind it.

"It's bothering you that much?"

"It's just a joke, Chloe. My leg's fine. It's good that I can joke about it, right?"

"Of course it is. Sorry." He was definitely becoming touchy about the subject. She made a mental note to give the leg thing a rest for a while.

"So tell me about the body," he probed, changing topics.

"Ugh. I really could have gone my whole life without talking about dead bodies again," Chloe sighed. "I didn't really get the scoop on it. The kids wanted to stay and watch, so I took Uber back to get my car. I'm sure I'll hear all about it tomorrow." She twisted to see the clock on the nightstand. "Speaking of tomorrow, I'd better go. It's after midnight here and I'm supposed to be at Reese's in the morning to work things out."

"It'll be fine, Chlo. God's got a plan in all this."

"Yeah, I know. I just wish he would've let me in on this part of it before now."

* * * * *

Jack slid his cell into his pocket, then sipped the last of his drink, easing back into the modern leather chair in the corner of the posh hotel bar where the movie studio had put him up in Los Angeles. A long, glossy black bar ran the length of the opposite side of the room. Tall mirrors paneled the walls, kept dark by the low level of light in the room. Even so, he was close enough to his reflection to see that he was looking pretty run-down. His normally bright green eyes were dull and his shoulders seemed to sag. He wondered whether, if he stood, he would be shorter than his standard six feet two. Even his chestnut hair, which usually spiked at the crown, was lying flat.

The noise in the room had grown to a dull roar over the last few minutes, with things getting going now that the night crowd had started trickling in. They were just firing up, and here he was, ready to call it a night. Every inch of him wanted sleep. Even his bones were weary. Whatever he had told Chloe, his leg was killing him and he was tired of thinking about it. He glared at it, frustration gnawing at him. The stupid thing still ached as if he had been shot yesterday instead of seven months ago.

Not to mention that, on top of just generally wanting a break from the pain, he had a five a.m. call time in the morning. Bed was where he ought to be. But it would have to wait a little longer.

The heavy feeling he had been suppressing during his conversation with Chloe surged. *I wonder if she could tell I was keeping something from her,* he thought, swirling his crystal tumbler round and round, the lone ice cube tinkling against the sides. Hoping not, he pushed the guilt down, and with the rhythmic thump of bass from the music of a younger crowd pounding away, he waited for her to arrive.

SEVEN

Crisp autumn light streamed through the sheers covering the floor-to-ceiling windows of Chloe's robin's egg-colored bedroom. She opened her eyes slowly, taking in the gentle scent of lavender on the linens. She had slept a full seven hours without waking once. Chloe stretched, surprised. Given the events of the night before, she expected to have trouble falling asleep. But apparently her exhaustion had overcome the shock of everything.

She had told Emma to tell Reese she would come by around nine, which gave her plenty of time to take the morning slowly. After a quick shower in the pristine black and white-tiled bathroom, she headed down the spindled wooden staircase in search of coffee.

The room to the left of the foyer had high ceilings, wooden plank floors and two tables extravagantly laid with linens in preparation for breakfast, which she had been told would be served at eight o'clock. Crossing to the room on the right side of the foyer, she found a cozy, crimson-painted sitting room with a floral couch facing out a window that overlooked the side yard's small English garden. A Keurig coffee maker sat on the sideboard, stocked with a variety of coffees, sweeteners, and creamers.

Anticipating the energizing brew, she started a cup of French Roast, noting that the small trash bin beside it was empty. If there were other inn guests, they weren't up yet. Normally she loved the conviviality of bed and breakfasts. Often it was the best way to get an insider's view of a locale. But today she was thankful for a few moments of solitude as she added enough French vanilla creamer to her coffee to turn it the color of butterscotch.

She walked to the front window and sipped the hot drink. A fat sparrow was perched on the tiered, concrete birdbath positioned beside a well-trimmed row of low hedges. A large oak, perhaps planted when the house was built in 1892, had decorated the lawn with its shed leaves of red and russet. Fall had definitely arrived.

"Hello?" a voice called from behind. Chloe turned to see the innkeeper that had checked her in the night before, a gentleman in his late fifties, white-headed and smiling.

"Oh, hey. Morning, Derrick."

"Good morning. Did you sleep well?"

"Great, actually."

"Good. Give me fifteen minutes and I'll have breakfast for you in the dining room, right across the hall."

"Great, I'm starving," she said, not realizing how true that was until that moment.

"You're the only one staying with us right now. So any special requests? How do you like your eggs?" he asked, as he finished tying on a spotless, starched apron.

"Over-easy? With toast?" she asked.

"Absolutely."

Breakfast turned out to be a heavenly combination of perfectly done fried eggs, lightly toasted sourdough bread, a small cup of berries drizzled with honey and yogurt, and the gooiest cinnamon roll she had ever tasted. All this with hot tea served in bone china.

"This was fantastic," Chloe praised, as Derrick whisked her empty plate away. "Best cinnamon roll I've ever had."

"It's from Merridee's, a bakery and restaurant one block from here, just right off Main Street. You can get there through the alleyway just to the left of the house."

"I may run over there. I was going to head down to Main Street anyway to get my bearings, maybe check some places out."

"Well, nothing else really opens until ten a.m., except for Starbucks and maybe a couple of the other restaurants. And here," he said, sliding a typed sheet in front of her. "It's a list of the things to do around here—historical sites, shopping, antique shops, ghost tours—"

"Ghost tours?"

Derrick nodded. "Been on a couple of those. Lots of fun. Anyway, when you mentioned the article you're writing, I thought this might help."

After savoring the last bit of tea, she slipped upstairs for a light jacket and her camera, then headed out, anxious to get a feel for the place. Instead of the alley, she walked just half a block to the town square that she and Reese had run across the night before. The marble statue of the Confederate soldier rested atop a granite shaft that had to be at least thirty feet tall. This time she stayed on the sidewalk, going left past a red brick building with massive white columns. A historical marker declared it to be the original courthouse from the early 1800s. Ironically, it now was positioned adjacent to a Mellow Mushroom restaurant, most definitely not an original from the 1800s.

Main Street itself was extremely well-preserved, with two- and three-story brick buildings lining both sides, some painted, others not, but all in keeping with a very traditional Southern scheme. Many of the buildings were a century or more old. There were a few chain stores, including an Anthropologie clothing store, but most were independent shops with specialty merchandise. Clothing, linens, gifts, china, jewelry—the list was endless. And the windows rivaled that of any Manhattan Fifth Avenue store. They were elegant, intriguing, whimsical—Chloe hated that she would have to wait until later to get a better look.

She snapped a few photographs of the more interesting ones, then turned left at the light. A bright blue banner heralding "Merridee's Breadbasket" hung outside a doorway on the opposite side of the street. Hustling across illegally, she swung the heavy wooden door open and stepped inside.

A symphony of vanilla sweetness, bacon, and a dark, nutty roast enveloped her. The place was packed, clearly a favorite of the locals. There were a lot of suits, and Chloe suspected many had business that morning inside the current, modern-day courthouse positioned just across the street. Exposed, rustic wood adorned nearly every surface—wide wooden floor planks, hefty wooden columns, and an exposed beam ceiling. Woven baskets hung from the beams and dark brick covered the walls. As she approached the counter, a waitress walked by with a plate of cream cheese-stuffed French toast that almost had Chloe ordering a second breakfast. Instead, she ordered a half-dozen cinnamon rolls to go and a latte for herself.

While she waited for the order, Chloe curled up in one of the leather chairs in the corner and pulled out her cell. She had been using an app that offered up a daily Bible verse, and lately, in light of her impending meeting with Reese, she had opted to focus on ones about forgiveness.

Forgiveness. This had traditionally not been a strength for her. With the exception of Tate, whom she had forgiven anything and everything, forgiving others had not come easily. Faces floated through her mind of people that had once been in her life, but, because of some transgression, had been plucked from it and tossed aside like weeds in a garden. It wasn't that she set out to be harsh. It was simply a matter of self-preservation.

But now, this strategy seemed to fly in the face of what she was learning about God's take on forgiveness. God forgave her. Every time. Even when it was obvious that she wasn't perfect and might fail again. And he was pretty clear that he wanted her to do the same. But the idea of just letting Reese off the hook still pained her, clashing with her sense of justice. It just seemed wrong.

So, of course, the verse that popped up for that day was Hebrews 10:17: "Then he adds: Their sins and lawless acts I will remember no more. And where these have been forgiven, sacrifice for sins is no longer necessary."

Chloe sighed, wishing again for the kind of compassion that would help her understand what that truly meant. It was such a great mystery to her, how God could not only forgive, but not even remember the sins any longer. It was hard to imagine ever forgetting the damage her father had done. Her moving on was one thing. Giving Reese permission to do the same was something else altogether.

The clerk called her name and she shot up to retrieve the bag of warm pastries and steaming latte. She took a swig of the vanilla-laced coffee, chasing away any last remnants of morning grogginess as she headed out the door, its bell ringing in her wake.

EIGHT

Chloe knew something was wrong the moment she turned onto Reese's street. A white patrol car emblazoned with the "City of Franklin" logo was parked right in front of the house. She pulled ahead of it, parked and got out, her gaze drawn to two police officers standing near the front door, taking photos and writing on a clipboard. It wasn't until she was at the front steps that she saw why. A large box, dripping with what looked like blood, sat on the top step. Written across the step in the same red liquid were the words, "BACK OFF OR ELSE."

"Is that…that's not blood, is it?" Chloe gasped as the officers turned towards her.

"Ma'am?" the female officer on the right said, starting towards Chloe. "Ma'am—"

Reese flung the door open, looking exhausted and a bit surprised.

"It's fine. She's fine," he said, waving them off. "It's my daughter," he explained further, glancing at his watch and shook his head. "Sorry. I had no idea it was this late already. It's been…well, if you could just come around to the side."

"Sure," Chloe said, leaving him and walking down the driveway that extended down the length of the house to a small porch and side entryway. Reese met her there, opening the door and ushering her inside the kitchen where she was immediately hit with Emma's angry voice. "Dad, I told you, I'm staying here today. I'm not leaving Tyler!" Emma shouted.

"Emma, look, please. He's fine. Just go to school. I'll be with him."

"Yeah, right. A lot that's worth." Emma looked past Reese. "Chloe, you get it, right? I can't leave him. He's too shaken up."

Chloe held her hands up in surrender. "I don't need to be involved in this."

"Well somebody needs to be because *he* is refusing to listen—like always!" Emma bellowed, followed by Reese starting in, their voices competing with one another in escalating fashion.

"Nice way to start off the morning, eh?" came a voice from behind Chloe. She swiveled to find Holt Adams standing in the space leading from the kitchen to the front foyer, a wry smile on his face. His thick, wavy hair was spot-on again today, almost too perfect, and Chloe wondered briefly if he had a stylist at home. A sharp, charcoal gray suit and Brooks Brothers wingtips finished off the fine-tuned look. As the battle between Reese and Emma raged louder, Chloe stepped past Holt into the hallway behind him, discreetly attempting to get as far away as possible. He kept pace with her, till both slipped sideways into the dining room, the first room off the front foyer. The walls were painted a serene tone of neutral gray, with decorative white panels and molding covering the bottom third. An oblong cherry table sat in the center, covered with a multitude of papers—files, photographs, printouts—all stacked and sorted. Pens, paperclips, and other sundry supplies littered the tabletop. An open laptop occupied the space at the head of the table, perched precariously on what appeared to be some kind of legal text. Emma had not been kidding about Reese bringing his work home with him. Chloe doubted many family dinners ever happened in there. She turned back to Holt, who pulled a face as Emma roared indistinctly in the background.

"Wow, she's loud today," Chloe remarked, her eyebrows rising.

He shrugged. "She's seventeen and at war with the world. She's a good kid, really. Just blustering."

Chloe nodded, remembering what it was like to be seventeen. "You're here awfully early," she noted, wondering if Reese normally had law partners over at this time of day, or if this was an exception because of the box on the porch.

He smirked. "I'm guessing somebody filled you in on who I am?"

"Emma said you work with Reese."

He held out a hand and she shook it. "Holt Adams. Reese and I are law partners. He called me after they found it. Thought he might need some help juggling the kids and the cops."

"That was nice of you."

"I pitch in where I can. I'm kind of fond of his little family."

Though she was sure it was unintentional, his words stung a bit, and she wondered whether and how much he knew about her place in Reese's "little family."

"So was that blood out there?" she asked, gesturing towards the front door.

"Nah. Just paint."

"It looked awful."

"Yeah," Holt agreed. "Unfortunately, Tyler found it. He went out to grab something from his backpack this morning and saw it from the driveway. Poor kid thought it was a package from Amazon or something and went running over. It really spooked him."

"I'll bet."

Holt nodded. "Ran upstairs for his dad and hasn't come down since. Emma doesn't want to leave him. They're thick as thieves."

"What was in the box?"

"Empty," Holt answered, shoving his hands in his pockets and rocking back on his heels. "They were just making a statement with the fake blood and all. Too bad they weren't more clear about what that statement is."

Chloe thought about the message written on the steps. "Seemed pretty clear to me."

"'Back off or else?' Back off of what? It could mean any number of things, from any number of people. They should have been more specific. Reese tends to make a few enemies in his line of work."

"What do you mean 'his line of work'?" She knew Reese was an attorney, but didn't see why that would put him in a special category of people who should expect bloody boxes on their porches.

"Our practice is primarily criminal defense and divorce," Holt explained. "Sometimes people get upset when we represent certain defendants, especially if the crime they're accused of is nasty. Sometimes, in divorces, the opposing spouse lets their hatred for our client bleed over onto us—no pun intended here."

"So something like this has happened before?"

"A couple of times. There was a dismembered squirrel with a note attached on the side porch once. That was pretty gross."

Chloe's eyes widened. "How did the kids react to that?"

"Fortunately, Reese found it before the kids got to it."

"So he doesn't know who left it, what they're mad about, or what they want him to stop doing?"

He eyed her with keen approval. "So, you see the problem."

There was a knock on the front door, which opened slowly. An officer with the name plate "R. Tomlinson" entered, carrying a digital camera. "We need to speak with Mr. McConnaughey," she said, her gaze wide as she overheard the tirade coming from the back of the house. "Could you possibly ask him to come back out?"

"Um, sure. Just a second," Holt said, then turned to Chloe. "Don't go anywhere."

No promises, she thought as he headed down the hall. This whole debacle was causing her to consider again whether this reunion simply wasn't meant to be. She had expected that confronting Reese would be hard, but this was bordering on ridiculous.

Holt was back in half a minute, with Reese in tow. "Hey, Rita," Reese said, smiling thinly at Officer Tomlinson. "You guys finished out there?"

"Yeah. You think we could have a word outside?" Reese nodded and followed her out the front door, leaving it cracked behind him.

"Does he know her?" Chloe asked quietly.

Holt nodded. "He knows a lot of the officers. When you do as much criminal defense work as he does, you get pretty familiar with the police."

"Don't they hold his job against him?"

Holt scoffed good-naturedly. "No. Actually, they respect him a lot. He plays fair and doesn't bad-mouth them just to make points. Although," he grinned impishly, "they definitely don't like that we win cases as often we do."

"So he's good at it—being an attorney I mean?"

Holt smiled. "Yeah. He's good at it." He paused for just a nanosecond. "We both are," he finished, and unleashed that grin again. The cockiness should have been off-putting, but for some reason it just came off as likably confident. Chloe snorted softly, amused, as her cell buzzed in her pocket. Reaching for it, she saw a number she didn't recognize.

"Hello?" she answered curiously.

"Chloe, it's me. Emma. I'm upstairs." Her voice carried none of the rage from her argument with Reese minutes earlier. Instead, it nearly vibrated with excitement. "Wanna come meet Tyler?"

NINE

The Camry rolled away from downtown Franklin, out towards the western part of the county. He had stayed in McConnaughey's neighborhood just long enough to see a patrol car pull in. After that, he felt it wasn't safe to stick around, just in case they canvassed the area.

After leaving the package, he had parked down the street where he had been able to keep an eye on it. He had wanted to be sure that somebody found his gift. It turned out to be the kid. Screamed his head off too. He bet that boy wouldn't sleep for weeks.

Maybe now McConnaughey would take him seriously. If not, he had no problem taking this thing to the next level. Part of him hoped that's how it went down. A little violence tended to go a long way.

TEN

As Chloe slowly made her way up the stairs her heart suddenly began beating harder in her chest. *Why am I so nervous?* she thought. *It's just a little boy. It's no big deal.*

But she knew instinctively that this was a lie. It wasn't just a little boy. It was a little boy that might look like Tate. Move like Tate. Speak like Tate. And that was a very, very big deal.

She slowed as she reached the top landing, sucking in a breath just as Emma stuck her head out of a room two doors down on the left.

"Over here," Emma called to her, gesturing for her to enter and sharing what Chloe suspected was an uncharacteristic grin.

The boy sat cross-legged on a low bed built to look like a red race car. A bright yellow "52" adorned its sides. The walls were the same off-white as most of the rest of the house, with built-in-shelves showcasing books, sports paraphernalia and toys. A World Wrestling Entertainment poster hung beside the closet.

Chloe stared at Tyler, words failing her. Whereas Emma differed from her in every physical way, Tyler resembled Tate greatly, though with small differences, as if he was the product of someone who had tried to draw Tate from memory. He had tawny hair, wavy and short, with round, amber eyes, just like Tate's. And hers. The shape of his face was almost exactly as Chloe remembered an elementary-aged Tate, though Tyler's nose was a bit longer and his skin just a shade darker than Tate's had been. A heart-wrenchingly familiarity washed over her.

"Hi," Tyler said, peeking out at her from under his eyelids. Apparently she wasn't the only nervous one.

"Hi," Chloe answered, moving further in the room. "So you're Tyler?"

He nodded, the bill on his baseball cap pumping up and down. "So you're my sister?"

Chloe's chest tightened. "I am."

She eyed him and a growing sense of pity filled her. This was hard for him. Having your family reoriented like this would be scary for him—was scary, even for her—so, of course, he would be tentative. She glanced at Emma for some kind of cue, and she nodded encouragingly.

Chloe moved to one of the bookcases, zeroing in on a shelf that held a row of paperbacks. Seven Harry Potter novels were lined up in a row, their colorful spines a literary rainbow. The books were worn, the pages dog-eared.

"So you're a Harry Potter fan?" Chloe asked, pulling out one of the volumes.

Interest drew Tyler's gaze upward. He nodded. "Emma reads them with me."

"*Goblet of Fire* is my favorite. What about you?"

He pursed his lips, considering the question. "The first one. Because it's when Harry finds out he can do magic."

Chloe nodded and started to reply, but then Tyler continued, "But also, *Order of the Phoenix*, because there's a bunch of magic fighting. But that one's a little sad."

Chloe pressed her lips together, trying not to smile. "Yeah, that one is," she agreed, then glanced over at the baseball gloves. "You play?"

"Shortstop," he answered proudly.

"He was team MVP last year," Emma offered with a satisfied smile.

"Wow. I'd like to see you play sometime," Chloe said, tracing a hand over one of the gloves.

"Really?" Tyler asked, the tone of pleasant surprise in his voice.

"Sure, I would. I like baseball. My brother used to play when he was about your age—"

"Your brother? So…does that mean I have a brother, too?" Tyler looked to Emma for the answer, and Emma looked to Chloe.

"Um," Chloe said, searching for the right words, "well, yes…you did." Her heart winced. "But he died."

"Oh," Tyler said, clear disappointment cutting through. "I'm sorry."

Sympathy curved Chloe's mouth. "Thanks, Tyler. That means a lot. I'm sorry you didn't get to meet him. He would have loved you."

Tyler wrinkled his nose. "You think?"

"I know. I could tell you about him sometime. If you want."

Tyler nodded.

"Hey, bud, why don't you show Chloe your Avengers collection?" Emma suggested, pointing to a dozen action figures displayed on one of the shelves.

"You like the Avengers?" he asked Chloe.

"Love 'em," she answered. "Let me see what you've got."

They spent the next fifteen minutes talking about the toys and trading opinions about the best Avenger and the new movie that had come out over the summer. Emma chimed in a bit, but mostly just watched and smiled. It was clear that she truly loved Tyler. Whatever animosity she felt for her father did not extend to him.

"Chloe?" Reese stood in the doorway, looking haggard.

"Hey, Reese," she said, rising from where she'd been sitting next to Tyler on the bed. "Everything okay?"

He exhaled heavily. "Uh, yeah. Look, I'm so sorry but this thing is going to have me tied up. Between this and the explosion and two other cases I've got hearings on this afternoon, I won't be able to take off this morning like I'd hoped."

"Surprise," Emma mumbled under her breath.

Reese's eyes darted to her. "You're going to school, Emma. Tyler's fine."

"I'm not going."

"Yeah, you are. Because one of those officers down there owes me a favor and agreed to take you if you won't go on your own."

She glared at him. "Fine," she sniped, marching towards the door. "But I'm taking Tyler first."

"No," said Reese. "I can drop him on my way to work."

"I can take him," Chloe piped in, and they both turned to look at her. Tyler looked up, a grin on his face.

"That okay with you, bud?" Emma asked, all traces of angst gone from her tone.

Tyler nodded vigorously. "That's cool."

Reese's shoulders seemed to relax. "That would be great, Chloe. If you're sure."

"Definitely," Chloe insisted, putting an arm around Tyler. "How could I resist a fellow Potterhead?"

"And, if it's okay, I thought Holt could show you around a little, just till I get done? Maybe he can run you through town and point out some of the highlights? Just so you get your bearings. Then he can bring you by the office and you can see what we do there. If you're interested."

It was almost laughable. Obviously the box thing wasn't Reese's fault, but still, whatever the reason, here she was after all these years and her father was still too busy for her. *But, if I'm not leaving, I should make the most of it.* She did have a job to get done and it wouldn't hurt to have someone show her around. And if that came with the added bonus of picking the brain of someone who really knew Reese McConnaughey in order to get the real story on him, or at least another version of it, so much the better.

ELEVEN

Ten minutes in the car with Tyler was all it took for Chloe to fall in love with him completely. Far from the shy kid she had first met in his bedroom, he now babbled incessantly all the way to William Nelson Elementary School. By the time he got out, Chloe had learned that a boy named Mack was his best friend, that a girl named Kinsey wouldn't leave him alone, and his teacher, Mrs. Ellis, hadn't had to put his clothespin on the red light in two weeks.

"He really likes you," Holt noted after Tyler hopped out of the car and raced inside the school.

"Feeling's mutual."

"Wait till he meets your boyfriend. An ex-navy SEAL that works on movies? Forget it. The kid'll go crazy."

Chloe eyed him quizzically. "How did you know about Jack?"

Holt shrugged. "Reese mentioned him once or twice. Or three times." He turned to grin at Chloe. "I've never seen Reese use spare time to do anything but work, but that book your boyfriend wrote? He couldn't put it down. And then he kept going on and on about it."

Chloe smiled, a twinge of pride slipping out. "Jack's a good writer."

"So are you, apparently," Holt said wryly. "Reese told me. Bragged, actually. It was getting a little annoying."

Chloe sat quietly, digesting that unexpected nugget. Before she could come up with a reply, Holt spoke up again. "So, where do you want to start? I could drive you around a bit, give you the lay of the land and some ideas if you want."

"Are you sure this is okay?" she asked. "You're probably really busy and I'd be fine on my own."

"Are you kidding?" he insisted. "Perfect fall day, driving around, grabbing coffee and crullers…you're doing me a favor, giving me an excuse to be out. I'm supposed to check on something related to the Donner thing at some point today, but I don't know when that'll be. Till then," he grinned, "I'm all yours."

When she didn't relent, he whined, "Come onnnnnn—"

"Okay, okay," she laughed. "If you're sure."

"Good," he said, nodding his head to seal the decision as he turned his Audi A6 out of the school drive, headed back towards the center of town.

Franklin's streets were full at this hour, cars crawling along to work and school at a snail's pace, thanks to the traffic lights and four-way stops at the end of every block. Holt maneuvered down several of these, then pulled into the left turn lane at a red light and waited, the clicking of his turn signal droning in the background. Straight ahead, a couple of blocks from where they sat, the construction site loomed. Even from that distance, Chloe could see that the structure had been badly burned on multiple levels.

"You said you had to work on the 'Donner thing.' Donner's the angry guy from last night?"

Holt nodded. "Phillip Donner. He's the owner of the construction project—and the victim in the criminal trespass and assault case we handled for Kurt Sims."

"That's Emma's friend's dad?"

The light turned green and Holt pulled forward, turning left. "Yeah, that's right. I forgot. You met Jacob last night."

"The kids mentioned that Reese represented him."

"It was just a favor, really. A little pro bono thing."

"Pro bono?"

"Oh—for free. Kurt was picketing at the construction site—something he does a lot—and it got out of hand. Walked straight onto the property, started yelling at Donner. Sims says a gust of wind blew the sign out of his hands, accidentally cutting Donner across the face. Donner says that Sims attacked him with it. We pled it down. It was pretty simple."

"That was nice of you and Reese to help him out like that."

"Yeah, well…it's turned into the gift that keeps on giving. Now, any time there's a problem with Sims at the site, we get a call. Hence, our presence last night. It could've been worse, though. Originally Sims wanted us to represent him in his lawsuit against Donner over the construction, but he couldn't pay us for that either. Wanted us to do it 'because it's the right thing to do,'" Holt said, making air quotes with his right hand, apparently parroting what Sims had said to them. "A case like that—just the costs alone—we couldn't afford to handle it pro bono."

"What's he suing Donner for?"

He braked as they approached a four-way stop, then looked at her, amused. "You sure you want to hear about this? It's pretty boring stuff."

Chloe shrugged. "It wasn't boring last night."

He chuckled. "True. So you know that Franklin's known as a Civil War town, right? Site of one of the war's bloodiest battles and all that?"

She nodded. Her research had made that very clear.

"So most of downtown is protected by historical preservation ordinances, including at least part of the area there at Five Points—that intersection at the construction site. Sims fancies himself a historian-slash-preservationist, whatever that is, and wanted to put a museum and tour company there. It's a great location for tourism, great exposure. He figured he could make a living and protect the history at the same time.

"So Kurt spends a chunk of his savings getting plans drawn up, having surveys done, courting the owner, the business association, the historical society—not to mention convincing investors. He claims he finally had the whole thing locked down, when Phillip Donner swoops in. He claims Donner used intimidation and maybe even blackmail to get the owners to sell to him, stealing the whole thing out from under him. Kurt loses his dream and his savings, not to mention that Donner builds a retail space on what Kurt considers holy historical ground. I mean, Donner's having to include a small memorial park beside the building to satisfy the ordinances, but still, it's like slapping Kurt in the face."

"So, can he win? I mean, if he did, wouldn't you get paid then?"

"*If* he can prove his case, and *if* he can outlast Donner's money and lawyers, then, yeah, we might get paid at the end. But it's not our problem anymore. Another lawyer, Cecilia Tucker—that's Trip

Tucker's mom," he clarified, then added when Chloe looked confused, "Emma's other friend from last night?"

"Oh, right."

"Well, she stepped up. I think she felt bad for the guy. And there's a lot of press in it for her. It's a pretty high profile case and she's running for Circuit Court judge next fall, so even if she doesn't get paid she'll get something out of it. I guess she figures any press is good press. She's in practice by herself, so we've offered to help out if she ever has a conflict or something."

"And Donner's still just building away while the lawsuit's going on?"

"Yeah. Sims tried to get a temporary injunction to halt construction, but the judge wouldn't grant it. So Donner is still building, because he wants to finish the thing and sell it, to make his profit. But even if he completes it, he won't be able to lease or sell it until the lawsuit is resolved. So that site could sit finished, but unused and unsold for months, if not years. Sims, on the other hand, is still pushing his lawsuit, hoping to eventually get a permanent injunction and a forced sale of the property to him. If that happens, Donner will lose a bundle."

"Why doesn't Sims just go somewhere else?" Chloe asked, as Holt rolled up to another stop sign.

"I'm not sure he can. Like I said, he's spent a fortune getting to this point. Plus, there's the historical angle keeping him focused on the site. What you have to understand is that Sims is a 'true-believer.' A fanatic about what he calls the undoing of history. If you ever talk to him, you'll see what I mean. He's got a day job as a telemarketer, but he spends most of his time running the 'Society for the Historical Preservation of the South,'" Holt said, rattling the name off with a self-righteous air he was obviously borrowing from Sims. "From what I understand, he's spent a lot of time bouncing all over the Southeast fighting the good fight whenever landmarks or protected sites are endangered."

"And Donner really thinks Sims would blow up his building?"

Holt groaned. "Yeah, Donner definitely thinks that. I'm more concerned with what the police are thinking. Hopefully it won't come to anything, but..." He trailed off, shrugging.

"What about that corpse they found? Have they released any more information about it?" she asked as Holt banked hard around a ninety degree turn, causing her to lean slightly in his direction.

"Not yet. But I'm working on getting the story."

For a moment, silence filled the car. Through the opposite windows, Chloe could see the Harpeth River as it cut through the land on a path parallel to the road. The banks of the small river were thick with brush and overhanging trees. Though the water level was low now, she wondered if the tributary ever spilled into the roadway during extended periods of heavy rain.

She turned her gaze back to Holt as he slowed at yet another traffic light. "So that thing at Reese's house this morning—could it have something to do with last night?"

"Like what? Donner sending some kind of message?"

Chloe nodded.

Holt grimaced doubtfully, waggling his head back and forth. "I suppose anything's possible but that would be an awful risk for Donner on a case that he will probably eventually win anyway. Plus, technically, we aren't even on the case. And like you said earlier, if we don't know who left the box, we don't know what to 'back off' of. So if that was Donner's plan, it was a bad one." He shook his head, dismissing the idea. "My money's on one of the divorce or child support crazies. You should see a couple of the divorces we have in the hopper. There's this one nut-job spouse—"

A trilling sounded over the car speakers, interrupting him. Holt pulled out his cell and answered it. Several "mmm-hmms" and "all rights" were exchanged before he hung up.

"So," he said, accelerating through the next intersection, "that thing I was supposed to check on? That call was it. I need to handle this if you've got a few minutes for a detour. Shouldn't take long. It's close by."

Chloe shrugged. "Sure."

"Great. Then let's go see a man about a dead body."

TWELVE

"...stuffed in a hazardous waste drum," finished the burly man sitting across the table from Holt and Chloe, whom Holt had introduced as "Pax." Pax wiped a blotch of ketchup off his face with the back of his hand. "Thing was halfway dissolved already. You should have seen it." He turned to Chloe. "Had to mop the floor after."

Chloe smiled obligingly and swirled her glass of half-and-half tea, grateful that she wasn't eating. Holt had driven them to an out-of-the-way diner just south of town called "Greasy's," which most definitely would not be making it into the article. They had found Pax at a table at the back, already well into his plates of waffles, sausage, bacon, and eggs. Based on the pool of grease lining each one, the place lived up to its name.

"I'll take your word for it," Holt quipped, taking a sip of what smelled like mediocre black coffee. "How did they find it?"

"Fire hoses," mumbled Pax. "That high-powered water hit a row of some waste drums and flipped 'em over. Knocked a bunch of the lids off. Half of 'em were empty. This one wasn't. Good thing they saw that body before that water hit it full on, or it woulda' been nothin' but jelly all over the site instead of laying on a slab at the coroner's."

Pax shoveled in more food as Chloe cut her eyes at Holt. He had explained that Pax worked as part of the janitorial staff of the Tri-County Coroner's Crime Laboratory, which three of the area counties used for all their evidentiary needs. He had gone on to explain that in exchange for the occasional breakfast, Pax was sometimes willing to share information he had picked up around the offices, sometimes giving Holt tips or a heads-up on forthcoming evidence a little sooner than he would otherwise get it through the normal course of things. This had, on occasion, been very useful in planning defenses for existing clients, and even in getting new clients. Holt had assured Chloe that this arrangement was on the up and up, but the more she listened, the more questionable it seemed.

"So who is it?" Holt asked.

Pax picked a stray crumble of egg from the stubble on his jaw. "No idea. This one's too far gone for prints or facial recognition. Apparently they'd stored some sorta acid or somethin' in that drum. Heard 'em talkin' about dental. Maybe DNA even."

"Girl? Guy?"

"Don't think they could tell."

"So they'll ship it off to Metro Forensics for the autopsy."

Pax nodded. "Later today," he grunted.

"Getting that back could take a while."

"Depends," Pax mumbled.

Holt paused, waiting until Pax swallowed. When he had, Holt asked, "So are they looking at anybody in particular?"

Pax looked up from his hash browns and frowned. "They don't tell me stuff like that."

Holt eyed him warily. "They don't tell you anything, Pax. I'm not interested in what they tell you. I'm interested in what you hear. Or maybe those eggs are enough to fill you up this morning."

Pax leaned back, rubbed his stomach, and propped his fork up on the edge of the melamine topped table. "No. I'm pretty hungry today."

"Okay. So are they looking at anybody?"

"Just heard a name." He paused. "Sims."

Holt nodded. "Okay."

"Heard your boss's name, too."

That got Holt's attention. And Chloe's.

"You heard them talking about Reese?" Holt pushed.

Pax nodded. "They were tossing around whether he's up to defendin' an arson charge and a murder charge at the same time."

"So the construction site fire was arson. They're sure?"

"Oh yeah. Found the bomb and everythin'. Or least what's left of it."

"Why do they suspect Sims?

Pax shrugged. "Dunno. Figures, though, don't it? Him bein' behind the lawsuit and all," he answered, wiping excess yolk off of his hand with a paper napkin.

Holt breathed in heavily through his nose and exhaled. "That it?"

"That's it."

"Okay," Holt replied, rising as he crumpled up his napkin and tossed it beside Pax's plate, along with a ten-dollar bill. "Let me know if you hear anything else."

"Will do," Pax mumbled through the bacon he'd just stuffed in his mouth, and gave a frumpy two-fingered salute off the brim of his John Deere cap.

Holt nodded Chloe towards the door, when Pax interrupted. "Oh, and one other thing. They said somethin' about havin' concrete evidence or somethin'."

Holt stopped. "Evidence of what?"

Pax shrugged. "Did'n say."

Holt pursed his lips thoughtfully then ushered Chloe towards the door again. They made their way through the gravel lot to Holt's car and once they pulled out, she turned to him.

"So he tells you all that just for buying him breakfast at this dive?"

"Yes. Although," he baited, throwing her a glance, "that breakfast comes with a side of Ulysses Grant."

Chloe squinted, bemused. Then it clicked for her. "Your napkin?"

Holt nodded.

"That's got to be illegal."

"No. It's just good intel gathering." Holt smirked mischievously. "I actually researched it because I definitely wouldn't want to cross a line. Pax doesn't work for the lab. He's with a private service. And he's got no confidentiality agreement with any of the offices where he works. Although, if they were smart they would make him sign one. If they want to keep things to themselves, they ought to pay attention to who's around when they're yapping." He shrugged. "It's their own fault, really."

"And this guy just feeds you information all the time?"

Holt shook his head. "Nah. I don't have that much of a need for it. Only every once in a while. A guy I know that handles a lot more of the heavy criminal representation put me on to Pax a couple years ago."

"But I thought you weren't getting involved in Sims's case?" Chloe pressed.

"Reese told him we'd find out what we could. Just as a favor. It was pretty obvious they'd be at least considering Sims for this after the assault case."

"And who's paying for Pax's breakfast?"

"Sims. We just won't charge him for our time for this one. He can afford the breakfast. But after this, he's on his own unless he wants to put us on retainer."

"Mm-hmm," Chloe retorted. "So your generosity has its limits."

"Hey, a man's gotta make a living."

"Do you think they'll charge Sims?"

"Depends. But it does sound like they may have found something. If not," he mused, running a hand through his hair, "it would be a pretty far leap from an assault and a lawsuit to arson and murder. We'll just have to wait and see."

"That body…the way it sounded…I can't imagine."

"It definitely makes things interesting," he piped back, apparently unfazed. "So where to?" he asked her. "We've still got a couple of hours before I need to head to the office. You hungry?"

Chloe spread her hands wide. "This is your party."

"That's what I like to hear. Okay, so first, I'm thinking you need an orange-lavender latte from Frothy Monkey to carry you through to lunch—"

He stopped short as his phone rang and Reese's name popped up on the car's entertainment display. He answered on his cell, then, after a short conversation, clicked off. He faced Chloe, his expression apologetic.

"Soooo, Reese's schedule has ended up being even more packed than it was before. Turns out the police want to interview Sims."

"So you guys are getting dragged into it after all."

"Looks like it. And Reese is going to need help. He's just got too much to do today. I'm going to have to go in."

Chloe waved him off. "It's fine. Really."

"Reese said that he'd be home for an early dinner if you want to join them later."

"Okay, sure," she replied, without any confidence whatsoever that such a dinner would ever take place.

THIRTEEN

With everyone busy for the rest of the day, Chloe headed back to Main Street, determined to squeeze in as much of it as she could. Pedestrians of all sorts steadily streamed down the sidewalks on both sides, even during the Friday workday hours, passing a mix of designer, eclectic, and specialty stores offering something for every type of shopper.

The sounds of the bustling town serenaded her as she made her way from one shop to another, discovering treasure after treasure. In one she found hand-painted pottery in bright pastels depicting things like bunnies, cows or landmarks of the town. A few doors down she found a hip boutique filled with striking contemporary clothes and accessories. A black dress displayed in its window fit her better than anything she had ever owned, and she bought it as a splurge, thinking how much Jack would like it. She gave the owner her business card and took some shots before leaving for the next stop, a chocolate shop with every form of confection you could imagine: truffles, caramel apples, chocolate clusters, and homemade fudge cut on a marble slab. The heavenly cocoa smell was enough to send a person running for Weight Watchers. Telling herself it was all for the research, Chloe bought at least two dozen different sweets, leaving with a bulging paper bag that would keep her in a sugar coma till Christmas.

As she stepped out the sweet shop's door, a bright red and green trolley reminiscent of those in San Francisco, though without the electric lines, rolled by. Chloe made a mental note that she would have to take at least one ride on it before leaving town. She popped into the next store, which specialized in home decor, including velvety 2000 count linens on fanciful beds fit for a princess, and china and glass tableware displayed beautifully on a white rustic farm table with ivy and ceramic dove centerpieces.

After two hours her stomach started rumbling, so she stopped by McCreary's Irish Pub for a late lunch of the Dublin Pot Pie, a creamy mix of chicken, carrots, and corn in a flaky crust, served with homemade soda bread. By the end she was so full, she wanted a nap more than anything, but with almost half the street still to explore, she headed back out, moving down the paver-bordered sidewalk. This time she noticed that, spread amongst the common concrete pavers that ran the length of the curb, were many larger ones, about twelve inches by twelve inches, that contained inscriptions, probably purchased as part of a fundraising effort by the city. Some were memorials noting dates of birth and death. Others contained dedications to a loved one. Some marked milestones like anniversaries or graduations. One in particular caught Chloe's attention: "From Robert to Pauline, loving you since 1939." She snapped a photo of it as the early afternoon sunlight fell across its surface, highlighting the dimples in the stone.

However things turned out with Reese, she was definitely going to have to bring Jack back here to visit. Thinking of him, she realized she hadn't caught him up on the craziness of the morning. Spotting a nearby bench, she sat down, pulled out her cell and called him.

As she waited for him to answer, she looked back at the paver and couldn't help but think that maybe someday, somewhere, she and Jack would get a paver of their own.

FOURTEEN

"You stood me up," Jack said, tapping his fingers impatiently on the table. The leggy red-head slipped into the seat across the table as the wind whipped up. It jostled the bright orange patio umbrella hovering above them and flipped wisps of the woman's long, wavy hair back and forth before they settled across her ivory cheek.

Lila Bartholomew sighed and dramatically pushed her oversized tortoise shell sunglasses atop her head. "I know. I'm sorry. I…I just couldn't make it." Jack's ex-wife signaled the waiter and ordered a non-fat macchiato. Jack eyed her doubtfully, keeping a tight grip on the black coffee he had been nursing for the last twenty minutes.

"You said it was life or death," he replied. The little cafe in Burbank was busy this afternoon, its half dozen street-side tables occupied. The loud buzz of conversation and traffic zipping by kept their exchange private.

"It is. And I really appreciate you coming. I wasn't sure you would after…well after everything."

He hadn't seen her since before their long, drawn-out divorce was finalized last summer, but on the surface she looked exactly the same, ever-fashionable in her short, dark blue slip dress and suede ankle boots, gold earrings dangling. She did seem to move a bit differently than he remembered, with a little less…flare. And her eyes looked weak. It was surreal, being here, with this woman who had not only cut him loose for another man after just eighteen months of marriage, but who had also waged a vicious divorce against him for two years before finally walking away with a big chunk of his money.

She watched him, as if waiting for him to say something in return, but instead he just sipped his coffee. Finally, she inhaled sharply through her slight nose. "Alexander left me."

Jack's brow furrowed and before he could help it, an amused look stole over his face. "Really? Romeo took off?"

She pursed her lips at the dig, exasperation tinged with hurt swimming behind her eyes.

Jack noticed the latter and, surprising himself, actually felt a little bad. "Sorry," he apologized. An uncomfortable silence filled the gap between them. "I don't know what you want me to say."

She shook her head. "Nothing. Nothing about that anyway. It's not why I'm here. Well, not exactly." She eyed him appraisingly. "You look different."

"Yeah, well, a lot has changed."

"I heard about that mess in Miami."

Jack subtly reached for his bad leg. "It all turned out okay."

"I was worried."

"You shouldn't have been. I'm not your problem anymore."

Lila sighed again, a note of weariness slipping through. "Can we not do this? Please?"

How many times had he thought about this moment? A face-to-face with the person who had caused him so much misery. He considered all the clever comments and stinging barbs he had played out in his head over the years. Maybe that was one of the reasons he had shown up. For a chance to deliver some of those carefully crafted insults. To leave some kind of mark. He wasn't proud of the thought. But even if that was true, it wasn't the only reason he had come. He had also been drawn by the desperation in her voice when she had called. The rescuer in him couldn't help it. Something had just seemed off.

Now, laying eyes on her, he believed that he might have been right about that. Yes, she was the same person he had once found hypnotic, drawing him into a hurricane of a romance that ended just as chaotically as it began. But this version of Lila seemed more depressed than dazzling, and despite himself, his ire softened. "Okay," he surrendered. "We won't do that." She smiled faintly at the concession.

The waiter returned with her macchiato and she took a long sip on it before speaking again. "After Alexander left I was really messed up. Angry, depressed, no place to go—it wasn't the money," she interrupted herself, anticipating Jack's coming question when he moved to speak. "I'm fine in that department. It was emotional, you know?"

"Yeah, I know," Jack groused, his gaze fixed on hers as if trying to telepathically remind her that, not only was she the reason he was well acquainted with emotional misery, but that the reason she was fine in the money department was because she had taken so much of his in the divorce.

She seemed to get the message. "I'm sorry I was so hard on you," she said ruefully. "I really am. I didn't have to make it so difficult."

His first thought was, *If you feel so badly, you could just give the money back*. His second was that this was the first time he could remember Lila actually saying she was sorry. For anything. Before or after their marriage. He digested that truth, wondering what kind of power Alexander had held over Lila in order to elicit such a change by his leaving.

"What do you want, Lila? What's so life or death that you needed to see me after all this time?"

She paused, gathering her words as a woman strolled by on the adjacent sidewalk, a fluffy, cinnamon-colored Shih Tzu prancing several feet ahead of her on a long, crystal-studded leash. "Me, Jack. I'm the life or death thing." She twisted her hands in front of her. "I'm struggling, Jack. Really struggling. I see now how much I screwed up. *Really* screwed up. I had a good thing. You were the real deal, and I couldn't see you for what you were until you were gone. Well, until Alexander was gone, and then I finally got it. I was stupid and selfish and I should have never left you. I had everything—"

"Lila," Jack said, leaning into the table, his hands held out in front of him as if warding her off. "Don't."

"But Jack, I need to—"

"Lila, I'm with someone."

"I know. I heard that too."

"So then, why—"

"I'm here because I'm out of answers. I know you and I are done. I'm not crazy. But, look, throughout everything that happened between us, you had this, this stability, this foundation or whatever and you kept your head even when things were at their worst." A sheepish look crossed her face. "I've been remembering that lately.

Now that Alexander..." She faltered, instead waiving a careless goodbye to finish her sentence.

"Now that you've had your own heart broken?"

She nodded and looked off across the street again. "I'm losing myself, Jack. Something's got to give."

"And you think I'm the answer?"

"I don't know. But I know you had something that kept you going. And I need that."

"You know what it was. We've talked about this before."

"Your faith."

"When you boil it down, yeah."

"Then that's it. That's what I need."

Before this moment, Jack would have confidently bet that he would never, *ever* hear from Lila Bartholomew again. But that Lila would return, contrite and seeking answers about life and truth and what really mattered? For that bet he would have pushed all the chips to the center, cleaned out his bank account, and borrowed as much as the house would allow.

FIFTEEN

"Hey, not that way, go right!"

Chloe was standing on Reese's porch, and he had just opened the front door when she heard Tyler yelling frantic instructions to some unseen person somewhere further back in the house.

"That sounds serious," she commented, stepping inside as Reese closed the door behind her. She turned towards him and noticed that his eyes were weak, his clothes rumpled, and he gave off an overall air of exhaustion. The day had taken its toll.

"Video games are a serious thing for an eight-year-old. I'm glad you could make it," he told her, motioning for her to follow him down the hallway. They walked past the dining room, following the hallway to where it opened into a large white kitchen with a six-seat marble counter that divided it from a bright family room. In its center, two gray slipcovered couches faced each other over a trunk that served as a coffee table. Tyler and Emma's friend, Jacob, sat on the floor in front of it, energetically playing a video game that apparently set humankind against an army of zombies.

"They've been at it for an hour," Reese told her, smiling. "Her friends are actually really good with him."

"That's nice," Chloe said, then turned to see Emma and Trip standing at the back of the kitchen near the microwave.

"We're making nacho cheese," said Emma, holding up a spoon dripping with yellow goo. "You want some?"

"Chloe!" Tyler yelled, just noticing her. He jumped up, abandoning his controller, and ran over to her.

"Hey bud!" Chloe chuckled in surprise as he hugged her tightly and briefly around her waist before racing back to the game. She turned to Emma. "Thanks for the offer, but I'm okay for now. Think I'll hold off for dinner. Hey, Trip," she said, nodding at him. He smiled and nodded back.

Reese glanced at the microwave, then back at Emma. "Don't fill up on dip, okay? We're taking Chloe out in a few minutes."

Emma rolled her eyes.

"Out?" Chloe asked, surprised that they weren't staying at the house, which would have been a little more private. *Then again,* she thought, *that's probably why.*

"Oh," Reese said, hesitantly. "I hope that's okay. I'm not much of a cook—"

"Seriously," mumbled Emma.

"—and I thought going out would be better. We can come back here afterwards if you want."

"That's fine," Chloe said, wondering when, if ever, she might finally get a few minutes alone with Reese to do what she had actually come to Franklin to do. Maybe never. Maybe he had decided that he didn't really want time alone to discuss anything that might be uncomfortable after all.

"Come on in here for a second," Reese said, taking her through a short butler pantry into the dining room. The pseudo-office was beyond cluttered. It looked as if he had been working for hours. Papers covered the table in no particular pattern, the computer was on and a half-drunk cup of coffee perched precariously on a stack of files. "Holt just got here too. He's been bringing me up to speed. I haven't really gotten to talk to him today either."

"Hey Chloe," said Holt, looking up from a file he was flipping through. Contrary to Reese, whatever Holt had been doing over the last several hours didn't seem to have left him any worse for wear. He was still perfectly coiffed, his shirt still wrinkle-free, and his smile still energetic. "Good day?" he asked.

"It was, actually. Took in Main Street, got a lot of good shots, and probably gained about five pounds. You?"

Holt shook his head. "Nothing that interesting. Spent the afternoon in court on a custody hearing."

"So," Reese said, directing himself to Holt, "you were saying?"

"Oh yeah," Holt replied, turning in his seat towards Reese. "Based on what Pax said, they are really looking at Sims. And they feel pretty good about it."

"What evidence do they have?"

"He didn't know. But he said they had something concrete."

"Concrete? Already? On the arson or the murder?"

"Didn't say."

"Have you briefed Sims?"

Holt shook his head. "Not yet."

"We need to sit down with him, let him know they're looking at him and find out what this solid evidence is that they have. I don't know that we need to represent him much further than that, but at least we can gather something to give the public defender."

"You said you had photos?" Holt asked, casting around for a sign of them.

"Well, the same ones everybody else has." Reese moved to the computer and tapped a key, pulling up a slideshow. Chloe watched the two of them from the doorway to the butler pantry, wondering if she ought to give them a minute. "Donner released these to the paper. They went online this morning," Reese explained to Holt, as he began clicking through the photos of the damaged site, lingering a bit on each one to give Holt time to take it in. "I'll bet the investigators aren't happy about it. I'm not even sure how he would have gotten access to the site already."

She felt a presence behind her and turned to see Emma and Trip standing there, sharing a bowl of dip and chips between them, watching the lawyers click through the photos. "They're always like that," Emma said, as Trip lifted a goo-covered nacho to his mouth and crunched. "Working, I mean. They never stop."

The two teens stepped around Chloe to get a better look. "Dang, that really did some damage," Trip observed.

"Yeah," agreed Reese. "You can see the point of origin," he said, indicating a spot at the center of the damage displayed in one photo, then continued advancing through the rest, all depicting various aspects of the destruction—toppled scaffolding; debris scattered over recently poured, pinkish-tinted flooring on the lower level that looked gouged; frayed and burned orange netting; and more. "It's a mess and it lit up one heck of a fire, but it's not as bad as it could have been. Apparently it wasn't a very powerful bomb. Whoever did this wasn't trying to take the whole thing down."

"Daaaddd!" Tyler yelled from the other room. "I'm starving! Can we go now?"

"Yeah, sure," Reese called back. He turned to Holt. "Let's finish this later," he said, slapping the laptop shut and herding them all into the kitchen.

"Glad you had a good day," Holt said, stepping towards the kitchen side door to exit. "You guys have a nice dinner and I'll see you tomorrow, Reese. Trip, Jacob, Emma, Tyler," he said, throwing a wave at them before heading out the kitchen side door to the driveway, "see you guys later." Only Tyler returned the goodbye.

"So, where do you want to go?" Reese asked Chloe as the door closed behind Holt. "I was thinking—"

"Mellow Mushroom! Mellow Mushroom!" Tyler shouted in a sing-song voice from his position in front of the television, not taking his eyes off the on-screen action.

"Tyler, I don't think Chloe wants pizza," Reese countered.

"No, it's fine," Chloe said.

Reese wrinkled his nose questioningly, prompting assurances from Chloe.

"No, really. I like pizza."

"See, Dad? She likes pizza. She *likes* it." He fired and four more zombies went down.

"All right, all right. Emma," he turned, "you ready to go?"

Emma stopped, mid-chip crunch, eyeing him with disdain. She swallowed. "Yeah, sure." She cocked her head towards Trip. "You guys wanna come?"

"Um, no we were heading out anyway," Trip said. "I've got to get home, and I think Jacob's dad wanted him back tonight." He set the cheese bowl on the counter. "Yo, Jacob. Time to go."

Jacob slapped Tyler on the back as he tossed his controller down. "Next time, little man," he said as Tyler nodded, before firing one last time and shredding Jacob's on-screen player.

*****

After a long dinner over a very cheesy, gooey pizza, salads, and two pitchers of soda, Reese pushed open the door leading out of Mellow Mushroom as Tyler scrambled beneath his arm and onto the Main Street sidewalk. It was now nearly eight o'clock as the four of them walked towards the car. Tonight they had to park a few blocks away since parking on the square and Main Street was blocked off in preparation for Franklin's annual Pumpkin Fest, taking place the next day. A dark velvet draped the sky, autumn stars peeking out bleakly like pinholes in it, a complement to the flickering street lamps spaced along the road. Empty white tents lined either side of the road, waiting to be filled in the morning with what Chloe imagined would be all sorts of fantastic merchandise and goodies. Glancing back towards the square, she could see a flurry of movement as workers bustled around setting up an extravagant display of hay bales, pumpkins, and scarecrows.

"This festival," Chloe asked, as Tyler dragged Emma across the next intersection headed for a toy store halfway down the next block, "it's a big deal?"

Reese shrugged. "They're all a big deal. We have something like four of them a year. If you really want to see something, come back for 'Dickens of a Christmas.' If you've never seen two hundred people dressed like they belong in Victorian England dancing in the streets, you haven't lived."

Chloe chuckled. "Will the kids come tomorrow?"

Reese nodded. "They'll want to." He turned towards her. "Are you up for it? I need to work part of the day but I could take a couple hours off."

Chloe sighed. She had been hoping for more than a couple hours with Reese, but it was starting to look like a few hours at a time was the best she was going to get. "Sure. What time—"

"Oh, shoot," Reese growled as he pulled a fistful of dollars from his pocket. "I forgot the tip. Hold on for a second."

"Yeah, sure," Chloe called after Reese as he strode swiftly back toward the restaurant. Chloe stopped, watching as Tyler stood with Emma, pointing animatedly at something in the toy store window. *They're tight, those two,* Chloe thought, a memory of her and Tate telling ghost stories in the closet flashing in her mind. Distracted by the thought, Chloe barely noticed the swiftly moving figure entering from the side street between them and racing towards Tyler and Emma. Dressed in jeans and a sweatshirt with the hood pulled up over his head, he collided hard and intentionally with Emma, ripping her purse from her shoulder and continuing down the street away from them at breakneck speed.

"Hey!" Chloe heard Emma yell before charging headlong after the thief.

"Emma, stop! Don't!" Chloe shouted after her, sprinting towards where Tyler stood, confused and staring after his sister.

By the time Chloe reached Tyler, Emma had already disappeared down the block, having taken a hard left around the corner at Five Points to follow the thief.

"That guy!" Tyler yelled as Chloe took his hand. "That guy just *hit* her and took off! She went after him…"

The rest of Tyler's sentence was lost on Chloe as her mind frantically vacillated between what to do. She wanted to race after Emma, to help, to protect her, but Tyler was here and Reese was still inside the restaurant. She couldn't just leave Tyler on the sidewalk.

And then Reese stepped out the door and Chloe was hollering at him. "Reese! Reese! Take Tyler! Take him!" Reese instantly realized something was wrong and jogged towards them, picking up speed as he went. Chloe grasped Tyler's shoulder and looked him in the eye.

"Stay here! Wait for your Dad!" Chloe ordered, then took off after Emma.

Other pedestrians, witnesses to the shouting, were now eyeing Chloe strangely as she zipped past, trying to run as best as she could in the wedges she had worn to dinner. The two-inch heels were not easy to run in, and as she took a sharp turn at an old Presbyterian church on the corner, she rolled an ankle, struggling to remain upright. The street lamps ended here, and the darkness enveloped her as she charged down the side street. Halfway down the block, she could see Emma cutting again to the left, into an alleyway running between the buildings that made up the church complex. Chloe followed her into the alley, lit only vaguely by dim rooftop lights shining down from the corners of one of the buildings. Chloe squinted as she ran, just barely making out two figures tussling about twenty yards away.

"Emma!" Chloe shouted as she neared. The thief froze momentarily, looking up at Chloe. A ski mask covered his face. Recovering quickly, he seemed to use all his weight to shove Emma against a brick wall, while she scrabbled to take her purse back. The shove made her slip on some loose gravel scattered beside the wall and she twisted, falling awkwardly and landing with a yelp.

Chloe was just yards from them when the assailant briefly leaned over Emma, then quickly jerked up and barreled away in the opposite direction. Skidding on the same gravel, Chloe nearly fell over Emma before coming to a final stop.

"He stole my purse!" Emma bellowed, snapping her head in the direction her assailant had gone. "Yeah! You better run!" she yelled after him, clutching her arm.

"What were you thinking?" Chloe scolded. "He could've really hurt you!" She reached down to help Emma stand up, and the teen squealed at Chloe's touch. "He did hurt you," Chloe said, as Emma cradled her left arm close to her chest.

"He *stole my purse.* You're saying I should've just let him go?"

"Yeah. That's exactly what you should've done." Chloe breathed in deeply. "How bad is it?"

Emma looked at Chloe. "I dunno. Maybe broken. It feels weird."

"Come on," Chloe said, putting her arm around Emma and marching her towards the street. "Let's go find your dad."

"The idiot thinks I'm not going to report it," she said as they moved down the alley. "Fat chance."

"What?" Chloe asked, confused.

"He said to keep my mouth shut," Emma growled. "To keep what I saw to myself. But he's crazy if he thinks I'm not going to the cops."

"Emma!"

The frantic shout came from Reese who had just turned into the alleyway entrance with Tyler in tow.

"Great," Emma grumbled. "He's gonna love this."

SIXTEEN

The world looked so much different from down here, flat on his back, staring up at the patch of dark sky framed by the circle of trees in the little clearing. He noticed the stars now, each one, and oddly tried to remember the last time he had noticed them like this, but couldn't. As a boy, he had loved staring at them through his telescope, there at the beginning of life, at the start of whatever the journey held for him. He had loved imagining what lived beyond; what adventures he might have. How fitting that as his life slipped away, now that he was at the ending of all things, he was staring at the stars again. He involuntarily sniggered at the irony, or at least tried to, but the blood filling his lungs prevented it.

An ache grew beneath him, and he thought he must have fallen on stray tree limbs, or rocks or something. Or maybe the bullet had shattered something inside. It was hard to tell. His senses were beginning to fail him. Darkness crept in on the edges of his vision as the shooter stepped closer and closer, until standing directly over him. Their eyes met, and he found no sympathy in his killer's gaze. Just resolve.

Dread coursed through him as the killer raised the gun once more. He averted his eyes to the stars again, hoping for comfort. But none came. Instead, panic filled his heart because deep down he knew that, whatever came next, it would not be an adventure.

Not after all he had done.

SEVENTEEN

The ER waiting room of Middle-Tennessee Hospital was predictably stereotypical, with its unflattering fluorescent lights and uncomfortable plastic chairs lining the walls. An uneasy quiet hovered, as the sliding glass doors awaited the next panicked intrusion of someone clamoring for emergency treatment.

Chloe and Reese sat side by side in two of the pale gray chairs. Beside them was Tyler, asleep and leaning on Reese, his head tucked up under Reese's arm. Chloe checked her watch again. A nurse had taken Emma back thirty minutes earlier. Emma had not wanted anyone to accompany her. Chloe thought that was ridiculous, but didn't say anything when Reese acquiesced without a word.

"She doesn't like me around," Reese muttered, as if reading Chloe's mind. "It's just easier this way."

"You're wrong," Chloe contradicted confidently. "If anything she wants you around more than you are. This is just her way of sounding off about it. She told me you're never around. That you're always working. She wouldn't have said that if she didn't miss you being there."

Reese inhaled deeply. "I have to work. I bring it home as much as I can, so at least I'm around when they're around. I don't know what else I can do."

"I think maybe she means you're not *there* even when you are there, you know? That you're preoccupied." She noticed his shoulders sagging more deeply at this and felt sorry for him, which, again, surprised her. She was oddly moved to throw him a bone. "For what it's worth, I think most teenagers feel like that. You're doing the best you can. You're making an effort. She's just doing what teenagers do. If you really are around, then don't be too hard on yourself. She'll figure it out eventually."

"Maybe," he said, stroking the top of Tyler's head. "I know it's ridiculous to even try to apologize now, but even so, I'm sorry I was never there for you and Tate. I was an idiot. Selfish. Stupid."

He kept his stare on Tyler, unable, Chloe presumed, to look at her after making this admission. She rubbed her eyes, noticing for the first time how very tired she was. "It's done. We can't go back," she said, and like him, let her gaze drift to Tyler. "But for what it's worth, I'm really glad you're getting it right the second time around."

"It's worth a lot," he said, his voice soft. She didn't look at him, but sensed his gaze boring into her and guessed that he had finally looked her way.

A loud squeak sounded as the waiting room's swinging door opened and a nurse in cartoon-decorated scrubs came through, heading purposefully towards them. "Mr. McConnaughey?"

"Yes?" he replied, starting to stand before realizing a sleeping Tyler prevented it.

"Your daughter has a simple fracture," she reported. "We're going to set it shortly. We've got her pain under control and she's doing fine. She should be finished within an hour or so." When Reese nodded his understanding, she turned and walked back out.

They sat without speaking for a moment before Chloe asked, "How long before the police get here, you think?"

"Any minute, probably."

More silent moments passed.

"Did he hate me?" Reese's words, just whispers really, seemed to escape rather than be intentionally spoken. A heavy apprehension cloaked them.

"Who?" Chloe asked, though she thought she knew.

"Tate. Did he hate me?"

Chloe inhaled, her shoulders heaving. She still found it a bit unsavory to hear Reese speak Tate's name. "Hate's a strong word." She stopped there, intending to say more, but the truth was, she didn't know what to say. Tate had loathed their father. And he hadn't been alone.

"I don't blame him. Or you. It's what I deserve."

"He never had a chance to know you."

"Which is my fault."

Something in Chloe's heart twitched. For years she had imagined what it might be like to meet her father again, to torture him with tales of their broken childhood, their pain, Tate's dysfunction—but now, when it was hers to dole out, she found that pain was not something she wanted to inflict. She did not know Reese well yet, did not particularly like him or dislike him, and certainly felt no bond to him. But he was a person, sitting in front of her, in pain. And she had the power to ease it.

"He looked like me," she said, unbidden. "Same hair, same eyes. But we were really different on the inside. Liked different things—we could never agree on take-out. And he was really smart. I mean," she hedged, "I did okay, but he was a genius. Got a 35 on the ACT."

"I did well on the ACT," Reese echoed, his eyes brightening at learning of a connection, however slight, between him and his son.

Chloe smiled faintly. "Well I didn't even get close to that. He was an overachiever. An Einstein when it came to computers." She sighed, remembering. "It's what ended up getting him in trouble."

"What did he do with computers?"

"Wrote programming at first. In the end he was a hacker. He wanted a shortcut to a good life, and he found one. It just wasn't legal. Ended up getting him killed, and almost got me and Jack killed in the process."

Reese took that in, staring distantly through the windows, not really seeing. After several minutes, he spoke. "Your mother and I...we just..." Reese trailed off, words seeming to fail him. She understood why. There simply aren't any words that make abandoning your children okay.

Somewhere deep inside Chloe, knots of remembered worthlessness tightened. Reminding herself that she was not that eight-year-old little girl who had just been left by her daddy, her eyes flicked up to him.

"I know mom was hard to live with. I know she was an alcoholic. It couldn't have been easy. But you didn't have to leave *us*. Why? Why leave us?"

Reese's eyes reddened as he seemed to search for more words that wouldn't come. "It wasn't that I wanted to leave you. I just didn't see a way to stay. She would've made life miserable for me if I had tried to stay in Atlanta and be a part of your life. I was so tired. I panicked. I just wanted out. I never meant to stay gone forever. I figured that after a month or two, I would re-establish contact with you guys, re-enter your lives…but she wouldn't hear of it. I tried. I really did," he said, a hint of wetness appearing at the corner of his lids, "but she refused. Threatened to claim I had abused her. I was afraid of what that would mean. Afraid of losing my license. Of losing Andrea—" He cut himself off, apparently regretting bringing up Emma and Tyler's mom. The woman he had left them for. "Some part of me fooled myself into believing you two would be better off without the push and pull of divorced parents in your life. That she would give you more than I could."

"You were wrong," Chloe said, allowing herself the luxury of uttering the painful truth.

"I know. If I could do it over, I would do it differently. Do you believe me?"

He said it in the way a child would have asked, with uncertainty and timidity, begging with his tone the only answer that would give him any peace.

Chloe nodded.

"Do…do you think he would have forgiven me?"

Chloe's eyes flicked away, remembering Tate, his anger, his broken heart. She couldn't lie.

"No."

Reese nodded, snorting softly as if impressed with her unabashed honesty. He paused before asking, "Can you?"

Chloe turned back to him, biting her lip and fighting back her own tears, as she remembered the Bible verse she had read earlier in the day.

"Give me time."

EIGHTEEN

It was nearly one a.m. by the time Chloe crawled into her bed at the inn. It had taken forever for Emma to be discharged from the hospital. And though Tyler had fallen asleep in the waiting room, when they woke him to leave he had apparently gotten just enough rest to find a second wind. He had insisted on signing Emma's cast before going back to sleep, and Chloe had finally left them at their house while Tyler was still trying to decide which superhero to sign as.

Leaning into the half dozen down pillows, she lifted her cell to see the three texts and one voicemail Jack had left her that afternoon. She had intended to get back to him after dinner, but then everything with Emma had happened and there just hadn't been a good time to call from the hospital. She started to text a quick, *I'll call tomorrow*, but then realized it was two hours earlier in California. Maybe he would still be up. She smiled. *Those Hollywood types keep late hours, right?* The thought of hearing his voice sounded really good after the night she had been through.

Taking the chance that she might wake him, and hoping he wouldn't mind if she did, she tapped his name on the screen.

It only rang once.

"Hello? Jack's phone," answered an unfamiliar female voice. At eleven o'clock at night.

Chloe shot straight up, confused. "Um, I'm sorry," she said, thinking that despite the answerer mentioning Jack's phone, she must have called the wrong number. She pulled the screen down to check.

No. It was the right number. The screen wallpaper was a photo of her and Jack standing in Times Square, superimposed with the caller identification, "Jack."

"Oh, okay," the woman responded.

"No, wait—I'm looking for Jack Bartholomew?"

"Yes, this is his phone. May I ask who's calling?"

Chloe's stomach tightened. "Um, may I ask who's answering? Is he okay?"

"He's fine, just in the bathroom. I just answered out of habit. I can tell him you called."

Chloe's mind stumbled around the woman's words, her face scrunching in disbelief and the beginnings of panic. "Who are you?" she blurted sternly.

"I'm his wife," came the snippy response. "Who are you?"

NINETEEN

"Did you see that! Did you see that!" Tyler yelled, pointing at the pile of milk bottles he had knocked over with a baseball to win a prize that Chloe felt sure would not be worth the five dollars Reese had forked over for him to play.

The carnival was set up in a field just off Main Street beside an old silo that now simply functioned as a landmark. All the standards were there, including a Ferris wheel, carousel, mini-coaster, house of mirrors, and plenty of overpriced carnival games. Pumpkins and hay bales were scattered everywhere, and the tantalizing scent of cinnamon and apple spice floated in the air. Happy carnival music, piped out of speakers hidden behind the hay bales scattered throughout the property, added to the frivolity.

Chloe glanced over at Tyler, trying to pull herself out of the dismal thoughts that had plagued her all through the morning and now into the late afternoon. She had come along to the festival as promised after lunch, but her heart wasn't in it. All she could think about was the woman who had answered Jack's phone. *"I'm his wife,"* she had said.

His wife? What did she mean, "his wife"? That had to mean Lila, his *ex*-wife, didn't it? But as far as she knew Jack hadn't spoken to Lila in more than a year. Not since before their divorce had been finalized and he had fled to the Caribbean island of St. Gideon to recover.

St. Gideon. Where she had met Jack eight months earlier.

Why would they be talking now? And in his hotel room? Late at night? And worse, what if it wasn't Lila? What if there was someone else?

Some other "wife" she didn't know about? That just didn't seem possible. Not with the Jack she knew. But then…who had answered the phone? The heavy weight of doubt pressed down, and another wave of nausea rolled through her.

"That was awesome!" Emma praised, patting Tyler on the head as he swiped her hand away.

"Aw, quit it Em," he said, then leaned up on the divider separating him from the pimply teenager running the carnival game. "I want the purple elephant," he barked excitedly, before turning to Chloe. "You like purple, right?" he asked, apparently taking note of the lavender top she had on.

Chloe forced a smile. "It's one of my favorites."

Tyler grinned and presented her with the elephant. She took it, and this time, didn't have to work for the smile. "Thanks, Tyler," she told him.

"No problem," he said proudly before turning to Emma. "Let's go ride the Scrambler again!"

"I'm out," Chloe sighed. "Unless you want me to throw up on you." Tyler's face contorted in disgust.

"Um, pass," he called out, before grabbing Emma's hand and racing down the path between the carnival games and other rides towards the Scrambler.

"You too?" Reese asked, wrinkling his nose as he nodded in the direction of the ride.

Chloe watched the kids as she and Reese followed behind at a slower pace. "I haven't been able to do those spinning ones for years now. I can handle roller coasters, but the spinning ones kill me."

"Same here," Reese commiserated as they reached the fence surrounding the ride. They leaned against it while Emma and Tyler waited in line.

Everywhere she looked, happy faces moved along, laughing and smiling, the lively music providing a playful backdrop. But for Chloe it just underscored how miserable she was. She still had not spoken to or texted Jack, despite the fact that he had both texted and called that morning. She had not had the nerve to listen to his voicemail yet. The truth was she was just plain scared to do it. Maybe there was a simple explanation. But maybe there wasn't. Maybe the truth was as awful as she was imagining. And even if it wasn't, whatever the explanation was, Jack had been keeping things from her. Things like meeting with his ex-wife. And there was no scenario that made that okay.

As she and Reese silently watched Emma and Tyler move through the line, she wrestled with the possibilities. Secrets. It was the thing she hated most. The thing that had hurt her most in life. People keeping secrets. Jack had once kept secrets from her, lying to her about who he was when they had first met. He hadn't come clean until after she had discovered the lie herself and confronted him. He said, and it was true, that he had only lied to protect her, to keep her from running from him when she really needed him around. But she had hated the lie just the same. And she had made him promise never to do it again. He had sworn that he wouldn't. But now…this.

"You're awfully quiet," Reese observed, watching the kids as they boarded one of the cars.

"I just…have a few things going on," she answered noncommittally.

Reese nodded, running a hand through his salt and pepper hair. "You getting your work done? Your piece, I mean? For the magazine?"

"Working on it. I'm planning on hitting it pretty hard over the next couple of days."

Chloe's cell buzzed. It was Jack calling again. She slid it back in her pocket. She still wasn't ready to talk to him, and this wasn't the place to have that conversation anyway.

As if in answer to her phone, Reese's cell rang too. He answered his.

He listened for just a moment before exclaiming, "What?", followed by more earnest listening. "Wait, slow down. Slow down," he ordered the caller, whose frantic voice could even be heard by Chloe as a sharp, panicked buzzing. "Now say again—they did what?"

Tyler screamed and waved at them as one of the ride's shiny steel arms pushed the kids straight at them at breakneck speed before yanking them right back towards its middle. Neither Reese nor Chloe noticed though, as both of them were intently focused on Reese's call. "Don't do anything," Reese instructed the person on the other end of the line. "Stay right there with them. Give them my name, tell them I'm your lawyer and that I'm on the way."

He hung up. "Chloe I hate to do this, but can you stay with them?" he asked, nodding towards Emma and Tyler. "I can't stay, and I can't just leave them here. I could make them go home, but—"

"No, it's fine. What's going on?"

He frowned. "Phillip Donner is dead. They found him early this morning. The police are at Sims's place now with a warrant. They think he did it."

*****

The kids got in line to ride another time before finally exiting, laughing and hanging on one another. Chloe watched as Emma pulled out her phone to snap a quick photo in front of the ride and Tyler made a show of pretending to vomit on Emma's Converse sneakers. They started laughing again as they headed her way, breaking through the throngs of people.

"Niiice," Chloe drawled, squinting at Tyler.

"She almost did it for real!" Tyler teased.

"No way," Emma bit back, whipping her dark hair back over her shoulder. "Not even close."

"Where's Dad?" Tyler asked, looking around.

"He had to leave," Emma sniped. "Work."

Chloe eyed her, surprised. "How did you know?"

Emma shrugged. "It's always work."

Chloe felt for the girl. She knew what it was like to not have any faith in your father. In *this* father in particular. "It sounded pretty important," Chloe hedged, trying to make Emma feel better. "Something to do with Jacob's dad, actually."

Emma's expression softened and concern replaced the bitterness. "Is he okay? What's wrong now?"

Chloe bit her lip, not knowing whether it was appropriate to tell them. Or at the very least, whether it was something Tyler should hear. She opted to stay on the safe side. "Something's just come up. I'm sure Reese will explain later." She glanced over at the Ferris wheel, and jerked her head in that direction. "Who's up for a ride?"

After the Ferris wheel, they wandered back towards the square and Main Street, the fifteen dollars Reese had given Tyler to spend burning a hole in his pocket. They spent the next hour wandering the dozens of colorful booths lining the street, while Tyler grappled with the difficult decision of what he should purchase. Although his interest was limited to the toys, Chloe couldn't help noticing the variety of impressive goods represented by the local artisans. There were handmade soaps sliced from loaves that smelled of lavender, eucalyptus, and sandalwood; a series of original oil paintings of a red giraffe in various unexpected locales, like Times Square and the Golden Gate Bridge; and whimsical mobiles fashioned from scrap metal and soda cans. Chloe made mental notes and took photos as she went, making sure to take in as much detail as possible to include in her article.

Ultimately, Tyler's final contenders were a handcrafted wooden marshmallow shooter or a handcrafted wooden string puppet. Still unable to choose, Tyler opted to get his face painted like a lion while he decided. He was still in the artist's chair when Chloe's phone rang. It was a number she didn't recognize.

"Hello?" she asked tentatively.

"Hey, it's Holt. Is Reese with you?"

"How did you get my number?"

"Reese. Just in case. Is he with you?"

"No. He left over an hour ago to meet Kurt Sims. Something about an emergency."

"Yeah, I'm at the emergency. He called earlier, asked me to come on out here, saying that he needed to do something before he came out. I thought maybe he ran by the office or something, but he never showed and I can't reach him."

"I don't know. But I haven't heard from him."

Holt exhaled in frustration. "Okay, if you do, tell him I'm at Sims's place. It looks bad. I think we may be headed to the jail soon. Tell him to call ASAP."

"Okay," she started to say, but he hung up before she could get it out.

It was six o'clock and closing time at the festival before Chloe and Emma were finally able to drag Tyler away. As they walked the short mile down Franklin Road back to Reese's house, he marched his new puppet beside him, a chocolate-colored dog with a corkscrew pipe cleaner for a tail. An amber glow framed the sky above, first silhouetting the brick buildings of downtown then, after they had crossed the bridge over the Harpeth River, the ancient maples and oaks dotting the roadside. A chill settled in as the sun faded, and a slight shiver ran over Chloe's skin as they turned onto Reese's street.

Once in sight of home, Tyler took off running, heading for the side door. Chloe started after him, not wanting him to get too far ahead after what had happened at the house the day before. Apparently Emma had the same idea, because she started jogging too.

When she got close enough, Chloe saw that Reese's car was parked in the driveway, and a small bit of relief settled through her. As much as she had enjoyed spending the day with her siblings, she was ready to turn them back over and get some work done. *And deal with Jack,* she groaned inwardly, knowing that keeping her silence wasn't going to make anything better in the long run.

"Wait, Tyler. Hold up," Emma called after him. But Tyler bounded up the side steps, punched a code into the lock, and darted inside, Emma close on his heels. Chloe had just clasped her hand around the door handle when a shrill scream sounded from inside the house. Panic gripped her as, without thinking, she bolted into the house, her head swiveling frantically as she tried to detect where the scream was coming from. Realizing it was from the front of the house, she sprinted towards the front door, nearly stumbling over herself as she braked quickly to avoid trampling Tyler and Emma, both crouched on the foyer floor beside the unmoving form of their father, who lay at the base of the stairs. His body was twisted in an unnatural fashion, one leg tucked impossibly beneath him at an angle that certainly meant it was severely broken. Blood trickled both from his mouth and from an egg-sized knot on the side of his head. His children shook him, but he did not stir.

Messy, rust-colored words streaked the wall above where he lay. This was not paint. This was her father's blood. The words had been written in a hurry, with gaps in the lines and smears from letter to letter. But the message was clear.

I MEAN IT. BACK OFF. THE KIDS ARE NEXT.

TWENTY

For the second time in two days, Chloe waited under the halogen lights of a waiting room inside Middle-Tennessee Hospital. Only this time, it wasn't a broken arm. Instead the medics had thrown around words like, "head trauma," "tachy," and "non-responsive." Emma and Tyler sat in the corner of the small waiting room on the surgical floor, curled up on a sofa, their expressions vacant. Neither had said much of anything since arriving. Chloe had hoped they might drift off, but that had not happened either, despite the fact that it was now 10:00 p.m. and they had been busy since early that morning.

Reese was still in emergency surgery, something to do with swelling on the brain resulting from what appeared to be a blow to the head. The officers Chloe had briefly spoken with at the house as Reese was loaded in the ambulance said that, at this point, they couldn't tell whether the blow was from the fall down the stairs, or if Reese had been struck with an object. They did, however, find a golf club near the upper landing of the stairs.

Once in the emergency room, Reese had been triaged. In addition to being diagnosed with a compound fracture of his leg, a CAT scan had discovered the brain swelling for which they were now operating. That was three hours ago. Since then, they had only received one update from a nurse, who reported that the surgery was ongoing and that the surgeon would be out to speak with them when it was over.

Chloe felt numb. *How could this happen when she had only just connected with Reese? And how could it happen to these kids,* she thought, glancing over to see Emma, sitting cross-legged with Tyler curled up in her lap. *They've already lost their mother. What if Reese didn't recover?* What would they do then?

The door to the small room opened with a low whine borne from squeaky hinges. Holt stepped through, returning from hunting down whatever passed for coffee in this place at this hour. He had arrived at the hospital after they had, coming as soon as he had been able to break away from the Kurt Sims situation. The police had arrested Sims after all, and now he sat in a cell in the Tri-County Jail awaiting arraignment on Monday.

Holt walked over to the club chairs positioned across the room from the kids and held a foam cup out to Chloe, smiling thinly.

"This is the best I could do. Cafeteria's closed for the night. Had to use a machine." Chloe took the cup, thanked him, and cradled it. The aroma was stale but strong. She took a sip. "And, I finally managed to reach Andrea," he continued, taking the seat next to Chloe. They had been attempting to contact Reese's ex-wife ever since they arrived at the hospital.

"Is she coming?"

"Um, no."

Chloe's brow wrinkled in amazement. "Isn't she at least worried about the kids, if not Reese?"

"She says she's sure we've got it under control and there's no need for her to come all the way from Seattle. You know, she's not exactly a doting mother. They waited nearly ten years to have Emma and another ten to have Tyler. She even told me once she had never wanted kids. That the idea had been 'Reese's thing.'"

"Wow."

"Yeah. So I'm not surprised. Out of sight, out of mind, I guess, when it comes to the kids." He brought his cup to his lips and sipped. "Did they tell you anything new while I was gone?"

"Nope," Chloe answered. "Nothing."

"I'm sorry," Holt sighed, looking weary. "I should have gone looking for Reese when he didn't turn up. That's not like him. I should have known something was wrong."

To this point, every time Chloe had seen him, Holt had been a bright, confident, almost ebullient personality. A charismatic force. But sitting here now, he just seemed…less.

Chloe shook her head. "Don't be ridiculous. He's a grown man. You said yourself he told you he had something he had to do before meeting you. You couldn't have known he was hurt. Besides, you had a job to do."

"I'm not sure you can actually call that a job. More like charity work. Sims can't pay us. Reese only asked me to go out there as a favor to him because he's Emma's friend's dad. But that only goes so far. There's no way we would take on a murder case for free. I think we were just helping out until Sims could make other arrangements. He'll be able to do that on Monday at his arraignment and get a court-appointed attorney."

She sipped the coffee. It was odd to be discussing her father's business at a time like this. But they were here, with time to kill and nothing else to talk about. "So what happens to him now?"

"He'll just sit there till then. Bail won't be set until the hearing. But I doubt he'll be able to cover it. It's a murder charge, so bond will likely be set pretty high. Plus, Sims has a history of bouncing around, taking on one historical injustice after another. He's only lived here for a few years. And if they end up connecting him to the explosion at the site, and who knows, maybe even that other body, there may be no bond at all."

"Are they trying to do that?"

"Based on what they took from the house, I'd say so."

"Which was?"

"According to the inventory receipt, several boxes of ammunition, some clothing, shoes, and some random wiring and duct tape. No gun, though. They asked Sims to produce the one he owns, but he couldn't find it. Apparently it was missing from the box he keeps it in. Which doesn't look good. But the wiring and tape definitely make me think they're looking at him for the explosion. It makes sense, given Sims's history with Donner."

"What makes them think Sims killed Donner? Do they have any real evidence?"

"We won't know for sure until the preliminary hearing, which likely won't happen for at least a week. But I'm betting it's the missing gun."

A few moments of relative silence passed, the occasional sound of intercom announcements and muffled talking in the hall the only interruptions. Holt's interlaced fingers worked restlessly, apparently fueled by worry. Lines on his thirty-something forehead seemed more pronounced as he leaned forward on his knees, studying Emma and Tyler in the corner.

"Hey, by the way," Holt piped up, "the police released the scene at the house before I got here. I went ahead and called a service to clean the wall. I thought it would be better if that was done before the kids got home. Since I know the code, I just let them in before coming here. I hope that's okay."

"That's…great, actually. I hadn't even thought about that." She smiled at him appreciatively, glad that at least someone was thinking straight. "Thanks."

"No problem."

"It's nice that you look out for them like that. I mean, I know you and Reese are law partners and all, and you have reason to care, it's just that you seem…really invested."

The corner of Holt's mouth turned up slightly. "Yeah. You could say that. Reese is the reason I'm a lawyer. He's done a lot for me." He inclined his head towards the children. "And I've spent a lot of time around your family. They're important to me."

Your family. The words fell strangely on her ears. And it was odd to hear someone speak of her father this way, with endearment and gratitude. She had only ever heard his name spoken with bitterness and regret. "I'm glad he had a positive effect on you," she said. "I wish I could say the same." Her gaze flitted to the kids. "He seems to have done well with them, though. Emma's teenage angst aside."

Holt pursed his lips. "Yeah. It's hard, being a single parent with such a demanding job. Someday she'll get it."

The mention of the children spun Chloe's thoughts in a new direction and she abruptly changed the topic. "Why threaten the kids?" Chloe asked, revisiting the events of the afternoon and the violent threat against Emma and Tyler the anonymous attacker had left scribbled on the wall. "That's so extreme. And scary. It makes me want to find out who did it more than before, not less."

"Yeah," he conceded, cradling his cup. "I won't really feel like they're safe until we catch the guy."

"I don't get it," Chloe continued, processing out loud. "Whoever this is, they just left their box-on-the-porch-warning yesterday. Why make another threat so soon?"

Holt shrugged. "I really don't know. The closest connection, at least in time, is Reese getting called to Sims's place."

"It would be in keeping with someone not liking that you guys showed up to help Sims on the night of the explosion. Maybe somebody really doesn't want you representing him."

"That just doesn't make sense. If it wasn't us representing him, then he would have some other lawyer—will have another lawyer after Monday. Whoever it is couldn't possibly expect that Sims wouldn't have a lawyer at all. What good does it do to scare us off if someone else just steps right in?" Holt reasoned.

"What about Donner?"

"Well, with him being dead and all…I'd say it's unlikely he's behind it."

"No, I mean, what if it started with him and now that the stakes are higher, somebody in his camp is continuing with the pressure?"

Holt shook his head. "I can't see it. Like I explained yesterday, it seems like a stupid move for him to take that kind of risk when he'll probably win Sims's lawsuit anyway."

"What about someone that works for Donner? What if they wanted to help things along?"

"Unlikely," Holt muttered, squinting as he mulled the prospect over doubtfully. "From what I understand, Donner held the reins pretty tight. I don't see some lackey getting ideas of his own. Though I guess it's not impossible. But I'm still not one hundred percent convinced these break-ins are connected to Sims. There's still my nut-job client or ex-spouse theory. I can take a look at the cases we worked on late yesterday and see if there's a connection, and check any court rulings handed down yesterday, too, and see if something unfavorable was decided. Maybe this person just wanted to double down on his pressure and it's just a coincidence that it happened right as Reese was headed out to help Sims."

Chloe considered this. "Maybe."

Holt sniffed and rubbed his nose. "There's another possibility. One that I'm not keen about."

"What?"

Holt tilted his head, appraising her. "You won't like it."

"Tell me anyway."

He seemed uneasy, a look Chloe suspected was rare for the utterly confident counselor. "Reese could have something going on that I don't know about."

"What…like with a case?"

"A case. Or a client. I don't know everyone he talks to. Just like he doesn't know everyone I talk to. Or, maybe Reese is in deeper on this Sims and Donner thing than I know. What if there are more players in that situation, more risks than I'm aware of? If any of that's true, it might explain the messages—maybe they are vague to us, but not to Reese. Maybe he knows what they're talking about after all, and he just hasn't been in a position to explain them."

Nervous panic fluttered across Chloe's skin. "Deeper how? You mean, like he invested in the project? Or took sides somehow—"

"I don't know. I'm not suggesting Reese did anything wrong. But Donner's a shady character. That much I do know. I just wonder if Reese did something we don't know about to make an enemy in the situation."

She thought of her brother Tate, and his involvement in the money-laundering syndicate that killed him. That nearly killed her and Jack. Her heart skipped a beat. She couldn't do this again.

Holt threw his hands wide. "Then again, we could be looking at this all wrong." He heaved a sigh. "I don't think we'll know much of anything until he wakes up."

If he wakes up, she thought ruefully. "I just don't like that they're in danger," she said, eyeing the children. "What if something else sets this person off? What if something makes this person follow through on their threat against the kids? How do we protect them when we don't know what's really going on?"

"They won't be unprotected," Holt said, stout determination in his voice.

Two hours later Emma and Tyler finally slept. The waiting room lights were dimmed for the night, and Chloe and Holt sat quietly, fighting the drowsiness that occasionally caused one of their heads to bob down before jerking back up. At a quarter past one, the waiting room door swung open at last.

"He's made it through the surgery," the surgeon said quietly, as Holt and Chloe rose to meet her. "It went well. But we'll have to wait until he wakes up to really know. It may take some time for him to regain consciousness. The blood clot resulted in oxygen deprivation for a short period of time. We don't know what, if any, the long-term effects will be."

She continued talking, saying a lot of other things about Reese and the surgery that Chloe only halfway heard. Holt seemed to be taking it all in, but all she could think about was Emma and Tyler and the fact that their father could be lying in that hospital somewhere, suffering from brain damage. They were her siblings. Her sister and brother. An unexpected protectiveness swelled. She hadn't been able to save Tate. But these two…she could do something for them. And she would. Whatever it took.

*****

"You don't really have to stay," Chloe told Holt, after gently pulling Tyler's bedroom door closed, so as not to wake the sleeping boy inside. "We'll be fine."

"Yeah, you will, because I'm not leaving. Take the guest room—it's the one past the bathroom on the right. I'll sleep on the couch downstairs. I promised the kid," Holt reminded her. "It'll be better for him this way."

After the doctor told them there was nothing else to be done that night, they had gathered a groggy Tyler and Emma and headed back to Reese's house. When Tyler had roused enough to get a sense of what was happening, he had asked in a shaky voice if Holt could stay over "in case the bad guys came back." Though they had insisted the bad guys weren't coming back, Tyler wasn't satisfied until Holt had promised to stay with them.

"Besides," Holt continued, "despite what we told Tyler, we don't know enough about what's going on to be sure they aren't coming back. I don't want all of you alone here if that happens."

Deciding he had a point, she caved. "Okay, fine. You win."

"I usually do," he said, grinning impishly, before turning to head down the stairs.

The guest room was understated in furnishings, its only decor a jewel blue-toned Matisse print hanging in a thick wooden frame above the queen-sized bed. It was pristine and un-personalized, and Chloe guessed that few people ever stayed here. As tired as she was, she just crawled under the white duvet and closed her eyes. Within seconds, she had started to drift off, when a buzzing from her back pocket woke her. Her cell. She had forgotten it was there.

Not bothering to sit up, she pulled it out where she lay and read the name on the screen.

Jack.

She plopped the cell face down on her chest, squeezing her eyes tight. Then, disabling the vibration on the phone, she slid it onto the nightstand and retreated under the comforter, waiting for sleep to take her.

*****

"Where are you, Chloe?" Jack asked of no one, leaning back into the hotel room pillows and staring at his phone. He had called four times since speaking with her last and texted twice that much. She had not responded once. It wasn't like her at all. Not even in her busiest moments.

The television droned on in the background, one of the Jurassic Park movies playing without Jack taking any notice. He had only turned it on for the noise anyway, feeling distinctly alone tonight. To his left, a discarded room service tray sat on the bed, still holding most of the fish tacos he had ordered, then hadn't felt like eating.

Why isn't she returning my messages? he wondered, a familiar nervousness creeping into his being. He recognized this uncertainty. This self-doubt. He had felt it with Lila years ago, when he had first started to suspect her discontentment with their relationship. With him.

The dull ache that was so much his companion these days coursed through the length of his leg, extending to his hip. It was particularly bad today after so much standing on the set. He shifted, trying to take the pressure off it. The pain eased a little.

She's just busy, he assured himself. *There's nothing wrong.*

But the doubt persisted. Because it didn't make any sense. In the middle of meeting her father—something that had terrified Chloe for months—and after routinely calling and texting Jack for support every day, several times a day, she stopped communicating.

She knew him. She knew that this would make him worry. And if things were fine, she would not ever intentionally make him worry.

Only two possibilities made sense. And they were both awful. Either she couldn't contact him because she was seriously hurt or sick, *or* she wouldn't contact him and didn't care if he was worried.

If she's sick, who's taking care of her? he thought, starting to chase the nasty rabbits he had conjured down their nerve-wracking holes.

What if she's not sick? What if she can't call because someone from the whole mess with her brother Tate finally decided to come after her? That one was a stretch, but it made him want to jump on a plane right then.

And lastly, *what if it's neither of those? What if it's the other option—that she doesn't want to talk to me?*

His brow furrowed as he rubbed his temples with the thumb and forefinger of his right hand.

What if, after all this time, she's finally figured it out?

TWENTY-ONE

Sunshine and a door slamming snatched Chloe from the throes of a dream about Tyler and Tate trapped in a room, unable to escape, with the words, "Emma's next," scrawled in red on the wall. She woke with a start, catching her breath, as her hand flew to her chest. Chloe blinked, taking in her surroundings and remembering why she was there. Glaring sunlight streamed in from the windows facing east. She had not bothered to draw the blinds last night and now the sunshine spilled over the room, ushering in the day. She tapped her phone. It was eight in the morning.

Kids. Breakfast. Her brain finally kicking into gear, she rolled out of bed and headed downstairs. As she crossed the threshold into the kitchen, she was wondering whether cereal and milk would be too much of a cop out, when the scene that met her made the thought irrelevant.

"I told you you'd wake her," Holt chided Tyler, flipping a pancake in a frying pan on the stove as Tyler crawled onto one of the stools at the bar overlooking the kitchen workspace.

"Sorry," Tyler apologized, grinning sheepishly as he fingered a video game case. "I left this in Dad's car. I wanted to play it."

"No worries," Chloe said, smiling as she leaned against the counter. "What are we having today?"

Tyler smiled. "Holt's making *Star Wars* pancakes," he explained, his eyes alight.

"Wow, that's impressive," Chloe replied. Sure enough, Holt had a Yoda shaped pancake nearly browned to perfection in the pan.

Several forms in shapes that resembled icons from the movies were stacked by the stove.

"You want a ship? Holt can make one."

"Sure, buddy. Holt can make me a spaceship for breakfast."

"Coming right up," Holt replied, his back still to her. Like her, he was still in yesterday's clothes. For the first time, he looked a little sloppy, his light blue button-down untucked, hanging loose over his tailored khakis. She guessed he was just shy of six feet, and probably in his early thirties. His eyes tended to crinkle when he smiled, perhaps from the stress of the law practice. Chloe wondered what in his genes gave him that "just off the Mediterranean Coast" vibe, and guessed that there must be a good amount of Italian or Spanish buried in there. Whatever it was, somehow, even disheveled as he was, he still looked like this was exactly how he had meant to look today. He was obviously one of those people that never had a bad hair/face/clothes day. She caught a glimpse of her reflection in the microwave, tawny curls askew, left-over mascara smeared beneath her right eye, and was reminded forcefully that she was not one of those people.

"Where's Emma?" Chloe wondered aloud, flipping her hair and attempting to rub the black from under her eye.

"Still asleep," Tyler droned, sounding annoyed. "She never gets up early."

"Most teenagers don't," Chloe agreed.

Holt slapped a plate down in front of Tyler. "Here you go, dude. Yours will be up in a second," he said, cutting his eyes at Chloe and winking.

"This is really nice of you."

"No problem."

"You know, I can take it from here, though. I'm sure you've got things to do."

"Nah. I'm good for a bit."

They ate spaceships and aliens with syrup and bacon and orange juice. Emma eventually wandered down and joined them. She was quiet, only speaking to tell Holt thanks. Finally Tyler piped up.

"How's dad?" he asked, shoveling an alien head in his mouth.

"He asked earlier," Holt explained. "I said it was too early to know more."

"We don't know yet, buddy," said Chloe. "We'll go see him this morning."

Holt stood, slid his plate in the dishwasher and motioned to Chloe. "Can I talk to you for a minute?" He inclined his head towards the dining room.

"Sure," Chloe answered and followed him.

"Look," Holt started once they were out of earshot. "I actually do need to get some things under control today. I've got to talk to the police about Sims and Reese and take a look at what we've got going on over the next weeks. I'm going to have to handle Reese's caseload until he's back on his feet, and I need to wrap my head around what he has coming up and figure out how to work it all in."

"Of course. You've done plenty. More than enough," she said. "Go. We'll be fine."

He rubbed a hand over his head. "It's gonna be quite a mess. And I need to talk to Sims. I want to see if he knows anything more. Maybe pressure him a bit. The more I think about it, I'm not sure handing his case over to a public defender is the right thing to do now. I want to get a better sense of what's going on first. See if maybe we can find a connection to what happened to Reese."

"Can I do anything?"

Holt eyed her wearily. "I wish you could. I think it's going to be pretty hectic for a while."

"I want to help if I can. Whatever you need. I want to help you get to the bottom of this." She said it resolutely, hoping he understood how determined she was.

He nodded. "I'll call if I find anything out. In the meantime, just hang tight with the kids. Go see Reese. Oh, and I've already called the security company Reese uses here. They'll be by later to reset the codes. Just in case," he added, as if not wanting to worry her too much.

"Good idea. Thanks," she said.

After a quick see-ya-later to the kids, Holt headed out, leaving Chloe to marshal the kids for their return trip to the hospital. She gave them a half-hour departure time warning, then headed upstairs. Her plan was to shower here, then run by the inn on the way so she could change clothes. But that all changed when she checked her phone. Jack had called again. And sent her a text.

If I don't hear from you in an hour, I'm calling the cops. I'm so worried. CALL ME.

Her heart plummeted. She missed him. And she was angry. And she felt alone. She needed him, his strength, his encouragement. But he had lied to her. Or not told her the truth. Or both.

It was time. Sucking in a deep breath, she dialed him back.

*****

"Where have you been?" Jack's voice came over the phone, apprehensive and direct. "I've been trying to reach you since late Friday night! Are you all right?"

"I'm fine."

"What is it? What's wrong?"

"Nothing," Chloe lied. "It's just been crazy here. Reese got hurt and I've been dealing with that and the kids, and I haven't had a moment to really sit down and talk."

"Hurt? What happened?"

So he's not going to even mention "the wife," she thought bitterly, before plunging into an explanation. 'Someone broke into their house. After the thing with the box on the porch. They attacked Reese. Shoved him down the stairs. He's in the hospital. We're headed over in a little while to see him."

"Is he going to be all right?"

"I don't know yet. There was a blood clot. He was still unconscious as of last night." Her voice was deadpan, unable to muster any liveliness as she waited for him to come clean.

"Why didn't you let me know? Why didn't you at least text? I was scared to death something had happened to you. I nearly jumped on a plane. I started thinking that someone from Inverse had come after you. Honestly I didn't know what to think, I just—"

"I called your phone two nights ago," she interrupted. "Late. Your *wife* answered."

A heavy silence met her revelation. She let it linger, awkward and pregnant, waiting for him to break it. He didn't.

"She said you were in the bathroom. In your hotel room."

She heard him exhale. "I was going to tell you." It was a lament, an admission ripe with regret.

"Was it Lila? I don't understand, Jack. Help me understand."

"Look, it's not what you think. Lila came to me a few days ago. Her life's fallen apart. She felt like maybe I could help her. She didn't know what else to try. I agreed to talk to her. We had a late dinner, I went up to change and she waited in my room. She just sort of followed me, I didn't ask her up."

"Why didn't you tell me?"

"I didn't know you'd called. Lila didn't tell me. I don't know why—"

"How long have you been seeing her?"

"I'm not 'seeing' her, Chloe. Not like that. She's staying out here, and I'm just, I don't know, encouraging her. I felt obligated to try to help. I know she was awful to me, but she's finally asking questions about faith and I didn't feel right not trying."

"You could've told me."

"I was going to tell you. I just wanted to understand what was really going on first."

"You're keeping secrets."

"What? No—"

"We said no more secrets. You *know* how I feel about that. First Tate with the money-laundering thing, and then Reese keeping Emma and Tyler from me and now you—"

"Wait a minute. Don't lump me in there with them. I am not keeping secrets. This is just a matter of timing, not a matter of me hiding things."

"She didn't tell you I'd called, did she?

"No." He paused. "I don't know why she did that."

"Yes, you do. We both do. She said she was your 'wife,' Jack. Not your ex-wife. She said *wife*."

"I'll talk to her. I don't know what she was thinking. She shouldn't have answered the phone anyway. Look, I know Lila may be completely snowing me, but I felt like I had to make an effort. Chloe, I love you. You know that. This isn't anything for you to get worked up about. Seriously."

"Seriously?" she echoed sourly.

She didn't want to do this. Not with him. He meant well. She truly believed that. But his judgment on this…it was just wrong. Why didn't he get that? "I love you, too, Jack. I do. But this—we've talked about this. You swore you'd never keep anything from me again."

"Chloe, you know I wouldn't hurt you for the world. Believe me when I say I was going to tell you."

"But that's the thing. You didn't. Not even just now. Not until I brought it up." She sighed. "I don't know. I just don't need this on top of everything else. But I can't talk about it anymore right now. We're heading to the hospital to check on Reese."

"Chloe, this isn't okay. I'm not okay. We need to talk about this."

"Jack, right now I've got two kids waiting downstairs for me to take them to see their potentially brain-damaged father. I can't do this. Can we talk later?"

He paused, blowing a bit of breath out. "Yeah, sure. Of course," he said, his voice soft. "Do what you need to do."

"Thank you. I'll call you—"

"Wait, before you go, the break-in—did they catch the person?

"No," she said. It was so unfamiliar, this feeling that she didn't want to talk about something with him. But talking about it would have meant prolonging their conversation and right now she just didn't know what to say. Plus, if she gave him specifics about the threat on the wall and the murder and everything else he would want to get on a plane right then.

"I don't like this at all," he insisted.

"We're fine. There's a burglar system. They're changing the codes out today."

"You should stay somewhere else—"

"We're fine, Jack. Besides I can't uproot the kids like that." She pulled the phone down to glance at the time. Her thirty minutes was disappearing fast. "Look, I've got to go."

"Call me, or at least text me later. Let me know what's happening with Reese."

She glossed over his request, too focused on asking her next question. "Are you seeing her again?"

"Do you not want me to?"

She could feel her lips drop into a frown, as she shook her head. *Do I really have to answer that?*

Yes, she believed that Jack was telling the truth about wanting to help her. Yes, Jack was a rescuer and, according to his description of his ex-wife, if ever there was a person in need of rescue, it was Lila. And, yes, she knew that if the woman was actually seeking hope—though Chloe had her suspicions about that—Jack was doing the right thing by pointing Lila in the right direction. *But even so, did it have to be him?*

"Do what you need to do, Jack. I'll talk to you later," she said and hung up.

*****

It was after ten in the morning by the time they actually stepped inside Reese's hospital room. Somehow he looked so much smaller in the hospital bed than when Chloe had met him on his front porch just three days earlier. His face seemed drawn, almost gaunt, and his body, less, under the thin white sheet that failed to cover the multitude of tubes and wires stretching from his arm to equipment suspended over the bed.

"How long will he be like this?" Emma asked, her face ashen. It was the first thing she had said since they had been allowed a short, ten-minute visit. That was all hospital policy permitted since Tyler was under the age of twelve.

Chloe took stock of the teen, wondering whether the pallor of her skin was due to fear, anger, frustration, or an inexplicable combination of all three and more. "The doctor said it just depends on how he progresses—how long he needs to be in a medically induced coma to help him heal. At least a couple of days."

Tyler stood by the bed, holding Reese's right hand, the one free of any IV lines. A fat tear dropped from the boy's jawline onto the sheet. He too had been quiet. *Probably trying to be brave,* Chloe thought, as they stood around Reese waiting for the ten minutes to tick down.

According to Chloe's private briefing by Reese's nurse, there had been no significant change overnight, which was a good thing. His vitals had remained stable and he seemed to be resting comfortably. Due to the extent of the head injury, they had opted to keep him in a state of medically induced unconsciousness to reduce the stress on his brain and to get him through, what would likely be, the most painful hours of recovery. Assuming all went well, they hoped to bring him out of it within several days, perhaps a week at most. But they had made no promises.

The pings and whirring of the machines in the room made a disconcerting backdrop to their short, silent vigil, until finally the nurse stepped inside to politely inform them that their time was up. Putting an arm around Tyler, Chloe followed Emma out the door.

The path to the parking lot took them past a set of double doors on the first floor with large plastic letters over them that read "CHAPEL." Chloe paused for a moment, and for half a second almost turned inside, but then considered Emma and Tyler. She couldn't leave them outside, and she didn't know how they would feel about it. In the end, she continued walking.

"So who could eat?" she asked, once they were in the car and pulling out of the lot. "I think there's a Steak 'n Shake nearby." From the rear view mirror she eyed Tyler in the rear seat, his head still hanging low. "Chocolate shakes? My treat."

"Cookies and Cream?" he asked, his chin lifting slightly.

"Whatever you want," Chloe said, smiling, as even Emma's lip curled up at one corner.

Thirty minutes later, deep into a huge basket of fries and shakes thick enough to defy the stoutest straw, Emma turned towards Chloe, a shadow of seriousness covering her face.

"So what now? I mean, Dad's in the hospital for who knows how long. There's Mrs. Brinkley, but she can't stay with us overnight—"

"Who's Mrs. Brinkley?"

"Tyler's babysitter when I've got to work after school or whatever."

"She's not my babysitter," Tyler protested, half a fry falling from his mouth.

Emma rolled her eyes. "She picks him up from school sometimes and stays with him till somebody gets home. But like I said, she never stays overnight."

"And you don't have any family—grandparents or aunts or anyone that can stay with you? Just till your dad is better?"

"We have you." Her words carried no emotion, just fact, her eyes cold-locked onto Chloe's. "There is no one else."

"You could stay with us," Tyler proposed innocently, dipping another fry in ketchup.

The noise of the little burger joint with its plates clanking and food sizzling, and the greasy scent of frying hamburgers surrounded Chloe as she considered this. She could stay. She could grab her stuff from the inn and move into the little guest room upstairs until Reese was better. She could.

But did she want to?

Yes.

She might still have her issues with Reese, but these two were not part of that. They were her at age eight and age seventeen. And they needed her.

"Would you really want me to?" Chloe asked.

Emma's features lightened, a mixture of disbelief and something like hope stealing over them. "Are you serious? You would do that?"

"Of course I would."

Emma turned her head so that she was facing away, brushed something from her eye and nodded.

"So it's okay if I move in for a while? Just until your dad is back on his feet."

"It's more than okay. It's awesome!" Tyler grinned and took a long, slurpy drag on his milkshake.

Checking out of the inn was a painless process, and within the hour, Chloe was dropping her dark red suitcase on the hardwood floors of Reese's guest room. The kids were somewhere else in the house, doing who-knew-what, but she had told them she was going to take a quick nap and would be out in a little while.

The truth was, she needed a moment to process what was happening—with Reese, with Jack, and with these two siblings that she had now charged herself with protecting. The hospital chapel had been appealing, but this room was just as good.

Hoping for some guidance, Chloe laid down on the bed, closed her eyes and started to pray.

*****

Chloe realized she must have fallen asleep at some point, because the next thing she knew, she was roused by screams of "Chinese food!" coming from downstairs. She dragged herself up, groggy from the unplanned REM sleep she had obviously been enjoying, and toddled down the stairs in her T-shirt, yoga pants, and fuzzy green socks.

"Nice," Holt said jerking his head towards her feet as he stood over the kitchen island, popping open a silver-handled take-out carton embossed with a red Chinese pagoda.

She smirked and rolled her eyes. He was dressed down in dark jeans, a tailored black-checkered button down, and comfortable but expensive looking loafers she was fairly certain were the same Ferragamos she had considered for Jack before realizing they were nearly five hundred dollars a pair.

"Who wants Chicken Lo Mein?" Holt quizzed, the kids hovering by either shoulder.

"Me!" Tyler replied enthusiastically, raising a cornflower blue plate towards Holt. "But take out the carrots," he admonished, turning to Chloe who had sidled up to him. "I hate carrots."

Chloe started to comment that Tate—the brother Tyler had never known—had hated carrots too, but instead she choked back the words as a burning rose in her throat. Tate had always made her pick the carrots out whenever they had ordered Chinese food. She wondered how many more similarities she would discover between her two brothers and when, if ever, they would stop shocking her system.

The kids moved to eat in front of the television as Chloe fixed her plate. It was early, only just shy of five o'clock, but she was surprised to find her stomach rumbling in response to the tantalizing aroma heavy with ginger and garlic.

"Chloe and I are headed out front for a minute, guys," Holt told the kids, and received a silent, two-fingered salute of acknowledgement from Emma that she gave without taking her eyes off the episode of *American Ninja Warrior* they were watching.

Out on the porch the late afternoon sky was turning golden, the hazy rays illuminating dust particles floating benignly through the air. A breeze ruffled the ragweed that covered the horse pastures behind Reese's neighborhood, just visible between the houses on the opposite side of the street.

"Thanks for sending the text update on Reese earlier," Holt said, setting his iced tea on the small table between them. "I'm sorry he isn't doing any better."

"At least he's not worse," Chloe said, taking a bite and swallowing. "I feel like we ought to be there, but I just don't think it's good for them to sit there all day, wondering when he's going to wake up."

"No. You're right. They'll let you know if there's a change."

"And thanks for this," she said lifting a fork laden with rice noodles and chicken. "I hadn't thought that far ahead."

"It's nothing. I needed to bring you up to speed anyway. And you've got news for me too, I hear. They said you've moved in."

"It's just temporary. I don't know how long I can stay and who knows how long it'll be before Reese is back home and on his feet. Eventually we'll have to make other arrangements."

"Well, regardless, it's really, *really* good of you to do this." He paused, twirling a fork in his noodles. "I could've taken responsibility for them, but having you here is just better. And," he shrugged, "now you'll get to know them even better than you would have otherwise. Maybe that's the silver lining in all this."

"Maybe," she conceded.

They talked about the logistics of the kids' schedules, school and after school activities, including the babysitter, Mrs. Brinkley, and Emma's after school job at Philanthropy, a boutique on Main Street. The plan was for Chloe to get the kids off to school, spend the day working on her research and article, and then pick Tyler up. Emma, of course, could drive herself. Mrs. Brinkley had also offered to help, and could pick up or sit with Tyler whenever she was needed, though she wasn't able to stay overnight.

"She said she would pick him up every day if I wanted, but I think I'd rather do it. It's not like I have somewhere to be. And Emma can pick him up, too, if I need her to, as long as she isn't working."

Holt squinted doubtfully. "On the days Emma doesn't work, she'll probably want to stay out with friends, so I wouldn't count on her." He shifted, balancing his plate in his lap. "So, I have a request."

"Shoot," Chloe said, setting her fork down.

"Until Reese comes home and until we figure out who's behind all the threats, I want to stay here. I'll feel better—and I know Reese would too—if I'm here at night, just in case anything happens."

She shook her head. "I can't ask you to do that."

"You're not. It's my idea. I'll just camp out on the couch, that way I'm already downstairs if anything happens. You'll sleep better."

"But you won't."

"I'll sleep better than I would at home worrying about the three of you."

Chloe knew she ought to fight him on this, that she ought to protest and tell him that she could take care of herself. But the thing was, she wasn't just taking care of herself. There were two children depending on her. And having that responsibility lying solely on her shoulders made her nervous.

"Okay. All right. If you're sure. I think I would feel better. At least for now."

"Great," he said and gulped down some half-and-half tea. "Now," he continued, depositing his glass on the little table. "I have an offer for you. If you're interested."

"Okay."

"I couldn't get in to see Sims today. So I've decided to temporarily continue representing him, at least through his arraignment tomorrow, so I can get another chance to flesh things out with him. If you're up for it, I thought you could come with me. It isn't every day that you get to go behind the scenes in a murder case, and even though it's not something that would make it into your article—"

She laughed, interrupting him. "No, it's not."

"—it's pretty interesting stuff. And," he added, "it would be a chance for you to get a feel for what Reese does every day. Not that he handles murder trials every day—they're actually really rare—but criminal cases in general." He paused, refocusing. "Anyway, if you have a few hours to spare, it's not something most people get the chance to do."

"You're sure I won't be in the way?"

"No. And it'll help me to have another pair of eyes and ears when I talk to Sims."

She considered the offer. No, it wasn't going to help with the article. But he was right—it was a rare opportunity. And it was more than an interesting murder case. Not only was Emma's friend's father the accused, but the whole thing might be connected to the bloody box on Reese's doorstep and the attack on Reese. Maybe Sims could shed some light on what it was all about, and they could get some answers.

"Just tell me when to be there," she replied.

TWENTY-TWO

The Santa Monica pier was noisy, full of tourists venturing out after an uncharacteristic and quick early morning rain. Jack navigated the crowd, accompanied by a lanky young man with umber hued skin dressed in a Habitat for Humanity T-shirt and bright white Nike tennis shoes. About halfway down the wooden boardwalk he spotted Lila, leaning against the railing in a white sundress, her red hair piled up in a messy bun. She stared over the crashing water through the large round sunglasses that hid her eyes.

"Lila," he said impassively, moving to stand behind her.

She turned slowly, as if for effect. "Hey you," she answered coyly. Then noticing Jack was with someone, she straightened uncomfortably. "Um, hi," she said uncertainly.

"Lila, this is Evan. Evan, this is Lila."

Evan extended his hand and a warm smile. "Nice to meet you, Lila," he said. Lila shook his hand, her forehead wrinkling in confusion.

"So, why the early meeting Jack? I thought we were getting together after your shoot later."

He sighed. "You've put me in a bad position, Lila." He searched her face for a reaction, but the sunglasses were good emotional camouflage. "I talked to Chloe. Why did you answer my phone the other night? And why did you tell her I was in the bathroom?"

"What—I just, I don't know, heard a phone ringing and answered it—"

"You told her you were my wife."

"No, no, I—"

"Don't, Lila. Don't lie. She told me."

"Well she misunderstood. I said ex-wife—"

"You didn't and we both know it." For several moments neither said anything as they stared each other down. Lila bit her lip and shifted her weight to her other hip, but offered no further explanation.

"This is over. Done," Jack insisted.

"Wait, you can't—"

"I'm not sure what your goal is here, but your little stunt the other night makes it clear that this," he waggled a finger between the two of them, "does not work. On any level."

"Okay," she flipped her sunglasses on top of her head, revealing pleading brown eyes, "I shouldn't have done that. I know. I just...I don't know. Lost my head for a minute. I was just messing around. But I'm serious about this, about learning something here. I'm floundering. You can't just abandon me."

"You're right," Jack said and gestured towards Evan. "Evan helps out at the church I attend when I'm out here. If you really are looking for answers, he can answer any question you have, and probably do it a whole lot better than I could."

"But," she protested, dropping her voice as if Evan couldn't hear her, "I don't want *him* to help me. I want you."

"Honestly, Lila, I don't know what you want. But if you are searching for answers, and I hope you are, he can help you find them." Jack took a few steps back. "You don't need me for that. Either way, don't call me. Don't text. Don't anything," he said, then turned sharply, walking back the way he had come.

For a few moments, Lila simply bowed up, her entire body tensing. Her hands curled into fists as she charged several strides after Jack, then planted herself, stomping her feet.

"Jack don't. Don't! I'm sorry, okay? I'm sorry. I just...I was jealous, all right?"

Ignoring her, Jack continued walking, his back turned.

Apparently sensing her failure, Lila changed tactics, brash annoyance eclipsing the desperation that had previously dominated her tone. "Look, I need your help. Alex took everything. He cleaned me out. I have no one else to turn to. What am I supposed to do?" She stomped an espadrille on the boardwalk again. "Jack!"

At her shout, Jack halted, still facing away from them. After a few moments of contemplation, he looked back over his shoulder once more. “That’s a great question,” he admitted, then turned and resumed walking away, calling out as he went. “You should ask Evan what the answer is.”

TWENTY-THREE

The General Sessions courtroom was abuzz as the bailiff called the next case on the Monday morning docket. The room was packed, and from the snippets of conversation Chloe had caught, the crowd was due to Sims's scheduled bond hearing on the charge against him for the murder of Phillip Donner. Many in the gallery appeared affiliated with various local media outlets, while others seemed to be curious citizens hoping for a front row seat to the latest scandal.

The courtroom was a fair size, painted a nondescript beige with honey-stained oak benches providing seating in the gallery. The judge's bench was at one end opposite the double-door entryway, with the seal of Tennessee hanging on the wall behind him. The traditional wooden railing separated the court from the gallery where Chloe now waited along with everyone else.

It was 9:48 and Judge Seton R. Bricker had dispensed with several cases already. Sims sat in the jury box to the right of Judge Bricker with the other defendants who had been transported to court from jail. Like them, Sims wore an orange jumpsuit with the words "Tri-County Jail" inscribed in black on the back. He was even more disheveled than he had been when she had seen him at Five Points on the night of the explosion. His shoulder-length brown hair clearly had not had a brush through it in days, and his scraggly beard was desperately in need of a trim. He sat hunched over, shoulders sagging as he reached up with one hand to push his square-rimmed glasses up the bridge of his nose. She doubted he had looked in a mirror before coming to court, which seemed like an obvious misstep for someone trying to convince a judge he was a safe bet for a reasonable bond.

"I'll talk to him about cleaning up next time," Holt whispered, leaning in on her right, apparently thinking the same thing she was. "He looks terrible."

Chloe nodded just as Sims's name was called.

The entire hearing took less than five minutes, likely to the great disappointment of the media hounds hoping for more. In that time, Sims was escorted from the jury box to the defendant's table, where he was met by Holt, whose impeccable dress made Sims look even worse by comparison. After a quick reading of the charge of murder in the first degree, Holt made a well-presented argument that due to his familial obligations, namely his son, Jacob, and ongoing litigation, Sims was not the type of flight risk that justified an excessively high bond. Unfortunately, Judge Bricker did not agree, and set Sims's bond at half a million. He set Sims's preliminary hearing for later that week, after which Sims was ushered back to the holding area looking even more defeated than before.

Holt pushed his way through the swinging gate at the dividing railing into the gallery where Chloe sat. "Come on, let's go see him," he said, tugging on her sleeve as he passed her. She rose to join him as he strode from the courtroom.

Holt led her through several melamine-tiled hallways to an area where they kept the transfers from the jail before and after their court appearances. After Holt spoke briefly with a sheriff's deputy, they were taken to a small room containing a metal table and two utility chairs upholstered in charcoal pleather on opposite sides of it.

"Here," Holt said, motioning towards one chair as he sat in the other. "Sit for a minute before he comes in. We need to take care of something."

Chloe sat and Holt pulled a document from his briefcase and slid it in front of her.

"The attorney-client privilege that protects my communications with Sims ceases to apply if a third party—that would be you—is present. Technically, you could be called to testify about anything he says or anything that you and I discuss, unless you're part of his legal team, which," he slapped the paper, "you are if you're an intern for the firm."

"An intern?"

Holt grinned. "Unpaid, of course."

She eyed him skeptically. "Is this legal?"

His face contorted distastefully. "Of *course,* it's legal. I can bring in anyone I want to work for me. Technically I don't even need to have you sign anything, but this sets it out clear as day in advance, should anyone question the arrangement. But, it does mean you'll have to help me on the case at least a little. Maybe sort through some discovery, maybe make some notes about interviews, that sort of thing. You up for that?"

She had the time. And it was pretty interesting. Something she wouldn't normally get to experience. She could get back to taking photos later.

He pointed to the signature line. "Sign and date it below and we'll have Karen—our office assistant," he explained, when Chloe looked bemused, "—notarize it when we get back to the office."

He handed her a pen and Chloe scratched her signature out. Five minutes later, the door squeaked on its hinges as Sims walked through, escorted by a sheriff's deputy. Chloe half-expected Holt to offer his chair to Sims, but when he raised his eyebrows at her, she realized she was the one expected to stand. She was just an intern after all.

Chloe moved to stand behind Holt as Sims deposited his gangly frame in the chair she had vacated, looking like someone who had just had the wind knocked out of them. "Just bang on the door when you're done," said the deputy, before closing and locking the door behind him.

"How you doing, Kurt?" Holt asked, leaning forward on his elbows. "You're looking a bit rough."

"Don't even man," Sims started, shaking his head. "I haven't slept in two days."

"You've got to do better next time. I probably could've gotten the bail knocked down lower if you didn't look like you'd just been pulled from the drunk tank. Next time wash your face. Comb your hair. Something."

"Okay, yeah, I got it," he groused. "How's Jacob?"

Something about Sims's air made his question seem less like the inquiry of a worried father and more like a truant officer confirming his ward was where he needed to be.

"Fine," Holt assured him. "Emma says he's fine. He's staying with his aunt. That's your wife's sister, right?" Sims nodded and Holt continued. "He's at school today as far as I know."

"Good. He doesn't need to go screwing up his attendance over this. Doesn't need to damage his scholarship prospects. Make sure he gets to practice, okay? I don't want him taking it easy just because I'm stuck in here. He gets lazy if I don't stay on him." The words sounded worn to Chloe, as if they had been said to and about Jacob many, many times. So far she wasn't liking Kurt Sims very much.

"I'll check on Jacob later, but right now we need to talk about you. You heard the judge. Bail's set at half a million. Can you swing the bondsman fee?"

"I don't have fifty grand, man," he said, then changed gears, appraising Chloe and looking between her and Holt. "Who's this?" he asked.

"This is Chloe McConnaughey. She's Reese's daughter. She's helping me out."

His eyes lit up. "So you're taking the case? Hey, that's…look, I know I can't pay you now, everything I had is sunk into that project and the lawsuit but—"

Holt held up a hand. "Don't thank me yet. I still don't know if we can take this on, especially with Reese out of commission for a while, but I wanted to at least be here for you this morning."

"Was Cecilia here?"

Holt shook his head. "No reason for her to be. She doesn't handle criminal anyway. I'll bring her up to speed later."

"Wait…what do you mean Reese is out of commission? What's wrong with Reese?"

"Reese stopped off at his house before coming to meet you and someone attacked him. That's why he never showed at your house on Saturday. He's in pretty bad shape at the moment."

"Is he gonna be okay?"

"They think so. Eventually. But right now he's still unconscious."

"And you think that had something to do with me?"

"We aren't sure what to think yet."

"Well, I'm really sorry about Reese," Sims said, his eyes flicking to Chloe before returning to Holt. "I like him. And he's been good to me. And I'm not just saying that because I need him—need y'all—right now. But I do need your help. What can I say to convince you? I'm telling you I didn't do it. I did not kill Phillip Donner. I'm not sad the man's gone and I definitely imagined putting a bullet in him a couple times, but I wasn't serious."

"The gun, Kurt. The Smith and Wesson semi-automatic you couldn't find. What's the story with that?"

"I don't know. Honest. It was there last time I looked."

"How long ago was that?"

"Maybe…a week ago. Two? I just keep it around in case, you know? Sometimes you get crazies in my line of work."

"And so it's just gone? You've no idea how? Who has access to it?"

"Just me. I keep it in a shoebox on a shelf in my closet."

"Ever fired it?"

"Yeah, sure, target practice in the backyard. And I go to the range once or twice a year."

Holt made a few notes on his legal pad, then looked up. "Okay, I'm going to want to get in the house."

"Why?" Sims blurted defensively.

"Because I need to look around. See what I can see. Check if they missed anything."

"Like the gun?"

"Maybe."

"Is that possible?" Sims asked, his voice more hopeful.

"Unlikely. But you never know. So how can I get in?"

"There's a key. Behind the third bush down the garage side of the house."

Holt nodded. "Okay. And you really need to start thinking about what might have happened to that gun. Given the ammo they walked out of your house with, I'm guessing that gun has a lot to do with your arrest."

"What else did they take?"

"According to the receipt there were shoes, wire, duct tape—"

"Wire and duct tape? Why? What wire and duct tape?"

Holt shrugged. "They didn't show me. I had to stand outside the house with you while they searched, remember?"

"They didn't have to make us wait out there."

"Yes, they did, Kurt. Because you were throwing a holy fit by the time I got there."

"Well, they had no business—"

"It is *exactly* their business. And you need to get control of yourself, clean up your act and start playing the role of reasonable, believable, concerned citizen, instead of hot-headed, loose-cannon zealot with a grudge, or you'll have no chance of a not-guilty verdict if this thing goes all the way. You hear me? The wires and duct tape? Think about it. They're looking at you for the explosion too. And guess what? There's another body attached to that situation. Start behaving, or you're going to find yourself slapped with two murder charges and an arson charge, along with who knows what else."

Silence filled the tiny room. Finally, Sims broke it. "Okay. Okay, I'll try," he grumbled. "So what happens next? How long will I be in here?"

"Your preliminary hearing's been set for Wednesday. The prosecution will gather its evidence and present just enough to convince the judge there is probable cause to have your case bound over to the Circuit Court. If that happens, the Grand Jury will hear it as soon as possible after that. If they deliver a true bill—"

"A what?"

"A true bill—meaning if they find there's enough evidence to justify trying you—then an indictment will be issued. You'll enter a plea and then the case will proceed to a jury trial unless a deal is made."

"A deal? I'm not making any deal for something I didn't do!" His tone was intense, his voice beginning to shake at the reality Holt was laying out. "Look, you have to help me. I swear I didn't do any of it."

Holt glossed over Sims's plea, pressing on. "The police also confiscated something listed as 'unknown red particles' from your house? What is that?"

Sims looked bemused, his eyebrows wrinkled together almost to a point. "No idea. Look," he continued, "if they say my gun is involved, then I'm being framed. That's the only explanation."

"Who would want to do that? Who would want to kill Donner and blame you for it?"

Sims fidgeted restlessly in his chair. "There's got to be a long list of people who hate Donner. He made a lot of enemies in his time. He's ruthless in business. I'm just an easy target because of what happened with me hitting him with that sign and the lawsuit and all, but if you dig a little, there's got to be somebody else. Because I know it's not me."

Holt exhaled laboriously. "Reese's attacker left a message warning Reese to stop doing something, but for some reason the attacker didn't specify what that something was. Maybe he thought it was obvious, but it's not to any of us. It might be completely unrelated to your situation, but with the timing, it seems possible that someone left that message because they don't want us to continue helping you. Do you have any ideas about who that might be?"

"Yeah, whoever's framing me."

"I meant a name, a lead, or something."

"No, man. I don't have a name. But I know where you might find one."

TWENTY-FOUR

Chloe gazed outside the passenger window of Holt's car as they motored towards Sims's house on the southwest side of Franklin, about ten minutes from the courthouse. She watched the oak-lined streets zip by while Holt was on the phone, trading "hmms" and "uh-huhs" with Cecilia Tucker on the other end of the line. After about five minutes, he dropped the cell phone onto the car's center console cup holder.

"So, Cecilia's going to send us the discovery materials Donner's attorneys produced to her in the lawsuit. Apparently it's too massive to copy—too expensive since neither one of us may ever get paid—but she was fine with us looking through the originals." Back at the courthouse, Sims had explained that after months of legal wrangling and a hearing to force the issue, multiple boxes of papers had finally been delivered to Cecilia in response to their discovery requests in the civil suit. Sims believed that the materials might contain clues as to who was involved in Donner's killing and the explosion at the site. "*You go through that,*" Sims had said, "*and you may find something that can help.*"

"She actually sounded glad about it," Holt remarked, turning onto Sims's street. "The boxes only came last Friday and she hasn't even started sifting through them. I told her we'd give her a heads up if we found anything useful."

Sims's house was a little orangish-red brick rancher that looked like it was built in the 1950s. The firehouse red shutters stood in contrast to the Kelly green artificial turf that had been applied to the front steps and landing. The house had a kept feel about it, the yard mowed and bushes trimmed, but with a minimalist approach. There was no landscaping to speak of along the front of the house itself, no pots with flowers, no personalization of any sort. It gave the impression that Sims exerted only the minimum amount of effort necessary to keep it clean, and no more.

"So what are you hoping to find?" Chloe asked as they got out.

"No idea," Holt replied, heading over to the bush Sims had indicated and retrieving the key beneath it. "But I just want to take a look around. You never know. Maybe we get lucky and find the gun stashed somewhere else in the closet."

"You really think that could happen?"

"No," Holt replied, unlocking the door and swinging it open. "But I have to check. After you," he told Chloe, waving an arm to usher her in.

The inside of the house was a completely different story from the outside. It was clean, yes, but monumentally cluttered. The place looked like an episode of *Hoarders*. Magazines, newspapers, and books of all sorts occupied almost every free square inch, most of them related to either history or politics. In the living room, the walls boasted thumbtacked posters of dozens of historical sites around the south, a few in the north, and photos of Sims at what appeared to be multiple demonstrations related to proposed demolitions. A strong, musty odor, like an old basement or stacks of old books, assaulted them.

"Whoa," Chloe remarked.

"Yeah, I know," Holt agreed, following behind and closing the door. "Come on, his room's down here," he said, heading down a hallway to the right.

The same level of clutter continued through the rest of the house, with the exception of Jacob's room, which was excessively tidy for a teenage boy—no clothes on the floor, no trash, no used dishes—adorned sparingly with his sports trophies for football and basketball. Several team photos were pinned to a bulletin board that hung over a small desk in one corner.

"Acorn fell far from the tree," Holt remarked as they walked past Jacob's room to the last door on the left.

"Apparently," Chloe replied. She bit her lip, weighing her next comment, before sharing. "He's a bit unlikable isn't he? Sims, I mean?"

"A bit?" Holt replied sarcastically, nearing the last door on the left, which was pulled shut. "Wait till you've spent more time around him. But Sims was never the reason Reese was helping out in the situation." Holt put a hand on the knob. "Reese likes Jacob. He's a good kid and good for Emma. So Reese wanted to do what he could," he explained.

"What about Sims's wife? Jacob's mom?"

Holt shook his head. "Jacob's mom passed away about three years ago. Leukemia, adult onset."

"That's awful."

"Yeah. But even so, Jacob seems to have it together. Definitely more than his dad does. From the little Emma's told me, he's killing it at school and on the field. He's a running back on the varsity football team," Holt explained, opening the door and stepping through with Chloe on his heels. "UT is already looking at him."

Sims's bedroom was more of the same, if not worse than the rest of the house. Dozens of white office boxes filled the room in haphazardly stacked columns of various heights, all of which looked as though a good breeze would topple them like dominoes. Papers crammed inside jutted out from beneath crooked lids, some spilling to the floor. Labels like "Mobile plantation demo" and "Briarwood sit-in" were scrawled across the sides in permanent marker.

"Yikes," Holt said.

"At least they cleared a path to the closet," she said, eyeing the gaps between the boxes.

"Yeah," Holt said, stepping over a stack of *Time* magazines on the floor, and reaching for the knob to the accordion-door closet. "So, let's see if—"

Suddenly Holt flew backwards as a black-clad figure leapt out of the closet, ramming Holt into Chloe, sending them both sprawling into the piles of papers, books, and random mess collected in the center of the room. Chloe fell into one of the teetering box stacks which crashed down around her.

"What—*hey*!" Holt shouted, scrambling up and over Chloe to charge after the intruder already sprinting out the door.

"Holt! Don't! Wait!" Chloe yelled, shoving off a box that had fallen on her leg. Jumping up, she hurtled after them just in time to see the intruder speed out the front door with Holt in pursuit. She skidded to a stop on the front porch, where she saw the tail of Holt's jacket whip around the house. She bolted after them, intending to follow, but when she turned the corner, both of them were gone.

* * * * *

Stupid, stupid, stupid!

He panted, trying to catch his breath as he continued running between houses, darting amongst trees and bushes in the hopes of staying hidden. He hadn't heard anyone following him for at least a couple of backyards now, but he wasn't slowing down. He wasn't taking any chances.

Why did I try in the middle of the day?

And why were they there?

His heart pounded like racehorse hooves against a track as he turned another corner and jumped a fence. He landed to the sound of angry barking from a German shepherd charging towards him from the back porch. Ignoring another wave of panic, he turned on the speed, pulling himself up and over the next fence just in time to avoid the dog tearing into his leg.

The message he had left at the McConnaughey house hadn't worked.

Clearly it was going to take something even more serious to get them to pay attention.

* * * * *

Chloe was sitting on the turf-covered steps of the front porch, legs-crossed and an elbow propped up on one knee when Holt reappeared around the corner, his chest heaving as he sucked in labored breaths.

"Lost him," he replied, walking towards her, his suit rumpled and shirttail pulled loose.

"You all right?" Chloe asked, concern evident in her voice.

"Yeah, yeah," Holt said, leaning against one of the wrought iron supports that propped up the small porch awning. "That sucker was fast."

"That was pretty stupid," Chloe chastised, standing up.

Holt eyebrows arched at the unexpected admonishment. "What was I supposed to do?"

"Umm, maybe *not* chase after him? Call 911? Wait for the police?" She eyed him sarcastically. "Stop me when I get to something that sounds good."

"Yeah, well, it doesn't matter. He took off."

"What do you think he was after?"

"I don't know," he said, pulling out his cell and dialing. "But it can't be good."

"Who are you calling?"

"Who do you think I'm calling?" he quipped, a plucky smile behind his eyes. "I'm taking your advice."

TWENTY-FIVE

After an hour long detour with the Franklin police, Holt and Chloe made it back to his law office, where Sims's discovery boxes had already been delivered.

Holt's shoulders drooped as they stared at a half dozen of the things. "She wasn't kidding," Holt groaned. "Cecilia said it was too much to copy. There's probably several thousand pieces of paper in each one of those."

"So what now?"

"We start going through them," he said, rubbing his forehead, as if warding off a headache. "I can do a little bit this morning, but I've got hearings later this afternoon and a trial in two days. It will just have to wait."

"I can do it."

He swiveled towards her, a look of amused skepticism on his face. "You don't want to do that."

"You said that as your 'intern' it would be good if I did some actual work, right? And I want to help. If sifting through all this," she waved a hand at the boxes, "will move this along, then it's what I want to do."

"It'll take hours. Hours upon hours."

"So? I've got time to kill now that Reese is in the hospital and I'm staying with the kids. I've already called my editor and taken some family leave."

"But, look," he said, exhaling uncomfortably. "I can't pay you. You don't owe Sims anything. It's not your problem."

"I'm not doing it for him. I'm doing it for the kids. If there is something in here that can point us to whoever hurt Reese and threatened Emma and Tyler, then I want to find it. If Sims benefits, so be it."

Holt surrendered. "All right, but when you go blind from boredom, don't say I didn't warn you."

"Fair enough."

Squirreling themselves away in the conference room, they tried to make some headway. After an hour, the table was covered from one end to the other with stacks of papers of varying heights, each one representing a different type of document. The piles were their attempt to bring some sort of organization to the mass of paper Donner's attorneys had provided.

"It's a blitzkrieg," Holt had explained. "There are two ways to go about discovery. Most often attorneys strip a request down and try to produce as little as possible. Unless they go the other way, and produce everything under the sun, even things you didn't request in order to mask anything that might be relevant, which is what they did here. Now there's so much that finding anything helpful is like hunting for a needle in a haystack."

He was right. So far they had not come across anything remotely useful. On top of that, there was no order to it all. It was as if Donner's attorneys had played "fifty-two card pickup" with the documents, then randomly boxed them up. Consequently, Chloe and Holt had decided to start by sorting the documents into categories as best they could, to be gone through a second time once they had a better handle on what they were looking at.

"Here's an electric bill for power usage at the construction site. I mean, what good is this?" Chloe fussed.

"Sims's requests were open-ended and Donner's attorneys ran with it. I can't blame them," he admitted. "It's a good strategy." He checked his stainless steel Rolex watch, tossed a final sheet on one of the piles, and pushed back from the table. "I've got to get ready for my hearings. Will you be all right here?"

"Definitely. I'll do what I can. I have to leave by 3:00 to pick up Tyler."

"Just let Karen know when you go."

Chloe nodded.

"How about I take you guys out for dinner tonight? All of you. There's a bar and grill downtown that the kids love. It's got karaoke. Maybe it'll cheer them up a bit after you check on Reese."

"Karaoke?"

A confident grin erupted on his face. "One of my specialties. Tyler loves it."

"All right, burgers and karaoke it is."

Chloe spent the rest of the day finishing sorting through the first box, just doing quick scans of documents to determine whether they belonged in the 'correspondence with city,' 'correspondence with seller,' 'construction related,' 'contract related,' or any of the other dozen or so piles they had separated the papers into. She had just dipped into the second box, when she realized it was a quarter to three and decided to call it a day. Thinking she might have some time after Tyler went to bed, she grabbed the box and headed for the lobby. After explaining to Karen what she was doing, she put the first box in the car, then went back for one more.

"Okay, this is the last one," Chloe told Karen as she passed by the mahogany desk where the receptionist sat typing away, her plum-colored nails clacking on the keys. Karen had a round face and amiable smile, and had been very pleasant all afternoon, even bringing Chloe a glass of tea halfway through her time there.

"Two boxes," Karen noted, her eyebrows rising. "That's pretty ambitious."

"Probably," Chloe admitted. "Thanks again for the tea and everything. I guess I'll see you tomorrow."

"No problem," Karen said, her short brown hair bouncing gently as she spoke. "It was really nice to finally meet you, Chloe. I know Reese is glad you're here." She paused and her eyes glistened a bit. "I'm really worried about him. And the kids. Please let me know if there's anything at all I can do to help you. If you get an update on Reese, would you let me know? Just text or call or whatever," she said, slipping Chloe her number on a yellow sticky note. "Day or night."

"I definitely will," Chloe assured her.

It was a short drive to the school, where Tyler hopped in the car and immediately began asking about his father. Chloe assured Tyler that Reese was on the mend and that they would go visit him as soon as Emma got off work, even though her multiple calls to the hospital had only resulted in reports that he was stable—no better and no worse. When Tyler continued to look fretful, Chloe suggested ice cream at Baskin Robbins on the way home as a distraction. This seemed to perk him up, and he chatted the rest of the way about the drama at recess when one of the boys had found a frog on the slide.

Baskin Robbins was housed in a little brick building just off the square. Tyler insisted on one of their signature creations—an upside down cone iced to look like a clown—while Chloe opted for a single scoop of lemon custard. They stepped out onto the little paver patio in front of the store, the shop's bell jingling as they exited. A light wind ruffled Chloe's hair, nearly sending it into the sticky sweet cream just before she snatched up the curl and tucked it behind her ear.

"Can we go see Emma?" Tyler asked, jumping on and off a concrete bench on the patio.

"Lead the way," Chloe answered.

Tyler took her free hand and they walked two blocks down Main Street to Philanthropy, the clothing and gift store where Emma worked after school and on weekends. The windows were beautifully decorated with old trunks, flouncy dresses, and burlap ribbon, lending the shop a sophisticated bohemian air. Burning candles, as wide as salad plates, in rustic tones of orange and russet, beckoned patrons inside.

Hints of cinnamon and vanilla from the candles wafted over Chloe as they entered. Old wooden planks, possibly the originals, comprised the floor, and walls of exposed brown brick stretched throughout the space. Every square inch was packed with thoughtful, creative displays of unique merchandise: jewelry made from antique spoons, photo frames assembled from reclaimed wood, and hand-dyed scarves from Africa.

"Emma!" Tyler shouted, running up to his sister who was hanging a group of deep aqua sweaters on a rack.

"Hey, buddy," Emma responded, putting one arm around him as he hugged her waist.

"Sorry," Chloe said sheepishly. "I know you're working but he really wanted to see you."

"No problem," Emma told her, crossing her arms. "I see he talked you into the clown."

Tyler's gaze shot to Chloe, guilt flushing his cheeks.

Chloe narrowed her eyes at Tyler in mock disappointment. "Should he not have?"

"Just watch out for the sugar rush in about thirty minutes," Emma warned.

"Ahh. Gotcha."

"Thanks for the texts about Dad earlier."

"Of course," Chloe said. "I thought maybe we could go by after you get off work."

"Um, well, I thought I would go see him by myself after work and then head over to hang out with Jacob and Trip. If that's okay? Jacob's having a tough time."

Chloe wondered whether Reese would think that was okay or not. Did he let Emma stay out on school nights? But then, this was such a special situation. "Sure. If you think it will help, that's fine."

"Thanks. I should be home around ten thirty or so."

Chloe nodded. "I don't know the rules, so whatever rules you have with Reese work for me." She realized as she said it that she would just have to trust Emma because she had no way of knowing what Reese's parental rules actually were.

"Excuse me?" A customer asked, approaching Emma through a large opening that led to an adjoining space that had probably been another shop at one time, but was now an expansion of Philanthropy. "Could you help me with some sizes?"

"Sure," Emma replied, accompanying the woman as she retreated back into the other side.

"Come on," Tyler said, taking Chloe's hand. "I want to show you the wall."

Wondering what he meant, Chloe followed him through the opening that Emma had just gone through. Like the other side, this part of the store was replete with clothing and gift items. But it also contained large displays of colorful handmade items sourced from struggling regions where people sold the products in an effort to create self-sustaining industries. Descriptions accompanied the goods, some showcasing lovely photographs of the artisans, connecting customers even more personally to the vibrant handwoven bags from Uganda, beaded jewelry made from brightly-hued recycled paper by women in Kenya, and multicolored canvas shoes cut and sewn by Chilean villagers. Chloe ran a hand over the soft fabric of the shoes.

"What a great idea."

"Yeah, they help people. Okay, so come here!" he said excitedly, motioning her to follow. She slowed as they moved past a whimsical display piled high in the center of the room consisting of stacked wooden crates topped with mounds of old books and, scattered amongst those, robin's egg blue pottery filled with dried ivory hydrangeas. At the pinnacle of the mound was a painted Queen's Anne chair reupholstered in creamy velvet, standing crooked on a gravity-defying single leg, counter-balanced by a thick rope secured to the ceiling by way of an old factory pulley. The inventive decor alone was reason to award the shop a feature spot in her article.

Impatient, Tyler took her hand, dragging her the rest of the way to a waist-high narrow table made of reclaimed wood pushed against one wall. The space directly above the table was covered by rows and rows of horizontal wooden planks pierced every several inches by large, square-cut nails. Every nail had dozens of old-fashioned, manila shipping tags hanging from it, each tag containing a message penned in different handwriting. Tin pails on the table held more blank tags and several pens. A stenciled sign declared this to be the "Prayer Wall."

"See," Tyler said, pulling a tag from the pail and choosing a pen, "you write your prayer on this, then hang it on the nail. Then you take somebody else's prayer and you pray that for them." He began scribbling on his tag as Chloe perused the ones others had left behind.

Some were sweet scrawls in kindergarten-like fashion, asking for help for 'Sam my golden retriever,' or 'Grandpa Jim.' Others were penned in flowing cursive, asking for 'peace after my husband's passing,' or strong, block-print letters requesting prayers for a new job. She touched one, imagining the person who wrote, 'heal Anne's cancer,' and wondered who Anne was, and how she was doing.

"And then," Tyler proceeded, clicking his pen and dropping it back in the pail, "you put yours on a nail for somebody else to take." He hung it on the nail closest to him. "Get it?"

"I do. Tyler, this is beautiful."

"Yeah, I like it. I take one every time I come in."

"You do?"

He nodded. "And I pray too. For the person on the tag. Do you ever pray, Chloe?"

Chloe smiled. "I do, Tyler. I do."

"Well, here," he said, pulling a tag off the wall. "You take this one and pray for," he squinted at the message, "Ellen's surgery, and then you put your prayer on this," he handed her a blank tag, "and leave it."

"That's a great idea, Tyler," Chloe said, pocketing Ellen's tag and taking a pen from the pail.

* * * * *

Before heading home they went by the hospital to check on Reese. She felt guilty for not spending more time there, but as the nurses continued to tell them, there wasn't really anything they could do but wait. Even so, it was good to go by there, squeeze Reese's hand, and let Tyler tell him about his day.

On the way home, Zach, a friend of Tyler's, called his cell to ask if Tyler could spend the night. Apparently, his mother heard about Reese's incident and wanted to help. After speaking with the mother and texting Emma to confirm that it would be okay to leave Tyler with this family, Chloe took Tyler home to pack a small bag, then dropped him off at Zach's house where he was attacked with a Nerf gun before even making it inside.

By 5:00 p.m., Chloe was back at Reese's house, alone. It was an odd feeling after all that had happened there over the last several days. She was just about to pour herself a glass of merlot from the stash Reese kept in the kitchen, when the doorbell rang.

"Got some hungry kids in there?" Holt asked when she opened the door. His hair was ruffled and shirt loose at the waist. His tie and suit jacket were absent and there was an air of exhaustion about him.

"Hard day?" she asked.

He nodded. "Started out chasing some idiot through a neighborhood and it went downhill after that," he grinned tiredly. "I went by to see Reese," he explained, seeming to sag a little more. "It's tough seeing him like that. Going out might be a distraction for us all."

"Holt, I'm sorry but both of the kids are out. Emma's with friends and Tyler's sleeping over at a buddy's. I should have called."

"Oh," he replied, genuine disappointment in his voice. "Okay, well," his eyes brightened, "you've got to eat, right? We can still go. I promise not to keep you late. A little karaoke can go a long way. You'll feel like a new person."

She was hungry. And not particularly looking forward to hanging out in the house by herself all night. She was about to accept when a generic, white delivery van pulled to the curb in front of the house.

"Hi there! Sorry," the driver called out, exiting his door and sliding open the rear door of the van. He pulled out a large vase of salmon-colored roses, intermixed with airy fern branches and snowy baby's breath. "Last delivery of the day. We were running a bit behind," he explained as he approached them. He glanced at the attached envelope. "Chloe McConnaughey?"

"Yeah, that's me."

"Great." He thrust the vase into her arms and jogged back to the van. "Have a good night."

"The boyfriend?" Holt asked, his hands in his pockets.

Chloe didn't answer, instead withdrawing a small blue card from the envelope.

I'm sorry. Take your time, but please call me. This isn't what you think. I love you. Jack.

"Yeah," she confirmed, sliding the card into her pocket. "It's from Jack."

"You don't sound too happy."

"We're just…in a rough patch at the moment."

"Sorry to hear that."

Chloe shrugged. "It'll pass." The roses offered a heady clove scent, unusually strong for store-bought flowers. A pang of regret pinched her, though her uneasiness over Jack's decision to keep his interactions with Lila from her had not dissipated. She would call him soon. She wasn't punishing him. It was just that she honestly had not decided how she felt about the whole thing and had no idea what she would say.

She cleared her throat. "Maybe we should do karaoke another night?" she suggested, feeling that maybe it was better to just stay in. "I brought a couple of the discovery boxes home with me and I should probably just work through those. I mean, the faster we get through them all, the faster we figure this thing out."

"Tell you what," Holt said, adjusting his stance. "Why don't we both work through the boxes? Otherwise, you're right, it'll be that much more staring us in the face tomorrow." He waved her inside. "Come on. Pizza's on me."

* * * * *

"It's nearly ten," Chloe said, reaching for the last piece of pepperoni and mushroom pizza despite her better judgment. She was bored with this and eating gave her something else to do. She followed the bite with a sip of ice water. She had switched over after her glass of merlot. A headache in the morning was the last thing she needed.

"I know," Holt said, dropping the last piece of paper from the box they were working on into one of the piles they had made on Reese's dining room table. "I just want to finish this box." He leaned back, looking somewhat satisfied.

Chloe shook her head. "Look to your right," she drawled.

He squinted at her, then turned, his eyes landing on another inch-high stack on the far corner of the table. "Ugh. I thought I got it all," he grumbled, snatching up the papers and leaning forward again. Holt snapped half the stack to her, which she took with exaggerated dismay.

"Not a word," she chastised, skimming a page and sending it to the 'project planning pile.' "It was your idea to help me tonight."

"Yeah, yeah," he answered.

Chloe perused the next page and relegated it to the 'communications pile.' Looking up, she noticed Holt's eyes narrowed on the sheet he was holding. "What is it?"

He pointed to a list of three names at the bottom of an email from Donner's company updating the Main Street Business Council on the project's progress. "These companies were copied on this email. Don't know why." He turned, tapping the communications pile. "I've seen several names here and there, copied or included in the mailings for different things. I think we should make a list. Then track down what they had to do with the project. Maybe it's nothing, but maybe we get lucky and find someone with a vested interest in Donner's project or a bone to pick with him. It might help us get a better picture of the scope of things."

Changing gears, they started skimming the documents related to communication, looking for names other than those directly associated with Donner's company. In another hour, they had compiled a list of eight businesses and individuals.

"I recognize a few of those from some of the documents I sorted at the office today, but I wasn't looking for names then, so we'll need to go back through those. And there's still three boxes we haven't opened yet," Chloe pointed out.

Holt shrugged. "It's enough to start on. We can add to the list and eliminate as we go." He pulled the laptop to him and started typing. Finding contact numbers for most of the names was relatively easy, requiring only a few minutes of searching. Two of the businesses, Marble Properties, LLC, and Vettner-Drake, Inc., did not return anything in his internet searches, and neither had a website, Facebook page, or online presence of any kind. "Okay. Let's go at this another way," Holt said, resuming typing and entering, 'Tennessee Secretary of State' in the Google search bar.

"So, every corporation doing business in Tennessee has to register and identify the person designated to receive service of legal documents on behalf of the company," he explained, typing in the first corporate name and slapping the 'Enter' button. "We can find out who it is and go from there." Within two minutes he had pulled up the entity information pages for both companies and jotted down the listed agents and their addresses. No phone numbers were offered and a search of the agents' names online did not reveal any.

"So what now?" Chloe asked.

"The ones with numbers we can call, at least initially, but we'll have to go see the other two in person," Holt said, waving the slip of paper he had jotted the information onto. "They aren't far. We could knock both of them out in a couple hours tomorrow. What do you say, Nancy Drew? Up for some sleuthing?"

She was.

TWENTY-SIX

Holt finally left around eleven o'clock, having deciding that since Tyler was sleeping at a friend's house, it might be an opportunity to get some really good sleep in his own bed.

"I'll be back tomorrow night," he insisted, though Chloe told him they would be fine alone. "I don't want Tyler worrying when he's here," Holt pushed, refusing to take 'no' for an answer.

Emma noisily arrived home a few minutes later, flinging the downstairs door open in typical teen fashion, without regard to anyone who might be sleeping. Proclaiming exhaustion from a night hanging out with Jacob and Trip, she headed to bed with barely a word and was out again by seven thirty the next morning. One quick hello and an update on Reese given through bites of peanut butter toast was all Chloe managed to fit in before Emma was zipping off to school.

Tyler was a different story. The boy was super chatty on the phone, assuring her he was fine and almost ready for school, before abruptly hanging up to get in on the cinnamon rolls made by Zach's mom. Chloe took advantage of the next couple of hours by herself to chart an outline for her Franklin piece, until Holt rolled into the driveway at nine thirty and honked.

After first asking about the kids and Reese, Holt explained that he had already managed to get in touch with three of the names on the list they had made the night before. "They were either friends of Donner or people he had done business with before. One said Donner had asked him to invest in the project, but it wasn't for him, so he passed on it. The others will probably be more of the same, but it's good to check. Less legwork for the public defender when Sims finally gets one."

They decided to first head over to see Charles Scott, the registered agent for Marble Properties. The address listed on the Secretary of State website was in Murfreesboro, about forty minutes east of Franklin. When they arrived, they found that the address was for his personal residence. Scott was at home and more than happy to talk. He explained that the business was a small, family-owned construction company that would invest in, develop, and then sell small properties. Scott was the owner, managing partner, and registered agent. His relationship with Donner had been a personal one, not business, though Donner had also approached him about investing in the Franklin project.

"Not the right market for us at the time, though," he said, explaining why he declined Donner's invitation. "Too rich for our blood. And, given what's happened, I'm glad we opted out. Shame about what happened to him."

They traded perfunctory sympathies and chatted about Donner's business for another fifteen minutes, until it was clear they had exhausted his knowledge of the subject. Then Chloe and Holt were back in the car, headed to the office because Karen had called, asking Holt to sign a few documents that needed to be filed that morning. After that detour, they struck out again, this time to find Eli Drake of Vettner-Drake, Incorporated, located in south Nashville.

They settled into a comfortable silence as they drove north into the city by way of Hillsboro Road, one of the pre-interstate thoroughfares into Nashville. Holt promised her that it would be more interesting than I-65 and would allow her to get a better feel for the area. As they rolled through Franklin and the suburban areas linking it to Nashville, they passed a variety of sprawling scenes: young neighborhoods sporting the latest stone veneers and craftsman beams; older homes—some renovated, some not—with long concrete drives cracked from age; century-old, stacked stone walls; open fields with brown, grazing cows. The roadside was packed thick with bushes and trees, dotted every so often by a church or school or the odd business building. Green was everywhere, though tinted with the slightest hint of brown, signaling the quick approach of coming cold days and the changeover to winter that would soon strip the color from most of nature for several long months.

After about ten minutes, the landscape began to change, the wooden fences replaced by iron ones crowned with gated drives leading to mansions rivaling anything in the best neighborhoods in Atlanta. Holt explained that they had moved on from Franklin and were now in what was referred to as the Forest Hills area. One particular jaw-dropping structure was stone, with three stories of floor-to-ceiling windows, wrought-iron balconies, and a pebbled circular driveway quartering what looked like a Porsche.

"These houses are insane," Chloe told Holt, eyeing another gate that zipped by on the right, this one flanked by six-foot-high white stucco walls, each boasting a metal sculpture of the letter 'E.' The drive behind the gate snaked between rows of giant oaks that bent over it worshipfully, likely leading to an equally impressive residence hidden further back on the property.

"I know. I never get used to it. I used to drive by here all the time headed into Green Hills—it's the shopping area just north of here. Our house was on this side of Franklin, so this is the way I'd usually go."

As he said it, she realized how little she knew about him, aside from the fact that he worked for Reese. "Okay, let's hear it. Tell me your story."

"Not much to tell," he shrugged. "High school dropout makes good. That's it really."

"You were a high school dropout?"

He groaned. "You really want to hear this?"

She nodded.

"We lived in a nice house in Cottonwood—a little subdivision on this side of Franklin. My dad was a banker in Brentwood. My mom was a housewife. Pretty cut and dry, actually. But I got bored. You know, I was one of those annoyingly privileged kids who isn't interested in anything resembling work. I skipped, shoplifted—the whole shebang. I actually had to repeat my senior year. That's when I quit school. Moved in with a buddy that was a couple years ahead of me. Figured I could make it on my own."

"And did you?"

He cut his eyes at her sardonically. "'Course not. It was awful. I was a cook at this little grease pit grill on West End in Nashville, living on a ratty couch in some dude's apartment. I was twenty years old, broke and pretty convinced I had screwed up my life when this guy walks into the grill one day. He's just got this look about him and so I ask him, 'What do you do?' And he says, 'I'm a private detective.' So I ask him about it and he tells me all the crazy stuff he does and how much he gets paid. At the time, it sounded like a million dollars. Long story short, he needed help at his office and agreed to teach me the tricks of the trade while I worked for him."

"At twenty?"

"I might have been a dropout, but I was smart. I guess he saw that. I got my GED and entered community college. Took classes while I worked for him. I got accepted into Lipscomb University for the last two years and ended up with a business degree."

"When did you meet Reese?"

"He was a regular client—divorce work and such—and said he saw a spark in me. He convinced me to go to law school. Said I was wasted as a P.I. It didn't hurt that I had seen the kind of money a lot of the attorneys we worked for were making. The cars they drove. The clothes they wore. I was tired of struggling. I wanted what they had. So I entered the Nashville School of Law. Worked by day, studied at night. Got through in four years."

"And he hired you when you got out?"

"I had clerked for him and a couple of other attorneys during the summers, but your dad needed the help the most. He had more work than he could handle. This was right after Emma and Tyler's mom left, and he was pretty stretched learning how to play single dad. As soon I started my final year he offered to make me his junior partner. He needed help and I needed a job. The rest is history."

"Your parents must be proud."

"Relieved would be more accurate. At least I'm not the disappointment of the family anymore. But it's a lot more intense work than I thought it would be. And definitely not a get-rich-quick scheme."

"Really? You look like you're doing okay?" she said, tilting her head towards his watch.

"What? This thing?" he asked, lifting his hand off the wheel and shaking it. "No. It's nice and all, but I got it secondhand at this store in Alabama that sells stuff found in lost luggage. I mean," he hedged, shrugging, "I *do* have a weakness for nice clothes—"

"And shoes."

"And shoes," he admitted, "but everybody's got something they splurge on, right? I'm doing fine. It's just that criminal defense attorneys in practice for themselves in small towns don't generally top the list of high earners in the legal field."

"Did you ever think about working for a larger firm?"

"Thought about it. But those guys always seem even more tired, more strung out. I like setting my own rules. Life's too short as it is."

"Yeah," Chloe agreed without any hesitation. "It sure is."

* * * * *

4912 Thorne Road was squirreled away in one of West Nashville's older, more secluded areas. The towering Mediterranean-style home sat squarely in the center of a huge property and looked like it belonged in Madrid, not in a southern American town known for banjos, biscuits, and barbecue. Holt turned into the long, aggregate drive that steadily climbed up the grassy hill leading to the front door. At the summit, he pulled into one of several parking spots against a stone retaining wall.

"Wow," Chloe remarked as they exited the car and walked up the front steps.

"Yeah," Holt agreed, then turned to her, a playful look on his face. "Okay. What's your guess?" he asked, deep chimes sounding as he rang the doorbell situated to the right of a double set of mahogany doors with textured glass and scrolled iron insets.

"What?"

"You think he'll answer himself or have a full-time housekeeper? My money's on the housekeeper."

Before Chloe could answer, an indistinct shadow moved towards them from the other side of the doors. She straightened up as a lock clicked and the right door swung inward with a creak, revealing a man in his early fifties with thinning brown hair and horn-rimmed glasses. He was dressed in a starched white shirt and charcoal gabardine pants, with a stiff attitude to match.

"Yes?" It was more an accusation than a question, emphasized by the annoyance reflected in his eyes.

"Guess I lose," Holt muttered to Chloe.

"What?" questioned the man.

"Mr. Drake? Of Vettner-Drake, Incorporated?" As Holt asked the question, Chloe sensed something immediately altered in him. Chloe's gaze flicked to him, noting that the tenor of his voice seemed sharper, more direct. Cutting. Even his stance was steely. Someone had flipped a switch and now Holt was all business.

The man at the door stalled a good three seconds before answering. "Yes. Who's asking?"

"I'm Holt Adams. I'm an attorney in Franklin. I apologize for the unannounced visit but we weren't able to locate any phone numbers associated with you or Vettner-Drake. We're here because we found Vettner-Drake listed on some documentation produced by Donner Properties and we hoped to ask you about the connection. I represent Kurt Sims—he's been charged with the murder of Phillip Donner, someone I think you may be familiar with. If we could just ask a few—"

"I'm not talking to you," Drake declared, his eyes narrowed in suspicion as he moved to slam the door.

Holt shoved his foot between the door and the frame. "You don't want to do that. Mr. Drake, we just want to ask you a few questions. If you've got any insight into Mr. Donner's dealings, it could really help us prepare a defense for Mr. Sims."

"Why would I care about that?"

"You wouldn't want an innocent man going to prison for a crime he didn't commit, would you?"

"Who says he's innocent?" said Drake.

"He does. Look, you can shut the door, but if we can't get answers from you then we'll just have to start digging on our own to find them. There could be subpoenas…press conferences…"

Drake huffed begrudgingly. "Fine," he grunted, opening the door a few more inches, but keeping it as a barrier between them. "How did you get my name?"

"As I said, Vettner-Drake was listed on some documentation provided by Donner Properties as discovery in a civil suit Mr. Sims filed against it. We weren't familiar with the name and wanted to check it out before crossing it off our list."

"Well, you can just cross it off already. We had nothing to do with Phillip's project. Yes, he was an acquaintance. We were friends socially. But, no, we weren't involved in the project."

"So Vettner-Drake wasn't an investor in Mr. Donner's Main Street project?"

"Like I said, no. Not an investor." As if anticipating Holt's next question, he continued, "Vettner-Drake is a real estate investment and management company. Privately held. I'm its sole employee.

Phillip asked me to invest in the project. I said no. But he kept including me on those invitations and updates anyway. I presume he was hoping I'd change my mind about investing." He looked at Chloe, sizing her up, then back at Holt. "Do you work with that woman that represents Sims in his civil suit?"

"No, we're a different firm. We just have the criminal case."

"Look," Drake replied dryly, "I may not have invested in Phillip's project, but I've got no interest in undermining it by helping the man suing him."

"We just want to know if you have any idea who might *have* wanted to undermine it."

"You mean someone other than your client?" Drake sniped, his voice dripping with sarcasm.

Holt exhaled loudly. "We aren't trying to cause you any problems, Mr. Drake. We're just talking to people who had a connection to Donner or his company to gather as much information as we can."

"Well, I don't think I can help you."

Their eyes locked for several tense moments. "You know what?" Holt finally surrendered, touching Chloe's arm to signal a retreat as he took a step back. "This isn't getting us anywhere. I'm sorry to have bothered you, Mr. Drake. We'll have to go about this another way."

"What's that supposed to mean?"

"It means you should call your lawyer," Holt said over his shoulder as he turned towards his car. "We'll be sending some documents your way shortly."

Chloe had just turned her back when the front door swung all the way open.

"Stop," Drake said. They turned back to him in unison. "I don't want to get pulled into this. I have interests in the area and it wouldn't do for me to be seen as aiding your client. Especially given that, from all reports, your client happens to be a nutcase. But that aside, I also don't want to get dragged into a paper war."

"Okay," Holt said, folding his arms. "Great. So what can you tell me?"

Drake sniffed and looked away, apparently weighing his words. Finally his determined gaze returned to Holt. "You need to talk to that other attorney."

Holt squinted, perplexed. "What other attorney?"

"The one handling Sims's lawsuit." A significant silence followed Drake's clarification.

"Cecilia Tucker?"

"Exactly. And that," Drake said, taking a definitive step backwards into the house and reaching to push the door shut, "is all I'm going to say."

*****

"I don't understand," Chloe opined as the Audi purred, racing along at sixty miles per hour, headed back to the office. "What's that supposed to mean? 'Talk to the other attorney.' It sounds cryptic."

"Yeah, I don't know. It was weird. I don't know why he thinks Cecilia can tell us anything—that she hasn't already, I mean."

"What has she told you?"

Holt twisted the wheel to the left, whipping around a slow moving car and gliding back into the right lane. "Generalities about the lawsuit, and we filled her in on Sims's arrest. We talked about discovery in the civil suit, obviously."

"Well, maybe he just meant that talking with her could be beneficial. Maybe he was just giving you a helpful push in the right direction."

"I'm pretty sure he wanted to push me, but not in a helpful sort of way," Holt said sardonically. "That exchange did not feel very 'helpful' to me. Did it feel helpful to you?"

"Not really."

"If Cecilia knew anything about another potential suspect in the murder case, she would have said something when we talked this morning. She knows I'm looking for another way to spin this."

"Why did you press him?"

"What?"

"I mean, you were different with him than with Charles Scott. Why? Maybe he just doesn't like people showing up without calling first."

"Gut feeling, I guess. Did you notice how unhappy he was when he realized who we were?"

"I'd guess 'unhappy' is a pretty standard reaction to a lawyer showing up at your house without warning, asking questions."

"Maybe. Initially. But Charles Scott was fine with it once we explained why we were there. There was no reason for Drake to be so cantankerous."

"So what now?"

"We go talk to Cecilia, get that weird question answered ASAP." He glanced at the clock. "It'll be time for lunch soon and we've got to eat, right? I'll call her, see if she can grab lunch."

Chloe's phone buzzed and she checked the number. She didn't recognize it.

"Hello?" she answered, listening quietly for about half a minute before speaking. "Can you hold on for a second?" She pulled the phone down and turned to Holt, relief and concern washing over her face in equal measure.

"It's the hospital," she said. "Reese is awake."

TWENTY-SEVEN

Reese's blanket rose and fell rhythmically with his breathing as Chloe watched from a chair pulled to his bedside. Though he had been awake earlier, after briefly communicating with a nurse he had passed out again. His skin held more color than it had a day before, a good sign. Emma perched beside him on the bed, one leg tucked under her, the other hanging off the side. Chloe had found her there, holding Reese's hand, when she and Holt had arrived a quarter of an hour ago. She had beaten them there, leaving school as soon as Chloe had called with the news of Reese regaining consciousness. Dogged concern creased her features, something Chloe would not have expected. It seemed that the news of her father's awakening, quickly followed by a descent back into unconsciousness, had unlocked something inside the teenager.

"Dad," Emma whispered, squeezing his fingers tight, "come on. We're right here."

Several minutes of tense waiting passed. "Maybe it's best if we let him rest," Holt suggested. "Sometimes these things take a while. We could come back later when—"

Something like choking issued from Reese. He shook and Emma, startled, jumped off the bed. "Dad? Dad?" she gasped, moving back as if frightened of him.

"It's okay, Emma," Chloe assured her. "Reese. Can you hear us? We're all here."

Reese's eyes flickered. "Emma?" His voice was gravelly, dry from days of non-use.

"Yes, Emma's here. And Holt. And me, Chloe."

Reese exhaled, his breath hissing as if let from a tire. "Tyler?"

"He's at school," Chloe said. "It's Tuesday, around noon. You've been out for a while."

"Tuesday," Reese grumbled, groggily.

"Reese," Holt started, "do you remember what happened? Do you know who did this to you?"

"Ski mask," Reese groaned. "Dressed…in black." He was struggling to speak. "Water," he grunted, his eyelids half-shut.

"Emma, why don't you go to the nurses' desk? Tell them he's awake again and asking for water."

"Um, okay," Emma said timidly, sliding to the door, then slipping out.

"Emma…here?" Reese asked, a hint of surprise in the question. "Wouldn't have…expected…" His words trailed off as he exhaled heavily.

"She's more attached to you than she'd like to admit," Holt noted sagely.

Something like a smile tugged at the corner of Reese's chapped lips. "Good…to know."

"Can you tell us what happened?" Holt pressed.

Reese struggled to turn his head to the side. It looked like he was trying to shake it. "Not…much. Came home before…meeting Kurt. Heard something upstairs. Surprised him," Reese paused, coughing and licking his lips. "Fought…Fell down stairs."

"He left a message, Reese," Holt said. "On the wall. Said to back off or the kids would be next."

The little color in Reese's face paled at this and he worked to open his eyes more fully. "The kids? He…threatened…kids?"

Holt nodded. "And right now it looks like it's the same person that left the box on your doorstep."

Reese grimaced as he shifted. "Leg…killing me."

"Don't," Chloe told him, placing a firm hand on his torso to keep him from squirming. "You broke it in two places in the fall. And you took a hit on the head. You had swelling on your brain, but it's better now. They had to do surgery, though."

"Brain…surgery," Reese echoed slowly, taking that in for a few moments. "Who are…kids staying with?"

Chloe bit her lip. "Me. Well, I've been staying with them."

Even in his drugged state, a noticeable wave of surprise rolled over Reese's face. "You would do…did…that?"

Chloe nodded. "I hope it's okay."

Reese exhaled. "You stayed."

Chloe nodded again. "Yeah. I stayed."

"Reese," Holt started, "about Kurt Sims—"

"Holt," Chloe said, shaking her head, "maybe now isn't the best time."

"It's important, Chloe. We need to know—"

"What about Sims?" Reese interrupted groggily.

"We need to know if you can think of anyone who wouldn't want you helping him. Anyone other than Donner, obviously," Holt pushed, as Chloe frowned.

"You sure…this…is about Donner?"

"Well, it could be about something else, but right now the connection to Sims is the best lead we've got."

Reese exhaled and seemed to sink further into the bed. The short conversation was visibly draining him. "Maybe," he started as a red-headed nurse in pink scrubs arrived with Emma on her heels, "you could…try—"

"Mr. McConnaughey?" the nurse interrupted, inserting herself into the mix and pulling Reese's tray over his midline. She set a large plastic cup with an accordion straw on the tray. "I'm Carol, your nurse. Your daughter tells me you're thirsty? Why don't you try some water?"

She put the straw to his lips and he seemed to take in just a bit of the liquid before pulling back from the straw. "So tired," he uttered, closing his eyes completely.

"Understandable," Carol agreed, raising her gaze to meet Chloe's. "It might be time for some rest. Maybe continue the conversation later?"

"Of course," Chloe acquiesced, standing. "Come on, guys. Let's let him sleep." She gently touched his arm before rounding the bed, headed towards the door. "We'll be back later. And I'll bring Tyler by."

"Dad," Emma started as Chloe passed her, "I'll be back. I'll…I'll see you soon." Reese's breathing had already smoothed and slowed, a sign that he was likely in the process of slipping back into sleep. He didn't respond.

The trio moved into the hallway with Holt bringing up the rear. He was about to close the door behind him when a muffled noise, something like an incomprehensible "wfff," sounded from inside the room.

Holt turned, perplexed, and stepped back inside the room. "What is it, Reese?" he said, moving to his partner's bedside and bending low over him, despite Carol the nurse's disapproving stare. "What was that again?"

"Wfff. Talk to…Donner…wife."

TWENTY-EIGHT

After sending Emma on her way back to school, Holt and Chloe headed downtown to meet Cecilia Tucker for lunch. They spent the ride tossing around ideas about why Reese would have pointed them in the direction of Donner's wife.

"Honestly," Holt started, as he pulled in the parking garage just off Main Street, "going to the wife is a pretty standard route of inquiry. It may just be that and nothing more."

"Maybe," Chloe said, as Holt got lucky and found a spot on the first level, "but he seemed so intent on getting that out before he fell asleep again. Seems like it was important."

"I'll definitely try to get a meeting with Donner's wife, but it's gonna be tough. Aside from the fact that we represent the man accused of killing her husband, Sims was also suing their company for a whole lot of money. I doubt she'll be very chatty."

They exited the cool shadows of the garage, stepping onto the sidewalk and into the bright sun of midday. Even so, the temperature was mild and the air breezy, and Chloe wondered if outside seating was possible. Holt pointed across the street to a bright red door covered by a black awning emblazoned with the name "Puckett's." "That's it," he said, taking her arm and pulling her with him as he jaywalked across the street.

To the left of the front door hung an old-fashioned metal sign suspended from iron scrollwork that further elaborated "Puckett's Gro. & Restaurant - Groceries, Eatery, Live Music." Holt pulled the door open and they were immediately enveloped by a vibrant hum of noise. Dozens of tables surrounded by ladder-back chairs filled the room, and nearly every seat was taken. Rustic paneling covered the walls, while strings of lights, dark now but probably cheerfully blazing in the evenings, stretched in rows across the exposed ceiling. To their left was a small, raised stage, the wall behind it decorated with multiple guitars and old, framed photos of musicians. A poster declared the live entertainment schedule for the rest of the month, including a guitar and fiddle duo called *The Bellinghams.* Tall white shelves formed a perimeter against the walls, displaying cans, jars, and jugs of food-stuffs like an old-fashioned general store. A large painted sign heralding "GROCERY" was propped on the top of the middle shelf. The scent of barbecue, rich and smoky-sweet, settled thickly on Chloe as they scanned the room.

Holt's gaze landed on a woman with strawberry blonde hair and glasses seated at one of the polished wooden tables in a corner across from where they stood. Her attention was consumed by a thick legal file she had spread out on the table, rendering her oblivious to what was happening around her.

"What exactly are you going to say?" Chloe prodded uncertainly.

"Just come on," Holt urged, before wading into the throng.

No one paid them any mind as they navigated the buzzing room. Half the diners were dressed in business attire, and Chloe presumed that given its proximity to the courthouse, Cecilia Tucker wasn't the only lawyer who frequented the place for lunch. Her nose remained solidly buried in the file as they sidled up to her table.

"Cecilia," Holt quipped, "fancy meeting you here."

Cecilia Tucker looked up, and a smile broke out on her face. "Hey Holt," she said, pushing back slightly and straightening.

"Thanks for waiting for us. I'm sorry we had to push it back."

"No, it's fine. I'm thrilled Reese woke up. Is he all right?"

"He's in and out. But on the mend."

"Well, here, sit," she said, waving a hand at the open seats. She flipped her file shut and swept it into the briefcase beside her chair, then extended a hand to Chloe. "So you must be Reese's daughter."

"Yes, Chloe," she said, nodding and shaking Cecilia's hand as they sat.

"Trip told me he met you at Emma's house," Cecilia explained. "I didn't realize Emma had an older sister."

"Well, Reese hasn't—" she paused abruptly, fumbling for an explanation that wouldn't cast Reese in a bad light. "Well, we haven't seen much of each other in recent years."

"Oh. You know, I think a lot of Reese. He's an excellent lawyer. And a good person. He's always been wonderful to Trip, and Emma has been a good friend to him too."

"I'm glad," Chloe replied, slightly wrong-footed by someone so fervently praising her father. It was odd to let the comments go without offering a different, more negative opinion.

Cecilia Tucker was petite and favored light makeup that did not hide the fact that she was somewhere in her mid-forties. She was well-dressed in a navy pantsuit and cream silk blouse adorned with a fashionable long gold necklace with a large pendant of white and gray crystals that tapped the table as she leaned forward.

"I would have ordered for you, but I wasn't sure what you wanted," Cecilia said.

"It's fine," Holt replied, turning to the approaching waitress. "Hey, Haley," he said, "we'll have the same as Ms. Tucker here. And two half-and-half teas?"

"Sure," she said, smiling a little too widely.

"You're a gem," he said, winking at her.

"And you're ridiculous," Cecilia told him, smirking as she turned to Chloe. "It was the same way when he worked for me. Had the clerk's office wrapped around his little finger."

Holt shrugged, feigning humility. "I can't help it if people find me irresistible."

Chloe's brow furrowed. "Did you say he worked for you?"

Holt clarified. "Cecilia was one of the attorneys I clerked for in the summer between my first and second year of law school."

"Reese hired him before I could make an offer," Cecilia said regretfully.

"You snooze, you lose," Holt teased.

"Uh-huh. Chloe, watch out for this one," Cecilia warned wryly. "He'll break your heart."

So," Holt said, changing the subject, "we've been seeing a good bit of Trip around."

"He's even more joined at the hip to Jacob than usual with everything that's going on," Cecilia said, then sipped her water. "He's worried about him."

"We all are," Holt agreed. "The other night he mentioned that Keeley's recording again."

Cecilia smiled. "Yeah. She is. It's going really well. D.B. thinks this might finally be the right time."

Holt leaned over to Chloe. "D.B. is Cecilia's husband. He's a music producer—his studio is just a few blocks from here. Keeley's her daughter. And the next big teen in country music."

"If you listen to D.B., anyway," Cecilia hedged.

"Oh, come on. Have a little faith," Holt chided.

"Well, she loves it. So as long as it makes her happy, I'm good."

They chatted briefly about Keeley's prospects, D.B.'s music production, and the other studios in Franklin until Haley returned with their orders, which turned out to be fried green tomato BLTs on wheat berry bread, with hickory smoked bacon and chipotle bacon ranch sauce. A mound of fries covered the little bit of the plate not taken up with the sandwich.

"This looks amazing," Chloe said.

"Chloe works for a travel magazine. She's doing an article on Franklin," Holt explained, before taking a bite. He swallowed roughly. "I've got a feeling Puckett's might make it into the story."

Chloe nodded silently, her mouth full.

Between bites, the conversation covered anecdotes from Holt's time as Cecilia's law clerk, including one story where he came to the office on Halloween dressed as Tom Cruise from *Risky Business*. "Someone from the clerk's office had bet him he wouldn't do it. Apparently," Cecilia said, cutting her eyes at him, "they didn't know him very well."

"I figured she'd make me change as soon as I got there—"

"But instead I made him go to court wearing the whole getup, sunglasses and all. Of course, I gave the General Sessions Judge a heads up, but still…" Cecilia trailed off, grinning.

"Guess I didn't know you very well, either," Holt remarked, wiping his mouth with a napkin.

Cecilia pushed her plate away slightly and leaned back in her chair. "So you said you wanted to talk to me about something in the murder case."

"Yeah," he said, putting down his napkin. "I need to know if you can think of anyone, anyone at all, with an axe to grind against Donner or his project or Sims."

"I mean, not right off the top of my head. Other than that they obviously had axes to grind with each other." Cecilia's nose wrinkled. "Have you decided to stick with the case after all? I thought you were turning it over to a PD."

Holt waggled his head back and forth. "Right now we're still only filling in until he gets a public defender. But we're hoping to flesh out the case as much as we can before passing it on."

"Well, you know if there had been a glaring alternative suspect I would have told you right off. What about the discovery documents? Have you gotten through those?"

"We're working on it. It's a lot."

"Yeah, I know. I'm counting on you sharing information with me once you get through it."

"Are you sure there isn't something else? Has anybody ever mentioned, or even hinted at, any ill will that someone other than Sims might have had for Donner?"

"No. There's nothing." She eyed him quizzically. "Why do I get the sense that this is more than you just being thorough?"

Holt sighed. "Like I said, we've been going through the discovery you lent us. We found some names—people and businesses—but no information about their connection to Donner Properties. So, we decided to run them down, just to see if they knew anything helpful."

"Sounds smart," Cecilia offered.

"Yeah. I thought so. One of the names we came across was Vettner-Drake, Incorporated."

Cecilia shook her head. "Never heard of it."

"It's some kind of private real estate management firm. Anyway, we—"

"Wait, who's this 'we'?" Cecilia noted, raising her eyebrows as she cut her eyes at Chloe.

"Yeah, well, with Reese out, work is piling up. Chloe offered to help out, and I thought it would be good for her to get an insider's view of what Reese does. She's now an official, unpaid intern."

Cecilia seemed to consider this for a few seconds, then continued. "So what about Vettner-Drake?"

"This morning we spoke to Eli Drake, Vettner-Drake's agent for service, and who knows what else."

"And?"

"And, he says his firm isn't involved in the project. But he was very unhappy about us being there and pretty belligerent."

"Ahh, finally someone you couldn't charm," she said, tossing him a satisfied smile.

"Very funny. But the thing is, when I threatened to drown him in paperwork and depositions, he caved and said that the one thing he could tell us is that we should talk to you."

His words hung there, poised in the air above them, begging for a reaction. Cecilia sniffed, straightened a bit in her chair, and shifted her weight.

"Kept that to yourself long enough," she drawled, the temperature of her voice notably cooler.

"What do you think he meant by it?"

"I think he meant to give you a reason to get off his doorstep, which is exactly what you did."

"Come on, Cecilia. Maybe there's something there—maybe something you forgot or didn't realize you knew—"

"Oh, my gosh. You're right. Now that you mention it there was this guy who came in my office the day before Donner was killed, waving a gun around and threatening to take him out."

"Okay, look—"

"No, Holt. I'm feeling ambushed here. What did you think I was going to say? If I knew something don't you think I would have told you? This guy—Drake—wanted to get rid of you and he succeeded. He must know that I'm representing Sims in his civil case. He baited you and you bit."

"Is it possible," he said, pressing harder, "that you've overlooked something? Can you think of anything, maybe something that doesn't even seem related at first glance, that might be worth a second look when it comes to Sims and Donner?"

Cecilia responded wordlessly with a disgruntled grimace.

"I wouldn't keep asking, Cecilia, but whoever attacked Reese isn't done. They've made threats and they're saying the kids are next. It's important we find out the names of anyone—"

"What do you mean, 'the kids are next'?" she interrupted, her grimace melting into genuine concern.

Holt breathed heavily. "Whoever attacked Reese is delivering messages saying that if we don't back off, they will come after Emma and Tyler next."

"Back off of what?"

"Exactly. We don't know. At least we aren't certain. From the standpoint of timing, it seems likely that it's all related to Sims and Donner and our involvement in Sims's representation. The perpetrator has been very cryptic for whatever reason, probably not wanting to leave anything specific enough to solidly link him or her to the acts. Without knowing more, all we can do is ask ourselves, 'who wouldn't want us to help defend Sims?' The only answers that make sense right now are someone with a grudge against Sims, or—"

"Or the person who actually did kill Donner and doesn't want to be found out," Cecilia finished for him.

"Right," Holt agreed, "and that means finding anybody else with a possible motive to murder Donner."

"From what I've been told, Donner could be very difficult. The list of people that didn't like him may be very long."

"Probably. But we had to start somewhere. We decided to start with the discovery and it led us to Vettner-Drake. And then to you."

Cecilia's visage tightened, an undertone of worry peeking through. "I had no idea Reese's family was being threatened." She put a hand on Holt's arm. "You know I would do anything to help. If I had information that I thought would lead to something, I would share it." Holt nodded as Haley approached to refill their glasses. "But I don't know anything about the relationship between Sims and Donner other than what Sims has told me," Cecilia asserted, clearing her throat and taking a sip from her refilled glass. "I've only ever met Donner once in person, in court during the temporary injunction hearing."

Holt's eyes pinched, and he waited to speak until the waitress had moved away. "Okay. But will you just give it some thought? Just in case there's something you've overlooked?"

Cecilia sighed and nodded. "Of course," she said, rising from the table, a loud grinding coming from the chair as she pushed it back. "I've got to get back. I've got a deposition this afternoon. It was so nice to meet you, Chloe," she said, shaking Chloe's hand. "Please give Reese my best."

"I will," Chloe echoed, and they watched her go.

"She's lying," Holt announced quietly, his eyes following Cecilia as she disappeared out the front door.

"What?" Chloe asked.

"The throat clearing thing. It's her tell." He swiveled his attention back to Chloe. "One of the things I learned while working for Cecilia was that she has a definite tell. Whenever she made any statement that was less than one hundred percent truthful, she would do that throat clearing thing she just did."

When Chloe looked bemused, he clarified. "Okay, for example, her home life wasn't the model of happiness she wanted everyone to believe it was. I don't know the specifics, but I do know that her husband, D.B., is apparently hard to live with. One minute she would be using me for a sympathetic ear, complaining about how awful her Saturday with him had been, and in the next, she would be telling someone else how great her family's weekend was, all the while doing that throat clearing thing. That's when I first picked up on it. Eventually I started noticing her doing it in all kinds of conversations."

"So you think she does know something about Donner? Something she's not telling?"

"Maybe. "

"Like what?"

He huffed. "I wish I knew."

TWENTY-NINE

Cecilia Tucker slipped quickly inside the door to her office and shut it behind her. Leaning against it she put a hand to her chest to steady her pounding heart. Panic swelled within, and even her hands had become shaky since leaving Holt and Chloe at Puckett's.

Deep breaths, she told herself, forcing her diaphragm to extend, then contract, expelling a heavy hiss of air. "Get yourself together," she grunted.

Who is Eli Drake and how had he known about her? she wondered, her pulse quickening again. Weakness threatened her knees and she sank into her black leather desk chair for support.

No one knew. No one but Donner. And he certainly wasn't telling anyone now. *But what if…what if he had told someone. As insurance, just in case.* She tried to breathe deeply again. *No. He had sworn that he had kept it to himself. It was the whole reason—*

A knock on the door sounded.

"Come in," answered Cecilia.

The door swung open, and Cecilia's assistant stepped inside. "You've got about twenty minutes—" She hesitated, concern crossing her face as she eyed Cecilia. "Are you all right? You look really pale."

"No. I mean, yes," Cecilia sputtered, discombobulated. "I'm fine, Allison. Sorry, I'm just exhausted already." Cecilia cleared her throat and forced a smile.

"No problem," Alison replied, still looking wary. "I just wanted to tell you that you've got about twenty minutes until everybody starts arriving for the Pyles deposition."

"Got it. Let me know when the client gets here."

Alison nodded, closing the door behind her. Cecilia inhaled another settling breath.

If Holt knew anything more he would have told you, she assured herself. *He wouldn't play games with you. He knows you, likes you.*

Trusts you.

But it wasn't Holt she was most worried about. It was this Eli Drake person. Someone who apparently had reason to believe that she had special knowledge that would be of interest to Holt as he investigated Donner and prepared Sims's defense.

Her thoughts assaulted her for several more minutes until Allison buzzed in, letting her know that her client had finally arrived. She told Allison to wait five minutes, then send him in.

She reached for the client's file, her mind still spinning. *Was that all Drake knew? That she "might" have information relevant to Donner's murder? Or did he know more?*

And if he did, how long would it be before everyone else knew it too?

THIRTY

The California sun shone down pleasantly on the oversized golf cart driven by the *Ending of Days* production manager, Todd Michelson, as it rolled through the movie lot. It rocked as Jack shifted in the passenger seat.

"Come on, Todd. You can spare me for a few days," Jack insisted. "This can't wait."

Michelson sighed laboriously as he slowly navigated the cart through a congested thoroughfare on the PremiereMax Studios backlot. "Look, if I didn't need you, I'd say go. But we're already behind schedule. If by some miracle we catch up, or heaven forbid, we need to reshoot something and you're off in who knows where—"

"It's Nashville, Todd, not Timbuktu."

"Whatever, I just know it's not Burbank. You know what a day's delay costs around here?"

"I do. But it won't happen. There's no way we're catching back up at this point. Right now, you aren't scheduled to need me until Monday at the earliest. I'll be back Sunday night."

"I don't know." Michelson scrunched up his face and rubbed it.

"Look, I've really messed up. This…she…is very important. I need to fix it."

Michelson studied him for a minute. "This is about a girl, then?"

Jack's eyes pleaded with him. "It's about *the* girl."

Michelson pursed his lips and huffed, turning to watch a group of Victorian-costumed actors entering a large sound stage to their left. "I wish I could say go. I really do," he uttered, genuine regret in his voice. "But it's just not possible. If I tell you to go and then they decide they need you, it'll be my head. Or worse, my checkbook. Can't you just call her?"

"No. I need to fix this, and I need to do it in person. The thing that matters most to me is on the line here."

Michelson shook his head. "You know as well as anybody here—sentimentality plays well on screen but it gets you nowhere with the studio. You're scheduled to be off this weekend. If you really need to go you'll have to wait until then. *And* you'll have to be back Monday."

Jack sighed, squinting in disappointment. "Fine," he said, hopping out of the cart while it was still rolling, his bad leg catching just a bit. "But don't think I won't remember this when you try to schedule reshoots next spring."

"Come on, Jack," Todd urged, slamming on the brakes and rocking the cart to a halt. "Get back in."

Shaking his head, Jack waved him off and turned, walking in the opposite direction.

Saturday was still half a week away. *Too long,* he thought, ducking between two horse-drawn carriages headed for unknown parts of the lot.

I need to fix this.

Now.

THIRTY-ONE

Holt had a full afternoon of court appearances and office appointments, so after Puckett's, he and Chloe split, giving her time to do research on local shopping venues. From Main Street she took the trolley to The Factory, a shopping and arts complex just blocks from Reese's home. Built in 1929, the assortment of old brick buildings with high glass windows and wrought iron stairs had served as a factory for a number of concerns, including a stove works and a bedding company before being abandoned. After sitting vacant for decades, it had been renovated and repurposed, preserving the historical look of the place while giving it new life. Now it was jam-packed with unique shops and galleries that would keep any tourist busy for several hours.

Chloe walked through the mall, strumming gleaming hand-crafted guitars at Artisan Guitars and stepping inside to watch a bit of an open, live-model class at SouthGate Art Studio. At one of the gift stores, a stunning turquoise bracelet caught her eye. Knowing her friend and editor, Izzie, would love it, she bought the unique piece for her as a "thank you" for giving her extra time off to stay with Emma and Tyler.

She canvassed several more boutiques specializing in distinctive clothing, gifts, and home goods, all tempting and making her second-guess the current state of her wardrobe and home decor. But, summoning her will power, she settled for stopping by Five Daughters Bakery for a '100 Layer' Milk Chocolate Sea Salt Donut which, she was informed, took three whole days to make.

She topped it all off with the best Cafe Americano she had ever had at Honest Coffee Company. Sitting on a polished cherry stool along the wall opposite the barista, Chloe spared a few moments to dunk her doughnut, sip the steaming brew, and scan through the hundred or so photos she had taken for her article over the last hour and a half. To her left, a couple sat in the corner, laughing and sharing earbuds as they listened to whatever music they had pulled up on a cell phone. She couldn't help but think of Jack. Of what he might be doing right then. Who he might be talking to. Laughing with.

Without thinking about whether she should, she checked her texts just to make sure she hadn't missed one from him. True to his word, he had not contacted her since sending the flowers. He was giving her plenty of space.

But did she want that much space? Yes, she had needed to sift through how she felt about his omission about Lila, and yes, that wasn't something she could do in one day. But this was starting to feel like too much. Like a spinning top that had gotten away from her. In the end, it wasn't that complicated. Of course she would forgive him. Of course she would let it go. So why had it taken her this long to come to that conclusion?

"Because you're stubborn," she mumbled, then drained the last drop of coffee from the cup and stood. *I'll call him tonight,* she vowed to herself. *After the kids go to bed.*

Chloe lingered as long as she could before having to leave to get Tyler, making a pass through Antiques at the Factory, a warehouse comprised of several dozen dealers offering antiques, estate jewelry, industrial pieces, and other rare finds. Finally, she pulled herself away from an early 1900s Chippendale desk and walked the three blocks back to Reese's house to get her car.

When she reached the head of the school carpool line, Tyler dashed into the passenger side, slamming the door and immediately launching into a full description of how he and his friend, Sam, "completely owned Mac and Ethan in football during recess." When Tyler finally took a breath, Chloe managed to tell him about Reese waking up briefly, at which point he insisted on visiting his father. Emma wasn't due home from work until 6:00, so after swinging through a drive-thru to get Reese's favorite shake, they headed for the hospital.

"Just remember," Chloe hedged as they pulled in, "he's probably still asleep. The hospital would have called if he had woken up again. So don't be disappointed if he can't drink the shake."

"But chocolate's his favorite, and if he knows it's there maybe that'll help," Tyler reasoned.

As expected, though, the nurses informed them that Reese hadn't regained consciousness since Chloe's visit earlier in the day. After Chloe promised Tyler that they would return the next day, and one of the nurses agreed to store the shake in the refrigerator in the lounge, they headed home.

"Chloe?" Tyler asked from the back seat as they drove, his gaze directed out the window at a passing field bordered by a long white fence. A solitary horse stood on the crest of the meadow, his mane nearly even with the setting sun.

"Yeah, bud?"

"Is Dad going to be okay?" His voice was shaky, like he was trying to be braver than he felt.

"I think so. So do the doctors. He was awake today, talking and everything. His body just needed some more rest. The doctors said he will probably be up tomorrow, or the day after at the latest, and that everything looks good."

Tyler turned to face her, his eyes big. "So I guess our prayers are working?" The remark was completely genuine, without sarcasm or doubt. Just a child-like, frank assessment.

Chloe smiled. "Well, I definitely think God is answering them. But you know, even if things hadn't turned out this way, it wouldn't mean God didn't hear you, or didn't care. It would just mean He had a different plan." She briefly cut her eyes to him and saw he was still gazing intently at her, waiting. "You know, I had to learn that the hard way. I didn't really have anybody that explained it to me when I was growing up. But now you know and you can trust that whatever happens, God still loves you. Even when we don't always understand why some things happen."

"Like Mom leaving." Again the words were not a challenge, just a statement of fact. Chloe was reminded that even though Reese had done immeasurably better as a single parent than Chloe's mother had, Tyler's abandonment by his mother still left raw wounds on the little boy.

"Yes. Like that."

"It still hurts sometimes."

"I know," she commiserated, reaching over to squeeze his arm. "Better than anybody. But you have to know that her leaving wasn't your fault, and that God still, even in that, will have a plan for you."

"Emma said Dad left you like Mom left us." His words struck a nerve in her heart. She hadn't known how much Tyler knew about the rocky past she and Reese shared.

"Yes," she answered gently, hoping honesty was the best policy in the situation.

"Does it still hurt?"

She sighed, knowing the truth wasn't an easy answer to give.

"Yes. And for a long, long time I was really, really mad."

"Me too," he admitted as his face drifted downward.

"But you know what? Eventually I realized something."

"What?" he said, his countenance perking slightly.

"When your dad left me and my brother, Tate, he was very broken. And broken people do broken things. It doesn't make it right, but it's why he chose to do what he did."

"Because he was broken and he made a mistake?"

Chloe nodded. "And once I realized that, I realized we're all broken in different ways. I mean, I've done things that I wish I could take back. Things I needed to be forgiven for."

"Yeah," Tyler agreed.

"And that made me a little less mad. And it made me realize I need to forgive him."

"Is that why you came? To forgive him?"

Chloe reached over to tousle his hair. "You're pretty smart for an eight-year-old."

"But it's hard to forgive people sometimes. Like one time, Sam at school pushed me off the slide at the top and it really, really hurt. The teacher made him sit out of recess for a whole week, but I was still mad. I didn't want to talk to him anymore."

"Yeah. Sometimes it is hard. And that's when I have to ask for help."

"What kind of help?"

"Well, I ask God to help me forgive the other person the way I ought to. Even when it's hard."

Digesting this, Tyler turned back towards the window as they pulled in Reese's driveway.

"Maybe that's why God didn't let Dad wake up yet," he began sagely. "Maybe that was His plan so you'd have to stay and you'd get to know us and you'd decide to really, really forgive Dad for real."

The insight floored her and once again she was stunned by this child's ability to see something that would have eluded most adults. Including her.

She switched off the engine and reached over to hug her little brother. "Maybe so, Tyler," she said as he hugged her back even harder. "Maybe so."

THIRTY-TWO

"Not over there!" Tyler yelled. "They're waiting for you!" Jamming his fingers on the controller, he fired a barrage of bullets at an oncoming zombie horde.

"I...can't...move fast enough!" Chloe wailed as a huge red 'X' flashed obnoxiously on her side of the screen, signaling her player has died its last death. "I'm dead. Again!" she whined, falling back against the carpet to stare at the ceiling. "I give up."

"Yeah, you're awful at this," Tyler conceded, taking the horde on all by himself as a knock sounded from the side door.

"You expecting someone?" Chloe asked, noting as she rose that Emma wasn't due home for another half hour. Consumed by the game, Tyler ignored her as she moved through the kitchen to answer the door. A quick peek through the blinds revealed Holt standing on the landing.

"Seriously," she said, opening the door, "aren't you worried about wearing out your welcome? I thought you were headed home tonight for some peace and quiet and a good night's sleep." She leaned in the doorway, blocking his path.

"I *was* until little man there texted me a half hour ago and begged me to stay again. He said you would feel better if I was in the house tonight."

Skepticism wrinkled Chloe's brow. "And this was Tyler's idea?"

"Completely unsolicited. Although, truth be told, I'm still not one hundred percent comfortable with you guys all alone in the house, so I don't mind. But hey, if you've had all of me you can handle today…"

He stood there, self-assured as always, looking a bit worn but handsome, still dressed in his suit from a day of lawyering. She was surprised by how cheered she was at his unexpected arrival. Surprised, then bothered.

"Are you going to invite me in or do I stand out here like an idiot?" he asked, his eyebrows furrowed quizzically.

"Sorry…sure. If it makes *Tyler* feel better," she said, smirking as she stepped aside to let him in.

He dropped his satchel on the kitchen counter. "I may commandeer Reese's bed though. Today was exhausting and I don't think I can do another night on the couch. I had four hearings—only one of which was mine. I was filling in for Reese on the rest. He had another one that I had to get continued—it's a child support and custody case he's been dealing with. It's just too complicated for me to handle without knowing the details. I didn't want to step in and muck it up so—"

"Hey Holt!" Tyler called without turning around, still focusing on saving the human race.

"Hey, little man," he answered, pulling a soda from the fridge and popping the top. "So," he continued, turning back to Chloe, "I had the hearing pushed back another week, but I'll have to give it my best shot after that. The mom's been waiting too long already for some relief." He took a swig of soda.

"Deadbeat dad?"

"Stereotypical," he said and took another drink. "I hear there's been no change in Reese since this morning."

Chloe shook her head. "None." She paused. "How do you know that? I mean, I don't mind, but I didn't know the hospital handed out information to people other than immediate family."

He grinned smugly. "The courthouse isn't the only place I've got wired. Reese's day nurse—Anne—seems to like me," he boasted charismatically, wiggling his eyebrows.

Chloe fought a grin. "I can't imagine why."

"It's a mystery," he said, raising a mock toast with the soda can as he turned away. "So little man," he called to Tyler as he plopped beside him on the floor. "Want me to show you how it's done?"

"You wish," Tyler goaded him, tossing Holt a controller while still blasting away.

Chloe leaned against the couch. "Hey, um, Tyler and I were going to head out soon to pick up dinner before Emma got home. But now that you're here, do you think you can stay with him while I run out for it?"

"Go, go, I've got this," Holt replied, both hands furiously gripping the controller, "and—BOOM! Four at once!"

"Lucky shot!" she heard Tyler exclaim as she slipped out the side door. "Just a lucky shot!"

*****

Chloe headed north on Franklin Road towards Nashville, driving for about ten minutes before reaching the Hot Chicken House, one of three tenants in a small strip mall. The place was packed, and there was no parking out front. She followed the signs for additional parking, which led down a wide alley to another lot behind the building. By the time she had parked and walked back to the restaurant, dusk had set in and the sky was quickly giving way to darkness.

A rush of sound hit her as she pushed the restaurant's front door open, the warmth of the space beckoning against the slight chill that accompanied sunset. The strings of multi-colored lights that were looped across the walls burned brightly, adding to the festive atmosphere as a guitarist set up on a small stage at the back of the dining room.

Tyler had insisted that dinner come from this place, one of his favorites. So Chloe had ordered enough hot chicken, honey biscuits, fries, slaw, and banana pudding to feed four, just in case Holt showed up. Which he had.

A twenty-something with a man bun stood near the register at the front, tallying tickets. "To go for McConnaughey," Chloe told him, leaning against the counter as the guitarist started picking a little bluegrass on his Gibson.

"Just one minute, let me check on it," he said, sliding out from behind the counter and half-jogging towards the kitchen. After a few minutes, he returned with a large brown paper bag filled with foam boxes and set it on top of the counter. Pulling the stapled ticket off the side of the bag, he turned towards Chloe and declared, "Thirty-four, sixty-eight." She paid and, leaving the sounds of the cheerful guitar behind her, stepped out into the night.

She had just turned the corner into the alley that led to the back parking lot, when a sleek, black Mercedes zipped up beside her, slamming to a halt and trapping her between it and the brick wall, leaving her nowhere to go.

THIRTY-THREE

There was no guard posted outside Reese McConnaughey's hospital room door.

At first it surprised him, but then he realized that there had been no reason for them to think anyone would actually come back to finish the job. His warning had been about the kids, not further damage to the man inside the room. But still, it would have been smart to put someone there. Just in case.

After all, here he was now, just feet away from Reese McConnaughey and there wasn't a person in sight to stop him from finishing what he had started.

The stainless steel door knob turned soundlessly, and he entered the dimly lit room. Reese, still unconscious or sleeping, lay in the bed beneath a thin sheet. The lights of the monitors on the rolling stand beside him kept watch over his blood pressure and heart rate, silently blinking.

He looked small in the bed. Harmless. But that would all change if he woke. He could do so much damage if he started talking.

He walked up to the railings that prevented any accidental rolling out of the bed. The metal was cold against his skin as he reached over it and fingered the intravenous lines in Reese McConnaughey's arm, pumping in pain meds and who knew what else.

A loud banging out in the hallway jerked him out of his thoughts. It was busy, and the shifts would change soon. If he waited too long, someone would almost certainly interrupt him.

It was time to do what he came to do, and get out.

THIRTY-FOUR

"Hey!" Chloe bellowed at the same time a hulking, besuited man exited the front passenger door of the Mercedes, leaving it open so that she was further blocked in. "What do you think you're doing!" Chloe snapped incredulously, as he stepped to her, then opened the rear door, giving them both a direct view into the back seat.

"Good evening, Ms. McConnaughey." The calm greeting issued from a petite woman dressed in a pale pink linen business suit. She looked to be in her early sixties, her silver hair curled in a loose bob that framed her lined face.

"Good evening?! What's going—?"

"Ms. McConnaughey, I'm a friend. I'd like to speak with you for a moment."

The man extended an arm, as if ushering Chloe into the back seat. Chloe eyed the woman like she had escaped an asylum and was still wearing the hospital scrubs to prove it. "Absolutely not. I am not—"

Before she could finish, the man beside her had muscled her into the car and shut the door behind her.

"Hey!" Chloe yelled, scooting back against the door and trying to wrench the door open. It was locked. "Let me out!"

"I'm sorry, Ms. McConnaughey. Abraham must have misunderstood you. He thought you wanted to get in and was just assisting you." The car started moving.

"Yeah, right!" Chloe exclaimed, panic setting in as she was forcibly reminded of being stuffed into a car less than a year ago by the syndicate in Miami that had ultimately tried to kill her. "I want out. Now."

"Of course. We'll be happy to let you out."

"Sort of hard to do while the car is moving," Chloe sniped, as he pulled onto Franklin Road.

"Pearson," the woman said, directing her comments to the driver, "let Ms. McConnaughey out as soon as you come to a safe spot to pull over."

Jabs of fear sliced through Chloe as she evaluated her situation. They weren't going that fast. There were a lot of people around. She could probably jump out without causing any real damage. But the door was locked.

"Unlock the door," Chloe ordered.

"We aren't here to hurt you, Ms. McConnaughey."

"You've got a funny way of showing it," Chloe barked, anger and fear trading punches in her gut.

"We're here to offer assistance. If you'll give me a few moments, I'll be glad to explain." The woman's voice was clipped, but with a hint of Southern sweetness to it. It was disarming and daunting all at once.

"You'll take me back to my car?"

"We're circling back around to it now," she said, as the driver pulled into a left turn lane at the light. "By the time we get there I'll be done. Sound good?"

"Who are you?"

A well-manicured hand showcasing a simple, diamond-encrusted band, slid a business card to Chloe across the cocoa leather seat. *Elise Banyon, Banyon Associates, Memphis, Tennessee.*

"What—you're a lawyer or something?"

"Or something. But I do represent Mr. Eli Drake and Vettner-Drake. I understand you visited Mr. Drake today seeking information regarding his involvement, or rather lack of involvement, in Mr. Donner's Franklin project."

"Holt Adams—he's Kurt Sims's attorney—asked Mr. Drake some questions. I was only there as an assistant." Chloe's nerves hummed as she tried to maintain her composure.

"I see. Well, either way, we want to reach a mutual understanding regarding Vettner-Drake's lack of involvement in said project and avoid any further unnecessary entanglements."

"I'm not sure I—"

"As Mr. Drake explained today, neither he nor Vettner-Drake had any financial interest in Mr. Donner's project, having declined on multiple occasions to make an investment."

"That's what he said. So why are you here now?"

"Because your Mr. Adams made it clear that, despite what Mr. Drake told him, he believes Mr. Drake has information on the subject. Mr. Adams also made it clear that he is willing to drag Vettner-Drake through the legal mill, if you will, to get it. We would rather avoid that. I'm sure you can understand how expensive and time-consuming a wild goose chase like that would be."

"I'm sure." Chloe struggled to keep her voice steady as more adrenaline kicked in.

"If you'll examine Mr. Donner's financial records with regard to the project, you'll find that what Mr. Drake has told you is true. You are wasting your time looking into Vettner-Drake."

"Well, we don't have those records. Or at least," she hedged, thinking about the discovery documents they had yet to go through, "we wouldn't know it if we did. And I doubt Mr. Donner's people are going to just hand them over."

Banyon reached towards Chloe and turned the business card over in her hand. A time and address were written on the back. "In the case of Donner Properties, Mr. Donner's 'people' consist of his accountant and his wife. Donner Properties was a closely held outfit. You have an appointment with them, at Donner's home, at ten o'clock tomorrow, at which time they will make available to you everything that you need to confirm Mr. Drake's comments to you."

"Just like that?"

"Just like that."

Chloe eyed Banyon. "You seem to know a lot about Mr. Donner's business for someone whose client wasn't *involved* in that business." She delivered the barb with more confidence than she actually felt.

"I never said Vettner-Drake wasn't involved with Mr. Donner. It simply had no involvement in this particular project. Mr. Drake knew enough about Mr. Donner's project to know it wasn't the right investment for Vettner-Drake." She stiffened. "So, after tomorrow, we would appreciate it if you would avoid contacting Vettner-Drake or Mr. Drake regarding this matter. As I'm sure you'll realize, further contact would not be beneficial to anyone."

"Is that a threat?"

Banyon snorted gently. "No dear. It's just the reality of the situation and an attempt to avoid an unnecessary waste of everyone's time and money. And now," she said as the car rolled to a stop, "you're back at your car. As promised."

They were, in fact, already back in the parking lot behind the Hot Chicken House, and the driver had stopped directly behind Chloe's car. It unnerved her even more that they knew which car was hers. The man Banyon had called Abraham was out his door and had already opened Chloe's door before she had shifted her weight off it, causing her to fall out a little before regaining her balance. Breathing deeply, she gathered herself and stepped out onto the pavement. Refusing to turn her back to them, she took small steps backwards towards her car. Abraham closed the rear Mercedes door behind her and returned to the front seat. As Chloe reached blindly for her driver's door handle, the Mercedes's rear window rolled down again, revealing Banyon once more.

"Ten o'clock tomorrow. Don't be late."

Ignoring the internal warning her gut was sounding to get out of there while she could, she pressed Banyon one more time.

"Why not just call Holt with this information? Why go through me?"

Banyon's mouth rounded into a condescending smirk. "Ten a.m. tomorrow, dear," she replied, just before her window rolled up and the Mercedes pulled away.

* * * * *

"Holt!" Chloe's voice boomed through the kitchen as she barreled inside, her purse swinging from one arm, the take-out bag in the other. "Holt!" she bellowed once more, setting the bag on the counter. "Ho—"

She spun around and slammed into him. "Hey, I'm right here," he said, taking her by the shoulders and setting her back from him. "We were about to text you to see where you were. Listen, you've got—" he cut himself off, taking in her frantic manner. "What's the matter?" he said, eyeing her more closely, concern breaking out on his face. "You don't look right."

"This, this…woman. Elise Banyon. She threw me in her car and—"

"Wait, what? Slow down."

Chloe inhaled deeply and started again. "This woman had her car pull right up next to me and had some thug throw me in the back seat. She said she wanted to talk—"

"Is everything okay?"

The words sounded from the door behind her, spoken by a voice deeper and richer than Holt's. Chloe snapped her head up.

Jack Bartholomew stood in the doorway, worry furrowing the brow above his narrowed emerald eyes.

THIRTY-FIVE

"Jack!" Chloe yelled, throwing her arms around him and hugging him tightly.

"You okay?" he asked, pulling back so he could see her face and better gauge her answer.

She nodded, her face split in a wide smile. "It's nothing. Just…oh, I'm so glad to see you." She kissed him, then pressed into his chest while he wrapped his arms around her.

"You didn't sound okay just now. You sounded really upset."

She pulled back, just enough to see his face. "Oh, it's nothing. It's just—well, I'll explain in a minute."

"It didn't sound like nothing to—" Holt started under his breath, before Chloe shot him a repressive look. He stopped talking as she turned her attention back to Jack.

"I can't believe it," she said. "What are you doing here?"

"I came to see you. I couldn't wait any longer."

Pounding sounded from the stairs, followed by Tyler running into the kitchen. "Hey, Chloe. I'm starving! Is that it?" he asked, pointing at the take-out bag, as Emma walked in behind him.

"He's been whining about it for half an hour," Emma said, eyeing Jack, whose arm was still around Chloe.

"Emma, Tyler, this is Jack," Chloe said.

"Yeah, we met earlier," Emma explained, while Tyler tossed Jack a head-nod that Jack returned.

"Can we eat in the den?" Tyler asked.

"Sure, buddy. Just keep it off the carpet," Holt told him as the kids ripped into the bag and started doling food onto plates. "Look," he said, turning to Jack and Chloe, "I'm gonna head out."

"Don't," she said, taking his forearm, not noticing Jack stiffen ever so slightly at the gesture. "I've got plenty of food and I need to fill you both in on what happened earlier. Stay."

He mulled this over for a moment. "All right. Dinner. But I don't think you need me staying over tonight."

"He's been staying over?" Jack asked.

Chloe's eyes cut to Jack. "For the kids. They know him, and they were scared with the intruder still out there…"

"Oh. Right. Makes sense," Jack agreed, although there was a whiff of skepticism in his tone.

"But obviously," Holt piped in, "you've got a Navy SEAL here now so…"

"So," she continued for him, narrowing her gaze as a caution to cut it out, "grab some chicken and let's talk."

Following her lead, the two men took their food into the dining room, away from prying ears. As they ate, Chloe filled them in on what had happened when she left the Hot Chicken House. She handed Banyon's card to Holt.

"She's set it up for ten in the morning."

Holt examined the card, flipping it back to front. "A little vague for a business card."

"I asked if she was an attorney or something," Chloe explained. "She said 'or something.'"

"So we're just supposed to show up tomorrow and Donner's people will just hand us everything we need to eliminate Vettner-Drake from this investigation? Just because she says so? You know, I made a call to Donner's wife earlier today." He shook his head. "I got nada. Zip. She made it quite clear she wasn't speaking to anyone representing the man accused of murdering her husband. But this Elise Banyon shows up and suddenly we've got a meeting? There's something screwy here."

"And why approach Chloe?" Jack asked, his hand resting on her arm. "Why grab her up that way? Why risk it just to make a point?" For most of the discussion, Jack had sat quietly beside Chloe at the dining room table, where they had made a small clearing for their plates in the forest of files. Now he tensed as he spoke of Chloe being forced into the car.

Holt shook his head. "They wanted to be intimidating, and that was a pretty good way to do it. Catching her alone, on the street like that? They wanted us to know they're serious about being left alone. And Banyon's really not risking much by doing it. She'll just argue Chloe misunderstood the invitation to talk. They dropped her at her car within five minutes. No real harm done."

"Still. It seems like a lot of trouble to go to if Vettner-Drake really isn't involved," Jack argued. "Why not just turn the papers over, let you see that there's no connection, and have it be over and done."

"Again, the intimidation factor. Maybe Vettner-Drake's involved with this project and maybe not, but either way, I'm guessing that it's not a completely above-board operation. They don't want us looking too deep. My guess is they're hoping their actions tonight unnerved us just enough that we'll go look at the documents tomorrow, and when we don't find anything, we'll just decide it's not worth it to push the issue anymore and we'll just walk away."

"But I'm guessing you don't scare easy," Jack appraised.

"Nope. But, the ironic thing is, Drake might be telling the truth. His company might not be involved with Donner at all. In which case, I wouldn't have really cared what they're doing. If there's no connection, I would have been more than happy to drop it. But now, with this stunt, they've got me curious."

"So you think we should go in the morning?" Chloe asked.

"We?" Jack echoed, concern evident in his voice. "Why do you need to go?"

"Some lunatic is threatening the kids," Chloe said, her head gesturing towards Emma and Tyler, blasting away on their video game in the other room. "I won't feel good about leaving until we know who that is. Reese is out of commission and Holt's on his own. I want to help end this if I can. As soon as possible."

In the uncomfortable silence that followed, Holt seemed to second guess his presence. "Umm, you know what?" He glanced at his watch perfunctorily. "It's probably time for me to go. I actually have hearings tomorrow afternoon that I need to prepare for." He rose, moving to gather up his plate and utensils.

"Leave it," Chloe said. "I'll get it."

"Here, let me," Jack offered, collecting the used plates and heading toward the kitchen. Chloe and Holt followed behind, carrying the glasses. Chloe put hers down, then went to retrieve the kids' plates. When Holt set his glass in the dishwasher, Jack caught his eye. "Hey, I want to thank you for looking out for her," he said, nodding at Chloe. "And her family. It means a lot to me."

"Not a problem. Reese's family means a lot to me too."

"I can see that," Jack said, his tone genuine, but heavy.

"So," Chloe said, returning with the kids' plates and pushing past Holt to load them in the dishwasher, "I'll walk you out?"

"Yeah, sure. Thanks. Good to meet you Jack," he said, shaking Jack's hand, then calling out a barely-acknowledged goodbye to Emma and Tyler. While Jack continued clearing the kitchen, Chloe escorted Holt to the kitchen side door, where he turned after stepping onto the outside landing.

"So that's your mystery man, eh?" he teased in hushed tones.

"Stop it."

"I thought you were on the outs."

"I never said—we aren't on the outs."

He didn't look like he believed her. "You still planning on coming tomorrow?"

She nodded. "Definitely."

"I don't think he'll like that. And I don't think he likes me."

"Don't be ridiculous."

"I'm just saying. Did you see the way he looked at me?"

"He's just worried."

"Yeah, but about what?" he said, raising his eyebrows suggestively.

"Not funny."

"Yeah," he admitted, grimacing, "probably not smart to antagonize somebody that knows how to kill you in forty-seven different ways."

"Forty-eight," she corrected blithely, a tiny smile turning up the edge of her mouth. "So, I'll see you in the morning?"

"I'll leave for the meeting at nine thirty. If you're not at the office by then, I'll assume you're not coming along."

"I'll be there."

"Hey," he grinned, a mischievous twinkle in his eye, "if I brought a copy of his book over, do you think he'd autograph—"

Rolling her eyes, Chloe closed the door before he could finish.

*****

As much as Chloe wanted some time alone with Jack, there were the kids to think about. And it was a good opportunity for Jack to get to know them. So for about an hour they played one video game after another, before finally sending them upstairs to do whatever homework they had before bed. On the way to the stairs, Emma passed Chloe, flicked her eyes in Jack's direction when he wasn't looking, and mouthed, "Not bad."

Chloe popped Emma on the head as she scrambled up the steps.

"They seem like great kids," Jack said, standing in the doorway to the kitchen with a glass of wine. "Here."

"Thanks," she said, taking it and sipping the zinfandel as they moved back to the family room and sank into the couch. "They've really grown on me."

"I can see that," he said, twirling a bit of her hair. "You're a natural."

"It's weird being the older one."

He eyed her dubiously. "Tate was only three minutes older than you."

"Well, he never let me forget it," she said, smiling wistfully. "I always felt like the baby of the family."

"Well, they seem to like you too," he said encouragingly as she leaned into him and he put his arm around her. She breathed in deeply, soaking him up as he broke the silence. "So…before we get to anything else, I want to tell you about what happened with Lila."

"Okay," she replied, listening as he explained how he had ended things with Lila, and how he had passed her on to Evan to handle her questions. "Of course, that was if she really ever had any," he finished somewhat skeptically. "And that was it. Haven't heard from her since. I know I should have told you—"

"Don't," she interrupted him gently. "You already apologized before. I was actually going to call you tonight when I got home. I know I overreacted."

He had an odd look on his face that she couldn't decipher. "What?" she asked hesitantly.

"Was that before or after the thing with Banyon?"

"What?"

"Just…did you decide to call me before or after the thing with Banyon?"

"Before."

"Are you sure?"

"Uh, yeah. I'm sure. Why…what difference does it make?"

"Because…are you sure you didn't decide to call me just because you got scared?"

"What? No. It had nothing to do with that."

He eyed her carefully, then straightened up and pulled away. "I want to ask you something, but I don't want you to freak out."

"Okay," she drawled uncertainly.

"Sometimes…I don't know…I worry that maybe part of the reason you're with me is because…because of what happened before. On the island and after."

"What do you mean 'because of what happened'?"

Jack looked grim as he explained. "I kept you safe on the island, then I got you off the island to Miami, then I pulled you out of a house full of armed captors—"

"Hey," she said gently, "stop. What—you think I developed some sort of savior complex about you or something?"

He shrugged. "Maybe. Sometimes."

She sighed. "No. No way. And you weren't the only person doing the rescuing, remember? What about Riley?" Jack's old SEAL buddy, Riley, lived in Miami, and Jack had recruited him to help when Chloe was kidnapped. "He was involved in all that and I didn't fall in love with him," she teased, gently jabbing her shoulder into Jack, in an attempt to lighten things.

"Chloe, I'm serious."

"And I'm serious. This is ridiculous."

"No, look," he turned towards her, "it happens. With people who have been through extreme circumstances together. They develop this bond because of what they've been through and misinterpret it as something more. Then down the road one of them realizes what it really was and wants out—"

"You want out?"

"No! No. I need to know that you don't want out."

"Of course I don't want out! Jack, you know how I feel about you." She studied him for a moment. His steady, but pained expression made it clear that this was not easy for him. Her eyes drifted to his bad leg, and she gestured to it. "Is that what this is about?"

He blinked just long enough to let her know she was on target. "No."

"I don't believe you. You've been acting oddly ever since they told you it might not heal completely."

"It isn't about the leg." He squinted. "Well, not really about the leg itself. But, I don't know, it's got me wondering."

"About what?"

"About whether, now that I'm not one hundred percent anymore, you might look at me differently. That you might start asking questions about why you're really with me."

"That's ridiculous."

"Are you sure?" he pressed.

"I'm not that shallow."

"I'm not saying you're shallow."

"It sounds like it," she said.

"No. Sorry. I'm not saying this well." A heavy silence filled the space between them.

"Jack, I'm not confused about my feelings. I'm not with you because of what you did. I'm with you because of who you are." He stared at her, his mind clearly circling something. "What is it?" she pushed.

He pressed his lips together and swallowed. "Okay, so you had already decided to call. So then, why didn't you call me right after Banyon grabbed you? If you'd already made up your mind to call anyway, it would've been a natural time to do it after something crazy like that."

"What?"

"You had the whole drive here after that happened and you didn't call me." There was no condemnation in his voice. It wasn't an accusation. Just a wistful statement of fact.

Something in her stomach rolled, as she began to sense something significant being unearthed. "I was a little shell-shocked. I just wanted to get back."

"Yeah I heard."

"What do you mean?"

He looked away, down at her hands, and placed one of his over hers, rubbing her knuckles absentmindedly. "When you walked in, you were yelling for Holt."

"I needed to tell him what had just happened."

"Exactly." The word was just a whisper. Then he looked up, his gaze determined, but sad. "The first person you ran to was him. Not me. Before this week I would've been the first one you reached out to." He pushed a curl away from her chin. "Tonight it was him. And I saw the way he was looking at you."

"Okay, now you really have lost it." Chloe shook her head. "Holt is Reese's business partner. I'm helping him with his case. He's helping me with the kids."

"I'm sure he is."

Chloe cocked her head, any semblance of a smile choked back by burgeoning angst. "Jack Bartholomew. Seriously, stop it."

"This thing with Lila—it was so easy for you to shut me out, Chloe. I know I should have handled it differently, but it was one mistake. Granted, I know it hit a raw spot because of your past—but still, one mistake and you stop talking to me. For days."

Chloe's shoulders sank. "I know. I'm sorry. I shouldn't have reacted so severely."

"That's not what I'm saying. The thing is, it was so quick, so complete. It made me think that somewhere in there, some part of you is looking for a way out."

She held his gaze, her eyes steady. "Absolutely not."

"I want to believe that."

"Then believe it because it's true," she said, and kissed him, momentarily driving all thoughts of Holt and Banyon and interfering ex-wives far, far away.

THIRTY-SIX

Chloe rocketed up, gasping for breath, her heart slamming against her ribs at a strength that threatened to break several of them.

She had had the nightmare again. The same one she had been having on and off since they had gotten back from Miami months earlier. Only this time it was different. And much worse. Like all the other times, Tate was dead, only he wasn't. And he had chased her to the Caribbean where he threatened to throw her off a cliff into shark-infested waters. Only they weren't sharks. They were men; the same men that had tried to kill her—Sampson, DiMeico, Vargas—the very men Jack had saved her from. Only this time in the dream, at the point where Jack usually grabbed her arm to keep her from falling off the cliff, he let her fall, yelling after her, "I'm not sure you really want me here. Maybe I should go…"

And that was when she woke up. She steadied herself, remembering the night before. Jack was there. He wasn't going to let her fall. She took a deep breath. She understood why he had his doubts, but she was going to prove to him that they were unfounded. They would be fine, and when all this was over in Franklin, they would go back to Atlanta and be great, just like before.

The clock read 6:45 a.m. "We'll start with breakfast," she said, deciding to make Jack's favorite banana pancakes, and go from there. Tiptoeing past Reese's room where she had put Jack up for the night, she crept down the stairs, determined to make a huge breakfast for everyone. She pulled out a skillet and reached for a mixing bowl, when she spotted a folded note addressed to her on the counter.

Dear Chloe,

I'm so sorry to leave like this, but I had to catch a super early flight back because I'm supposed to be on set later today. I sort of skipped out on them without permission. I hate that our time was so short, but it was the best I could do. I couldn't let this go on any longer without seeing you. I thought it would just be better to let you sleep. I'm not sure I could have left otherwise.

About last night—I meant what I said. I know you said I'm wrong, and I hope I am, but I want you to really think about it, to really be sure. I want to be with you more than I've ever wanted anything. But it only works if you want to be with me for the right reasons. And, given everything, I just need to make sure that's true.

Whatever you might think, I know what I saw last night. Holt is more interested in you than you realize. As much as I hate to admit it, I definitely sensed something between you two. It kills me to say this, but please just think about it. Pray about it. Make sure you want me for me, not because you fell for some guy that pulled you out of a tight spot once upon a time.

I've got another week and a half in California before I can come back. I'm not going to call or text or anything between now and then, to give you some time and space to really think. When you're ready, I'll be in Atlanta waiting. I'm not going anywhere.

I love you,

Jack

Shock rolled over Chloe as she gingerly sat on a bar stool at the kitchen counter. She had only just set the note down when her cell rang. A pang of disappointment struck when she saw it wasn't Jack.

"Hello?"

"Could I speak to Chloe McConnaughey, please?" replied an oddly official voice.

"This is she. Who is this?"

"Middle Tennessee Hospital, ma'am. Something's happened with your father."

THIRTY-SEVEN

"Where is it?" Holt bellowed urgently, striding into Reese's hospital room and nearly knocking over an exiting nurse.

Chloe looked up from her seat by the window, next to where Reese's bed should have been. The absent bed left a significant space in the room. She nodded her head at the police officer standing in the opposite corner, speaking with a second nurse.

"And you found it where?" the officer asked the nurse, a pad and pen ready to record her response.

"Underneath the bed. It must have fallen between the mattress and the railings. I didn't spot it until we moved him for testing downstairs."

Holt eyed the plastic bag the officer was holding, then glanced up. "Officer Richards," he acknowledged, nodding at the policeman.

"Holt," replied the officer, returning the nod, obviously another acquaintance of Holt's.

Holt gestured at the bag. "May I see it?" he asked.

"Help yourself," Officer Richards said, setting it on a nearby tray table before returning his attention to the nurse.

Holt stepped up for a closer look. Inside the zip-locked bag was a small square of blue-lined paper containing a handwritten warning.

Don't forget. Stop. Next time I finish the job. Or maybe break her other arm.

Holt moved closer to Chloe, leaning over her as he spoke.

"'Break her other arm'?" he said quietly. "Did you tell him—"

"I explained that it probably means Emma," she said in a hushed tone, so as not to disrupt the officer's conversation with the nurse.

"So either it's the same guy from the alley," Holt muttered, "or someone who's watching all of you very closely and knows about her broken arm."

Chloe nodded.

"…And you found nothing else out of order?" Officer Richards continued with the nurse.

"No," she answered, a bit flustered. "Nothing. I've searched everywhere. Security did too."

"Yeah, I've already spoken with them downstairs," replied Officer Richards. After jotting down the nurse's contact information, he dismissed her and she strode out, clearly wanting to step away before he thought of any more questions.

Officer Richards turned his attention to Holt. "They sent me over to take statements, but Detective Laney will be here shortly. She's the one assigned to Reese's assault."

"Did anybody see anything?"

"Nah. 'Course we haven't talked to all the shifts yet. Just this morning's, so you never know. Evidence has already been by to dust the room, but I wouldn't hold out much hope for fingerprints. They're pulling the security video now for the floor, but there isn't a camera directed down this hall. Still, we'll see what we get. At the very least we can get a look at the elevators. Unfortunately, since the note fell under the bed, there's no way to know how long it's been there. It could've been left at any time since the last time he was moved, which they said was Monday."

"Okay," said Holt.

Officer Richards focused on Chloe. "Like I said, Detective Laney should be here soon. And, for the time being, we'll post an officer outside Reese's door until a better threat assessment can be made."

"What about his kids?" Chloe pressed, her voice pinched. "The threats are against them too."

"You'll have to talk to the detective about that. But, if they determine that the kids are at risk—"

"If they determine?" Chloe sniped a little too sharply, her volume climbing steadily higher. "There are multiple threats, a broken arm, swelling on the brain…" Frustration punctuated her every word. "What more do you need?"

Officer Richards's face tensed sympathetically. "Ms. McConnaughey, I assure you that we are doing everything we can."

Heat flushed Chloe's complexion. "Well, it's not—"

"It's okay," Holt interrupted, clasping Chloe's forearm to cut her off. "Thanks for the information, Jim. We'll wait to hear from Detective Laney."

"Yeah. All right," he said, nodding at Holt and clapping him on the back as he left.

"Do you know everybody in this town?" Chloe muttered, biting her bottom lip.

Holt's mouth twitched. "Hey, if you want, I could catch him before he hits the elevator. Bring him back, let you take a few punches. Just so you're not swinging at me."

Chloe exhaled, her whole body deflating. "Uhh, Holt. I'm sorry. It's not you."

"It's fine."

"No, it's not. It's just…some guy takes a crack at Reese—twice—and now threatens the kids again, and this," she held her hands out wide, "is the best we can do?"

"I know it's frustrating, but they're doing what they can. Trust me, the law enforcement community in this town is top notch, really thorough. They'll check for fingerprints and review the video, and I'm sure they'll do some more interviews of the staff, but it'll be hard to get answers without a better sense of when this happened."

Worry lines crinkled Chloe's forehead. "I know, but…the kids. Someone has to be watching them all the time. If one of us can't be there, we'll have to arrange for Mrs. Brinkley to sit with them. We've got to keep them safe."

"We will. We'll figure it out," Holt said, turning and leaning against the window sill next to her chair. He glanced at the space where Reese's bed should be. "Why did they take him for tests?"

"They're concerned about additional swelling because he hasn't regained consciousness again. He was scheduled for a CT scan at six this morning. That's when they found the message." She bit her lip. "This has got to be about Sims, right? I mean, it's all you're working on right now. Somebody doesn't want you doing that."

"Well, no, it's not the only thing. I'm working other cases too."

"But any as significant as this? And what about the guy you chased off at Sims's house? Has that happened in any of your other cases?"

Holt shook his head. "No. You're right…at this point the most likely culprit is the Sims case."

"Okay, so if we assume this is about Sims and your firm representing him, that suggests that all of this is to get you and Reese to back off of helping him. Why? Why would somebody do that? What difference would it make if you dropped Sims as a client? Wouldn't he just get another attorney?"

"He doesn't have the money for it. Nobody will take this case on for free."

"So he gets a public defender."

"True, but they're all overloaded with cases and probably wouldn't have the same time and resources to devote to a murder case that a private firm like ours would. Maybe someone is hoping for that."

"But the box on the porch happened before the murder."

"But not before we were involved with representing Sims in his criminal matters. Remember the assault charge from when Sims hit Donner with that sign? And the box happened *after* the explosion. We were down there with Sims at the construction site that night, remember? Whoever this is could have easily seen us there, helping him with the cops. Maybe this someone wants him hanged for all of it." He rocked his head from shoulder to shoulder, as if considering something. "And there's always another possibility. It's pretty far-fetched but one the prosecution might latch onto."

"What?"

"That this is being done by someone in league with Sims, to cast suspicion in another direction. That someone is helping him make it look like he's been framed."

"Yeah," she sighed. "I guess."

For a moment they were quiet, each of them staring off into a different part of the room. A gurney rolled by outside the door, clattering obnoxiously, and Chloe exhaled, running a hand along the windowsill absentmindedly.

"You gonna be okay?" he asked, his brow furrowed in concern.

She sighed. "Yeah. Sure."

"Where's Jack?"

"He left," she said, her face dropping away from him.

"What? Already?"

"He couldn't stay. Had to be back on set."

Holt folded his hands together and hinged forward slightly, turning his face so he could see hers, which was downcast towards the floor. "What happened?"

She cut her eyes at him. "I don't want to talk about it."

"If I said something last night that—"

"You didn't do anything. Really. I just…don't want to talk about it. It's fine. I'm fine."

He watched her skeptically. "Maybe you should skip this today. I can go by myself."

She turned towards him. "What? No. I'm going."

He sighed. "Chloe, I don't think that's a good idea."

"I'm going."

"Chloe, if I could, if it didn't feel so wrong, I would get off the case myself. Just to keep everybody out of harm's way. But I've been thinking about it and I can't. I know I said I was planning on just staying on through the hearing on Monday, but if Sims is innocent, I can't just leave him hanging out there in the wind. I may not be a huge Kurt Sims fan, but it wouldn't be right—"

"No. I get that."

"—and I couldn't do that to Jacob. That kid has already suffered enough. First his mother dies, and now his father is going to be tried for murder and probably arson. If Sims ends up going to prison, Jacob will have no one. If Sims isn't guilty and that happens because I didn't see this through…I couldn't forgive myself."

"No. I get it. I'm not asking you to drop it," she replied emphatically. "We have to see this through."

"No. *I* have to see this through. *We* don't have to do anything. I might not be able to walk away, but you can."

"If you're still doing this, then the kids and Reese are still in danger. So I'm helping. Period. The more help you have, the sooner you can figure this out, and the sooner everybody will be safe."

"You do realize that you're one of Reese's kids, right? So technically you're at risk too."

"And you're at risk as Sims's attorney," she countered, stiffening.

His shoulders dropped as he ran a hand across his forehead and sighed. "But you don't have to be as connected to this thing as you are. The more space we put between you and anything the firm is doing, the safer you're going to be. I don't want something to happen to you." A quiet determination brewed beneath his features. "Look, don't be so stubborn about this. Take care of the kids. You can stay with them all the time and make sure they're okay. Take care of Reese. Write your article. This isn't your problem."

She shot up off her chair, swiveling to face him. "It is my problem. It's my family being hurt here. I'm not going to just sit back and hope you figure this thing out. I know I'm not much help, but I'm free labor at least, right? I can look through documents, I can talk to people—look, Banyon approached *me*—"

His voice grew steely. "You don't have to do this."

"I do have to do this!" Her eyes widened as she yelled it, her volume surprising even her. They locked eyes for several moments before Chloe spoke again.

"I do have to do this," she said, keeping her voice soft but firm as she regained her composure.

Holt's dark gaze traced her face. He shifted his weight from one foot to the other, killing seconds, until finally speaking again. "Why?"

She sniffed, then turned away from him towards the window, leaning against the windowsill and focusing on a flock of starlings just before they disappeared over the roof. "I have my reasons."

Holt made a sound like a game show buzzer. "Eeeeep. Wrong answer. Try again."

Chloe's eyes narrowed. "What do you mean, 'wrong answer'?"

"I mean you just started yelling at me like a crazy person because I suggested you ought to bow out of participating in an investigation that's gotten your father attacked and left in a coma, a bloody—albeit fake—box on his doorstop, your sister's arm broken, and—oh yeah—last but not least, quite possibly a building *blown up*. So, yeah, while I appreciate the help, it's probably gone far enough, and 'I have my reasons' just isn't gonna cut it."

She sucked a breath in, releasing it slowly. "How much do you know about Tate? About what happened with him in Miami?"

Holt shrugged. "I know what Reese told me. And," he admitted, looking a bit chagrined, "maybe what I Googled about the case."

She was quiet for several moments, breathing in deeply and rhythmically, trying to still her internal storm. He waited silently. She pressed a hand against the cool glass of the window, staring out at nothing in particular.

"Did Reese tell you that after he abandoned us, and our mom died, all Tate and I had in this whole world was each other? Tate was my family. My only family." Her unfocused gaze drifted to the traffic outside and lingered. "And in the end there wasn't a thing I could do to save him from the people who were after him. Not one thing. By the time I figured out what he was mixed up in, it was too late. He was already dead. Gone. I would have given anything for the chance to make a difference. So if I can do something, anything, to make a difference for Emma and Tyler," she caught herself, "for Reese even—then I'm going to do it."

The words felt wrenched from her, as if each syllable was torn from that part of her still grieving the loss of her brother. The ache of it changed the air in the room, the air between them, and Holt stayed quiet as the words settled over them.

When he didn't respond, she tilted her head up at him and blinked, her eyes glistening. "Okay?"

The fight seemed to leave him as he placed a hand on her shoulder and squeezed gently. "Yeah," he said, also turning to gaze out the window at nothing in particular. "I guess I'm okay with that."

THIRTY-EIGHT

The Camry trailed right behind Emma McConnaughey's bright red Hyundai as she pulled into the William Nelson Elementary School parking lot. Rather than follow her in, since he didn't have a student to drop off, he pulled onto the shoulder of the road and watched.

The boy, the younger brother, hopped out and waved, swinging a navy blue and green backpack up and over one shoulder. Just like he had the last three times he had followed the boy to school. It was routine. Predictable. Which was a good thing.

He would know soon if his plan had worked. Fortunately, Reese McConnaughey was still out of it and certainly wasn't going to be causing problems anytime soon. But that other lawyer…Adams…he would have to see if he had finally gotten the message. If not, he would have no choice but to move into Phase Two. That was when the school schedules would come in handy.

The little red car pulled forward, rolling towards the exit. As he watched, he took a long drag on the cheap cigarette that was his second of the day. When he chased it too quickly with a gulp of bitter, fast-food coffee, he started coughing, spluttering drops of the dark liquid all over the dash. Cursing, he smeared the wet drops with the sleeve of his shirt, his weak attempt at cleanup leaving the dashboard worse than before.

Growling, he hunched down in his seat. *McConnaughey better hope that Adams backs off,* he thought. *Otherwise, when he wakes up, if he wakes up, he's gonna find he's lost a whole lot more than a couple of days.*

THIRTY-NINE

The address Banyon had given them was just a few blocks southwest of Five Points, in an area populated with houses built during the latter part of the nineteenth century. In keeping with Franklin's reverence for all things historical, the majority had been renovated, restored, and updated, both preserving the past and increasing their value.

"Wow," Chloe said, peering out the passenger window as they parked on the curb in front of 1004 West Main Street, an enormous French blue Victorian boasting a two-story tower on the front right corner, topped by a spectacular spire. This flanked the asymmetrical front porch, lined with arches painted a sharp contrasting cream, and backed by an expanse of rectangular windows. Gray stonework lined the foundation, at least three feet high, and continued up the chimney on the side of the house opposite the tower. A historical sign mounted in the front yard read "McKinley House, 1892."

"Yeah. Not bad," Holt echoed. "Wonder if Donner bought it like this or renovated it."

"Either way he spared no expense."

They walked up the concrete path to the front door and rang the bell, setting off a chime version of Clare de Lune.

"You gotta be kidding me," Holt quipped. "I have to hear that again." He reached forward to depress the ornate button again, when the latch clicked, and the front door swung open to reveal a blonde dressed in a gray, silk jumpsuit and four-inch high, open-toe heels. Chunky gold bracelets capped the long sleeves on each arm, mirrored by an equally stunning gold-link necklace hanging almost as low as her wavy tresses.

"Holt Adams?" she asked, glaring coldly at him.

"Guilty. And you must be Claire Donner. My condolences for your—"

"Save it," she snapped, her red lipstick forming an angry line. Her eyes shot to Chloe. "Who's she?"

"My assistant. We were told—"

She huffed and spun around, walking back into the foyer before Holt could finish.

'Wow,' he mouthed silently to Chloe as he ushered her inside and pushed the door closed.

Claire Donner's heels clacked gaudily on the marble floor as she led them through the foyer, then turned right into a dining room painted a merlot shade of red, with clean white wainscoting skirting the lower third of the walls. A Colonial-style mahogany table surrounded by twelve gold and gray damask chairs occupied the center of the space. The wall to their left was nearly completely obscured by an imposing cabinet showcasing elegant bone china and numerous crystal pieces, while an aged fireplace sat idle on the wall opposite them.

"Hello, Mr. Adams," said a barrel-chested man dressed in a gray suit and red tie that almost matched the walls. His hair was far too dark for his skin tone and unnaturally thick at the front in a manner highly suggestive of surgical assistance. He stood directly behind the chair at the head of the table, where a small stack of papers rested.

"Come on in," he called, waving them further inside, the chunky ring on his pinky flashing obnoxiously, competing with the rainbows reflecting off the four-tiered, crystal chandelier suspended imposingly over the table's center. Chloe and Holt moved to stand beside the table, while Claire Donner planted herself several feet away, leaning disinterestedly against the china cabinet.

"Thank you for coming. I'm Trevor Jernigan. I am…was…Phillip's accountant. Personal and business," he clarified quickly. "And you are Holt Adams. And Chloe McConnaughey." He extended a hand towards Holt, who considered it, then shook it reluctantly. Jernigan nodded at Chloe.

"You're not Mr. Donner's attorney?" Holt asked, mild intrigue creasing his brow.

"No. No, I'm not. We saw no need to involve attorneys in this small exchange. I apologize for the odd meeting place, but there really wasn't another suitable location. There's a trailer on the job site, but well…this seemed better."

"I have to admit, we're a bit surprised to be here. Given how reluctant Mrs. Donner was to talk to me yesterday."

Claire sucked in a breath, as if readying to shoot back, but Jernigan waved an admonishing hand at her. "She had a change of heart," Jernigan offered. "With Mr. Donner's passing, Mrs. Donner is now the sole owner of Donner Enterprises. After reconsideration, she sees the benefit of working with you to reach an understanding, rather than jumping through expensive legal hoops only to arrive at the same destination."

"Of course I didn't want to talk to you," Claire interjected scathingly. "Your client killed my husband."

Jernigan shot her a look. "Claire, please."

Holt eyed her confidently. "Mrs. Donner, my client maintains he is innocent. And we plan to prove that. But," Holt said, turning his attention to Jernigan and placing a hand on the back of the chair in front of him, "if she didn't want to talk to us, I'd love to know how Vettner-Drake convinced you to take this meeting?"

"It's simply a matter of convenience," Jernigan assured him. "Donner Enterprises maintains a business relationship with Vettner-Drake, though," he added, "not in connection with the Franklin Project. As you know Vettner-Drake elected not to invest in that particular project."

"So we've been told. Repeatedly."

"Yes, well, as a favor to Vettner-Drake, Donner Enterprises has offered to disclose to you certain documents that will make that fact readily apparent."

"That was awfully nice of you."

"As I said, we have a business relationship that we would like to maintain for future potential projects. So if we can help Vettner-Drake avoid unnecessary expense and trouble by answering a few questions—"

"You know what's not so nice?" Holt interjected, slicing through Jernigan's spiel.

Claire Donner looked up from her nails. Chloe, who had been intently watching Jernigan's face, zeroed back on Holt.

"I'm…I'm sorry?" Jernigan stumbled.

"Do you know what's not so nice?" Holt repeated, giving it a few moments to sink in. "Throwing my associate here in the back of a car."

"Wait, now, I'm not sure—"

"Yeah, well I'm very sure that's exactly what happened." An uncomfortable silence curdled the space between the two men. "In the future, if you or Vettner-Drake have something to say, you say it to me? Got it?"

"Mr. Adams, I don't know—"

"And just so we're clear, if anything like that happens again, 'unnecessary expense and trouble' won't begin to describe the pain Vettner-Drake will be feeling." As he spoke, a brooding, protective strength replaced Holt's typically easy-going persona. Subconsciously, or maybe consciously, he had angled himself so that he created a barrier between Chloe and Jernigan. Before Jernigan could react, Holt plunged on. "So," he said, pointing to the documents, "let's see what you got."

Jernigan cleared his throat and gestured to the chair at the head of the table, apparently happy to pretend the intense exchange had not occurred. "Have a seat," he said, and moved to sit on Holt's right.

"No, she'll sit there," Holt countered, nodding at Chloe.

"All right, fine," Jernigan said, annoyance finally bleeding through his tone as he switched to the opposite side of the table.

Chloe took the seat, unable to stop herself from a quick glance at Claire, who was glaring daggers at Holt. Chloe fought the corner of her mouth that ached to turn up. Holt was clearly more than enjoying himself.

"All right, then," Holt said, sitting and pulling the stack of papers to him. "Walk me through this."

*****

"So," Jernigan said, leaning back from the table, "hopefully that makes things clear for you."

Holt sat with the stack of papers still opened before him, casually thumbing through the last of them for the second time. As promised, Jernigan's guided tour through the documents had demonstrated that the Franklin Project had been funded by investments by Donner Enterprises, Phillip Donner personally, two individual investors—

Mark Vellum and Lynn Hope, out of Nashville—and a loan from First Capital Bank, also out of Nashville. Donner Enterprises was named as sole owner of the project, with all other funding being treated as loans to be repaid. Various financial documents outlined the specific amounts loaned and outlined the terms for repayment over time.

There were only about twenty sheets of paper in the stack and it had taken about that many minutes to go through it. Chloe had watched quietly, shifting her attention between Holt, as he perused intently, and Claire, who only left her spot against the cabinet long enough to retrieve what looked like a Bloody Mary. She was back in her spot now, sipping and scowling.

Holt flipped over the last page and sat back. Jernigan took that as his cue. "Well, I trust that satisfies you as to Vettner-Drake's lack of involvement."

"That certainly appears to be the case."

"So you'll agree there's no further reason to approach Vettner-Drake regarding this matter."

Holt's eyes flicked to him. "That certainly appears to be the case."

"Mr. Adams—"

"Mr. Jernigan. Based on what you've shown me, I see no reason to bother Vettner-Drake any further. I will, however, need to contact the individuals listed in here." He tapped the stack and stood. Following his lead, Chloe rose as Holt reached for the papers, when Jernigan's hand flew to the top.

"I'm sorry, but you can't take these with you. We allowed you to see them, but you may not take them from here. Here's the contact information for the names listed there," Jernigan said, handing Holt a small folded sheet. "That should be all you need."

"I'll just get a subpoena."

Jernigan's expression hardened. "Then you do that. But until then, they stay here."

The two men faced off silently for several moments. Claire sidled up behind Jernigan, whether for support or to get a closer look at what came next was unclear, but her haughty smirk said she was relishing Jernigan's refusal to give Holt what he wanted.

Finally, Holt relented. His posture relaxed, an ill-fitted smile appearing on his face as he stood. "All right then. See ya around, Trevor," he said flippantly. "Mrs. Donner," he added, tossing a little nod in Claire's direction before turning his back to them and striding into the hallway. Chloe stepped quickly to follow him out.

"And don't bother getting up, Jernigan," Holt called jauntily over his shoulder. "We'll show ourselves out."

FORTY

"Was that a good idea?" Chloe asked as Holt navigated the A6 towards his office.

"What?"

"Provoking him like that? And what about her? I thought she was going to burn a hole in you with her eyes."

"Yeah, but it was fun." He grinned. "And productive." He turned down a side road to avoid the heavy noontime traffic on Main Street. "Did you see his face when I wanted to leave with the documents? I thought his hair plugs were gonna stand on end."

Chloe snorted, then said, "I don't get it. Why would they care if you took the papers? You saw everything on there."

"Showing me is one thing. But I can't memorize it all in twenty minutes. So letting me leave with all that information would have taken their cooperation to a whole new level. They weren't willing to do that. I think they still want us to get the message that we're supposed to walk away from this, not keep looking."

"But wouldn't they have produced the same documents to Sims? I mean, I know they would probably be buried somewhere in those boxes, but still, don't we already have them?"

Holt shook his head. "Maybe. Maybe not. It all depends on the wording of Sims's requests. If Cecilia didn't ask the right questions, they might not have had to share them. Or they may have found a loophole. Donner's lawyers would've found a way to keep back anything they really didn't want out there. We need to look, though, just in case. But I doubt we'll find them in there."

"It was just a bunch of financial information, names of investors—why would they care if that got out? What difference would that make in Sims's suit?"

"It's not about the documents. I can get them with a subpoena in the murder case if I need them. Investors make great potential suspects. We're entitled to that information, and they know it. That's why they handed us the names and contact info. Almost as if they *wanted* us to contact those folks. Like they were redirecting us. Whatever they are scared of, I can guarantee you that me talking to Mark Vellum and Lynn Hope isn't it."

"So why not just hand them over instead of being all weird about it and creating more suspicion?"

"Because today was about control. About controlling whether we do any more looking in their direction. Because for some reason, that really unnerves them. And Vettner-Drake. First, they go out of their way to intimidate us by accosting you. To send a subtle message that we *really* don't want to poke this particular bear. Then they follow that with getting all helpful, offering to show us who their investors are, just to prove they're telling the truth and drive home the point that we don't need to dig any further. I think it's their way of giving us an out. A way that I can say I've done my due diligence—I reviewed their documentation, offered by their accountant—and I've seen that Vettner-Drake isn't involved. I can drop it now and not be accused of failing to do my job. And that's what they want."

"But you're not going to."

"Part of me says it's not worth it. That I should just track down those two individual investors, confirm that they had no reason to want Donner dead—after all, they'd be less likely to make their money back if Donner's gone—and move on."

"But?"

"But," he smirked, "if I keep at it, there's a pretty decent chance I can get Jernigan's plugs to actually shoot straight out of his head."

"Come on, be serious."

"I am serious—who wouldn't want to see that?"

She raised her eyebrows impatiently.

"Look, I've got a pretty good sense of curiosity, and they've piqued it. They're hiding something, and for some reason, Donner's people are playing along. That whole show today? Innocent people don't act like that. People only act like that when they have something to hide."

"But what if that something has nothing to do with the reason Donner's dead?"

"That's possible. Heck, I'd even say it's likely. But what if it *is* relevant? What if this is the thread that unravels the case against Sims. What if it leads to the guy that attacked Reese? I think it's worth the risk. But listen, anytime you want to walk away, that's okay by me. I would prefer it actually. Then I wouldn't have to worry about you."

"Nope," she answered, cutting her eyes at him. "I don't scare easy, either."

* * * * *

They arrived at the office with a couple of hours to go before Holt's afternoon court cases, one of which was Sims's preliminary hearing. While Holt prepared, Chloe pulled out the next discovery box and spent an hour sorting more of the documents Donner had produced in the lawsuit. When Holt came to check on her, she had only gotten halfway through it.

"How's it going?" he asked, leaning in the doorframe, a can of Coke in his hand. He held it up. "Want one?"

"Thanks, but I'll stick with water. That much sugar would have me bouncing off the walls." She leaned back in her chair. "This is going to take forever just to sort. But, I did find a couple more names we might want to check out." She tapped the yellow legal pad beside her. "I'm adding them to the list."

"Okay, great," Holt said. "Let me see." He moved to lean over her, bracing himself against the table with one hand. "So, did you Google those yet?"

A tingle of alarm rippled through her. He smelled like leather and something woodsy that Gucci or Prada probably had bottled. And he was too close.

"Umm, yeah. They're local businesses. Contractors of some sort."

"Okay, just keep adding the names as you come across them. Then we'll do another round of checking."

She nodded, but he kept staring at her, a curious expression on his face.

"What?" she asked.

He eyed her impishly. "I don't know. You tell me."

"I asked you first."

"You've just got this look. I don't know…you look nervous."

"I'm not nervous. I'm bored."

"Hmm," he replied, pivoting away from the table and heading back to the doorway. "Well, sorry about that. Discovery can be like that sometimes. You sure I can't bring you a Coke? Caffeine might do you good. Coffee maybe?"

"Go. Keep getting ready. I'm fine." She waved him off, and he turned back to the lobby where Karen's desk was.

Chloe continued working, sliding one piece of paper after the other out of the stack and forcing herself to read it. But after only a couple minutes, the task couldn't hold her attention and she looked up, watching Holt in the next room, standing near Karen while reviewing papers and giving her instructions.

She was being silly. Her radar was way off. Holt was simply befriending the daughter of his friend and partner. Making sure that she was okay under these strange circumstances that had left her in such a bizarre position. Reese had been good to him, and he was just repaying the kindness. He was a flirt and a charmer and that was all there was to it.

Right?

Was there any chance Jack was right? Was Holt harboring some sort of…attraction to her?

No, she thought dismissively. *Jack's just feeling insecure. And he has no reason to.*

Just then, Holt looked up from the stack of papers Karen had given him to study, running a hand through several dark locks that were threatening to fall across his face. Out of the corner of his eye he caught Chloe watching him. An amused smile slid onto his face as he turned his attention back to the documents.

Chloe straightened up, forced her eyes down, and started reading the same sentence for the fourth time.

FORTY-ONE

Judge Bricker's courtroom was packed when the afternoon criminal session began at 1:00 p.m. on the dot. The judge was graying, in his late sixties by Chloe's estimation, with a Brooks Brothers bow tie resting just above the collar of his black robe. He wasn't a large man, but something about his presence was imposing, and Chloe was glad she wasn't in the position of having to go before him.

Holt had three cases set for hearing. The first was called early in the lineup, an aggravated assault in which the defendant was accused of getting into a bar fight and sending the other guy to the hospital with multiple knife wounds. Holt's client towered over him, and most definitely looked like someone who could pull that off. The victim was still in the hospital recovering, but from the sound of the grumblings coming from the back of the courtroom, he had a few friends who had shown up to make sure the wheels of justice were spinning. The prosecution called two of them to the stand to testify, and both claimed the defendant had laid into the victim after the victim had beat him in a round of pool and demanded the defendant pay up on their bet. Their friends got a little noisy when Holt cross-examined each of the witnesses, suggesting that the victim was actually the one that had thrown the first punch when the defendant had refused to fork over the money to settle the bet. After a stern warning to the peanut gallery, Judge Bricker found probable cause and bound the defendant over to the grand jury.

Holt's second case was a civil matter set for hearing upstairs in Family Court. After letting Judge Bricker's clerk know where he would be, they headed to the second floor. In this case, Holt represented a mother against a dead-beat dad who had failed to pay child support for the last two years. Even so, he still insisted on sporadically visiting his elementary-aged boys with no warning and not in keeping with the visitation agreement, even threatening their mother when she protested. The mother had finally had enough and filed a civil petition for collection and contempt as well as seeking a restraining order. The mother, a thirty-year-old with wispy hair and no makeup, wore a flowered sundress much too lightweight for the last part of October, which made her look even more fragile. She sat next to Holt on the first row behind the plaintiff's table, folded in on herself, as if trying to disappear completely.

After about ten minutes, the case was called, and Holt escorted the mother past the divider to the plaintiff's table in the main area of the courtroom. The defendant father was not present. The court noted the defendant's absence from this hearing, as well as his absence from earlier attempts to hear the motions at issue, and his failure to secure counsel of record or respond to any of the motions. After taking minimal testimony from the mother to establish the arrearage and the father's failure to abide by the terms of the visitation order, as well as his harassment of her and their boys, the judge granted her petition and ordered payment of the arrearage.

"I'm setting another hearing one month out to revisit this. If payment on the arrearage has not been made by that time, I will be inclined to order the defendant to serve an appropriate jail sentence due to his repeated and willful refusal to comply with the prior support orders. I'm also revoking visitation and granting an order of protection with respect to both the plaintiff and minor children." With that pronouncement, the judge called the next case and Holt guided the mother back to the gallery. After a few whispered comments between them, the mother slipped out into the hall and Holt returned to Chloe.

"Time to head back for Sims's case," he said, nodding at the exit. They left the courtroom quietly, maneuvering through the people grouped along the hallway.

"That whole situation in there is really sad. Your client looked scared to death," said Chloe, as they took the stairs again.

"She is. But she'll be better when this is over. I doubt she'll ever see any money, but at least the protection order will get her help from the police if he does come around again." He shook his head as they took the staircase back to the first floor. "I hate these cases. I hate seeing what people can do to their own families."

"You're helping," Chloe urged. "That's something."

"Yeah, I guess. So," he said, as they reached Judge Bricker's courtroom again and he opened the door for her. "Sims's case will likely be called last since it's such a serious one. Could be a while, so settle in."

He was wrong, though, and just twenty minutes later a side door at the front of the courtroom opened and a bailiff escorted Kurt Sims inside, handcuffed and still adorned in his jail-issued jumpsuit. This time it seemed he had at least made an effort to look somewhat presentable. His hair was slightly damp and combed back, and his beard looked less grizzly-ish. But there was still something defeated about his posture, and his dark eyes looked more annoyed than anything else. After wrapping up the case in front of him, the judge called out, "State of Tennessee vs. Kurt Sims." Holt moved toward the defense table, where Kurt was being deposited by the bailiff, and they sat down together.

The Tri-County District Attorney was a tall woman, probably in her early sixties. She was dressed in a tailored, charcoal pin-striped jacket and matching skirt, ecru blouse, and flats. Her curly white hair was tightly cut against her crown, a striking contrast against the bronze brown of her skin. She moved quickly, calling several witnesses to establish the basis of the murder charges against Sims. Within thirty minutes, the testimony of one police detective and a forensics specialist established that Sims's gun, a Smith and Wesson M&P semi-automatic pistol, was still missing, but that the 9mm bullets recovered from the murder scene matched bullets that had been previously fired from Sims's pistol. It turned out Sims had a bad habit of having shooting practice in his own backyard, which was not only illegal, but had provided the police with several bullets to compare with the bullets extracted from Donner's body. Also, the fingerprints found on the shells recovered from the murder scene belonged to Sims. On top of that, police recovered multiple threatening messages from Sims on Donner's voicemail, two of which had been left on the day of the murder. Additionally, Donner's cell records showed a one-minute call placed to him from Sims's phone at 10:30 p.m. on the night of Donner's murder. Forensic testimony put Donner's time of death between 11:00 p.m. and midnight. The final blow was testimony that the shoe prints at the scene matched a pair of hiking boots recovered from Sims's bedroom closet.

If any of this phased Holt, he didn't show it. Instead he took it all in, making notes throughout the testimony, and noticeably not speaking to Sims at all, even when he tried to get Holt's attention. Holt had no questions for the witnesses, and when the D.A. finally rested, Judge Bricker announced he found there was probable cause, and bound Sims's case over to the grand jury.

"Your honor, if I may?" the district attorney asked in follow-up.

"Yes, Ms. Linden?"

"The State has secured an arrest warrant for the defendant on the charge of first degree arson arising out of the detonation of explosives at the Donner Properties construction site located at Five Points in Franklin. The State—"

"What?" Sims bellowed, his handcuffs clattering against the table as he shot out of his chair.

"Shh, Kurt!" Holt hissed, squeezing Sims's arm and pulling him back to the table. Sims exhaled in disgust.

"Mr. Adams?"

"Sorry, your honor," Holt apologized. "Won't happen again."

The district attorney eyed Sims before continuing. "Although the events of the alleged arson are distinct from the specific events of Phillip Donner's murder, the State intends to seek joinder of the two cases. It is the State's position that the arson was part of an escalating series of events that ultimately became the motive for and led to Mr. Donner's murder."

"Mr. Adams, any objection to my setting bond on the arson charge at this time?"

"No, your honor."

"Fine. Bail is set at five hundred thousand on the charge of arson. The prior bail amount of five hundred thousand on the murder charge shall remain intact, for a combined bail amount of one million." Judge Bricker proceeded to set the preliminary hearing on the charge of first degree arson for the following Monday, then called a ten-minute recess before moving on to the next case.

"Holt, you got a minute?" District Attorney Linden had sidled up to the defense table. Holt rose to meet her, standing at least a full foot taller than she did.

"Sure, Annabelle. Just a second." Holt leaned over to the bailiff, who had returned to collect Sims. "Keep him in the interview room for a minute, will you?" Holt asked, and the bailiff nodded.

"Hallway?" he said, turning back to D.A. Linden.

Her head bobbed in affirmation, and she headed for the exit doors with Holt following.

He had handled dozens of cases against Annabelle. She was competent, thorough, and passionate about her job. And like Cecilia Tucker, she had a tell. A Cheshire-cat smirk that split the corners of her mouth whenever she had information that positioned her to send one of Holt's clients to jail.

It was that smile she had flashed at Holt, just briefly, when bobbing her head. Just long enough for him to glimpse it before she turned.

And that wasn't good. It was never good.

*****

"Your guy needs to plead this out." District Attorney Linden stood in a quiet corner of the large courthouse lobby, gauging Holt's reaction. Her arms were full of brown case files, with Sims's file, one of the thicker ones, balanced on top.

"Come on, Annabelle. You know I'm not pleading out. You haven't even been to the grand jury yet."

"Just a professional heads up. Thought I could save you some time. I know you're doing this thing pro bono."

"Really? You know that?"

Annabelle smiled. "Word on the street. Anyway, I just felt like you should maybe get out in front of this thing before we expend too much effort prosecuting."

"Talk to me after the grand jury."

"It doesn't get better, Holt." She pulled a smaller file from the bottom of her pile and handed it to him. "Go on. Take a look."

His eyes narrowed, then he set his briefcase down on the floor and pulled the folder open.

"Read the reports. The hiking boots we found? Not only did they match the tracks at the murder scene, but we found particles of dried, red-tinted concrete stuck in the treads. It just so happens that the night before the bombing, someone accidentally walked right through some newly poured, dark red-tinted concrete that was part of the flooring on the first level. Was going to be part of some sort of atrium or something. The workers finished pouring it right before punching out that night. Nobody else was on the property after that. Or at least they weren't supposed to be. The employees showed up the next day and found their newly poured floor tracked through. Ruined. They figured it was some kids just in there messing around, but after the explosion happened later that night, they felt it might be connected. They had repoured it before we could take impressions, but they were right. The particles are a match, Holt. Your guy's guilty of arson and murder. You should plead while we're in the mood."

Holt heaved a sigh. "Talk to me after the grand jury."

"Fine," she said, shrugging as if he was squandering an opportunity, "but before you decide," she paused, pulling a final sheet of paper from her stack and handing it to him, "you may want to ask your client about this."

*****

"You blew up a bulldozer?" Holt bellowed as he slammed his briefcase down on the table separating him from Sims. Whatever method Holt had used to rein in his emotions in the courtroom, he was not employing it now.

Sims looked surprised, but not surprised enough. "They found out about that? It was, like, thirty years ago. And those records were sealed."

"Yeah, Kurt. They found out about that. Of course, they found out about that. They're the police. That's what they do. They would have learned about the sealed file in the course of handling the assault charge Donner pressed against you. But that wasn't a felony, so they wouldn't have taken a look at the sealed juvenile charges. But in a felony investigation like this, they can look at the sealed records. What I can't figure out is why my *client* didn't tell me about it first."

Chloe watched the exchange from where she stood behind Holt, leaning against the wall with her arms crossed in front of her.

"Why would I bring that ancient history up?" Sims whined. "I was a kid. It was a demonstration stunt gone wrong. Nobody got hurt. I was trying to blow the tracks off the thing to slow down the demolition of a Civil War-era house. They were building a strip mall in Charleston for Pete's sake. The explosion just ended up being a little bigger than I thought it would be. Took out a couple of cars parked beside it. It was no big deal."

"No big deal?"

"Yeah, it got pled down to a misdemeanor. My dad knew the prosecutor. I got probation and some community service."

"And a record. Which popped up when they ran your name."

"So what? What does this have to do with Donner's murder?"

"Because you're not just being charged with Donner's murder, Kurt. Didn't you hear the D.A. in there? You're now being charged with arson over the construction site explosion."

"Yeah, I heard her," Kurt hissed, his frustration level rising to match Holt's. "It's a complete farce. I wouldn't even know how to do something like that."

"So I hear." Holt's eyes glittered black. "Did you really tell the officers at your house during the search that you wouldn't even know how to blow something up if you wanted to?"

Sims's eyes flitted down, casting around for a memory. "You mean when they were talking to me before you got there?"

Holt nodded laboriously.

"They were talking garbage, giving me a hard time, asking me if they were gonna 'find anything' in the house and whether I just wanted to confess to the murder so I could save them time. I told them to shove it and they said, 'well, what about the explosion at Donner's project? How about that?' and I yelled at them, said I wouldn't know how to blow anything up even if I wanted to. So what?"

"So, you *do* know how to blow stuff up, Kurt. *Have* blown stuff up. The bulldozer is Exhibit 'A'."

"They can't use that in this…can they?"

"Yeah, Kurt they can. Because now that you've misrepresented yourself, if you take the stand, they can introduce evidence of the bulldozer incident to show that you lied to the police and that you're not trustworthy. So the jury gets to hear that you're a liar *and* that you have a history of blowing stuff up when you're not happy about it."

"That's not right!"

"That's why I, as your lawyer, advised you to *keep your mouth shut* before I got to your house. You should have listened."

"What if I don't testify?"

"But what if we need you to testify, Kurt? Now we're gonna get hit with this if we put you on the stand. Then again, it may not even matter. It's possible they can get the conviction in even if you don't testify, on the grounds that it proves you possess the skills and knowledge necessary for such a stunt."

"But…but we don't even know whether it was the same kind of bomb! I mean I basically used a souped-up version of a Molotov cocktail on the bulldozer. That wasn't, couldn't have been, what was used at Donner's site. It wouldn't have been strong enough."

"Maybe, maybe not. We won't know more till we get the case materials from the D.A. Either way, it severely complicates things and, at a minimum, limits our options."

"Holt, I'm telling you, I didn't do it. Not the murder, not the bomb. I'm innocent."

Holt looked away, scratching his jaw. "See, Kurt, here's the thing. Your prelim on the arson is set for next Monday, but I doubt they'll present anything more than they've told me today. And frankly, they won't need to. Remember the 'unknown red particles' they took from your house? Well, it's *known* now. It turned out to be dried clods of recently poured, red-tinted concrete from the site near where the bomb was placed. It matches exactly. They found it in the treads of your hiking boots, Kurt. And on your closet floor. Like you tried to scrape it off, but didn't quite get it all." Holt paused to rub a hand over his mouth. "Back when all this started, right after the explosion, somebody said there was talk of 'concrete evidence' in the case. I didn't realize they meant that literally. And now they've matched it to you. 'We've got him red-handed—or at least 'red-footed,' the D.A. just told me, Kurt. She's so convinced that you're as good as convicted that she's making jokes."

A dull panic was making its way into Kurt's features. "Hold on. I didn't scrape anything off anything, man. I didn't step in any concrete because I wasn't at the site."

"It's not all they have, Kurt," Holt said, and proceeded to outline the rest of what the D.A. had shared with him.

"But I didn't make that call to him right before he got killed!"

"What about the other calls? The messages with the threats?"

"They weren't threats! It was just posturing. You know, like vague…comments…about how hard it was gonna be for him. Just trying to annoy him into walking away."

"And they'll claim that when that didn't work, you decided to take more serious action. Like with the bulldozer. Are you sure that the 10:30 call wasn't you harassing him again, with another 'comment'?" Holt asked, using air quotes.

"No!" Kurt blurted, standing to pace while wringing his hands. Then his face contorted in deeper worry as he seemed to reconsider his stance. "I don't know. Maybe. I've been drinking a lot lately. Maybe I called and forgot—"

"Oh, Kurt, come on."

"No, seriously! But I didn't mean anything by the calls. Not really."

"Come on, Kurt. That's not going to help at all. Besides, we'll likely never get to explain that to the jury because if we try, the first thing they'll hear is how you aren't trustworthy vis-à-vis the blowing up the bulldozer lie."

Kurt plopped into the chair, sagging forward, leaning his head on the table.

"I'm done for."

Holt turned to look at Chloe. His expression said that he didn't disagree.

FORTY-TWO

"I don't believe him," Holt scoffed as he and Chloe walked down the courthouse steps, the late afternoon light falling over the street and through the remaining bright yellow leaves still clinging to the trees spaced along the sidewalk. A pleasantly cool breeze tickled the skin as a couple walking their Goldendoodle passed by. The curly giant loped several feet ahead of his parents, tugging on his leash energetically.

"This is going to be a black hole," Holt groused. "And I doubt we'll ever get paid. At least not enough to make it worthwhile."

"But what if he's innocent?" Chloe replied.

Holt turned to Chloe as they stepped off the last step onto the sidewalk. "I know," he said, his shoulders dropping in surrender. "I know."

"Mr. Adams?"

The voice came from behind them. They both turned to see a young woman following them down the courthouse steps. "You're Mr. Adams?"

"Yes," said Holt.

The woman tucked a stray, wavy hair from her short blonde bob behind one ear and rocked nervously from side to side on her wedge boots. "Your secretary said you'd be in court. She said you weren't expected back in the office today and…well…this couldn't wait." She eyed Chloe questioningly.

Holt noticed the nervous glance. "This is an associate of mine," he said, twisting a hand towards Chloe. "She helps out in our office."

"Oh. Well, okay. I guess that's okay." She bit her lip. "That murder case? The one about, um, that Donner guy on the news? I saw your name in the article online. It said you were representing him—the guy they arrested?"

Holt nodded.

"Um, yeah. Well. I think I may know something." She anxiously cocked a hip and leaned on the strap of the Michael Kors handbag hanging from her shoulder as if hoping it would hold her up.

"What do you mean, 'you might know something?'"

She squinted at him, and exhaled slowly. It looked like she was still trying to decide whether to actually share whatever it was that brought her there. Finally she gave in. "I mean, like, something important. You know…something that maybe proves he didn't do it."

FORTY-THREE

The air conditioner whirred in the background as Holt leaned forward on his mahogany desk, elbows propped on the leather blotter. The woman from the courthouse steps, who had finally introduced herself as Amanda Parvel, sat across from him in one of two navy and gray tweed wingback chairs. Chloe sat in the other. Bookshelves flanked either side of the office door, home to rows of old editions of the Tennessee Code Annotated and Shepard's Citations. An engraved plaque from the local bar association acknowledging some achievement adorned the same shelf as a glass-encased baseball with a signature Chloe couldn't make out. Diplomas and certificates of admission to the bars of multiple courts hung in heavy gold frames on the wall behind the desk.

After several minutes of urging, they had finally convinced Ms. Parvel to come back to Holt's office with them. Even then, she had sat in her car for about five minutes before finally coming inside. Now she sipped the bottle of water Karen had brought her, clutching it like it was her only friend in the world.

"Better?" Holt asked.

She nodded. "Yes, sorry. It's just…I'm a bit nervous."

"I understand," Holt sympathized. "Why not just start at the beginning?"

"Okay," Amanda said, shifting in her chair again. The late twenty-something was having a hard time with whatever it was that had prompted her to seek Holt out. Chloe perched on the edge of her chair, willing the woman to get to the point. She knew they couldn't push too hard—they might spook her—but if she had information that could help Kurt Sims, maybe it would also shed light on the identity of the person threatening her family.

"So, I'm a…well, it doesn't matter," she qualified, before continuing, clearly filtering her comments as she spoke. "I've lived here a couple of years—came from Birmingham after graduation. Anyway, about four months ago I met this guy and we started dating. He was a little older than me, but he was good to me and fun, so the age difference didn't seem to matter."

Holt nodded, pressing her on.

She sniffed. "So, the night of that fire—the one at the construction site at Five Points?"

Chloe and Holt both nodded eagerly.

"Well, the next day, he and I were having lunch at Nero's Grille and—you know they have those flat screens on the wall—anyway, the news does a quick, little report on the explosion and when it's over, he says, 'Guess what goes around comes around.' I asked him what he meant and he just said, 'Never mind.' But then a couple of days later, the guy that owned the site, Phillip Donner, was found murdered. And that night, we were just hanging out, grilling, watching the game, you know. But I guess he had one too many, and whenever that happens he gets really, really chatty. He was going on and on about the SEC East, so just to change the topic I asked him if he had heard about the murder, and he started talking again about how Donner got what he deserved. Only this time, when I asked him what he meant, he said an ex-girlfriend of his had had some trouble with Donner. When I asked him what kind of trouble, he said that Donner had threatened to cause problems for her unless she went along with some scheme of Donner's."

"Who's the ex-girlfriend?"

She shrugged. "I don't know. He wouldn't say. But then he goes, 'Wouldn't put it past them.' Which didn't make any sense, right?"

"Sure," Chloe agreed.

"So I said, 'Put what past who?' And he said, 'Ending it once and for all.' So then I asked him, 'Ending what?' But then he just shrugged me off and changed the subject."

"Did you ask him about it later?" Holt prompted.

Amanda nodded. "But he wasn't having it. A couple of days later I came in—he was already annoyed that I had been at a showing all day so it was probably bad timing—but I asked him about what he meant, and he told me to drop it. It ticked me off that he wouldn't explain himself, so I pressed him. In hindsight, I should have just left it alone. Timing, you know? We were both exhausted from long days, and the whole thing turned into a fight until we were just yelling at each other. Then he threw a glass against the wall and I left."

Holt squinted disapprovingly. "Is he normally violent?"

"No, but after seeing that side of him, I broke up with him. I don't have time for that."

"You're gonna need to tell me who he is," Holt pressed.

Amanda bit her rose-painted bottom lip. "I don't know if I should say."

"Amanda, this information only helps us if we get his name. You had to know we would need it. Otherwise, why tell us this at all?" Holt asked.

"Amanda," Chloe interjected, offering a soft smile, "I know this must be hard, but, if you can help us, please do. You came here because you thought there might be something to this. If you're right, it could keep an innocent man from going to prison. Don't you want that?"

Amanda blinked. She looked like she might cry. "Of course, I do. It's just…I don't want to make trouble for him. I mean, I don't want to date him, but that doesn't mean I want to get him mixed up in the middle of something. It's why I came to you instead of the police. If you check this out, and find out that there's nothing to it, if it's not going to clear your client, then you can just forget about it, right? You don't have to give anyone his name."

"Look," Holt assured her, "if there's really nothing to this, then, maybe we can just forget you ever came here. But I won't know until I check it out."

She rubbed her pant leg and fidgeted. "No," she said urgently, shaking her head. "This was a bad idea. I shouldn't have come."

"Amanda—"

"No, I mean it," she snapped, slinging her purse onto her shoulder and jerking out of her chair in one forceful movement. "This was a mistake. I have to go."

She strode past Chloe and through Holt's door, headed for the lobby.

"Amanda, please," Holt called, following after her as the electronic beep signaling the opening of the office's front door sounded. When he reached it, she was already halfway to her car.

Holt stepped outside, calling out to her. "Amanda, if you change your mind, you know where I am." She stopped in her tracks, one hand on her open driver's door, still facing away from him. She didn't turn as he continued, "Please give it some thought, okay? A man's life may be on the line."

In answer, she climbed inside her royal blue Prius, slammed the door shut, and drove away.

*****

Holt walked back into the office to find Chloe leaning back into her chair, looking very disappointed.

"So now what?" she asked.

"Well," Holt started, then his eyes widened in alarm. "Oh man," he exclaimed, then ran to the lobby and ripped open the front door. Chloe followed him, watching as he disappeared onto the front porch. She looked at Karen who shrugged, apparently as lost as Chloe. She was about to follow him out when he reappeared in the doorway, looking grim. "I forgot to get her license plate."

"Could you run a search on it if you had?"

He tromped past her back to his office. "I know people who can," he said, sliding back into his chair and opening a window on his computer. "All right, let's see what we can find."

Chloe moved to stand behind him as he opened Facebook. A search for Amanda Parvel turned up no one even remotely resembling the woman who had just raced from his office.

"Google?" Chloe proposed.

Holt's fingers flew over the keyboard. A list of multiple people named Amanda Parvel appeared. He scrolled through them, clicking on a few with no luck. "None of these seem connected to our Amanda, as far as I can tell. The only one linked to Tennessee," he said, pointing to a commercial social connections site, "looks nothing like her."

"So, maybe she gave a false name," Chloe remarked. "Just in case."

"Yeah, probably so. But we may still have something. Did you hear what she said about the showing?"

"Yeah, I noticed that too. The thing about her boyfriend being annoyed that she had been at a showing all day. You think that means 'showing' as in showing a house? Like maybe she's a realtor?"

"Maybe," he said, clacking away on the keys again.

Chloe grimaced. "But, in the Nashville area there have to be, what—"

"Hundreds of realty groups, yeah. Thousands of realtors." As confirmation, he pointed to the screen, which displayed a multiple-page list of realtors produced by his initial search.

Chloe's shoulders sagged. "That'll take a lot of time to go through."

"Yeah. I've got a guy I can put on it. He's not too expensive for something like this." He picked up his cell phone from his desk and tapped on it, pulling up a photo. "I managed to get a really bad side angle picture of her while she was focused on you. With a little work, he can hopefully track her down, and maybe figure out who she was seeing."

Holt made the call on his cell, then frowned. "Voicemail," he said, as he waited for the beep then left a message asking for a return call. "He usually calls back within a couple hours."

Chloe sighed. "I was really hoping she might point us towards some answers."

"Well, don't give up hope yet," he said. "This still could pan out. This is a good thing."

And as if offering a counter to the notion that something could finally be going their way, Chloe's cell buzzed, her nerves revving up when the name across the screen identified the caller as 'Mid-Tenn Hospital.'

FORTY-FOUR

Reese's laugh boomed through the tiny hospital room as Tyler described the chaos that had ensued in his classroom earlier that day.

"...and then Jackson's dog jumped up on the counter where we keep the guinea pig and *turned the cage over!"* Tyler's eyes were bright, his hands shoving out in front of him to mimic the cage going on its side. "I've never seen a guinea pig move so fast! It was just this brown and white fur ball racing down the counter. Samba—the golden retriever—ran after him and knocked everything over. Mrs. Ellis dove for him, but she tripped on the books that he had knocked onto the floor and she fell on her butt!"

Holt snorted, while Emma cackled. "I would've loved to have seen that," she said. "Mrs. Ellis put me in time out once."

Emma sat in a chair near Reese's monitors, her feet propped up on his bed. Reese laughed at her comment, then squeezed her leg gently. The teen hadn't moved from the spot since arriving over an hour earlier.

Reese was flushed with color, and according to the monitors, his vital signs were good. Much better, in fact, than the last time he had regained consciousness. According to his doctor, this was promising and likely an indication that Reese would not slip away again. "He just needed a little more intense recovery time," the doctor suggested, before leaving the family to catch up with his patient. "Only half an hour more, though, all right?" he had insisted, not wanting Reese to tire out too quickly and overdo it. He didn't want a setback. No one did. That was forty-five minutes ago.

"Okay gang," Holt said, checking his watch. "We've overstayed. Time for Reese to get some rest. He can only take so much of you two," he said, ruffling Tyler's hair, "before he needs a nap."

Tyler leaned over to hug his dad. "I'm glad you're okay," he whispered. "I knew you would be. Chloe and I prayed for it."

Reese's eyes darted questioningly to Chloe. "You did?"

Tyler nodded. "So…I'll see you tomorrow, right Dad?"

"Definitely," Reese replied, "and bring me another story from school," he told him, as Emma took a turn to hug her father lightly before following her brother out.

"Will do!" Tyler called back as he stepped into the hall.

Holt stopped in the doorway and eyed Chloe meaningfully. "I'll run them home," he offered. "Why don't you stay for a minute on your own?"

"No, no," she said, rising. "You've been going all day. You should get home."

Holt shook his head. "It's no problem. I'll stay with them until you're done. I can work just as well from there. Reese," he said, turning his gaze to his mentor, "it's good to see you back in the land of the living."

"Good to be here," Reese replied, smiling.

Holt patted the doorframe in answer, then slipped into the hall.

Reese heaved a sigh, continuing to watch the spot Holt had just abandoned. "I can't thank him enough. I can only imagine what he's done this last week. And you," he said, turning to Chloe, "you didn't come here for this."

"Stop," Chloe said, holding up a hand to halt him. "It's been fine. Actually, it's been, well…good. I mean, not what happened to you," she backpedaled, "but me with the kids—that's been good. I've gotten to know them much better than if I'd just visited for a couple days."

"So you're a glass-half-full kind of girl."

Chloe pursed her lips contemplatively. "I haven't always been. But now, I'm trying to be."

"Sit," Reese said, gesturing to the chair Emma had abandoned. As Chloe complied, it occurred to her that this was the first time she and Reese had been alone since Emma's visit to the emergency room. Suddenly she felt uncomfortable, and absentmindedly began running her hand along the textured blue cloth of the seat. The fabric was bumpy and created an odd sensation as she moved her hand across it.

"Chloe…tell me about Tate."

Her eyes flicked in his direction. "Now?" she asked uncertainly. "I don't know, Reese. It doesn't seem like a good time to get into something like that. Something that stressful."

He grabbed her hand, taking her by surprise. "Now *is* the right time. I could have died days ago, and I would have done it not knowing my son. I know that's my fault," he added, getting there before she could. "It's entirely my fault. But I want to know him. As much as I can. Even if it's just in a small, secondhand way that doesn't do him justice."

"He deserved more," Chloe said. It wasn't a cruel comment, or meant to cut. It was just the truth.

"He did. But this is all I can do now. So please, tell me about Tate. All of it. Any of it. Who he was—the sports he played as a boy, the foods he liked, the movies he liked—I want to *know* him."

She thought of Tate as a boy, with that untamed curly shag of hair and the toothy grin that made his hazel eyes sparkle. She liked remembering him that way. And she liked the thought of someone else remembering him that way too.

She scooted forward in her chair a bit, resting her elbows on her knees. "Well," she began, "for starters, there were no sports. Tate couldn't throw a ball to save his life. As for food…he ate enough sushi to feed a small Japanese town. And movies…"

As she spoke, Reese's eyes began to glisten, then pool, until fat drops slipped down his cheek, striking the scratchy bed sheets one after the other.

FORTY-FIVE

"Come on down, you guys!" Chloe bellowed, dropping a bowl smeared with vanilla-laced whisked egg and milk in the sink. "Your breakfast is getting cold!"

Pale morning light filtered through the Roman blinds that topped the windows in the family room beyond Reese's kitchen, bathing the countertops in the promise of the coming day. Two plates stacked high with cinnamon French toast clattered as she set them on the raised bar in front of her, followed by the clinking of flatware as she set each of their places. The irresistible rich, sweet scent of the baked concoction enveloped the room, ultimately convincing her to forgo her promise to herself to watch her carbs today. She was wiping a bit of syrup from her chin when Emma and Tyler finally made it into the kitchen.

She swallowed a mouthful of French toast. "Syrup's on the counter," she said, nodding toward the plastic bottle between the two plates.

Tyler drenched his toast in the sticky, golden liquid, then snatched up his plate and fork. "Can I take mine over and watch TV for a minute?" he asked. As if anticipating Chloe's protest, he added, "Dad lets me."

Chloe looked at Emma for confirmation. She nodded and shrugged, her black hair bobbing in the high ponytail she had swept it up into.

"Sure, Tyler," Chloe told him, and he bounded off with a plate.

"So, you stayed with Dad until they kicked you out last night?" Emma asked, shoveling in a mouthful.

"I did," Chloe responded, chasing her last bite with a tangy glass of low-acid orange juice. She had remained at the hospital, regaling Reese with tales of Tate until he had finally fallen asleep in the early evening. She had stayed even after that, uncertain why, but feeling like she wasn't supposed to go. Somewhere around nine o'clock, she realized she was praying for the man lying in front of her. It wasn't a particularly purposeful prayer, but just general requests for God to move in his life, in their relationship—if that's what you could call whatever existed between them at that point—and in Reese's children's lives. She didn't remember starting to pray; somewhere along the line she must have just lapsed into it. The realization surprised her. Prayer was still a very conscious endeavor on her part. At least it had been. Maybe that was changing.

The nurses had kicked her out when visiting hours ended at ten. By the time she finally got home and relieved Holt, she was so exhausted that after checking on both kids, she dropped into the bed, fully clothed, and slept soundly for the next eight hours.

"How was Dad?"

"Fine. Great. Sleeping when I left. You should go by after school today."

"I'm working, but yeah, after that I will." Emma's cell chirped and she checked it, laughing at whatever message someone had sent her. An idea nipped at Chloe.

"Hey, Emma," Chloe continued, "I wanted to ask how Jacob is doing. His dad was asking yesterday at the hearing."

Emma shrugged, taking a sip of juice. "Yeah, Jacob told me about the hearing. He's dealing with it, I guess. He said he tried to visit his dad but Mr. Sims wouldn't meet him. Something about not wanting him to see him like that."

"It's got to be hard."

"Not too hard to keep him from laying into Jacob. The only message he sent back was not to slack off on football while he was gone."

"That's a bit harsh. How did Jacob handle it?"

"Jacob wasn't surprised. His dad is like that all the time. And like I said, Jacob's dealing. He hasn't missed school or anything, so his dad ought to be happy." Emma grabbed her backpack off the counter. "Come on, bud," she called to Tyler. "We're gonna be late."

Tyler groaned, then brought his plate back to the kitchen before heading out the door. Emma followed after him, but Chloe called out, stopping her in the doorway. "Hey, Emma?"

Emma turned and waited.

"Why don't you see if Jacob can come over for dinner one night soon."

"Yeah, sure. He'd probably like that."

"And you know, your dad is probably going to come home before long, which means, I don't know how much longer I'll be here. I was thinking, what if you left school early today so you and I can spend some time together? Maybe right after lunch? Unless you've got tests or something else you can't miss."

Emma's face lit up. "Seriously?"

The corner of Chloe's mouth turned up. "Yeah, seriously. I already talked to your dad and he's fine with it. He thinks you could use a little break, too."

Emma grinned. "You have got to be the best secret half-sister I didn't know I had ever."

Chloe returned the smile. "Right back at you."

*****

Once the kids were gone, Chloe took her tea over to the laptop, determined to take a shot at finding Amanda Parvel. She hated the thought of waiting on whomever Holt had called for help to get around to looking into it. Even though there were a lot of realtors, if she just kept looking, eventually she might stumble onto a photograph of the woman they had met yesterday, since every realty office maintained a website with photographs of their agents.

Maybe it won't be as hard as you think, Holt. But even if it was, it was worth some time and effort on her part to try. If she was able to find Amanda, it would be a real contribution to what they were trying to accomplish and, at the same time, save Holt some money. Money that, she knew, he wasn't getting paid.

It only took fifteen minutes to realize it would be exactly as difficult as Holt had anticipated. Not only did the Nashville area seem to have an excessive number of realtors, but many were one- or two-person outfits, meaning that there were hundreds of individual websites to peruse. She managed to get through a couple dozen before draining her first cup of tea. Realizing she was going to need a higher octane, she switched to French roast, black, and came up with a game plan. It made the most sense to start with groups based in Williamson County, hitting the large firms first, to see as many faces as possible on one site. Once she got through those, she would move on to the smaller ones. After that, if necessary, she would cast the net wider into the metro Nashville area.

She was halfway through the cup of coffee, having no luck whatsoever, when her cell beeped, alerting her to a text from Holt.

Hearing in federal court this a.m., it read. *Call u after lunch. Go have fun. Forget about Sims for a while.*

Will do, she replied, following it with a smiley face emoji, then immediately returned to the computer.

Hundreds of faces scrolled by as she sipped the earthy brew. Somewhere in the middle of her search, her thoughts drifted to Jack and what he might be doing. Was he thinking about her? Was he struggling with not reaching out to her? Did he have to continually talk himself out of calling? She hated that he felt she needed space. She didn't need any time away from him and it made her sad to think that he believed she did. She was ready for this separation to be over. To get back to Atlanta and her life with Jack, and figure this whole thing out. But she couldn't leave until Reese was home. Sighing, she shook her head and refocused on the photos on the screen.

After another hour the faces had started to blur into a featureless stream of blondes, brunettes and redheads, until Chloe realized what she was doing and reminded herself that she had to pay closer attention. It wasn't enough to just look at the hair. Amanda easily could have changed it.

After her second cup of coffee, she realized that she was feeling a bit jittery, not something that was particularly helpful for sitting patiently in front of a computer for hours on end. She paused long enough to fix a mug of herbal tea, then got back into it, adding name after name to the list of agencies she had already checked without success.

Another hour in and her eyes were beginning to glaze over. She had nearly convinced herself that it was time to give up and let Holt's man take a crack at it, when a familiar face smiled out at her.

"Gotcha!" she yelled, as she stared at a photograph of Amanda Parvel, one of eighty realtors listed on the page of agents that comprised Hogan and Hartley Realty, Inc., of Spring Hill, Tennessee. The photo she had used as her headshot must have been a recent one because the woman in the picture looked exactly as Amanda had in Holt's office. Blonde, messy bob, blue eyes, big smile. The only thing different was her name—Amanda Luther, not Amanda Parvel. A work email and phone number were listed beside the photograph. Hoping to reach Amanda and maybe talk her into divulging the name of her ex-boyfriend, Chloe snatched up her cell and started dialing. Just before pressing the call button, a thought occurred to her and she stopped.

What if I scare her off? What if, instead of convincing her to help, she ends up warning the guy not to talk to us?

Exhaling, Chloe set the phone down. She bit her lip as she thought, *Maybe I need to go about this another way.*

Returning to a window already opened to Facebook, Chloe searched for the name Amanda Luther. Her page popped up in three seconds. Though Amanda had gone to some lengths to keep her personal information from Holt and Chloe, she had made no such effort on her Facebook page. She had over 1,500 followers and nothing was restricted. It made sense that a realtor would need to maintain a public profile, and Amanda certainly had created one. All her information—birthday, workplace, favorite movies and books, and so on—was accessible by anyone.

"Didn't figure you for a *Band of Brothers* fan," Chloe mused, as she kept sifting through the information. Unfortunately, under relationship, there was no entry. Just 'single.'

Chloe moved on to Amanda's photo albums, hoping to find a picture of her with her mystery man. The woman was a compulsive poster. Photos of the KitchenChef home delivery meals she had prepared on multiple nights during the last week was evidence of that. There were also plenty of photos of nights on the town, friends having lunch, and family get-togethers, but nothing that resembled a shot of a couple dating. Either she had never posted photos of her mystery boyfriend or, more likely, she had deleted them after the break-up.

Refusing to give up, Chloe scrolled back several more months, to around the time Amanda had said she and her boyfriend had started dating. But still, Chloe found no photos that might suggest any kind of romantic relationship. There was one group photo, however, with half a dozen women and two guys, all having dinner and margaritas at a Mexican restaurant. It looked like a birthday celebration, based on the gargantuan black and silver-spangled sombrero propped on the head of the woman on the end. Wondering whether one of the men had become more than a friend, Chloe scrolled over their faces. Both had been tagged.

Chloe clicked the tag on the first one, and the Facebook page of 'Justin Perry' opened. He looked to be in his late thirties, and had a scholarly look about him, complete with glasses and a goatee covering a slight chin. Although his site was mostly private, he did share some posts and photos with the public. Chloe scrolled back just a few weeks and gasped as the timeline revealed several photos of Amanda and him together. From the looks of it they had definitely dated. For whatever reason, he apparently had not felt the need to delete them after their break-up. This was the guy.

Would it be possible to approach him directly?

Chloe leaned back in her chair, pulling her warm mug to her chest. Going straight to the source would have its advantages. They could skip convincing Amanda to cooperate. Then again, he might be even more skittish than she was. What if confronting him scared him off? Maybe they needed Amanda to grease the wheels first and convince him to meet with them. Fortunately, it wasn't her decision to make. Holt could field that one after she handed him all the information.

"So, Mr. Perry, let's see if we can give Holt an address to go with the name." Hunching over the computer again, she searched his name for matches in Franklin. Several people-finder sites that provided information about individuals returned hits on the name. She clicked on the first such site and waited for the results to appear.

The first possibility was listed simply as "Justin Perry," but he was only nineteen.

"Too young for Amanda's Mr. Perry," Chloe noted, and continued scrolling. The next entry was "Justin K. Perry," but at seventy-two he couldn't be a match either. She continued clicking on each name in succession, but none of them were the Justin Perry she was looking for. After the last listing for various forms of 'Justin Perry,' the site began suggesting similar names as possibly being relevant to her search. She sifted through the "Justin" and "Perry" permutations before finding one halfway down the list for a Justin P. Roberts, thirty-seven years old. The age sounded about right. Maybe 'P' stood for Perry.

She opened another window and searched Justin P. Roberts, Franklin, Tennessee. The top hit was for a licensed therapist with an office in downtown Franklin. She clicked on the link.

A black and white professional photo of the same man listed as Justin Perry on Facebook filled up one quarter of her screen as the website for Justin P. Roberts, licensed therapist, opened. It was definitely him. He must have used his middle name as a last name on Facebook in order to keep the page somewhat private. It made sense, given that he was a therapist. He wouldn't want clients stumbling onto his personal page too easily.

Her nerves firing, she clicked back to the people-finder site and ordered a full report on him for $1.95. When the report finally generated, it gave his latest address as 239 Breakstone Way, Franklin, Tennessee. According to Google Maps it was only fifteen minutes away.

"Nicely done," she told herself, already thinking about how satisfying it would be to tell Holt she had not only found Amanda, but also her mystery man.

Out of curiosity she returned to Justin's Facebook page to get a better sense of the man, and maybe gain some insight as to how they could best approach him. She noticed that the latest post was from just that morning—a photo of him standing in front of what was, presumably, his home. He stood beside a Lexus sedan, his arms in the air, giving the thumbs up. The caption read, "T minus one hour. Beach bound—Destin here I come!" She squinted at the photo. The time of the post was just twenty minutes earlier.

"You've got to be kidding me," Chloe groaned. This guy looked like he was about to leave for the beach any minute and Holt was stuck in court all morning. They were going to miss him.

Unless she did something about it.

FORTY-SIX

Holt checked his phone again, just to make sure it was in silent mode. The federal courthouse may have relaxed its rules about bringing cell phones inside, but it had a zero-tolerance policy on noise from them. He had been witness to more than one attorney getting dressed down in open court and slapped with a fine. Justice Janice Nixon, United States District Court Judge for the Middle District of Tennessee, was no different. If anything, she was considered more unforgiving than most. Consequently, the triple check of the phone.

The large open room was packed with attorneys waiting for their turn on the motion docket. The scent of stale coffee punctuated the air along with pockets of nose-hair-singeing aftershave worn by several of the more senior lawyers. A steady rumble of hushed whispering issued from the gallery, a droning background for whatever arguments were being made before the bench at any given time. Unfortunately, Holt's case was at the bottom of the docket, which meant he would be lucky to get called before lunch.

Holt represented the plaintiff in a lawsuit filed against her employer, claiming the company had intentionally failed to promote her because she was a woman. It wasn't the typical kind of case he handled, but he had caught it because the plaintiff's husband was a friend of his. After depositions, the company had filed the present motion for summary judgment, seeking to have the case dismissed. Holt had promised to call his client once he had a better idea of when the case would be called, hoping to spare her unnecessary hours on the gallery's hard wooden benches. Reconciling himself to a long wait, he pulled his cell out again to see if Chloe had texted him. She hadn't, but there was a text from Pax.

Call me ASAP.

Slipping out the back of the courtroom, Holt found a somewhat private corner in the marbled hallway and called Pax.

"Hey, man. It's me. What's up?"

"You know that corpse? The one from the Donner site?"

"Yeah," Holt answered impatiently.

"Well, they got the DNA back on it."

Holt's gut hummed. "And?"

"And I need to know if you're planning on buying my breakfast tomorrow."

"If this is good, I'll buy it for a week. Spill."

"Dude's name was Joe Bellamy. He's not from here. Hails from New Jersey. Or New York. Can't remember."

"You can't remember?"

"Yeah, whatever. They were sayin' a lot."

"Okay. Fine. What else?"

"The word 'mob' was mentioned."

Holt turned towards the wall, angling for more privacy. "As in, the *mob* mob?" he said, his words hushed.

"As in, like, the Sopranos, yeah."

"What mob? From where?"

"That's all they said."

"Did they happen to say anything about how Bellamy's body ended up in a waste drum on Donner's property?"

"Nope. But, they did say it looked like it had been in there a couple weeks. And, turns out, they found a bullet in the drum. They figure it fell out when the body decomposed. Acid did a pretty good number on the guy's—"

"But nothing else? Nothing that points to who did it?"

"Nope. Sorry. At least, nothing they mentioned."

"Did Sims come up?"

"Nope."

"Okay. Thanks. Keep me posted."

"Uh-huh. I'll be expecting that breakfast."

"Yeah," Holt said, tapping to end the call. He shoved the cell phone in his pocket and strode back into the courtroom, wondering how far he would have to dig into Donner's affairs before finding a tie to Bellamy and whether, if he pulled on it, he would find Elise Banyon and Vettner-Drake at the other end.

FORTY-SEVEN

The directions Chloe had pulled off the internet indicated that Justin Roberts's house was only fifteen minutes from Reese's place. But it seemed to take forever to get there as Chloe turned off Highway 96 West and continued down a series of winding country lanes leading, it felt like, to the middle of nowhere.

It was a beautiful nowhere, though, with brisk cerulean skies crowning open fields of snowy popcorn-like cotton begging for harvest. Chloe's Civic floated over the winding roadway, golden thickets on both sides towering over her car like sentinels, the tips of their branches stretching towards each other as if playing a game of London Bridge, creating an autumnal tunnel. It almost hurt to drive through it without stopping to photograph the brilliant fall display.

She flew over a rise and felt her stomach drop as if on a rollercoaster. She was going much too fast. But her fear of missing a departing Justin Roberts outweighed her fear of a speeding ticket. So she pressed down harder on the gas and zoomed on.

Her GPS dropped her in front of Roberts's stone-trimmed, French Country style home just seventeen minutes after rocketing away from Reese's house. She exhaled a heavy sigh of relief. Roberts's Lexus was still in the driveway.

Chloe slammed the car door behind her then jogged up the flagstone walk, wasting no time in banging hard on the plank cedar front door. When Roberts yanked it opened suddenly, she had to catch herself to avoid knocking him right in the face.

"Oh, hey, sorry," she apologized, stepping back. Tall and lanky, his pale eyes regarded her with curiosity from behind steel-rimmed glasses. The goatee from his earlier online photos had been shaved off.

"Can I help you?" he asked, standing in the doorway with one arm raised above him, holding the door open just about a foot or so.

"I really, really hope so," Chloe answered, then dove into her story.

*****

"Geez, Amanda…" Justin Roberts groaned, his voice trailing off as he rubbed his face in obvious frustration. He leaned against his porch railing, trying to process what Chloe had just told him. She leaned against the post opposite him and waited.

"She never should have said anything about that conversation. It didn't mean anything. I was just—" He cut himself off, huffing loudly as he searched for what he wanted to say. "It didn't mean anything. She shouldn't have come to you. She's just mad because I threw that glass."

"For what it's worth, she made it pretty clear that she really didn't want to say anything. But I think she realized that in a situation like this, if she could shed light on a murder investigation, it was too important to stay quiet."

"It doesn't shed any light on anything. I was just rambling. I'd had one too many and I shot off at the mouth."

"Amanda disagreed. She thought it sounded like you might know someone with a reason to hurt Donner."

His eyes pierced hers from behind the lenses of his glasses. "She's letting her imagination get the better of her."

Chloe squared her shoulders, refusing to back down. "Did she imagine you saying that you wouldn't put it past your ex-girlfriend to murder Donner?"

Roberts straightened, his nostrils flaring. "I didn't say that exactly. I was mad, okay? At the woman I'd been dating. Things between us ended terribly. There was a lot of animosity. When I said what I said to Amanda, I was just letting off steam."

"But—"

"No," he barked, interrupting her and waving her off. "You know what? I'm sorry, but I don't have to do this. I was on my way out of town and now," he checked his watch, "you're holding me up. I think it's time for you to leave. I don't have anything to say."

"We'll just talk to Amanda again."

"Well, then it'll be her word against mine."

He turned towards the front door, but Chloe caught his arm. He looked down at her grip on the sleeve of his button-down shirt, then flashed his gaze up, his nostrils flaring.

"I get it, Mr. Roberts, I do," she said. "And I'm really sorry for how this happened, I…it wasn't how I wanted to handle it. But I didn't have a choice." He shook her hand off, but stayed put. "This is too important to just forget about. So, you can either talk to me now, or, if you won't then we'll have to expand our investigation and share what little we know with the police and come at it that way. And then this becomes a whole other kind of frustrating. A very public, very official kind of frustrating."

In truth, Chloe had no idea what kind of leverage they had to hold over Justin Roberts's head. For all she knew, her ultimatum had absolutely no teeth. But she was willing to bet that, given his reluctance to talk, just the idea of getting the police involved would escalate things far beyond what Justin Roberts was willing to risk.

The twinge of panic that flittered across Roberts's features told her she was right. "You can't go to the police with this." His face had started to flush and his hands tightened into white-knuckled fists. She had struck a nerve.

"We don't want to do that, Mr. Roberts. Not unless we have to."

"What do you want me to say?"

"We want to know the name of your ex-girlfriend and why you thought she might be mad enough to get rid of Phillip Donner."

"It was just a stupid comment! It was nothing. I didn't mean it."

Chloe shook her head. "It was enough to scare Amanda into seeking us out, so she could tell us about it. From what she said, it sounded like Donner was trying to blackmail this woman into doing something. If you're worried about her finding out that you helped us, we can do our best to keep her from knowing it came from you. We can—"

"No," he seethed, stiff determination in his voice. "I can't. Don't you understand? *I can't.*"

His last words held more than anger. There was desperation in them. Whatever was going on, he was terrified of being forced to disclose it.

"Then we don't have a choice. We'll have to start talking to everyone you know. Trying to find out on our own who you've been dating who might have a connection to Donner. Your friends, family, your co-workers—"

"What? No!" He rubbed his face in his hands. "You can't do that. You just can't." His eyes pleaded with her. "It will ruin my career." He was rigid and pale, his lips clenched together.

What is he so scared of? she thought, her mind churning to come up with a set of circumstances that would put a therapist's career at risk, when it hit her.

Who was strictly off-limits for a therapist when it came to dating?

Chloe eyed him cautiously. "She wasn't a client, was she, Mr. Roberts?"

The chilly silence that met her guess confirmed that she was right.

"So the reason you can't talk about it is because the woman you were dating was someone you were counseling?" His head dropped a few inches, and he closed his eyes in remorse.

Chloe sighed, her shoulders sagging. This complicated matters. There was no way he was going to talk to her. Not unless it was better than the alternative.

"Okay. Just think through this with me. If you talk to me now, if you give me her name, explain what was going on, then maybe we can minimize the impact on you. I know there are rules about client confidentiality, but there are exceptions, aren't there, when a crime is involved? If you talk to us, we can keep you out of it as much as possible—I mean, I can't promise the relationship won't come out, but there's less chance of exposure than if we go rummaging around in your life—"

"No, it's not like that." He cut her off, his repudiation a sharp bark. "The problem—the issue she had with Donner—it wasn't something I learned about while counseling her. This isn't a client confidentiality problem. It was…a different kind of situation."

"Okay, what kind of situation?" Chloe pressed.

Justin's stature deflated even more, and he looked away for a moment, out over the yard, to the field across the street where white fences corralled a meadow of ash-black cows. He scratched his chin, maybe absentmindedly reaching for the goatee that was no longer there. His shoulders seemed to cave a little more in surrender.

"You realize that the board might have my license over this—dating a client?" He heaved a sigh. "What I tell you, I'm only telling you because I think it'll be worse if I don't. It'll be bad if I do, but..." He shook his head, letting the thought go unfinished. "Of all the ways I thought this might come back to bite me—this wasn't even on the list."

Chloe waited silently for him to continue.

"If this is going to come out, I don't want to get dragged through some investigation and I sure don't want it to look like I'm not cooperating. It's bad enough without that."

"Okay, so talk to me. What was this...situation...that your ex-girlfriend had?"

He snorted, as if she had said something funny. "That's just it. I *am* the situation."

"What's that supposed to mean?"

"It means that she wasn't just a client. She's a married client."

Chloe's eyebrows shot up. "Oh."

"Yeah. Exactly."

"And you were their marriage counselor?"

"What? No!" he denied quickly, almost sounding insulted by the insinuation. "Just hers. But the licensing board still won't like it."

Chloe ignored the comment and charged on. "So why would you having an affair with this woman create a situation for her with Donner?"

"Because Donner threatened to use the fact of our affair against her if she didn't cooperate with him. Said he would ruin her reputation, her career—not to mention her family."

"Cooperate? Cooperate how?"

"Don't know. She didn't say. Just told me to stay far away from her. Acted like I'd been blabbing about our relationship—which was ridiculous because it would've hurt me as much as her."

"How was this going to ruin her career?"

"She's running for an open judgeship next term. Something like that comes out and you don't stand a chance in a primary, forget the actual election."

Chloe's instincts pinged as she cocked her head. "She's running for judge?"

"Yeah," he said, a knowing look pinching his face as he recognized the comprehension in Chloe's eyes. "If you work for Sims, then you know her."

Chloe's stomach took a tumble. "Cecilia Tucker?"

"Yeah. I figured you'd met her."

"Yeah," she replied, her mouth suddenly dry. Chloe's mind raced as she tried to process what this meant, thinking of the lunch she and Holt had shared with Cecilia at Puckett's, and the woman's flat denial of knowing anything about Donner outside of Sims's lawsuit. "We've met."

"For what it's worth," he started, shifting uncomfortably, "I really don't think she's involved in what happened to Donner. We ended things very badly, and I really was just blowing off steam with what I said to Amanda." He eyed Chloe meaningfully, as if impressing the truth of his words on her before letting his gaze drift back to the fields, leaving Chloe to digest what this revelation really meant.

It meant that Holt had been right. It meant that Cecilia Tucker, Esquire, had been hiding something from them that day in Puckett's.

An honest-to-goodness motive for murder.

FORTY-EIGHT

"Come on, come on!" Chloe griped impatiently at the unanswered ringing sounding through her car's wireless audio as she sped down the road away from Roberts's place. The wind had picked up, sending crunchy, coppery leaves across her path just before her car tore through them, leaving them to dance in her wake.

Finally, Holt's voice came over the speakers. "Hey, how're you doing?"

"Hey, I can't believe I got you. I thought I'd have to leave a message."

"I got out early. Arguments were continued to another day—again. I'm headed to the office now. I've got some news to catch you up on. There's been a development in Donner's case."

"Well, I've got news of my own," she bested him, "and you're not going to like it."

It took her only a couple of minutes to deliver the short version of her finding and confronting Justin Roberts. When she told Holt about Cecilia Tucker, he cursed under his breath.

"I knew she was hiding something. But I never would have guessed it'd be something like this. This is serious stuff. She could be in real trouble." Disappointment tinged with concern curdled his voice. "Keeping something like that quiet? Blackmail, or whatever it was Donner was doing to her? And continuing to represent Sims?"

"I'm sorry. I know you two are friends."

He groaned. "Well, I thought we were."

"What about you? What did you find out?'

"No, look, I'll bring you up to speed when I get there. I need to think this through right now. Map out the implications in my head and figure out where we go next with this. Can you meet me at the office in twenty?"

"Sure."

Holt clicked off without another word. His abruptness surprised her.

This is hitting him harder than I—

Suddenly a violent impact at the rear of the car slammed Chloe into her seat, her head snapping into the headrest. She screamed as her gaze flipped up to the rearview mirror just in time for another jarring whack. As she grabbed the wheel to steady herself, she accidentally wrenched it to the right, causing her car to swerve onto shoulder of the road. She ripped the wheel back to the left, correcting the car's trajectory, then twisted, looking over her right shoulder to get a better look at who had hit her.

Nothing. But as soon as she registered that, she heard something roaring up on her left. She twisted in that direction, catching a brief view in her side mirror of a darkish blur as it slammed into her left flank, sending her into a spin. She had a fleeting glimpse of what might have been a sedan, flying away through the tunnel of orange foliage, before careening off the pavement.

* * * * *

Elise Banyon lowered herself into the supple, burgundy leather chair situated behind her desk and extinguished a cigarette in the smokeless ashtray beside the phone. The gadget was supposed to remove the majority of the smoke and odor before it ever permeated the room. But it never did the job completely. The smoking was a bad habit she had never been able to kick since starting in the parking lot of Beaumont High School as a junior in 1973. Over the years she had done away with two other vices, three husbands, and eight business partners. But smoking was one thing she had never been strong enough to cut out of her life.

This cigarette was her fifth of the morning. One might think that the repeated indulgence was a sign of heavy stress. But Banyon didn't get stressed when under pressure. She just got busy. And that's what she had been since arriving in the Memphis offices of Banyon Associates at six o'clock that morning.

Handling client needs, all sorts of needs, was the core of Banyon Associates' business, but it was difficult to pin down exactly what the firm did. The business license labeled Banyon Associates as a firm that provided "business strategy counseling services," but that was really too vanilla a description. Businesses and individuals came to her, by referral only of course, when something untenable crossed their path—some matter that the client couldn't, wouldn't or shouldn't handle. Always these situations required finesse, but sometimes, something more. Something akin to pressure. Perhaps that was the best way to describe the work she did here. She was a pressure placer. A compliance ensurer. A wheel greaser. She stepped in to make things happen for her clients. Or to keep them from happening. A conversation with a certain senator. A private meeting between competitive businesses. Providing a name here. Facilitating a payment there. She didn't cross lines that would get her in trouble with the law. At least not directly. And never on paper. Having been an attorney once-upon-a-time, she was quite savvy regarding how to avoid those sorts of complications.

Vettner-Drake had her on special retainer. The kind where they paid a premium to call on her services any hour of any day. So when Eli Drake contacted her at closing time several days ago about an upstart criminal defense attorney in Franklin who was threatening to poke around in their business, she had hopped on a flight and taken action. Her price for being on call to finesse a situation was high. But money had never been a problem for Vettner-Drake, or for its parent company.

She ran a hand along the neckline of her navy, Escada sheath dress until reaching the sharply-carved gold pin fixed above her heart, or at least, what some people would say passed for one. The piece was Italian, something she had procured on her trip to Milan last year, and she fingered it as she eyed the clock on her computer. It read *12:14*. He had said to expect the call at 12:15. And if he was anything, he was punctual.

The phone rang just as the clock ticked over.

*****

Chloe opened her eyes. Her heart raced frantically, and she grabbed her chest, willing it to slow down before it exploded. Sucking in a huge gulp of air, she shivered as she looked up to get her bearings. The car had come to rest on her side of the road, but facing the wrong direction. Somehow she had missed the telephone pole six yards up and the ditch just a few yards back. She hadn't struck anything and the airbags had not deployed. *Thank you, Lord. Thank you.*

She turned in her seat, snapping her eyes to where the other car had raced away, hoping to get a look at it. But it was long gone, having disappeared around the next rise and bend in the old country road. She would have no helpful description to give of the car or the driver. It had all happened so fast.

She took an inventory of herself, checking limbs for injury, but all seemed fine. Cracking open the driver's door, she looked to see if the same was true for her Civic. It wasn't, although it wasn't as bad as she expected. There was a shallow bowl-like dent just above and behind the rear wheel on the driver's side. There were a few deep gouges running the length of the dent, and several lesser scratches. Chloe leaned in closer. Inside a few of the gouges there were dark marks—black, or maybe dark gray or navy—which were probably paint marks from the other car. She surveyed the bumper, but those dents were smaller and there were no paint marks that she could see.

She thought about what would happen when she told Holt about this. He would definitely refuse to let her keep helping on the case. And Jack—well, he would want her out too. Not to mention that it would likely prompt him to come right back to Franklin. For the wrong reasons.

She leaned against the car, still trying to catch her breath. *Maybe they don't need to know*, she thought. It wasn't like the police could do anything. The best description they would get from her and the marks left on her car was that the culprit was a dark grey, blue or black 'sedan-ish' vehicle. There were no gas stations or traffic cameras around to help with identification. So even if she reported it, they weren't going to find the guy—or girl for that matter. And she would bring a whole lot of grief on herself.

Keeping quiet about it makes the most sense, she thought as she got back in the car and slammed the door shut. She went to crank the engine, and noticed her hands were shaking. The post-accident shell shock was setting in. She leaned back against the headrest and inhaled a deep, calming breath from her gut. After a few moments, she tried again, and the engine turned over on the first try.

*****

"I understand you were successful in making contact." The statement was actually more of a question, delivered by him in that intentionally tempered New Jersey accent of his.

"Yes," Banyon replied, fingering her pin as she cradled the phone between her ear and shoulder.

"And you think that you made your point?"

She sniffed, leaning forward in her chair. "I got their attention. They've seen what they need to see to start moving in some other direction."

"And have they?"

His imperious tone annoyed her, as it always did. She wasn't one of his hired hands. She was exponentially more critical to the organization than he was, as she was the handler for every single one of their investments in the southern region. Not to mention that she had twenty-five years of age and skill on him. But, he signed her checks, so for now she tolerated him, just like she would when the next guy stepped in to replace him.

"We'll have to wait and watch. The lawyer exhibited a good deal of bravado at the meeting, but I think he was just saving face. He hasn't made further inquiries since."

"That you know of."

"Correct."

"Stay ahead of this, Banyon."

"Absolutely."

He cleared his throat. "There's been a development with Bellamy. His mother just received a notification from the locals. He's dead."

"The body on the construction site."

"Yes. So what's your take on things now?"

"Not much has really changed. When Bellamy's cell showed him headed for Florida weeks ago, we assumed that was his attempt to misdirect us. We weren't wrong about that. We were just wrong about who was doing the misdirecting. Obviously, we know now it wasn't Bellamy. So we'll just have to step up our investigation before this gets away from us."

"Get a handle on it," he demanded. "And be prepared in case Bellamy's identification throws some heat our way. We could get calls from investigators looking into his connections. If we do, we're clean on our end, so it shouldn't be a problem unless the local connection where you are presents a risk."

"No. There's no paper trail, no risk. Someone would have to know what they're looking for or they could stare at it all day and never see it. It's under control."

"It had better be," he remarked flatly, his tone leaving no room for error.

FORTY-NINE

Cecilia Tucker's law offices were situated in a 1920s bungalow that, like so many others in the Downtown Franklin Historic District, had been renovated on the interior to serve as a commercial building. Eggshell-tinted walls and stately mahogany furniture spanned the lobby, perpetuating the historic feel, while a pairing of geometrically patterned rust and navy Persian rugs blanketed the original dark wood flooring.

"Hey, you two," she exclaimed, smiling pleasantly at Holt and Chloe as she entered the lobby from the hallway that led into the rest of the building. She eyed Chloe with concern. "How's your Dad doing?"

"He's better, thanks," Chloe said. "They tell us he might be able to come home soon. Maybe early next week."

A look of genuine relief washed over Cecilia. "Oh, that's great. Really. I'd like to visit, if I could, after he's feeling up to it?"

"I'm sure he'd like that," Chloe replied.

Cecilia glanced down at her rose gold Apple watch. "So Alison said you needed a minute? I'm supposed to be in court at 1:30, and I still need to prep, but I can talk if we can keep it short."

"Sure," Holt replied, nodding.

"Okay, come on back," she said, turning her back to them and leading them down the hallway that took them past the conference rooms to her office at the rear.

"Sorry I don't have longer," she apologized as they entered her office, motioning for Chloe and Holt to take the rice-hued linen wingback chairs opposite her desk, "but you know what it's like." She gently pushed the office door closed and stepped around to her desk chair. She dropped into it and removed her tortoise shell Kate Spade glasses from her face, setting them on the leather desk blotter. "So I'm guessing you need a word about Sims? Did something come up?"

Holt leveled his gaze at her. "Tell me about Justin Roberts."

Cecilia's smile evaporated instantaneously. The air bristled with tension for several seconds before she finally responded with a petrified whisper. "Who?"

"Let's not do this, Cecilia."

More silence. "Do what?" A slight quiver invaded her words.

"This. This little dance, or whatever. We've talked to him. We know about the affair."

What little color was left drained from Cecilia's face. For a moment she bowed up, as if preparing to go on the offensive, but then caved in upon herself, her head dropping low. "That idiot."

"That's rich," Holt fired sharply.

Cecilia cut her eyes to Holt. They begged for a reprieve. "You don't understand. This…it was impossible. There was no way…If Justin had just kept his mouth shut—"

"You should have opened yours, Cecilia! You should have said something about what was going on."

"Why in the world would I do that? You know what a scandal would do to my political chances. If the affair had come out—"

"The affair? That's what you're worried about? That's just the tip of the iceberg, Cecilia." Holt shook his head. "Come on."

Cecilia bit her lip, seemingly trying to judge what or how much to say next. "What do you mean?"

Holt's eyebrows shot up beseechingly, begging her to come clean.

"What?" she barked desperately. "What did Justin tell you?"

Holt sniffed, shaking his head in surrender. "That Donner knew about the affair. That he used it as blackmail to manipulate you in Sims's civil case. What—did he ask you to throw it? Take a dive on the motions, on the arguments in front of the judge? That's it, isn't it? He wanted you to throw the case, or he would go public about the affair?"

Cecilia brushed a wisp of hair back, stalling. When her eyes flitted back to Holt, they were full of resolve. "Did you have to bring her for this?" she asked, tottering her head towards Chloe. "It's hard enough. I would have expected more from you."

"I could say the same." His words carried a hard edge to them, uncharacteristic for Holt, and a testimony to how deeply this disappointment had cut him. When Cecilia again held her silence, he charged forward. "And yeah, I brought her. Because it's *her* father that's laid up in the hospital and *her* kid sister and brother that are being threatened because of this mess, so, yeah, I brought her."

Shock rippled over Cecilia's features. "I had nothing—nothing—to do with any of that. This," she waved a hand through the air, "has nothing to do with what happened to Reese."

"You don't know that."

"No. Look, I do. Donner came to me right after I took Sims's case. He confronted me about the affair, which, by the way, had happened over a year before that. It was short and stupid and I walked away from it, but…somehow, Donner found out. And, yes, he told me that if I didn't throw Sims's case, if I didn't pave the way for him to win, he would call the papers about me and Justin. And," she said, holding a hand in front of her, "before you ask me why I didn't just get off the case—Donner also said that if I did that he would call the papers, too."

"Okay, but then why didn't you say something? To someone? Someone that could have helped?"

"Because I would have had to admit the affair and if that got out, it would have ruined me. And not just because it might have kept me from winning the election. It would have utterly destroyed my family. You worked here, Holt. You've been around me enough to know that D.B. and I, we've had a lot of problems over the years. I tried to hide it, but I know people could see it. I've heard the talk. We came this close," she held her forefinger and thumb a half inch apart, "to divorcing more than once. But then we got a wakeup call through the kids. The conflict was killing them. Trip and Keeley were falling apart. School, friends, everything. They needed us to work. So we hunkered down and made the best of it. We even got counseling—not from Justin," she shot, anticipating the question, "and it was working. We were actually close to being happy, I think. Still are."

"Until Donner."

She shrugged defeatedly. "The thing with Justin happened when I was at a real low point. He was the counselor I was seeing before D.B. and I decided to work things out. Back then, D.B. was—" she sighed, stopping herself, "well, it doesn't matter. But I wasn't looking for it. It just happened. And it was over within weeks. We're doing okay now, but if D.B. finds out that I had an affair, he won't be able to let that go. My family will be done. Over. And it would destroy my kids."

"But," Holt reiterated, squeezing his eyes shut and rubbing his temples as if fending off a tension headache, "you agreed to *throw a case.*" He punched each word, every syllable a staccato indictment of her failure.

"No," she blurted, leaning into the desk as if trying to physically draw him into her perspective on things. "That's the thing—I didn't. I never gave Donner an answer. I'm not even sure he was waiting for one. I think he just expected me to capitulate. I was trying to buy time to think it through and also hoping for a miracle. I thought, if I got lucky, maybe Sims would drop the suit, or maybe, I don't know, Donner would move on, before we ever had the first hearing. But that didn't happen, and I knew I couldn't do what he was asking. So I went to the hearing and did what I was supposed to and represented Sims to the best of my ability."

"And Donner wasn't going to let that go," Holt surmised.

Cecilia shook her head. "No. He threatened me again, right there on the courthouse steps after the hearing. We didn't get the temporary injunction, but it wasn't because I didn't try my hardest. I'd done a good job and he knew it. But I flat out told him I wasn't going to do what he wanted. I was going to let the chips fall where they may. After that I just hoped that maybe he wouldn't follow through. That maybe he had bigger fish to fry or something. And then…he got shot."

"And just like that your problem disappeared."

Weak relief enveloped her. "I know. I couldn't believe it."

"But Cecilia," Holt sighed in frustration, "you see the problem, right? It's a textbook motive for murder."

She recoiled in disbelief. "You're not serious."

"I'm defense counsel for a client accused of the murder of the man that you also have a motive for killing. Frankly," he added, gesturing vehemently, "a better motive than my client has. So, yeah, I'm serious."

"You can't use this, Holt. It'll end me."

"You know as well as I do that if I can give the jury an alternative theory to the one the prosecution's pushing, it could help secure a not-guilty verdict. I've got an obligation—"

"No! Just—just get off the case. Let someone else handle it," she argued, her pitch rising, spurred by growing panic.

"What difference would that make? That lawyer would still have to use it. I can't keep this to myself. I hate that you've put me in this position."

"Please," she begged, wetness gathering on her eyelashes. "I didn't kill Phillip Donner. You know that. Just don't, Holt. Just let it go."

"Oh come on, Cecilia! And ruin my career too?" Holt rose and stood back from the chair. He ran a hand through his hair and heaved a sigh. When he looked up, there was something softer about his eyes. "You know that the last thing I would ever want to do is hurt you. But this is out of my hands. You and I both know that this is coming out one way or another."

"I didn't kill Phillip Donner!"

"It doesn't matter if you did or didn't. You had a reason to do it and that's enough. At least maybe enough to give a jury reasonable doubt in Kurt Sims's case."

"For heaven's sake, Holt, they've got evidence that Sims's gun was the murder weapon," she said with a note of pleading.

Holt sighed resignedly. "Yeah, and you're his lawyer—who has been to his house where he kept the gun before it disappeared and became the murder weapon."

They locked eyes for several moments, Cecilia's expression growing increasingly callous when Holt failed to yield.

"Get out," she finally muttered miserably. "Get out, now."

FIFTY

"Are you okay?" Chloe asked, as Holt sped through the square, horns honking to their right as he cut off a Bronco in the outer lane so as not to miss their exit.

"Yeah. Fine." His clipped speech offered evidence to the contrary.

"I know that was hard."

"It's impossible. I've looked up to Cecilia Tucker as an attorney for as long as I can remember. And now, I'm in the position of having to sacrifice her and her family on the altar of my duty to represent Sims." He exhaled. "And it's more twisted than you think."

"Why?"

He swiveled to look at her. "All of that," he swirled his index finger in circles, "back there? That doesn't just mean that Cecilia presents an alternative suspect theory. Think about it. What are the primary reasons people commit murder?"

"I don't know…what…money? Revenge. Jealousy. To protect themselves—"

"Exactly. Cecilia arguably could have killed Donner to shut him up, to protect her career and marriage. Who else might have wanted that same thing?"

"Her husband? That is, if he had actually known about the affair and that Donner was using it as blackmail."

Holt nodded. "Exactly."

"But he didn't know about the affair. He didn't know what Donner was threatening."

"As far as Cecilia knew. But what if she was wrong? Or what if she's lying to protect him? What if he did know about Roberts? Donner found out about him somehow. What if D.B. did too?"

"But that doesn't make sense. If D.B. knew about all of it, why would he kill Donner? Why wouldn't he have just left Cecilia like she said he would?" Chloe clenched the arm rest when Holt braked unexpectedly to avoid running over a couple of millennials who had decided to cross in the middle of the street.

"Geez, people. Come on," Holt groaned, waving them across, his eyebrows raised in condemnation. "Maybe he would have. Or maybe he would have envisioned that leaving would have destroyed his kids, just like Cecilia believed it would." He pressed on the gas. "Imagine—D.B.'s bent on keeping his family together, but knows that Donner's out there, waiting to drop a bomb on the public that will embarrass and humiliate his already emotionally struggling kids. Not to mention ruining the career ambitions of his wife, which would likely crumble Cecilia, gutting any stability they've managed to achieve in their relationship. But take Donner out of the picture, and whoosh," Holt waved a hand across the windshield, "the slate is clean."

"That's a stretch, don't you think?"

"Maybe," he conceded. "But my job is to hand a jury as many options as I can. A guy deciding to avoid the demolition of his marriage and his kids with one bullet? I could sell that."

"You're serious?"

"It's all about options. The more options the jury has, the less certain they can be about Sims." He scowled. "Normally, this kind of alternative theory would really get my blood pumping. Two other people with a motive, and one, if not both, with access to the murder weapon and the ability to frame Sims? It'd be Christmas come early." He paused. "But these are my friends."

"So…not great."

"Yeah. Not great. And it will kill Reese." He rocked his head back and forth, considering something. "On the upside, now we've also got Roberts."

She eyed him skeptically. "Roberts? Really? As a suspect? I mean, I know that what he did would look bad professionally, but is that a reason to kill someone?"

"He's a counselor who had an affair with a client mid-treatment. I can't imagine the licensing board would just let him off scot-free.

Even if they didn't take his license, they would make sure he was sanctioned. And the sanction would be public information. Searchable. Roberts would be finished in the counseling arena. Who's gonna seek treatment from a guy who has affairs with the wives he's supposed to be helping? If Donner had lived to tell his tale, Roberts's career trajectory would take a nosedive."

"But there's no real proof that any of them—Roberts, Cecilia or D.B—are involved."

"I don't have to prove it, Chloe. I've just got to plant a seed." When she pressed her lips together tightly and narrowed her eyebrows in response, he smiled sadly. "You're disappointed."

"No, I…" Her words tapered off, and she shrugged. "It just seems a little—"

"Wrong?" he offered, helping her out.

"Yeah, maybe."

A wan smile crossed his mouth. "Welcome to the juxtaposition of being a criminal defense lawyer. Wrong in this situation would be ignoring what we've learned in the last couple hours. Wrong would be not doing everything I can to secure a not-guilty verdict for Sims. You're mistaking me for a truth-teller, Chloe. I'm not."

"So what are you?"

"I told you—I'm an option-presenter."

"Still, officer of the court and all that."

"Look, I'm not going to lie or put on evidence I know to be false. That, most definitely, would be wrong. Under any paradigm. I'm going to lay out possible versions of what happened to counter the one version the prosecution is pushing. It's up to the jury to weigh them all and cull the truth from it. It's the only way the system works."

Chloe fidgeted. "I started helping you because I wanted to find the person responsible for the attack on Reese and all the threats against my family. I wanted to make sure that they're safe."

"And?"

"And you think this is the way to do that?"

"Well, I think I have an ethical obligation to represent Sims. And I think as we do that, as we keep rattling cages and following bread crumbs, hopefully, we'll shake out the guilty party. That is, if the assault and threats against your family are, in fact, actually connected to this case. I told you when this started, it's possible they're not."

"But, it makes the most sense that they would be."

Holt nodded. "It does. After everything that's happened, that's where my money would be."

"And what if we're just confusing things. What if it turns out Sims *is* guilty? That he's responsible for it all?"

Holt exhaled laboriously. "Why would Sims attack Reese and demand that we stop helping him when we're all he has going for him?"

"You said it yourself. Misdirection."

"I said the prosecution would *argue* that as a possibility," Holt said dismissively, "but I don't for a second believe Sims would actually do that. If we just keep doing our job, and we do it well, hopefully, the truth will come out. And if it does turn out that the threats against your family aren't related to Sims's case, then we'll just keep digging till we figure it out." His eyes locked on hers, his expression carrying the gravity of one making an oath. "I promise you that."

She let that sit for a few moments, marinating in the sound of Rush's "Tom Sawyer" playing quietly over the speakers on one of the satellite stations. "So what happens now?"

"Whatever we're going to do, we've got to move fast," he declared, braking a little too hard at the light and jarring Chloe forward again.

She eyed him dubiously. "How about I drive next time?"

He didn't respond to her jab, though a brief smile, appreciative of her sarcasm, flashed across his face. "Look, we can't let this sit. I've got a feeling Cecilia isn't going to wait for this to just explode in her face. If she really thinks I'm going to use it, she'll break the news to D.B. first. If that happens before we get to him, we won't have a chance to feel him out and see what he knows, if anything, before he's aware of what we're doing. I'm guessing she'll wait a couple of days in the hopes that I'll change my mind." He turned into the office driveway. "So we're going to have to figure out a way to get you in front of him by then without tipping off either of them."

"Me?"

"If I do it, he'll know something's weird, even if he isn't involved in this. He and I wouldn't have a reason to chat like that. But you? Pretty journalist? Doing an article on Franklin? It would be right up his alley."

"Why?"

"Well, one—pretty journalist. Two—free publicity. Record producers love free publicity. His studio recorded a song this year that almost made the Billboard Country Music Chart. He's on his way up and looking for exposure. You show up with a camera and he'll talk for hours," Holt said, shifting the car into park and rotating towards her. "Think you can handle that?"

She nodded, thinking that if he knew about the car that had run her off the road that morning, he wouldn't be letting her anywhere near D.B. Tucker.

"I also heard back from my private investigator. He's making headway on the names they gave us at Claire Donner's house and on this Joe Bellamy person, as well as Banyon's situation." Before leaving for Cecilia's office, Holt had explained to Chloe the information Pax had shared about Bellamy and the possible mob connection. "He said he would have a report for me soon. If we get lucky and find a link between Donner and any of it, we may have another potential suspect."

"I really don't get how that fits into all this. I have a hard time seeing Cecilia Tucker being involved with stuffing a body in an oil drum."

"Yeah. Well, I have a hard time seeing her doing any of it, but that doesn't matter. Maybe they're connected, and maybe not, but we don't know enough at this point to make assumptions about anything."

Chloe nodded.

"My gut says that Bellamy is part of the reason Vettner-Drake and Banyon didn't want us looking too closely into their relationship with Donner. But if we want to know what's really going on, we have to keep digging."

"So for now we just follow the bread crumbs?" Chloe asked.

"Exactly. And hope they lead us right to the witch's front door."

FIFTY-ONE

"Hey, hold still!" Chloe laughed, leveling the camera at Emma one more time. "I can't get the shot."

Emma had left school early as planned, and now stood about ten feet in front of Chloe in a vintage clothing booth at the Franklin Antique Mall, modeling a 1930s charcoal-gray cloche. The mall was twelve thousand square feet of home decor, vintage pieces, and antiques housed in a stand-alone brick building on Second Avenue, just a couple of blocks off the square. The nearly two hundred-year-old structure once served as Franklin's ice house, and before that, a flour mill, and was dripping with the kind of charm that would fit perfectly in Chloe's article.

"What do you think? Is it me?" Emma teased, puckering her lips and tossing a dramatic runway look at Chloe's lens, tugging on the bell-shaped hat just beneath the felt magnolia blossom that adorned its lower edge.

Chloe snorted. "You're a natural. Not sure the hat goes with your jeans, though," she said, casting a nod at the half-dozen fraying rips in Emma's black denim.

Emma wrinkled her nose. "Yeah, probably not," she agreed, replacing the hat on the cherry hall tree she had taken it from.

"Here, grab that," Chloe said, gesturing toward the tripod that held her strobe flash. "I saw a grouping of grandfather and cuckoo clocks in one of the booths down that left side when I scouted this place. I think I could do something with that."

"So is this what you do?" Emma asked, lifting the tripod. "Travel around taking photos of places other people want to go?"

"Well…sort of. What I'm actually trying to do is find new places for them to go. Places they might not have considered. They see my article in our magazine, and then maybe they decide they want to go there."

"And you get paid for that?" she asked, following Chloe as she moved down the aisle.

"In a manner of speaking," Chloe said, thinking of her meager salary. "It's not the best paying job in the world, but I do get to travel for free."

"What's the farthest place you've ever been?"

"New Zealand. Hands down. Twenty-three hours on flights and in airports."

"It'd be worth it to travel like that. I'd do anything to get out of here."

"Really?" Chloe challenged as they walked between the rows of treasures. "I kind of like it here. Seems like a cool place to grow up. Wait, it's right here," she said, as they reached the booth with the clocks. Chloe pointed to a spot in the aisle. "Set it up there."

Emma followed Chloe's directions, talking while she worked. "Franklin's fine," she conceded, securing the tripod legs. "I just don't ever get to leave. I'm stuck in this town, Dad's busy all the time, I'm always babysitting my little brother. It's brain-numbing."

"See, this interests me," Chloe said, lowering her camera and momentarily pausing from determining her shot angle, "because when I was a teenager, Reese wasn't around at all. I have no idea what he's like as a parent. Take…I don't know…dinner. Is he ever there? Or does he always miss it for work?"

"No, he's there, but it's all last minute, you know? Rolling in at six o'clock with whatever he's picked up on the way home."

"Okay, what about weekends?"

Emma huffed, lowering herself onto the edge of an old steamer trunk. "Completely boring. We don't *do* anything. He sits in that dining room he calls an office and works pretty much non-stop, unless Tyler's got a game or something."

"And what about your stuff? Your games or whatever. Does he go to that?"

"No. I mean, he did, when I was younger and had events—dance and stuff. I'm kind of not into the whole 'organized activity thing' right now."

Chloe considered Emma, clearly trying to decide how to navigate the next bit of their conversation. "See," she started, "here's the thing. The Reese I knew when I was a kid was never around. There was no dinner. Not at six. Not at seven. Not ever. And he sure never thought about us enough to care whether we had dinner made or to bring anything home. And he didn't have an office in our house. Come to think of it, I don't remember ever seeing him work on anything at home, because he left for his law office before I woke up and always got back home after I was in bed. I was in dance class from the age of three, and he never came to a single recital."

She paused, and when Emma didn't stop her, she continued. "I know you've had a horrible time with your mom leaving. Nobody should have to deal with that, and I know exactly what that's like. But the thing is, in your case, Reese stayed. He did the right and hard thing and raised you guys alone. Single parenting is brutal. My mom couldn't do it. Tate and I, we ended up in foster care."

Emma's mouth dropped slightly in disbelief. "You did?"

Chloe nodded. "But the point is—you didn't. You have a dad who loves you and is there for you. Reese is doing the best he can, and if that means take-out at six o'clock or working at home so he doesn't have to be gone all night and all weekend, well, that's not the worst thing in the world."

Emma pressed her lips together, processing that. "That's awful, what he did to you. I can't believe you even came here to see him. Why didn't you just tell him off and leave?"

Chloe shrugged. "I was going to. But, I don't know…it changed once I met him. For one thing, I found out about you and Tyler. And then…I guess…when I finally met Reese, when I actually had a conversation with him and saw him with you guys, I realized that the person I knew once upon a time just isn't here anymore. Your dad, the man Reese is now, he's different. He's trying. And from what I can see, and from what Holt tells me, he's doing a pretty good job by you and Tyler."

Emma grunted contentiously.

"I know he's far from perfect. But he is present."

"Okay, but even if he's changed," Emma pressed, "how do you forgive something like that? Something that awful? I don't know how you can stand to be around him."

"Well, it isn't always comfortable," Chloe admitted, "but I am trying to forgive him. I'm kind of…working through the process. You're right, though. It's not easy."

"I couldn't do it."

"Well, a year ago I wouldn't have been able to do it either."

"So why can you now?"

"A lot changed in the last year."

"Like what?"

Like everything, Chloe thought. "Jack and I…we met during a crazy time. Tate had, um, done some stupid things that got me in a lot of trouble."

Emma's eyebrows perked. "What kind of things?"

"He had…taken some stuff that some really bad people wanted back."

"Bad people, like criminal people?"

Chloe nodded as the clocks began a staggered chorale of various tunes, announcing it was three o'clock.

"No way."

"Yeah. But Jack helped me through it. And when things got really scary and I was struggling to keep it together, Jack told me about what helps him hold it together when everything's a mess."

"Which is?"

"His faith. Something about that surrender gives him peace, even when things are incredibly hard. Not that he still doesn't hurt," she added, thinking of his recent exit, "or struggle or sometimes do stupid things, but somehow, it's all just…different when you're also trusting God in those moments. It gives you another perspective."

"It sounds a little too easy," Emma said skeptically.

"That's what I thought. But eventually, after seeing the difference it made for him, I decided I wanted that peace too. And I was surprised as anybody to find out it actually exists."

Chloe let her words resonate for a moment, a thoughtful silence passing between her and Emma. As the teen actually seemed to be pondering Chloe's words, she let her be, and began snapping shots of the gilded clocks from multiple angles.

"I saw you," Emma finally remarked after a few minutes, shifting on the trunk to face Chloe better. "In the hospital when we visited Dad. You were eyeing that hospital chapel when we left."

"Yeah, well, praying helps me. And I definitely need all the help I can get because, like you said, forgiving the man that abandoned me is not easy. And," she said, standing as she clicked one last photo of a particularly old grandfather clock, "not something I would naturally do. But I keep feeling like, if God can forgive me for the things I've done, then who am I to deny Reese the same?" She glanced down the way at a booth showcasing a number of vintage bridal gowns and tossed her head in their direction. "What do you think? Would they make an interesting shot?"

Emma sucked in a breath and squinted at the dresses, holding her fingers up like a makeshift viewfinder. "Yeah, I could see it."

"Okay, come on then. Grab the light."

They moved about twenty feet down and Emma busied herself resetting the light, talking while she worked. "So…Jack."

Chloe smiled at the girl's less than subtle change of subject. "Yesss?"

"Holt said he's a Navy SEAL. And that he works on movies."

A faint but proud smile crested Chloe's mouth. "Yeah. Funny how those are the two things that always seem to stick with everyone."

"So has he ever introduced you to somebody famous?"

Chloe clicked her cheek in mock dismay. "Not yet, but I'm holding out for Chris Pratt."

Emma snorted, a dry chuckle escaping. "So if he's so amazing, why are you having problems?"

Tiny shockwaves of surprise coursed through Chloe, and she stopped checking her light meter. "What do you mean?"

"I'm not an idiot. He left in a hurry that morning after he showed up and you seem, I don't know, a little sad or something ever since he left."

"We're…working through something."

"Is it the fact that Holt likes you?"

"What would make you say that?" Chloe stammered.

"Oh, come on," Emma groused. "It's obvious. He hangs on every word you say, and he kept looking at Jack in this weird way the whole time they were waiting for you to show up the other night."

"You're being ridiculous. Holt's not like that."

"Not in front of you. But when you're not looking, he like, stares at you." A slightly evil grin had crept onto Emma's face.

Chloe forced a dismissive chuckle. "No. He doesn't. Holt's your dad's partner, and I'm just helping him because we want to figure out what's going on so everybody's safe. He needed somebody to pitch in while your dad's in the hospital, and I was here."

Emma smirked. "Yeah, whatever. But I gotta tell you, you don't even sound like you believe that. Where is he, anyway? You two are always together."

"We are not," Chloe contested vehemently, then looked a little sheepish as she provided an answer. "He's at the office for a deposition or something. He said if he didn't tend to some of his other cases he would get fired by the clients who are actually paying him. He said he'll come by for dinner with everybody tonight."

"Of course he will."

Chloe pulled a face just as her cell rang.

"Hey, Izzie," Chloe answered, doubly happy because not only was it her best friend, but it gave her an excuse to short-circuit the Holt discussion. "Can you hold on a minute?" She brought the phone down as she turned to Emma. "I need to take this real quick. Do you think you could run out to the car and grab my gold light reflector? I want to use it for the next couple of shots. I left it in my backseat." She dug her keys out of her purse and handed them to Emma. "It's folded up in a black circular canvas pouch."

Emma took the keys and headed towards the front of the building, disappearing behind a row of dining room pieces as Chloe returned her attention to the phone.

"So, how are you?" Chloe asked. "I miss you." She imagined Izzie sitting behind her editor's desk, her long, ebony hair tied back in a band, chomping down on the nicotine gum she had been chain-chewing since trying to quit smoking.

"Miss you too. I haven't heard from you in a couple days. You still doing okay?"

"Yeah. We're good." She filled her in briefly on Reese's improvement. "I'm with Emma now. Trying for a little quality time. And I'm squeezing work in, too."

"Ooh, I like the sound of that. How's it coming?"

"Great actually. I'll have everything I need to start piecing something together soon."

"Fantastic."

"How's Jonah?" Chloe asked. Her golden retriever was a regular guest at Izzie's house whenever Chloe went out of town.

"Wonderful. Better than my kids. At least he listens when I tell him to stay." They chatted happily for several minutes until Izzie interrupted Chloe's debate about which restaurants to include in the article. "Hey, can you hold on a minute?" she asked Chloe, before having a quick, muffled conversation with someone on her end. "Hey," she came back on, "I'm really sorry, but I'm gonna have to go. Can I call you later?"

"Absolutely. Don't forget."

"I won't."

After hanging up, Chloe resumed planning the gown photos, moving around to determine the best angle from which to shoot the collection of dresses given the faint lighting this far back in the building. She felt like the gold reflector would help give the shot an organic, warm feeling, but she would have to try it out to be sure.

When another few minutes ticked by, she looked up in the direction Emma had gone, wondering what was taking her so long. The disc should have been easy to find. They had parked down the street a bit because they had stopped in another shop before coming here and just walked the rest of the way, but it wasn't that far. She tried Emma on her cell, but she didn't answer Chloe's text or her subsequent call.

Concern growing, Chloe left her equipment and maneuvered through the aisles back to the storefront. Bypassing the clerk who tried to speak to her, she pushed through the front door. There was no sign of Emma in the antique mall's graveled parking lot. She returned to the front desk, her sense of danger escalating,

"So, how are the pictures going?" the clerk asked. "Getting what you need?"

"Yeah, um, it's fine, but—did you see the girl I was with? Did she come through here?"

"Sure, maybe…ten minutes ago."

"Did she come back in?" Chloe asked, thinking maybe Emma had ended up going down the wrong aisle.

"No. Not that I saw, and I've been right here the whole time."

Chloe flew out the door, headed for the street. As she landed on the sidewalk, she rounded a bank of trees that had previously blocked her view. There was her car, parallel parked about halfway down the street where she had left it. But Emma was nowhere to be seen.

What was I thinking, sending her out here alone!

"Emma!" she yelled, scanning the area as she frantically jogged toward her car. "Emma!"

Nothing. On the street, a plumbing company van rolled by, braking at the stop sign ahead before turning right. Chloe stopped, her eyes shooting to it. She wondered where it had come from, her imagination conjuring terrible pictures of Emma unconscious in the back. With desperate, jittery fingers, she tried Emma's cell again.

A phone rang faintly from somewhere ahead, in the same direction as Chloe's car. Charging towards the sound, she pleaded in her heart for a glimpse of Emma's oversized plaid shirt. The ring grew louder as she raced toward it.

There, on the sidewalk beside Chloe's car, lay Emma's abandoned cell.

Chloe gasped as she bent down to snatch up Emma's phone, then screamed when she spotted Emma lying face down in the backseat of her car.

"Emma!" Chloe yelled, yanking on the door handle, but it was locked. She pounded on the window and yelled Emma's name. This time, Emma flipped over, her eyes wide and cheeks tear-stained as she reached to unlock the door. When Chloe ripped it open, Emma flung herself into her sister's arms.

"Hey!" Chloe exclaimed, grabbing Emma's face and pulling her back to get a better look. "Are you okay? What happened? What were you doing in there?"

"He said," Emma started, her words choking off mid-sob, "not to move. Not to leave until you came out. He said he would hurt you."

"What? Who said that?"

"The guy—I came out here to get your stuff, and when I bent in the car to get it off the floor, he shoved me face down on the seat. Told me not to look, not to move. He said he'd hurt you if I got out. So I didn't—"

"And he just shoved you in here and left?" Chloe asked, completely perplexed. "Why would he do that?"

"Because," Emma continued, rubbing tears from beneath her mascara-smeared eyes, "he said he wanted me to give you a message."

FIFTY-TWO

After a full day of putting out other people's fires, the Vettner-Drake matter had landed on Elise Banyon's desk once again. She watched the smoke from the last cigarette of her current pack of Dunhills drift meagerly upward before ultimately falling victim to the draw of her electronic ashtray. It was just after six o'clock and a hint of brilliant sunset remained at the edges of the Memphis horizon, with the darkening sky increasingly offering a stark backdrop to the fluorescent-lit offices in the buildings surrounding her own downtown suite. Between buildings she could see the rolling water of the Mississippi River passing between Tennessee and Arkansas, the orange glow of sundown reflected hundreds of times over in the rippling current.

Being that time of day, she was already mildly craving the two fingers of Talisker 18 she allowed herself every evening as reward for a job well done. But that would have to wait. Tonight she still had work to do.

"Hello," he finally answered, after her call had been put through the standard series of protocols to avoid any unwanted listeners.

"We have a problem. I got a tip from someone in the probate office here. Someone's been poking around some holdings."

"Which holdings?"

"Donner's."

He expelled a vexed groan. "So take care of it."

*****

"Okay," Holt said, his eyes locked in on Emma, who sat in her family room with Chloe, Jacob, and Trip surrounding her on the couch. "One more time. And this time, say it exactly like he did. No paraphrasing."

Emma groaned, leaning back into the cushions, frustration starting to get the better of her after going over the scare several times with the police, her friends, and now Holt. From his spot on the sofa arm, Jacob reached in and squeezed Emma's shoulder in support. Chloe thought he looked exhausted and wondered if maybe the toll of his father's incarceration was overwhelming him. Even Trip looked haggard, like he too was losing sleep over his friend's plight.

"He said," Emma started, "'Tell them the lawyers need to stop. I'm done asking. It's your last warning.' Then he locked the door and slammed it and that's all I know."

"And you're sure you didn't get a look at him—"

"No," she interjected emphatically, "because I wasn't stupid enough to try to look at him after he said he would hurt Chloe."

"Yeah, no, that was smart. I'm just trying to fish out anything that might help us. Let's go back to his voice. Was there anything else, anything at all, other than that he sounded like he was doing a 'really bad Christian-Bale-Batman' impression?" he asked, quoting Emma's earlier, very colorful description.

Emma shook her head, no, her black hair swinging across her shoulders.

"What if," Trip suggested, rocking back and forth on his white Nikes, "you, you know, were able to, like, do a police lineup or whatever? Would that help?'

Emma shook her head again. "No. Even if I heard him again I wouldn't be able to identify his voice. I mean," she added regrettably, "unless maybe he did the Batman thing."

The doorbell rang, signaling the arrival of the lasagna takeout Chloe had ordered from Zolo's Italian Restaurant. Between the episode at the antique mall and dealing with the police in the aftermath, she had not had the energy to even think about cooking anything.

"It's about time," Emma grumbled, jumping out of her seat and chugging toward the front door with Jacob and Trip following.

"It's paid for," Chloe shouted after them, then turned to Holt, eyeing him pointedly. "So have the police come up with anything else?"

Holt shook his head. "No. I checked in with them again after I ran by to see Reese—he's really worried about you guys, by the way. I told him you'd call later."

"I will. I just couldn't go after everything today. I'll call with the kids after dinner," Chloe assured him.

"The detective I talked to said the prints from your car could take several days to process. But if this was the same guy that attacked Reese here or came by the hospital, I doubt he left any. He didn't leave any before, so I don't know why he would start now." Holt tiredly ran a hand through his hair. "On the upside, they are going to increase patrols past the house…drive by even a few more times during the night."

Chloe grimaced skeptically. "I'm not sure what good that'll do."

"Well, I already told them to do it. And we'll have to keep the kids close."

"I think it has to be school only, and then home. If they do go out, they'll have to be with one of us the whole time. No more going out of sight, even for a second. That was so stupid," she lamented, dropping her shoulders.

He put a hand on her arm. "It wasn't."

"Yes. It was. But it won't happen again, which means Emma will have to take a break from work for a while."

"She's not going to like that."

"No," Chloe agreed, "but it's got to happen. And what about Reese?"

"The police still have someone posted for now. But I don't know how long they'll be able to do that. We may want to consider hiring a private security guard. Just as a precaution." Holt sighed. "And I've been thinking about something else."

Chloe's eyes flicked up to meet his. "What?"

"I could just drop Sims's case. Just hand it over to someone else."

Holt's complete turnaround on this subject caught Chloe by surprise. She squinted at him dubiously. "Before now you were completely against dropping it."

"Before now whoever is threatening us hadn't actually gone after one of the kids. The thing in the alley with Emma could have arguably been a random mugging, but this…it's too much."

"But if you drop the case, whoever takes over will be the new target. And their family, too. You'll just be shifting the burden to someone else."

"Someone else that isn't my best friend's kids. Or you."

He looked at her, his gaze simmering with a level of concern and protectiveness that made Chloe slightly uncomfortable.

"What about Jacob?" she pressed, shooting a glance in the teen's direction, and lowering her voice as the kids started tearing into the takeout bags in the kitchen. "Whatever happens to Kurt, happens to him too. You can't just abandon him. Who knows what'll happen if someone else takes over. If Kurt Sims loses, Jacob loses."

When Holt remained silent, she pushed harder. "You overheard Trip talking to Jacob earlier, same as I did. Kurt's not taking this well. And he's taking it out on Jacob."

"Yeah, I know."

"And Emma told me the same thing. A couple of days ago she went with Jacob to the jail, and she could hear Kurt screaming at Jacob all the way out in the waiting room."

"Screaming about what?"

"Something about football practice not going well or something. Like Jacob's performance on the field has been slipping since this all started."

"What else did she say?"

"That Jacob seems to be doing okay staying at his aunt's. She says he's going to school, although she said she thinks he's gotten a couple bad grades, which is unusual for him. It sounds like he's managing pretty well overall, except for the football."

"I'll bet Kurt doesn't like that."

Chloe shook her head. "Apparently not."

"Yeah, well, I'll talk to Kurt, tell him to lay off. If Jacob manages to graduate with all this going on, it'll be an accomplishment."

"Exactly, and you getting off this case," she pleaded, "isn't going to help that situation. You've got influence with Kurt. You can sway him when it comes to dealing with his son."

"Not much."

"Well, more than a stranger would."

"I want to help the kid, I do. But the risk—"

"I know I messed up today, but it won't happen again. I promise you I can take care of myself. And the kids, if it comes to it," she said, and patted her hip.

Holt's eyes widened. "That's not what I think it is? Is it?"

"It's one of the first things Jack taught me after we met. And, after Banyon stuck me in her backseat, I decided it was better to have it on me than locked in the trunk of my car."

"Okay," he drawled. "So, why haven't you ever mentioned it?"

She shrugged. "It never came up."

"It didn't come up?" Holt repeated dubiously. "Really? And you know how to use that thing?"

Chloe straightened smugly, a reproachful gleam in her eye. "My boyfriend's a trained killer. So…what do you think?"

He exhaled disapprovingly, wrinkling his face before shrugging in submission. "I think I'm starving. Let's eat."

*****

This time he had parked the Camry down the road and walked to McConnaughey's house, just to make sure no one spotted it. After everything that had gone down, he expected that they might be keeping a better eye on things. So, here he stood, hiding in the shadows of the line of cypress trees across the street, keeping tabs. The invigorating scent of pine enveloped him as a shiver ran up his back, his gloves and barn jacket barely staving off the chill from the rapidly dropping temperatures, a courtesy of the cold spell that just arrived in time for Halloween.

The kids in the house had opened the front door less than thirty seconds after the delivery guy had knocked on it. Just opened it right up. This proved that the delivery guy thing was definitely his ticket in, as long as it wasn't Holt Adams that answered. He would just have to make sure Adams wasn't around to answer it.

Come to think of it, he had watched the McConnaughey woman get a flower delivery a few nights ago. *Wouldn't be hard to duplicate that either,* he thought. Maybe even better than pizza. They wouldn't be expecting a flower delivery, so they wouldn't refuse it just because it was a surprise.

Flowers. That would work.

All in all, things were falling into place.

*****

Hours later, well after Holt had departed and the kids had gone to bed, Chloe rolled over, tugging the heavy cotton blanket up around her as she fought for sleep. Nighttime was the hardest, there in the dark, when it was just her and her thoughts.

What was Jack doing now? It was midnight in Tennessee, so it was ten in L.A. Jack often headed to bed around that time. But since he wasn't calling or having any contact at all, she had no idea what he was doing. Was he having trouble sleeping too? If he was, was he out, driving around, his preferred way to clear his head?

She swiped left on her iPhone screen, pulling up a photo of her and Jack at a Braves game in early June. It glowed harshly in the blackened room, but the warmth of the image—Jack's smile and hers and his arm wrapped snugly around her—softened the intrusion.

Swipe. A weekend in Destin, the salty surf pummeling them as they posed for the shot.

Her heart ached at the sight of him, his imposed separation feeling all the more hollow tonight. She missed him, not because he kept her safe, or because she was lonely, but because she missed *him*. She didn't need any more time to figure out why she felt that way. She never had needed any. She knew, had known since last winter in Miami, that Jack was and would be, the only one for her.

So why doesn't he know it?

She wanted to share this whole experience with him. All of it—Reese, the kids, the case—with *him*. Not because she needed to share it with somebody, but because he was her somebody. Her person.

And her person had not been himself for some time now. The leg was bothering him more than he let on. And not just physically. His personality had slowly changed. He was more reserved. A little sad even. His affable confidence had morphed into self-doubt. Like he was in some kind of mourning.

A possibility nudged the edges of her thoughts. What if Jack's difficulties were actually a sign of something larger? Something he maybe needed help with? He had been through a lot during those first awful weeks together. He had killed people and nearly been killed. Maybe it had taken a larger toll than either of them had realized.

Tomorrow, she resolved. *Tomorrow I end this. I'll call him and tell him how wrong this is and drag him out of this funk, or self-doubt, or jealousy or whatever. Tomorrow I set him straight. And if he needs help, we'll get it.*

She brushed away a thin wetness collecting on her cheek, and drew a small smile from a photo of them on date night getting sushi in Buckhead.

Swipe. Their road trip to Athens for the University of Georgia versus Auburn football game, a sea of red and orange flooding Sanford stadium.

Swipe.

Swipe.

Swipe.

FIFTY-THREE

Chloe clutched her steering wheel nervously as she stared at the entrance to D.B. Tucker's recording studio from her front row parking spot. The stumpy red brick building was situated on Lewisburg Pike, about one mile southeast of downtown. From the outside, it didn't look like much. Chloe guessed that maybe it had originally been built as an office for an insurance company or something similar. It loomed tauntingly in front of her as she debated whether to go in or just drive away.

Emma and Tyler were safe in school. She had dropped them off personally, meeting with each principal to make them aware of the current safety risks faced by the kids. After being satisfied that they would be well watched over until she picked them up at three o'clock, she had gone by to visit Reese and assure him that his children—all three of them—were fine. She stalled a little longer, remembering their conversation.

"And you're not over-extending yourself, you're sure?" Reese had questioned, genuine concern creasing his face, which had finally regained its color after nearly a week in the hospital.

"No," she had opined. "I'm exactly where I need to be."

He had sniffed before announcing randomly, "Holt came by." He had kept his gaze trained on her, presumably to gauge her reaction.

Chloe's eyes had narrowed suspiciously, something in his tone sending up a red flag. "So he said."

"He's been keeping you pretty close."

"I'm helping him with this case," she had offered, a note of self-justification rippling through her words. "Because his partner," she had said, slapping at the lightweight knit coverlet cast over Reese's legs, "is out of commission."

"I don't like it. He shouldn't be involving you like this."

"It's fine," Chloe had insisted. "And for the record, he wanted me to drop it."

"Good."

"But I told him, no."

Reese shifted in the hospital bed, frustration seeming to unsettle him. "You tell me that the kids are safe because they're being watched one hundred percent of the time. But what about you? Who's watching you?"

"Stop worrying."

"Worrying's all I can do from here. It's driving me crazy."

Reese was bothered by Holt involving her. But the truth was, if Holt knew she was here now, he would be twice as annoyed as Reese. Because last night, over piping hot ribbons of noodles dripping with Bolognese sauce, he had changed his mind about having her talk to D.B. After what had happened to Emma, he insisted that she stay out of the line of fire. So, finally, she had agreed that she wouldn't go anywhere near D.B. Tucker for the time being.

But, in the light of morning, she had thought it was a terrible idea. Once Cecilia spilled the beans to D.B., their opportunity to surreptitiously find out what D.B. knew would be over. So, rather than argue with Holt about it, she just decided to make it happen. By nine thirty she had managed to reach D.B. at the studio, and like Holt had expected, he was thrilled at the prospect of being part of Chloe's article. Holt was busy with appointments and court today, so he wouldn't have to know a thing until it was already over.

"Okay, it's now or never," she told herself, finally grabbing her equipment bag and pushing herself out of the car and up the front walk.

A small brass plaque to the left of the front door read, 'Tucker Studios.' She pressed the entryway buzzer and waited. When no one answered after about a minute, she tried again. After another couple minutes, she had nearly decided to forget the whole thing when someone swung the door open.

"Hey there! I'm D.B.," he said brightly. D.B. Tucker was lanky with a head of dark curly hair. He wore a navy plaid button-down, its tails loose over dusty gray jeans ending at black boots. "You must be Chloe," he said eagerly. "I'm so glad you're here. Sorry about the wait," he apologized as she stepped inside. "I've got a guy in the back laying down vocals this morning."

"No problem."

"Can you hang back with me for just a second? I'll get things going and then I can show you around." His reaction to her seemed perfectly pleasant. If Cecilia had warned D.B. about Holt and Chloe, he wasn't letting on.

The inside of the building was a complete one-eighty from what the outside suggested it would be. Varying textures of stone, wood and brick covered every surface, creating a warm, rustic vibe. Chloe followed D.B. through a knotty pine-paneled hallway that ended in a large, open control room where this styling continued, creating the sensation of being in a mountain lodge. A mixing console comprised of six feet of columns and rows of dials and sliders was positioned in the middle of the room, directly facing three separate glassed-in, sound-proofed rooms. The one in the middle was largest, flanked by two smaller booths. An engineer sat behind the console, expertly fiddling with the controls, as a male singer sporting large headphones in the booth to the left spoke to him through a shiny condenser microphone. Faded kilim rugs in muted reds and oranges carpeted each area, complimenting an overstuffed red velvet couch at the back of the control room to which D.B. directed Chloe.

"If you can give me just a minute, I'll get this going and then we can talk," he promised.

As D.B. conferred with the engineer, Chloe sat patiently and took in the room. A white board beside the door set out the schedule for the current and upcoming month. Chloe noticed that many of the days for November were blocked off with a myriad of names. According to the calendar, the singer in the booth, someone named "D. Freeman," was there to record vocal tracks. The wall opposite was paneled in a darker wood, decorated with black and white photos of people Chloe presumed had used D.B.'s studio. She moved closer to inspect the names engraved on little brass plates beneath each frame. One in particular, a picture of a young pre-teen girl with long straight blonde hair and perfectly white teeth, caught her eye. The name beneath it was "Keeley Tucker."

"Okay, David, you ready?" the engineer asked the singer through a microphone. When the singer nodded in reply, the engineer started working the controls and music flowed into the space.

"All right, I'm all yours," D.B. said, stepping over to where she stood by the photos.

"Is this your daughter?" Chloe asked, pointing to the girl's photo.

D.B. grinned exuberantly. "Sure is," he gushed. "She's something. We just finished her demo last week. Should be mixed and ready to make the rounds by the middle of November. That girl's going to be the next Taylor Swift."

"Wow. Seriously?"

D.B. nodded confidently. "We've already got interest from two labels. Hopefully the finished demo will attract more."

"She must be special."

"She is. I knew it when she was four years old, watching the CMAs, jumping up on the coffee table at home and belting it out along with the stars. Next year this time, some little girl is going to be singing a Keeley Tucker song." He walked over to the console and pulled a CD from a drawer and handed it to Chloe. The cover was another photo of Keeley, this time propped against a brick wall and holding a Gibson acoustic guitar. "It's a few of her best."

"Thanks," Chloe said, then pointed to the phrase, 'Recorded at Tucker Studios,' printed just below Keeley's name. "I take it if Keeley becomes successful, that would help your studio."

"Absolutely." D.B. jerked his head towards the white board. "We stay about sixty percent booked, and our reach is expanding across the South. Plus, our clientele genres are widening. We handle mostly country and some contemporary Christian artists like David," he said, gesturing to the singer, "but next month, we've got a couple of pop artists coming in. We're growing, but yeah, it wouldn't hurt to have a big name get their start here."

"I imagine it's hard to get a studio like this going. How long have you been at it?"

"Eight years. Hard isn't the word. You could throw a rock and hit twenty studios from here to Main Street alone. Everybody wants a piece of the Nashville pie."

"Holt said you had some success earlier this year with one of the songs you recorded here."

"Yep. Nearly made it onto the country streaming chart. We got some business off that one. I'm really hoping Keeley can do the same for us."

"Keeley looks a lot younger in the photo on the CD than the one on the wall," Chloe observed.

"Yeah, well, the one on the wall is more recent. She…we…kind of took a break for a little while there. You know teenagers. Angst and all that. She had a, uh, difficult year last year. But," he quickly qualified, maybe concerned that he had said too much, "that's all over with. She grew out of it real quick and now we are primed and ready to go." A big grin hitched onto his face. "So," he said, rubbing his hands together, "tell me about this article you're writing."

FIFTY-FOUR

"This is too rich for my blood," Tom Erickson avowed, kicking back in the vinyl booth and taking a long gulp on his second Michelob of lunch. "I give you this and I'm done. You want any more digging done, you gotta find somebody else."

Holt spun the straw in his Coke and leaned back in his seat, the last booth in a long row inside a greasy shotgun diner on Broadway in downtown Nashville. For some reason, the private detective across from him loved the place, and always insisted on taking meetings there. Holt thought he was nuts. The ear-splitting sound of dishes being carelessly cleared and dropped into a busing tub just barely overpowered the noise from the argument between the fry cook and the waitress over a misunderstood order of a patty melt that, apparently, should have had no onions. The onions had been grilled, however, and their tangy odor saturated the place.

"Two beers at lunch?" Holt questioned, ignoring Tom's comments.

Tom plucked one of the last fries swimming in the watery pool of grease that was the sad remains of his double bacon cheeseburger and popped it whole in his mouth. "Well," he said, licking the salt from his fingers, "it's a two-beer-lunch kind of day. Matter of fact," he continued, signaling the waitress that he wanted another, "I'm thinking it's probably a three-beer kind of day."

From the looks of Tom's waistband, Holt thought three-beer lunches probably weren't all that rare. Or double cheeseburgers, for that matter.

"So what's got you so spooked?" Holt asked, leaning forward.

Tom had asked for the last booth, as usual, insuring a certain amount of privacy in the noisy hole-in-the-wall which, for reasons Holt had never understood, was always busy. Tom quickly swept the room with his eyes, before pushing a thin manila file across the table to Holt.

"I think you have finally gone and tripped in it, son."

Skepticism punctuated Holt's expression. "Come on, Tommy," Holt drawled. "I've never known you to shy away from a case."

"You ever been to a scary movie, Holt?"

"Uh, yeah," Holt answered uncertainly. "Sure."

"You know, one of those where some creepy thing is going on in the attic or basement or somewhere and one of the characters, you know, some idiot blonde teenager, she knows something weird is going on because her friends keep kicking it?"

"Okay."

"But instead of walking away and living out her life, this idiot decides to *go in the basement.* And the whole time, you're like, yelling at her, saying, 'Turn around, don't do it,' but she does it anyway because the curiosity just gets the best of her."

"Yeah," Holt answered, his brow wrinkling further.

"And then, like we all knew she would, she gets an axe through the head or some ghost strangles her, and we're all thinking, *if you'd just walked away.*"

"Yeah, okay. I get it."

"You're the idiot blonde. I'm the guy in the theater screaming at you."

"Yeah, I said I get it."

"And if you have half a brain, you will *not* go in this basement. Because anybody can see that if you do, you're gonna end up with an axe in the head."

"Tommy, come on…"

"Or in this case," he said, holding two fingers to his head like a gun, "two taps and a swim in the Hudson."

Holt squinted, sizing up Tom's meaning before leaning forward and in a steely voice demanding, "Tell me."

Tom took a quick swig of the amber bottle the waitress had dropped off, then deposited it on the chipped melamine tabletop with a hard thud. "All right, then," he relented, ripping open the folder. "It's your funeral."

*****

Half an hour later, Holt sat in his car, contemplating his next move. Tommy wasn't wrong. The contents of the file were trouble. He might have poked the wrong hornet's nest.

Cars zipped by his parallel parking spot on Broadway, just a hair's breadth between the vehicles and Holt's Audi. He didn't notice.

What he held in his hand was a definite lead. An alternative theory to Sims being the guilty party in the arson and Donner's murder. It might be the key to getting Sims home to Jacob and ending the threats to them all.

Or it might be putting an even larger target on their backs.

The afternoon docket was starting soon, and he had a hearing set on it. He would have to decide this later, after talking it through with Reese. Now that his partner was awake, alert, and out of the woods, it was time to bring him back into the loop.

And cut Chloe out of it. Before she got hurt.

A spot opened up in the eastbound lane as the traffic light down the block triggered. Holt swung out headed for I-65 south back to Franklin—just like the graphite Ford F150 that pulled out when he did, dangerously cutting across two full lanes to follow him.

FIFTY-FIVE

Chloe shut her driver's door and waved goodbye to D.B., who was still standing in the entranceway giving her a proper and hopeful sendoff. When he finally went inside, she exhaled loudly, releasing the tsunami of nervous energy that had been building for the last couple hours.

On the one hand, she now had a memory card full of great photos and a new angle to add yet another layer to her piece on Franklin. Showcasing the music business side of the town that was home to not just country music artists, but also so many other musicians, would definitely boost the interest value of the destination. That was a plus.

On the other hand, after strategically gathering information during the course of her interview, she was now pretty sure that both of Trip's parents had a motive for murder.

That was not a plus. *Not a plus at all.*

* * * * *

Holt barreled up to the front door of his office building, colliding with it when it remained stoically shut despite his twisting and shoving the knob.

"What…oh," he said, catching himself as he realized the time. Karen was still out at lunch. He ripped his keys from his pocket, fumbled for the right one and unlocked the door.

Slamming the door behind him, he raced back into his office. He was late for court and unless Karen had planned ahead for him, he still had to gather—

"Aww, Karen. You are too good to me," he gushed, spotting a small stack of files and working notes gathered on his blotter. Right in the center was a yellow sticky note with '1:30 docket' written on it. Grabbing the pile, he hustled right back out the way he came, turning to lock the door behind him as he left.

"Whoa, there, counselor."

Holt turned around to find two men flanking him. They were dressed down, both in jeans, one in a plaid button-down, and the other in a black T-shirt with a whiskey label printed across it in white.

"Um, sorry, but if you're here to make an appointment, you'll have to wait till my secretary gets back. I'm late for court just now," he said regrettably, pushing past them and shuffling down the stairs to the parking lot. "She should be back in, fifteen minutes or so, if you want to wait," he said without turning. "Or you could just call a little later."

At his car, he reached out to open the door, when two hands forced it shut again.

"Hey!" Holt called out, spinning to find himself cornered against his own vehicle by the two men, who had obviously bolted down the steps to catch up to him, "Look, I'm really sorry, but I can't do this now. If you've got an emergency—"

"I think you're the one with the emergency."

Holt cocked his head and squinted at the shorter, stockier man on the right in the plaid shirt, whose slicked back hair had seen more than its share of gel. "Excuse me?"

"Well, I'd like to, but it seems it's too late for that."

Holt tensed. "I think you'd better step off."

"Mmm, not yet. We've got a message for you."

With glaring eyes, Holt appraised the two men, making some quick calculations about the situation. "Yeah, well, I already got that message when your boss shoved my friend in her car," he countered.

"I'm not sure what you're talkin' about." Plaid shirt was apparently the spokesperson for the team.

"Sure you are. Your boss lady crammed my friend in her car and threatened her. Wasn't very nice."

"Mmm, nope. Doesn't sound like our style."

"Oh yeah?" Holt baited, his patience faltering. "And what *is* your style?"

The second guy, muscled but thinner, his dark jeans sagging loosely on him, snorted in amusement, while plaid shirt grinned.

"Gotta tell you, brother," he said, shaking his head. "You are gonna be sorry you asked that question."

FIFTY-SIX

Chloe had just driven through Five Points on her way to Holt's office when her cell rang. It was Karen.

"Hey, I'm sorry to bother you but I'm looking for Holt. I can't reach him. Is he with you?" Karen's voice was higher pitched than normal, and she seemed nervous.

"No. I haven't seen him today. I thought he had court this afternoon."

"He did but he didn't show up for the docket. The judge's clerk called looking for him."

Chloe's nerves began churning. Something wasn't right. "Does that ever happen?" she asked, already suspecting the answer.

"No. He never misses court. And if he's going to be late he calls to give them a heads up. I don't want to overreact, but with everything that's gone on—"

"No. You're right. We should track him down."

"That's just it. You were my last resort. I already called his house. No answer. If he's not with you…Chloe, his car is still here. Wherever he is, he either walked there or somebody else drove him."

"Can you go out to his car?"

"Yeah, sure. Hold on, I have to walk outside—"

"Is there anything in it, around it? Anything at all that suggests something happened?"

"Okay, hold on, I'm just getting there. I'm really worried, Chloe. He would've checked in by now—okay, I'm at the car. No, I don't see anything—oh, no," she uttered, her voice turning grave.

"What? What is it?"

"His phone." Fear punctuated Karen's voice. "It's in the front seat of his car. With his keys."

*****

When Holt was eleven years old, the class bully and a couple of his cohorts tricked him into going into the woods behind their neighborhood by telling him they had found a puppy. When they finally got deep into the trees, where no one would be able to hear or help, the three cornered and pummeled him until, bleeding and sore everywhere he had skin, they left him in the dark, alone and scared. He had laid there on the ground in a ball, thinking it might hurt too much to ever move again, until eventually he cried himself to sleep. Sometime later, he woke to his older sister, Kimberly, shaking him. She had picked him up, brushed him off, and walked him home, every step of the way stabbing his nerves like knives.

Now, laying on the ground in a field somewhere in east Williamson County, the pungent scent of raw earth mixed with blood filling his nostrils, Holt thought that this felt a lot like that. Although this time, there was no Kimberly to come to his rescue.

FIFTY-SEVEN

Chloe paced inside Reese's hospital room, fear driving her steps. "Where could he be?" she asked him for the third time. "Are you sure you don't have any ideas? You don't know any place he might have gone?"

Reese's face was wrinkled with concern. "No, like I told you, I haven't talked to him since yesterday." His eyes narrowed as he straightened slightly. "This is the end of it, Chloe. I want you off this case. I mean it. I don't care that you want to help. I want you to go back to Atlanta—"

"I cannot just leave you and the kids here to fend for yourselves when you're incapacitated."

"I'm not incapacitated—"

"You can't leave here yet. And what are you going to do if someone comes after the kids?"

"I'll hire security. I'll—"

Chloe's cell phone rang, cutting through their argument like a bell in a boxing match. She snatched it out of her pocket.

"Hello?" she squawked, unable to keep the stress out of her voice. She listened briefly, as relief flooded her face. "Okay. Thanks. I'll be right down."

She hung up, her gaze flashing to Reese, who was waiting expectantly. "Well? What is it?"

"It's about Holt," she said, gathering her purse and striding towards the door. "He's in the ER downstairs."

*****

"What happened?" Chloe exclaimed as she burst into Holt's private room in the ER. His face was swollen, one eye threatening to shut completely. Blood streaked across the width of his forehead, apparently left by someone's poor attempt to wipe it clean. He sat in the bed wearing a hospital gown stained here and there with red, hunching forward holding his torso, as if trying to keep from moving.

"*Who* happened," he corrected, his voice not much more than a growl. "And I don't know. I do know they can throw a pretty good punch. Though I don't think that'll help the sketch artist much."

There wasn't a chair, so she sat on the edge of his bed and reached over to squeeze his hand. He winced at the pressure.

"Sorry, sorry!" she apologized.

"It's fine," he groaned.

"Holt, come on," she said, her face pained. "Tell me."

He shrugged, as if she was asking him something as benign as what he had eaten for lunch. "Two guys grabbed me outside the office. Took me to a field about five miles outside of town and beat the stew out of me. That's about it."

"And then what?" she said, her tone rising.

"Well, after they did their worst, they told me to stay down and count to one hundred. I did. When I looked up, they were gone. I had to walk about a mile before I came across a house. Used their phone and called the cops. They picked me up, drove me here. They left just a little while before you came. Took a statement, although a lot of good that's going to do them. I couldn't really give them much to go on."

"You gave them a description, right?"

"Yeah, but 'fat guy in plaid shirt' and 'less fat guy in T-shirt' doesn't go very far."

"And you've got no idea who sent them? Did they say anything at all?"

Holt shrugged again, wincing as he moved. "Other than 'kick him one more time in the gut and I think he'll puke'? No. They didn't say anything helpful."

"Could they have been with Banyon?"

"Well, I asked them, but surprisingly, they wouldn't own up to it." He smiled weakly. "But even if there is a connection, to Banyon or Vettner-Drake or anybody else, we probably won't be able to find it since we have no idea who they were. They did bring up Sims's murder case, though."

"Really?"

"Mmm-hmm. They said if I was half the lawyer I thought I was, I'd be looking in a different direction. 'If I were you, I'd be taking a good, hard look at the wife. It's always the wife,' one of them said." Holt rubbed his jaw, which apparently was aching from talking. "I did manage to land two good punches and one mighty kick to the groin that plaid shirt won't be forgetting anytime soon, though, just in case anybody's keeping score—"

"Holt, come on. Be serious."

"I am. It was a really good kick. Ice-for-two-days kind of kick."

She groaned. "So, what now?"

"Now, I start looking into the wife a little more closely, just in case. Whoever they were, I would have expected them to warn me off the case altogether, but instead they pointed me in her direction. It might be just a diversion, but it's probably worth exploring a little more. I'll put Tom on it as soon as I can get my fingers to dial a phone again," he said miserably, wiggling his bruised digits.

She offered him a sympathetic smile, then bit her lip, as if keeping words back.

"What?" he asked sagely. "You look like you know something."

She hesitated, not sure if this was the right moment. But he needed to know. "I have news, too."

Holt's eyes sharpened. "What do you mean 'you have news'? You aren't supposed to have news."

"Well," she started sheepishly, "you know how I promised I'd stay away from D.B.?"

Holt groaned. "Spill it."

Chloe filled him in on her time with D.B., then shared her theories. "So, here's what I'm thinking. D.B. has a lot riding on Keeley. He was pretty forthcoming about the fact that she's making headway in her recording career and that if she gets picked up by a label, it could change a lot for his studio. Right now, he's only booked about half the time. I don't see how he can be making a go of it as a legitimate business."

Holt pursed his lips and wagged his head in agreement. "He and Cecilia have sunk an awful lot into that studio. Financed most of it with their savings. There's a lot riding on it succeeding. It's been the source of a lot of tension between them since he started it."

"And," she continued, "he let it slip that Keeley had to 'take a break,'" she used air-quotes around the words, "last year because she was having such a bad time in general."

"That was the year they were going through all their marriage troubles."

"Exactly. Which fits with what Cecilia said about her kids falling apart over it."

"True."

"But now, according to D.B., Keeley is feeling better and she's raring to go. So I'm thinking, here's D.B., desperate to have a studio that can support itself, with 'the next Taylor Swift' as he puts it, ready to launch a career. If she takes off, so does his studio. But that requires her to be happy and healthy. Able to work. Focused. What if he found out about Justin Roberts? What if he found out that Donner knew about Roberts and was using it to blackmail his wife? And, what if he figured that Cecilia ultimately wouldn't give in to Donner, that she would stand up to him, come what may? If he thought the information about the affair was going to come out and ruin the stability he and Cecilia had finally achieved for their family, which would undermine Keeley's state of mind and likely her career—"

"Not to mention the studio's potential future success riding on the coattails of that career," Holt interrupted.

Chloe nodded, Then that would give him—"

"A motive for murdering Donner."

"Exactly." She watched as a grimness settled over him. "What? Are you worried about what this means for Cecilia?" she asked.

He eyed her closely for a moment before launching in. "You did a good job with D.B. Really. It'll help Sims. But," he continued, "I really need you to hear me."

He leaned towards her, grimacing at the movement, then offered a slight smile. "You said you weren't going to meet with D.B. And you did anyway. Alone. You raced off to Roberts's house. Alone. I *know* it's important to you to help with the case. I get that you feel like you're atoning for some kind of failure with Tate, but I really think your judgment is getting clouded. Look at what just happened to me. It could have been you."

He paused, as if measuring her reaction. "Be there for Emma and Tyler—and for Reese. He'll be coming home soon. They need you. Let me handle this. Okay?" His gaze narrowed on her with an uncharacteristic dark focus. Though he had posed it as a question, his tone made it clear that it wasn't one. "Whatever it is that you think you can do to help, however sooner you think you might help bring this to an end, it's more important for you to be safe." He tensed almost imperceptibly, as if expecting a fight.

But she wasn't going to give him one. She had known it would come to this as soon as she had rushed in and seen him sitting there, bruised and bloodied. And as much as she wanted to bring this to a head, as much as she wanted to end it, she had to admit that this may have finally moved beyond her. She couldn't deny the pattern, the escalation, or the determination of whoever was behind all these actions. If she kept on, there would be another incident. And she didn't want to be responsible for whatever horrible thing happened next. Not to mention that if something happened to her at this point, there wouldn't be anyone to watch over Emma and Tyler. Holt might not be able to drop the case, but she could keep her family as far removed from it as possible. She nodded her agreement.

"Really?" he pressed, surprised at her quick capitulation. "No argument? I know how strongly you feel about it."

She shook her head. "I guess I just don't think it's the best way to protect them anymore."

His shoulders relaxed. "Good. And, speaking of news, you're not the only one that has some."

The faint lines around her eyes tightened in disbelief. "What...you've got something other than being dragged off and beaten to a pulp?"

Despite the fact that it hurt to talk, he couldn't keep the excitement out of his voice.

"Do I ever."

FIFTY-EIGHT

Jacob Sims hardly lifted his gaze to meet his father's, who sat across the table from him in the cramped space that served as a visitation room at the Tri-County Jail. Crowding it further was Trip, who leaned against the wall behind Jacob, his arms crossed.

"You skip school to be here?" Kurt Sims barked, his gruff tone reeking of accusation.

"No, Dad," Jacob muttered. "School's out at two thirty. I came right after." His voice was languid, his posture deflated.

"You can't be ditching school."

"I'm not, I'm—"

"He's not, Mr. Sims," Trip interrupted protectively, speaking over Jacob. "He hasn't missed a day so far."

"I wasn't talking to you," Kurt snapped, glaring at Trip, before once again directing his ire at Jacob. "Why'd you bring him anyway? Can't stand to be with me for five minutes on your own?"

"No, Dad, Trip's my ride. The car stopped working two days ago—"

"What? The car did what? Why didn't you say something?"

"To who? You can't do anything about it from in here. And Aunt Meghan has enough to worry about."

"Did you tell Adams?"

"No, Dad, I didn't because it's not Holt's problem. He's busy enough taking care of you."

"Adams is doing his job."

"It's not a job if you don't get paid," Trip grumbled under his breath, just low enough to avoid Sims's hearing.

"Tell Adams. I can't have you missing practice because of the car."

"Fine." Jacob's reply was a whisper, barely audible.

"What?"

"I said fine," Jacob repeated sharply.

Sims adjusted in his seat, running a hand through his unkempt hair. "So how's practice? You still working hard? You can't slack on my account."

"I'm not slacking," Jacob said, hardly looking at his father. "I've been every day."

"I need you to keep it up. Get that scholarship. Your future depends on it, and I won't have you losing out because you got weak." Kurt reached across the table and squeezed Jacob's arm. When he let go, a telltale red impression lingered. "You hear me?"

"I'm not weak, Dad," Jacob said, jerking his arm back and shoving it under the table.

"You'd better not be. And I don't want you coming back here. You don't need the distraction."

"I just wanted to see how you were."

"I'll be fine unless you ruin everything while I'm in here. So get it together," Kurt ordered, standing and knocking on the door to signal the guard that he was ready to go. Within seconds, the guard had opened the door and stood aside to allow Kurt to exit. Kurt stepped into the hall, catching Jacob's eye one last time. "Don't let me down, kid," he growled. "Don't you dare let me down."

* * * * *

"Tell me." Chloe stared expectantly at Holt. He was clearly exhausted, sore and hurting, but the hint of fire in his eyes told her that he must be on to something.

"So, like I told you before, after Sims was charged with Donner's murder, I had my P.I. start looking into things—into Donner, his business, any problems he had— pretty standard stuff for a charge like that. The story is that Donner, through Donner Enterprises, has been in the real estate development business for over twenty years. Typically, what he does is buy a piece of property in a prime location—one that's either already empty or he demolishes whatever's on it—then he constructs a huge commercial development. He fills it with tenants, gets it nearly profitable, then sells it. He reaps a balloon profit and dumps the burden of managing the property. You can imagine the kind of revenue that generates after doing it a couple dozen times."

"If it's successful. If the property's marketable once it's developed."

"Exactly. And for years Donner was extremely successful at it. He built all across Tennessee—Nashville, Memphis, Knoxville—and also in smaller locales that had an established or growing tourist industry, like—"

"Like Franklin."

"Right. Donner made tens of millions and because he was the sole owner of Donner Enterprises, he didn't have to share that with anyone. Now, he did typically have a couple of private investors in each project, as well as short term development loans from various banks to float the projects while he held onto them."

"Which is pretty much what his people told us."

"Right, except that starting about five years ago, Donner stopped being so successful."

"What happened?"

"Whatever crystal ball he had been using to select his properties must've cracked because he had three in a row that went under."

"Ouch."

"Yeah. So by the time he covers his losses on those and pays his investors back, Donner Enterprises is cash poor. And now, he can't secure the same kind of bank loans or private investors for future projects, because his track record has been damaged. Now, according to Tom, my P.I., despite whatever financial troubles Donner started having, he still maintained an impressive personal asset portfolio. His house in Franklin, one in Vail, and one in Key West, not to mention an apartment in New York, a yacht—you get the picture."

"I imagine Claire Donner needs a pretty big allowance, too."

"I'm sure. But, the thing is, when Donner started having his financial troubles, he didn't change any of his spending habits. He didn't sell anything. As far as we can tell, he kept everything and kept spending as if nothing was happening."

"So he's got lots going out and nothing coming in."

"Less than nothing, actually, since the properties continued to cost him until he sold them. So what does a real estate developer do when he's got to make some money, pay back existing investors to avoid bankruptcy, and rebuild his business, but no one will lend him anything?"

Chloe shrugged.

"He gets creative financing." When Chloe seemed to struggle to catch on, he continued. "Okay, so apparently, just after things started going sideways for Donner Enterprises, the company started successively buying little pieces of run-down property here and there all over the state. About half a dozen that Tom could find, and that's just in Tennessee. Who knows if or how many he bought elsewhere. Anyway, they were all undeveloped tracts or had buildings begging to be demolished. Typically, they would be located in urban areas, failing parts of town, but on the edge of some area of redevelopment. Far enough away to be really cheap, but close enough to take the chance that someday the property would become part of the advancing renewal, and the value would shoot sky high."

"How did buying more property that he would have to wait to sell help him in the short term?"

"Because each time, usually less than thirty days after he purchased it, someone else would swoop in and buy it from him for a lot more than he paid. Quadruple his purchase price in some cases. So suddenly, he's not cash poor anymore and he can afford to start and flip more projects. The money would have kept Donner and Donner Enterprises alive."

"That seems awfully coincidental."

"And that's not all," Holt agreed. "Tom did a little bit more digging on the properties he was flipping. Turns out that within six months of each of those sales Donner made, all of the properties, except for one, were bought a third time, by other corporations, again at significant premiums."

"Why did the values keep going up so fast?"

"That's just it. They shouldn't have. As far as we can tell there would be no reason for anybody to want to pay so much for any of them."

"So what, you think Donner was doing something illegal?"

"Well, I don't know about illegal, but something was definitely up."

"So who were the buyers?"

Holt smirked. "This is where is gets even more interesting. The buyers were all corporations chartered in the Caribbean."

"That sounds sketchy."

"Mm-hmm. And, unfortunately for us, that's as far as we can take it, because it's pretty hard to get information on corporations based there. Which is usually the reason people incorporate there in the first place." He smiled. "But I've got a theory."

"Of course you do."

"Imagine you're Donner, and your business is failing. You need money, but a traditional bank won't lend to you anymore because your balance sheet is debt heavy and you're too high of a risk. You can't get it from your current investors because you don't want them to know there's a problem. You can't attract new investors, because your most recent projects have failed and trying to get capital that way would risk being exposed to your current investors. So, instead, you go to an alternative lending source."

"What's an 'alternative lending source'?" she asked. In response, he raised his eyebrows, as if encouraging her to think creatively. She did. "What, like a loan shark?"

Holt nodded. "Just follow me, here. Donner goes to some outfit for a loan. This outfit agrees, but only at a very hefty rate of interest."

"Okay," Chloe said, following his train of thought.

"But this lender has two issues. One, the lender might run into some trouble enforcing that kind of interest depending on usury laws. He might find himself unable to enforce his claim on the interest at all. But that's really not the primary problem."

"What is?"

"This kind of lender wouldn't tolerate default. So if he has a customer that ends up not being able to pay the money back with the interest, or even looks like he won't be able to, this lender would take very serious and probably violent steps to prevent that from happening."

"Like what? Breaking legs or something?"

"Maybe. Maybe worse. Depends how much money is at stake. But think about it. If you're that lender, and you want to be able to enforce collection in that manner, then you'll want to keep the loan quiet so that if you do have to press your right to collect and that customer ends up in the hospital—"

"Or the morgue—"

"Or the morgue, you don't want your name out there as a potential suspect. So what do you do? You hide the loan as a real estate transaction. It lets you move lots of money very quickly for seemingly legitimate reasons. The customer buys a piece of crud property for next to nothing. You then buy it from him through some shell corporation or straw man individual for a whole lot more than he paid for it."

"And that's the loan," Chloe surmised.

"Exactly. Then you give the customer six months or whatever to pay you back. How does he do that? He buys the property back from you through some other shell corporation at an even higher price, say, double what you paid him. The lender gets the principal back with interest and the other guy got his loan, albeit at a very high price. And if for some reason he can't pay the loan back when it comes time, the lender can exert all the pressure he wants because nobody will ever know about the loan—"

"Or suspect that the lender has a motive for murder, or maiming the guy or whatever they do to him."

"If it comes to that."

"And you think that's what happened here? You think Donner borrowed money in some sort of scheme and then didn't pay it back, and the lender, whoever it was, got to him?"

"Well, I don't have any proof. It's just a theory really."

"It's pretty far-fetched, Holt.

"Yeah, I agree. But there's a couple of really interesting things. Remember I said there was one piece of property that didn't sell for a second time within the six-month period?"

"So?"

"So—the six-month period ended three weeks before Donner died."

"You're saying there was a payment due?"

"Maybe. So think about it. Sims files his lawsuit and drags the whole project into court. So now, Donner can't flip the property because it's tied up in legal proceedings. If he can't flip it, maybe he can't pay the lender back. And maybe the lender gets tired of waiting."

"Well, if they kill him, they never get paid. So that doesn't make much sense."

"Unless you're convinced he either can't or won't ever pay and you want to send a message to other customers."

"But even if you're right, who's the lender? Do you think Banyon or maybe even Vettner-Drake is involved?"

"That I don't know. I don't have anything connecting them to it. Yet."

"Well, it doesn't do you any good to have a theory without anyone to point to, does it?"

"Well, yes and no. I mean, it's awfully circumstantial, and I'm not even sure I could have any of this admitted into evidence. But if I can convince a judge that it isn't complete speculation, even without a name, it gives the jury another option. Something else to help muddy the reasonable doubt waters for Sims."

"But it's just a bunch of conjecture."

"Well, it's a bunch of conjecture that my detective told me and within one hour I was lying in a field bleeding half to death."

"You really think that the timing of you getting this information in relation to when those guys came after you proves that the two are connected?"

"The timing isn't the only thing that convinced me."

"What did?"

"Remember Joe Bellamy? The corpse?"

"Yeah…"

"According to Tom, he's from New Jersey. Years ago he was licensed as a private investigator that did work for a lawyer up there, by the name of Richard Arjulio." Holt took a breath, wincing slightly as he grabbed his aching ribs. "That remaining piece of property? The one that hadn't resold in the six months? We can't find out who the owners of the Caribbean chartered corporation are, but guess who's listed as the U.S. agent of service?"

Chloe finally saw where this was going. "Richard Arjulio?"

"Richard Arjulio. I may not have absolute proof, but I've got a corpse on Donner's property who once upon a time had a link to the lawyer who works for the corporation that bought one of the inflated value properties from Donner. It might be enough. At least, enough to create doubt in the jury's mind."

"Yeah, maybe," she agreed somberly. "But I'm worried," she said eyeing his wounds, "that it might also be enough to get you killed."

* * * * *

When the doctor finally entered Holt's room on rounds, Chloe slipped into the hallway outside to call Reese to update him on Holt's situation. She could have gone upstairs to tell him in person, but she wanted to get back in to see Holt as soon as the doctor left. An orderly came around the corner pushing a gurney bearing an unconscious patient, and she pressed against the wall to avoid her toes being run over. Turning and gripping the cell phone, she strained harder to listen over the metallic rattling of the gurney's wheels.

"And he's okay?" Reese asked. "You're sure?"

"Yes. They said he should be released in about half an hour."

"And you're done with this, okay? Right?"

"Don't worry. We've already talked about it. I'm going to step back."

"Good."

"Look, I'm going back in there to see what the doctor says. I'll update you if I learn anything else."

Chloe disconnected and slid back inside Holt's room just as the doctor walked out and nodded at her. Holt sat up a little straighter as she entered.

"He says that other than a couple of broken ribs, I'm fine."

Chloe narrowed her eyes at him. "You're lying."

Holt pursed his lips in exaggerated contemplation. "Not exactly lying. Downplaying, maybe. But he did say I could go as soon as the paperwork's done."

Chloe checked her watch. She would have to leave in twenty minutes to pick up the kids from school. She took in Holt's battered form once more as she resumed her spot on the edge of his bed. Concern crept in and she reached out to gently grip his arm. "Listen, I'll do what you want and drop all this. I won't butt in, and I will leave all the lawyering to you. But you have to be careful, too. I know you have to do what you have to do, but you can be smart about it. Safe, about it. I don't want anything to happen to you, either."

He eyed her with amusement. "It almost sounds like you're worried about me."

"Of course I'm worried about you." Several seconds passed as she measured what she wanted to say. "I really wish you would let Sims find someone else to represent him. Is any client worth," she gestured to his battered face, "that?"

Holt shrugged stoutly. "I like to live on the edge."

Chloe's lips set hard in frustration. "I mean it, Holt. You're not taking this seriously enough. I care about what happens to you. The kids care about what happens to you." Her eyes were bright and intently sincere. "You can't be this cavalier about it."

His shoulders relaxed, and he bent toward her a little. "Hey, I'm just messing around." He placed his hand on hers and patted it gently. "It'll be fine, I promise. This isn't the first time I've been threatened over a case."

"Is it the first time somebody actually took a crack at you?"

"Well," he started reluctantly, "maybe. But it's not that bad."

"Not that bad? Holt. Come on. Look at you."

"Well, I would, but," he pushed a loose twist of dark hair from where it hung over his swollen left eye, "I'm not seeing so well at the moment."

"I'm serious."

"I know you are," he replied gently as his gray eyes locked onto hers, a quiet intensity radiating from him. She sensed something different in his tone, all sarcasm and brevity gone, replaced with something deeper, more piercing. A nervous twinge flickered in her stomach, and suddenly he was pulling her to him.

FIFTY-NINE

"Don't."

Her command was hushed but unyielding. She had pulled back sharply from him, only milliseconds before he had completely closed the distance between them. Even so, he remained there, poised as he had been when just about to kiss her. She held his gaze firmly.

"I'm sorry," she said, and she meant it. There was no anger in her voice, just empathy. "Holt, I'm so, so, sorry. If I did something to—"

"Stop," he said and heaved a labored sigh. Tossing her an understanding smile that couldn't hide his disappointment, he sank back into the head of the bed, propped up on pillows. "You don't have to say anything. I just…I guess I thought there was something here," he said, waving between them. "And, I don't know, maybe it's the painkillers or the knock on the head, but it sort of seemed like the moment."

She spoke gently. "I'm with Jack. You know that."

"I know that he ran off and left you here for no good reason. I know he hasn't called for days and that you've barely spoken to him since I've known you. And I know you deserve better."

"You don't know him. He's got good reasons for doing what he's doing, even though I don't agree with it. He just wants to do the right thing. We'll work through it. I love him, Holt. I'm sorry if I led you to believe any differently. You've been amazing."

"Not amazing enough apparently," he said wryly.

"You've been an amazing *friend.* To me, to Reese—to all of us."

They were quiet for a minute, the occasional beeping of his monitor the only sound in the room. "So," he finally said with an awkward smirk, "is this going to be too weird now? Have I messed things up, or can we still be friends?"

"Of course we can still be friends."

"Mmm. Easy for you to say," he said. "You're not the one that just made a complete idiot of himself. Maybe it'll be too weird for *me* now."

"No, it won't," she insisted.

"I mean, my ego *is* pretty fragile," he said, subtle sarcasm in his tone. "I'm not sure I want to be reminded of my crash and burn every time I see you."

The corner of Chloe's mouth ticked up as a knowing smile emerged. "Really?" she chided with amused skepticism. "*Your* ego is fragile?"

He made basset hound eyes at her. "What can I tell you? I mask it well."

She laughed. "Okay. Whatever you say." She bit her lip hesitantly. "So we're good?"

Holt squinted, wrinkling his nose, and nodded. "Yeah, we're good. Now go on. Get outta here. Before Emma decides she's sick of waiting and catches a ride with somebody else."

*****

Cackles of laughter erupted from the family room, while Chloe sat at the dining room table in the front of the house, scrolling through the Franklin photos she had taken so far. While waiting for the rosemary chicken to roast for dinner, the kids had started a movie and she had endeavored to make a little headway on her article. Her present task involved creating a list of the photos she liked best and making sure that she had a good balance between the historical, entertainment, and culinary aspects of the vibrant town.

It was slow going, but she had gotten through about half of the shots. Presently she was sifting through the ones of Sweet Cece's frozen dessert shop at Five Points. The rustic shop's hot pink and Kelly green decor and rainbows of candied toppings in glass dispensers for the frozen yogurt and ice cream jumped off the screen. As she studied the photos taken from various angles, her mind drifted to her conversation with Holt, as it had a dozen times already during this process.

He had been right about one thing. This tension between Jack and Chloe wasn't good. It was time she ended it.

The photos could wait. Jack couldn't. She closed the laptop and pulled out her cell. Would he answer? If he wouldn't take the call, then what?

I could fly out there tomorrow. I could take the kids with me, she thought. *They would probably be safer out there anyway. Reese couldn't argue with that. We could do Disneyland with Jack. Maybe see the ocean—*

The doorbell rang, interrupting her mental planning. She swiveled in the direction of the front door, eyeing it suspiciously. "Hey," she called out, still watching the foyer, "are you guys expecting someone?"

"Uh, no," Emma yelled back over Tyler complaining that he couldn't hear the television with all the shouting.

Chloe rose from her chair and took a hesitant step towards the front door. "You didn't order pizza or anything and not tell me?" she called out.

"You're cooking in there. Why would I order pizza?" Emma hollered back.

Chloe took several steps towards the door, trying to suppress her overactive imagination. *It's just a doorbell. It's not a hitman.* All the same, she patted her holster, checking for her pistol, ready to use it if need be. *It's probably just…somebody checking on us. Maybe Holt decided to come by*. She lifted the peephole cover and peeked through.

A bouquet of at least two dozen red roses, so large that it blocked any view of the delivery person, filled the entirety of the lens. Relief flooded her as, grinning, she unlatched the deadbolt and opened the door.

SIXTY

Chloe screamed as the caller lowered the paper-wrapped bouquet of roses, revealing his face. She threw herself at him and he caught her with his free arm, hugging her tight.

"Hey you," Jack said, burying his face in the amber curls around her neck.

"I can't believe you're here!"

"I'm here," Jack whispered in her ear. "To stay."

She pulled back, cautious optimism shining from her eyes. "What do you mean? You're done? You're staying?"

He nodded vigorously.

"But I thought—you said—"

"Yeah, I know what I said. Dumbest thing I've ever done."

She dropped her head onto his chest. In the span of fifteen seconds the world had righted again. She was warm and whole again for the first time since driving away from Atlanta. "I don't need time, Jack. I never did."

"I know. I was an idiot."

"But you're my idiot," she grinned, blinking back tears as she breathed in the familiar scent of soap on his skin.

Grinning back, and without seeming to spare a thought for the kids that had come running to see what the yelling was about, he dropped the bouquet, cupped her face, and kissed her.

* * * * *

After a long dinner of explanations and having Emma and Tyler play several rounds of 'guess the famous people Jack has met on movie sets,' the adults were left to clean up while the kids returned to their movie.

"So, not that I'm complaining," Chloe remarked, wiping out the roasting pan with a non-scratch pad and rinsing it beneath a fresh stream of water before handing it to Jack to dry, "but you still haven't said what exactly changed your mind about things. That's a pretty good one-eighty you did."

"Yeah, it was, wasn't it?" he agreed humbly as he took the pan and began drying it with a Williams Sonoma plaid kitchen towel. "I'd like to say that I came to my senses on my own, but the truth is, it was Riley."

Chloe smiled at the mention of John Riley, Jack's old Navy SEAL buddy and the man that had helped Jack rescue her from Tate's killers in Miami.

"I called him a couple days ago. I needed a fresh perspective from someone I could trust. He told me I was being an idiot."

Chloe chuckled. "I always did like him."

"Personally, I often find him to be a pain in the rear, but, in this case…he was right." Jack stopped drying and turned to lean against the counter. "And not just about me being an idiot." He paused, as if hashing out in his mind what he wanted to say before he said it. "Coming here and seeing you with Holt, how he was with you, it definitely sparked jealousy—"

"Jack—"

"No wait, let me finish. But I trust you, Chloe. And I know how you feel about me. So why did I make it about something so much bigger? How could I just walk away, just give up and leave? That isn't like me."

"No, it's not."

"No. Riley says that maybe I overreacted because all of the stuff going on—your reaction to the thing with Lila and your friendship with Holt and your relying on him—tapped into the fact that I've been feeling sorry for myself since what happened with my leg, and that it's possible I'm not processing what happened to me very well, and that maybe I've even been feeling like less of a person because I'm not as capable as before."

"Of course you're as capable—"

"You know I'm not."

"So you're a little slower. Who cares?"

"I care, apparently."

She inhaled heavily, thinking on that for a second. "And Riley came up with that in-depth analysis on his own?"

"Well, what he actually said was that I needed to stop throwing a pity party and get my head straight."

"That sounds more like him."

"But I read between the lines."

"Why in the world would you think any of that could ever affect how I feel about you?"

"I don't know…I guess that maybe part of me thought that if I saw myself as less than I was when you first got involved with me, then maybe you did too. And maybe you wanted a way to bow out gracefully."

"Did you really think that I might be looking for a way out because the guy I fell for ended up with a bad leg?"

"Well, when you say it like that it sounds ridiculous."

"Because it is ridiculous."

He took a copper pot she had finished washing and rubbed the cotton cloth over it, absorbing the water clinging to its sides. "It isn't just that. Riley thinks there may be more going on. That maybe I overreacted because I'm having a harder time processing the leg and everything else that happened in St. Gideon and Miami than I realized. It might even be cumulative…building on issues left over from my Navy days."

"What, like some kind of PTSD?"

"I don't know. That's what Riley thought. He also thought I should see someone. You know, to work through it. Deal with any ghosts rattling around in there." He paused apprehensively. "What do you think?"

She smiled at him, turning and slipping her arms around his waist. "I think Riley's a smart guy."

He kissed her forehead. "I'm really sorry about everything."

She shook her head, dismissing his apology. "Look, I overreacted too. About Lila. We both have our stuff to work through."

He nodded. "How about you don't assume that I'm secretly seeing someone if they happen to answer my phone, and I promise not to assume that every guy that smiles at you is trying to worm his way into your life."

Chloe's face flushed. "Umm, about that…"

SIXTY-ONE

Trevor Jernigan leaned forward on his elbows, resting his full weight on the modern steel-framed glass desk in his office. A stream of morning sunlight lasered through the partially opened blinds on the eighth floor of the CoolSprings Business Complex that housed his accounting firm in north Franklin. He held the translucent orange bottle up to the light, examining the two little white pills resting on the bottom. A few hours ago there had been three pills, but he had taken number three in the hopes of getting some sleep. No such luck.

His nerves were shot, as evidenced by the quaking bottle in his hand. He gripped it, contemplating another Xanax. Just to take the edge off. But that would only leave him with one. And with it being Saturday, there was no way he would be able to get a refill until Monday, if even then. He had already gone through this bottle way too fast.

He yanked a drawer opened, dropped the bottle in, and slammed it shut. The violence of it calmed him. It felt good to unload on something. Because there was absolutely no person he could unload on. Not without risking everything.

He ran a thick hand through his oily hair. Things were getting too close for comfort. They had identified Bellamy and now they knew. Or at least suspected. And unfortunately, suspicion was all these people needed. So he had slept on the couch across from the desk last night, banking on it being safer there than in his house. The office had a better security system, and it was unlikely they would expect him to stay there through the night.

His one hope was that they hadn't connected him to it yet. So far nothing suggested they had, but eventually they would get there. He just needed a little more time. Then he would be home free.

*****

"They put him in the hospital," he told Banyon matter-of-factly, though his sharp Jersey accent was bleeding through, letting her know that frustration was getting the better of him. "It'll draw attention."

"It's what it took." Banyon fought back the growl she wanted to unleash. She didn't like it when clients told her how to handle her business.

"Any sign of the money?" he asked.

"No," she told him. "But that's not a surprise. He wouldn't keep it where someone could stumble onto it."

"What about Adams? If he persists, will we be kept out of it?"

"I don't know. It just depends how deep he digs. But the more nicely wrapped a gift we hand him, the less likely he or anyone else will feel the need to keep going."

"I pay you to make sure that's the outcome we get."

Banyon's lips pinched angrily. "You know as well as I do that if I'm handed a cow chip cake, I can only make it taste so good. Next time listen to me when I tell you how to get out ahead of something. And have Drake handle things better on the front end. A little cooperation on his part when Adams first showed up could have avoided all of this. We could have laid it on the wife from the get-go. His approach was a miscalculation, which if you recall, I warned you about."

Brooding silence filled the space between them. "I don't normally tolerate that kind of insolence from my employees," he said.

Banyon took a long drag on her Dunhill, trying to decide whether or not this was the moment. It was. She blew out the toxic smoke with purposeful force, just so he could hear it all the way in Clearbay, New Jersey. "Well, good thing I'm not one of your employees, then, *Paul*." She brandished his name, speaking it with an exaggerated southern drawl that left no room for confusion about who owned whom. "I don't work for you. I partner with you in a profitable business arrangement that benefits us both on an as-needed basis. Emphasis on your need, not mine. I've got two dozen prospective clients on my waiting list, anxiously awaiting the day when I fire one of my present clients who has finally become just a little too demanding, stupid, or unwilling to do things my way. So, if you've forgotten how this works, maybe that day has come for you."

It wasn't a bluff. She would walk away without a thought. It was a move without financial or personal risk for her. In addition to the steady stream of individuals seeking her services, like all of her clients, she had more than enough dirt securely packaged for effective release on Paul's outfit, should the need arise. It was quite sufficient to ensure she would not end up as part of the foundation of some construction site somewhere.

But it wouldn't come to that. Paul was the son of a semi-retired, self-made 'business' owner in New Jersey and had inherited the position he now held, having sacrificed nothing to actually earn it. On the contrary, she had been hired by his father back in the day and had earned that man's trust and respect a hundred times over. In a contest between her judgment and Paul's, the father would side with her every time. Like most sons desperate for a father's approval, the last thing Paul would want to have to explain is why he fired the company's most reliable fixer, leaving the company in untold jeopardy.

As she knew he would, he caved. "Just fix it," he growled and hung up.

She smiled. They were all the same. Little yappy dogs with big dog egos, marking their proverbial fire hydrants until she finally had to remind them that she was the one holding the hose.

SIXTY-TWO

Duct tape. Check.
Zip ties. Check.
Duffel. Check.

He had waited all day, until finally darkness had fallen. Now, in the cover provided by the night, he finished his preparations in the makeshift driveway in his front yard. Reaching around to grab the black duffel off the ground beside his car, he set it in the trunk beside the case of bottled water. If he wanted the boy to last, he would have to keep him hydrated. And fed. The box of chocolate chip granola bars crammed in next to the water should take care of that.

Somewhere in the woods nearby a coyote howled, answered quickly by another. He ignored them, too focused at the moment on surveying his handiwork. The trunk space actually looked pretty cozy with the food and water and the thick wool blanket he had laid across the trunk bottom. Heck, he had even thrown in a pillow for good measure.

He wasn't a monster. No matter what Holt Adams said.

SIXTY-THREE

"You look fantastic!" Reese praised as Tyler ran around his hospital room in his newly bought Iron Man Halloween costume, stopping only to shoot imaginary foes with energy blasts from his hands.

"I know!" Tyler agreed, much too loudly. "Jack got it for me!"

Jack rubbed Tyler's head as the boy darted by, headed to intercept whatever evil villain he imagined lurked in Reese's bathroom.

"You didn't have to do that," said Reese.

"I wanted to," Jack assured him. "I've got a little catching up to do in the getting-to-know-you department, and a little bribery never hurts."

"I guess not," Reese said, chuckling.

From where Chloe leaned against the narrow window ledge, she smiled at the easy grace with which Jack had inserted himself into their newly formed dynamic. Reese had taken to Jack immediately, and although she wasn't craving Reese's approval in this matter, getting it made the whole situation feel even more right.

"You ready to come home tomorrow?" she asked Reese.

"More than. I can't eat any more Jell-O."

"Jell-O?" Tyler squawked, detaching from his universe-altering battle. "Who's got Jell-O? Can I have some?"

"We just ate," Chloe declared in disbelief. "You had two cheeseburgers. You cannot be hungry."

"He's a little garbage disposal," Emma taunted from where she leaned against the wall near the head of Reese's bed, not pausing to look up from her cell phone.

"Am not," Tyler argued, and blasted her with an invisible laser.

"We're taking Tyler trick-or-treating as soon as we're done here. He wanted to wait until dark," Chloe informed Reese.

"Only babies go when it's light out," Tyler groused.

"What about you?" Reese asked, directing himself to Emma.

She shrugged. "I want to hit the hay maze out near Carnton Plantation."

"We're going afterwards. All of us," Chloe said, emphasizing the latter part.

Perturbed disappointment flushed Emma's face. "I can go by myself. Trip and Jacob are coming with me."

Chloe wondered again if they had made the right choice, not telling the kids the whole story about what had happened to Holt. They knew someone involved in a case had gotten mad and started a fight with Holt, but Chloe and Reese had made the decision to hold back the information that these same people had probably threatened the kids too. If they had told Emma all of it, she might be more amenable to being chaperoned.

"Chloe's right," Reese echoed. "Until everything settles down, it's just better if someone's with you."

Emma shrugged again, but didn't fight back, possibly remembering what had happened when she had been shoved in Chloe's car.

"Holt agrees with us," Chloe added, hoping that would lend more credibility to the decision, given how highly Emma regarded him. She had actually been so concerned about him that she insisted on going by to see him at his place. Chloe had taken her over earlier that afternoon, while Jack stayed at home with Tyler.

"Yeah, I know. He told me," Emma said with a finality that made it clear she was done talking about it. "I guess me, Trip, and Jacob'll be your wingmen tonight," she told Tyler, just as he grabbed the end of Reese's bed and started to propel himself up and over the foot of it.

"Whoa!" Jack bellowed, catching Tyler before his knees landed on Reese's bad leg. "Watch your dad's leg buddy," he said, setting him on the floor. "He's still got a way to go before he's Avenger-ready."

Tyler tossed Jack a quick salute before tearing off down the hall.

Emma rolled her eyes. "If you think this is bad, wait until tonight after he's had two pounds of chocolate."

*****

By seven thirty, the pint-sized Iron Man was still going strong, fueled by a steady intake of Milky Ways, M&M's, and sour gummies. Having hit every house in Reese's neighborhood, they had moved on to the Harpeth Meadows subdivision just one street over to continue the pillaging. Tyler's neon orange plastic jack-o'-lantern was overflowing, and Chloe's pockets were full from collecting the escaping bits of candy that marked his trail.

Porch lights gleamed through the darkness at the Halloween-friendly homes, beckoning trick-or-treaters to ring their doorbells. Several of the more festive yards sported scarecrows or blow-up characters with pumpkin hats or plastic skeleton arms digging their way out of otherwise innocuous flower beds. One ambitious house had even trimmed the roofline with strings of purple and orange lights, blinking in sequence like some kind of twisted take on Christmas. Miniature ghosts, superheroes, and princesses swarmed the curbs, giddy with their hauls.

Chloe and Jack had purposefully fallen back a bit to give the older kids some space and at least the illusion of independence. Emma, Tyler and Jacob, who had opted for zombie make-up, white T-shirts and jeans, had actually turned out to be a big help, taking charge of Tyler as they went door to door. "Don't get too far!" Chloe yelled, trying to make out which of the older kids had Tyler's hand now as they headed for the next house, a couple of lots away.

"We're still good," Jack reassured her, as Emma, likely thinking the same thing, waved her off.

But Chloe was still feeling nervous, as a row of pines temporarily obscured the kids around a bend.

"It's fine," Jack said, as if reading her mind, and took her hand tightly, squeezing it confidently. "See," he said, as they cleared the pines and spotted the four kids again. "All good."

When Tyler's bucket strap broke from the weight of the candy, Chloe and Jack finally convinced Tyler it was time to head over to the maze next door to Carnton Plantation on the outskirts of

Franklin. The teens piled into Trip's car, again for the sake of some independence, while Chloe, Jack, and Tyler followed behind in hers.

When they got to the maze, the place was packed. Between that and the traffic at Carnton Plantation, which was across the street and down a bit from the property hosting the hay bale maze, there was hardly a parking spot to be found.

As they made their way from the lot to the maze ticket booth, Carnton Plantation loomed in the distance, its front illuminated by landscaping lights. Built before the Civil War, the plantation had quite a history, not the least of which was that it had served as a makeshift military hospital during the Battle of Franklin, one of the bloodiest battles of the entire Civil War. The house still had its bloodstained, original wood floors, and a Confederate cemetery covered a portion of its grounds. Both were rumored to be haunted. Halloween tours of the house often included costumed guides for patrons seeking potential real-life ghost interaction. The whole thing created a conveniently spooky backdrop for the hay maze.

Jack insisted on buying tickets for everyone who wanted to go, and had barely handed them out before the four kids dashed off towards the maze entrance, marked with towering hay bale pillars on either side and a white banner suspended between them that read, "Enter if You Dare."

"Hey, hold up!" Chloe yelled, and they all turned around. "Seriously, do not lose sight of Tyler in there," she ordered.

"Got it," Jacob said, grabbing Tyler's hand. "Let's go, little man."

"I'm not crazy about this," Chloe droned as the kids disappeared into the maze's depths.

"They'll be fine," Jack said, wrapping an arm around her. "Let's head for the exit. We can wait for them there."

They maneuvered through the crowd to the opposite side of the half-acre maze, where they stood, waiting for the kids to reappear. Chloe knew it was an overreaction, knew they were completely safe here, but her nerves stayed on edge, and would until all four turned back up. She compensated by stress-eating several mini-chocolate bars she had collected earlier from Tyler's goody trail.

"You're gonna be sick if you keep that up," Jack cautioned, watching her down her third Snickers.

"Well, we can't have that," came a familiar voice from behind them. They turned together and saw Holt, darkening bruises and all. "We don't need another McConnaughey in the hospital."

"You should be at home," Chloe chided, disapproval piercing her tone.

"The kids called. Tyler said I had to see his costume. He texted a little while ago. Said you all were headed here. Didn't have the heart to disappoint the little guy. They come through it yet?"

Chloe shook her head. "Still waiting."

Holt extended a hand to Jack. "So you're back?"

Jack nodded, clasping his hand around Holt's and shaking it.

"Well, I know she's glad to have you here." For half a second, an awkwardness passed between all three as Chloe's gaze flashed to Jack then back to Holt. Jack's focus never wavered from Holt. It was piercing. Knowing. And definitely message-sending. "Oh," Holt said, sniffing as the import of the situation registered. "So…I guess she told you."

Jack nodded lightly, his gaze still boring into Holt.

Holt looked away over the noisy crowd, as if stalling for the right response. When he turned back to them, a charismatic, though slightly sheepish smirk curved his mouth. "You're, uh, not gonna hit me, are you?"

A small, appreciative smile crept onto Jack's face in response, as he shook his head from side to side. "Looks like somebody already took care of that."

"Yeah," Holt answered, groaning, "well, wish I could say 'you should see the other guy' but as I was on the ground most of the time, I didn't even get a good look at him myself."

Jack snorted. "Can't say I haven't been there."

"So," Holt said, re-extending his hand in truce. "Are we good?"

Jack shook it and nodded. "Yeah. We're good."

As thrilled as Chloe was that it looked like the two of them were going to let bygones be bygones, she couldn't help but wonder whether she might get flattened by the tsunami of testosterone that had just rolled by.

"Great," Holt said, slapping Jack on the back. "So now that we're friends, can I ask you something?"

"Sure. Shoot."

"I hear you meet some famous people now and again out there in Hollywood land."

Jack tossed him a practiced look. "It's been known to happen."

"Great. So I was wondering if maybe you could get me Jennifer Lawrence's number…"

*****

After fifteen more minutes of waiting at the maze exit, Jacob and Tyler finally emerged, high-fiving.

"Nice, man," Jacob yelled, slapping Tyler's open palm.

"Hey, Holt!" Tyler exclaimed, spotting Holt and running to him. He jumped on his friend before anyone could ward him off. Despite the obvious pain it caused, Holt hugged the boy before setting him down.

"Hey buddy, you look great! Perfect Iron Man impression. Robert Downey Jr., has some competition."

"Who did your makeup?" Tyler asked, squinting at Holt's face in the moonlight. "It looks really real."

"Yeah, well, it feels really real," Holt grunted, gently rubbing the arm he had held Tyler with.

"You guys beat Emma and Trip," Chloe told them. "They still haven't come out."

"No, they left," Jacob said.

The words ran through Chloe like ice in her veins. "What do you mean they left?" she asked sharply.

"Emma left her phone at the house when we dropped off the candy. She wanted to get it, so Trip took her home. They're coming right back." Catching sight of Chloe's panicked look, he added, "They'll be back really fast. They left about ten minutes ago, so it'll be, like, just fifteen more minutes. She'll be okay. Trip's with her."

"Call her," Jack urged, though Chloe was already dialing Emma's cell. "She can stay on the phone with you till she gets back."

"Is Emma okay?" Tyler asked, worry creasing his young brow.

"She's fine, buddy," Holt reassured him, though he was unable to hide the concern behind his eyes.

"She knew she wasn't supposed to go off on her own," Chloe moaned, holding her phone up to her ear. After several seconds, she pulled it down. "She's not answering."

"Come on," Jack said, placing a hand on her back and ushering her towards the parking lot. "Tyler, Jacob," he continued, reaching for Tyler's hand, "come on. We're going."

"Why don't you guys stay here with these two?" Holt suggested as he walked alongside them. "I can go check on Emma and Trip."

"Not a chance," Chloe said, as her walk to the car turned into a run.

SIXTY-FOUR

"Emma!" Chloe hollered as they stormed through the backdoor of the house. "Why isn't she answering her texts?"

"She's a teenager," Jack reasoned.

Visions of Emma lying at the bottom of the stairs in the way they had found Reese bombarded Chloe as she flew through the first floor, desperate for a sign of the girl.

"She's probably fine," Jack assured her again as he kept pace with her.

"Probably, but till I know…" Her words trailed off as she barreled towards the stairs. The house was quiet, but there was a path of switched-on lights leading from the back of the house all the way to the second floor. As if someone had turned them on as they went in, but had forgotten to turn them off when leaving.

Chloe breathed a sigh of relief when she reached the bottom landing of the stairs. No body. No bloody words inked on the wall like when they had found Reese. *See, she's fine,* she told herself. *Stop overreacting.*

"Emma!" she called out, charging up the stairs headed for Emma's room. Like the downstairs, the lights were on, but there was still no Emma or Trip. Jack arrived just as she darted out into the hall to check the other upstairs rooms. Nothing.

"I left Tyler with Holt downstairs," Jack said as she passed him again headed into Emma's room. "You should try her again."

Chloe nodded and dialed for the twentieth time. "They've been here," she said, as she waited for an answer. There wasn't one, and she pocketed her cell again. "The lights are all on," she pointed out, then, noticing the light on in Emma's private bathroom, stuck her head in there.

"Anything?" Jack asked as she returned. Chloe shook her head.

"Well, they probably got what they came for and left again," he reasoned.

Chloe stood in the center of Emma's room, then turned in a circle, scanning for something, anything to lay her fears to rest. "Her laptop is open," she said, spotting the computer on the desk, "and running."

Something didn't feel right to Chloe. "The lights are all on, Jack. And the computer. The door downstairs wasn't locked either. I just ran in." She inhaled heavily. "Something's not right. It's like they flew out of here."

"Maybe. But you've also just described the way every teenager leaves a house. Don't jump to conclusions."

Jacob walked in, his body tense. "Any sign of them?"

Chloe shook her head no.

"I'm really sorry. She just told me she was going. I didn't think it would be a big deal."

"It's not your fault," Jack assured him, clapping him on the shoulder.

"Hey, um," said Holt, his voice coming from the hallway. "I'm out here with Tyler, and he's a little worried. Can we come in?"

"Yeah, of course," Chloe said, as the two appeared in the doorway. "It's okay, Tyler," she said, offering a confident smile to the boy, even though she didn't truly feel it. "She's probably headed back to the maze by now. I just don't like not knowing where she is."

"Hey," he said, spotting the glowing laptop screen on Emma's desk. "Maybe Trip just wanted to show her a picture."

"What?" asked Chloe.

Tyler nodded towards the photo currently pulled up on Emma's computer screen. "Trip asked me about Emma's computer a few days ago. He said he wanted to surprise her by printing out some photo for her. But I didn't know the password."

Chloe shifted her gaze to the screen. As the photo on it resonated with her, a foreboding chill rippled through her body.

"Holt." The severity of her tone immediately changed the atmosphere in the room. She leaned over the fuzzy black chair, positioned where Emma would normally sit, to get a better look at the screen.

"Yeah?" Holt answered, sidestepping Jack to move closer to Chloe.

"The thing. The thing that your friend said he overhead about the evidence they had against the bomber."

"What thing?" Holt replied, looking over her shoulder at the display.

The screen displayed an enlarged JPEG file, expanded to take up nearly half the monitor.

"About the evidence. At the scene. Something about how good it was—that it would nail whoever was responsible."

"Concrete," Holt offered, his tone low. "They said they had concrete evidence."

Chloe raised her hand, pointing to the photo on the screen. It was the one she had taken of Emma, Trip, and Jacob on the night of the bombing, with the fire in the background. More specifically, it was the first one she had taken, the one Emma insisted on re-taking because all of their shoes were propped up on the table, almost blocking out their faces. Chloe's index finger landed in the bottom right corner of the photo, pointing to Trip's sneakers, the treads of which were thoroughly and unmistakably caked from toe to heel with dried-in, dark red-tinted concrete.

SIXTY-FIVE

"I don't understand," Jack said, one arm wrapped protectively around Tyler, while Holt continued staring at the screen in disbelief.

"Red-footed," Holt muttered, then stepped back from the desk. "The D.A. said they had the bomber 'red-footed.' It was a play on 'red-handed.' A joke. She thought it was funny."

"Still not getting it," Jack pressed.

"The night before the bomb went off, someone—presumably the bomber setting the bomb—trespassed on the construction site and tracked through some recently poured red-tinted concrete," Holt explained.

"I saw this," Chloe mumbled, pointing at Trip's shoes again and sounding somewhat dazed. "For just a second that night. I took the photo. But later…I never put it together."

"Trip couldn't have done this," Holt countered. "It doesn't make any sense."

"Maybe it does," Jacob said, moving in closer, a heaviness settling into his features.

Jack, clearly concerned about little ears hearing whatever might come next, jumped into the conversation. "Hey, um, Tyler? Buddy? Why don't you go play in your room for a minute and let us talk?"

"But I want to know what's going on. What did Trip do?"

Jacob knelt down. "Nothing, Tyler. Probably nothing. So could you go hang in your room for a minute? I promise to catch you up when we're done."

Reluctantly, Tyler went. Jack held up a finger, then slipped out to make sure Tyler's door was shut. When he returned, Holt fired off a question, sounding much more like an attorney than a concerned friend now. "Why wouldn't that be crazy, Jacob? Why would you say that?"

"Trip hated Philip Donner. He talks about it all the time. He won't say why, and if I ask him he gets angry, so I don't anymore. But he was really happy when that building went up in flames. Said Donner deserved it. He was even happier when he heard the guy was dead."

"And he never said why?" Chloe pressed.

Jacob shook his head. "Just that Donner had hurt people. He said that if my dad did it, Donner really deserved it." Though the adults' eyes lingered on Jacob, clearly inviting further elaboration, the teen had nothing else to offer.

Chloe took a deep breath, steadying herself after the torrent of information just unleashed on them. Trip had red concrete on his shoes. He hated Donner. He had access to Kurt Sims's house whenever he wanted it. And he knew the code to Reese's house, which meant he could get in there whenever he wanted to without actually breaking in. Like the afternoon Reese went home and found an intruder. And was attacked by that intruder. Her stomach plunged.

The laptop had been left open to an incriminating photo. The lights were on. The doors unlocked. As if someone had run out of there fast. As if they were running from someone. Had Emma stumbled onto the photo and Trip panicked? Had Trip pulled it up and Emma stumbled onto him? Did he chase her out? Or worse…had he done something to her?

"We have to find Emma," she said. "Now."

"How?" Holt asked desperately.

Chloe turned in the room, looking for something. Anything. "I don't know. I don't know what to do. Jacob?" she asked, scrutinizing the teen. "Where would they go?"

He groaned. "I…I don't know," he stuttered apologetically. "I mean, there are a couple places we hang out. There's an old house, a shack, about a half mile down the railroad line from her dad's office. And we kill time at Sonic when we're bored. He likes that old cemetery by Kroger…"

"It's not going to be somewhere obvious. Not if this is what we think it is," Holt said.

"Her wallet is still here." From the foot of Emma's bed, Chloe picked up a small black fabric wallet attached to a lanyard. "She doesn't go anywhere without this. And that," she pointed emphatically at the computer screen, "that's a problem. She figured something out and now he…" She caught her breath, squeezing her eyes shut, forcing out the thoughts in her head that were accusing her of failing another sibling.

A sharp ding, like a glass mallet striking a bell, cut through the air in the room. All eyes flicked up, as the question, *Whose phone is that?* ran through each brain.

"It's mine," Jacob said, ripping his phone from his pocket. After a quick glance down, he held the phone up for all to see. "It's her. It's Emma." He pulled it back to read the text. "'Come quick. I need help. It's Trip,'" Jacob read, his voice quivering slightly, as he finished the message. "'Overlook.'"

Jack grabbed Jacob's phone, scanning the text for himself. "What does she mean, 'overlook'?"

A new level of gravity punctuated Holt's features as he answered, "Wilton Hollow Overlook. It's a trailhead in the woods, several miles southeast of town. It's where they found Phillip Donner's body."

*****

The sound of the car peeling out of the driveway startled him, jerking his attention up from the gun range video he was watching on YouTube.

"What the—" he muttered to himself as the car that had been parked in McConnaughey's driveway raced down the street, followed closely by a second car, the one that had been parked in front of McConnaughey's house.

What were they doing? He had just followed them home from that maze. He had expected them to stay put for a while. Where were they headed in such a hurry? Tossing the phone aside and depositing his half-finished Budweiser between his legs, he cranked the car and slammed it into drive.

*****

They followed Highway 96 west out of Franklin for nearly ten miles, past most commercial developments. The utility street lights drifted farther and farther apart, until ceasing altogether.

"Okay, you're coming up on it," directed Chloe, who was watching Google Maps while Jack drove. "Turn left here!"

"I see it," Jack told her, wrenching the wheel to turn onto Butcher Road. The sharp turn threw everyone to the right, especially Tyler in the back seat.

"Hey," Tyler yelled, sounding excited and a little annoyed at the same time.

Chloe spun to check him. "Sorry, hon. We're trying to get there fast."

"I'm good," he promised, and offered another salute. This was an adventure to him. A real-life superhero adventure. There was no point in telling him otherwise. The fact that he was there sickened Chloe, but they couldn't leave him at the house and there hadn't been time to take him anywhere else or call Mrs. Brinkley.

"Anything?" Jack asked, and Chloe knew he was referring to the dozen texts she had sent Emma.

"Nothing. No response." Her jaw set tightly. "I don't know why she just texted Jacob. I mean, okay, if not me, then why not Holt? She trusts him. If she's in trouble—"

"I don't know. Who knows how teens think? I mean, she might be just as worried about Trip getting in trouble as she is about her own safety. Holt's a lawyer. Maybe she's afraid of what that would mean for Trip."

"But she said she needs help, so that has to mean…I don't know…" She let the tail end of the thought hang without resolving it. Because there wasn't a way to resolve it. None of it made sense.

She cast a determined look at Jack, whose eyes were riveted to the road, his face flushed. An electricity she hadn't felt in him since the days in Miami seemed to be radiating from him now. An invisible powering up that both beckoned and warned off any danger that might be looming. He was in his element. This was Jack in his truest form. No matter how gentle, how kind a man he was, he was and always would be a soldier waiting for deployment.

But it wouldn't do any good to have him there if they were too late. Gravel and dust spit up off the road as they flew through the increasingly wooded countryside. The poorly paved secondary road was clearly never meant for vehicles traveling over thirty-five. And they were already going sixty-five.

"Faster," she told Jack, ignoring the speed limit sign that flashed by. "Faster."

He pressed on the gas just as Holt, following right behind in his car with Jacob, whipped out and passed him, then swerved back in front.

"He's leading us. He knows where they are," Chloe said.

Jack nodded, then braked suddenly as Holt flipped on a turn signal and made a sharp right. Jack followed, tires squealing as they followed the road that dipped in a stomach-dropping lurch before inclining again. They followed the gravel lane that was barely more than one car length wide for about a half mile, into what was an undeveloped, forested area. Thick brush and trees too high to see the tops of in the dark lined the lane, like something out of a Brothers Grimm fairy tale. Finally Holt turned off, following a dirt road about thirty yards before slamming on his brakes.

They were in a dirt-covered cutout, a parking lot more in theory than reality. The ground was well beaten down by the hundreds of cars that had come here over the years seeking hiking opportunities or privacy.

Emma and Trip's cars sat side by side at the back of the lot, haphazardly parked catty-cornered to one another. Two cars was a good sign. He couldn't have done something to her if she drove here. *But why would she follow him? Or did he follow her?* Chloe thought, panic rising again.

"Stay here!" Chloe ordered Tyler, her tone harsher than normal. "I'm serious, Tyler. Do not leave this car. Jacob," she commanded, as the boy reached her, "stay with him. Give him the keys," she told Jack, who threw them over the hood to Jacob. "If we aren't back here in one minute, you call 911. Got it? And if anyone comes out of here other than us, you drive off. You hear me? Don't wait for us."

Jacob shook his head. "No. Look they're my friends. I need to go in—"

"She's right, Jacob," Jack insisted. "We need you here and we can't risk something happening to you. Please."

Jacob's jaw was set hard and it was obvious he was not okay with the plan. Nevertheless, he nodded reluctantly and got in the car with Tyler. Satisfied, Chloe, Jack, and Holt charged down the narrow dirt path leading out of the back of the lot into the wooded darkness.

The worn path was well-traveled, and led to a small grassy clearing surrounded by towering evergreens and birch and ash trees. Multiple hiking paths branched off the main clearing. The rear of the space ended at a ledge that plunged off to the valley below. There, silhouetted against the inky sky were Emma and Trip, facing off against each other, the weak moonlight highlighting their features—as well as the gun Trip pointed at Emma.

"Trip." The voice was Holt's, but both deeper and softer than usual. He stood beside Chloe, whose heart had frozen at the scene before them.

The teens turned in unison. Trip's face was stricken, tear tracks dragged through his costume makeup, creating the odd illusion of a bawling zombie. Emma's gaze locked onto Chloe's with wide-eyed fear, as Chloe tried to telepathically send the message to the girl that everything would be okay. To not panic. But as she wasn't sure she believed it herself, she wasn't confident the message got through.

"Trip," Holt repeated, stepping towards the boy. Trip matched his movement with a defiant step backwards and raised the gun a half inch, reasserting his aim at Emma.

"You don't want to do that," Holt insisted, grabbing Chloe's arm and holding her in place when she instinctively lurched towards Emma. "Why don't you put the gun down?"

"She followed me here!" Trip spluttered, angry tears starting again. "I didn't…I told her to go, but she won't!" he barked, jabbing the gun at Emma again.

"Emma, why don't you step away from Trip," Chloe said encouragingly, reaching a hand out to the girl. "He doesn't want you there."

"No!" Emma shouted, her backbone straightening as she held her ground. "He'll just hurt himself."

"Emma, we don't want *you* getting hurt, either," Holt explained, gesturing for her to come to him. "Trip will be all right—"

"No, he won't! He'll kill himself. He said so before you got here. It's what he drove out here to do!"

In that moment the scene reoriented for Chloe, and understanding pierced the chilly Halloween air. Trip wasn't holding Emma at gunpoint. He was holding her *off* at gunpoint.

"Just let me be, Emma!" Trip hollered, choking back a sob. "I can't—I just can't anymore. I just want it over."

"But you don't, Trip," Holt insisted. "You don't. You want a way out. That's not the same thing." Holt directed himself to Emma. "Emma, I need you to trust me. Can you do that? Can you trust me?"

Emma's doe-like eyes flicked to Holt and stayed there. "He'll shoot himself, Holt. Or throw himself over," she moaned, jerking her head towards the outcropping's edge, just beyond Trip's back foot.

"No, he won't. Will you?" Holt asked, now firing a look at Trip. "You wouldn't do that while Emma stands six feet away, and force her to relive that over and over for the rest of her life."

Trip's shoulders dropped incrementally, and the gun shook in his outstretched hand.

"You wouldn't do that to Emma, or me or Chloe. Because whatever's happened, whatever you've done, you care about the people here in front of you and you wouldn't do that to them."

The boy's head swiveled left and right, his gaze drifting over each onlooker.

"Good. Okay," Holt said, taking Trip's silence for acquiescence. "See, Emma, it'll be okay. Just go to Chloe. Now."

Emma bowed up, uncertainty seeming to plague her resolve, until finally she hesitantly followed Holt's instructions and moved towards Chloe.

"Okay, good. Okay," Chloe cooed, taking the girl's arm as soon as she was near enough, and pulling her in close. Barely a moment passed before Trip reacted, jerking the gun to his temple.

All three of them screamed at once, bellows of "Trip," "No," and "Stop!" ringing through the backwoods. Holt charged him, bending low to take him out like a lineman sacking a quarterback, when Trip brought the gun down and fired.

SIXTY-SIX

"What are they doing in there?" Tyler asked, fidgeting in the backseat of Chloe's car, which had grown chilly in the dropping temperatures. "I'm getting cold."

Beside him, Jacob bounced his leg nervously, answering without looking because his eyes were trained on the entrance to the path to the overlook. "They're helping Emma and Trip. They'll be back any minute."

"Are Emma and Trip hurt?"

"No," Jacob assured him, hoping it was true. "Trip's just upset, we think. It'll be—"

The resounding, unmistakable crack of a gunshot shattered the air, causing them both to jump.

"What was—" Tyler started.

"I gotta go," Jacob said, already unlatching the door. He stepped out, then spun around, leaning over into the backseat. "Here, take this," he said, tossing his cell to Tyler, "and dial 911. Tell them you're at Wilton Hollow Overlook and to come quick, okay?"

"Yeah, okay, I know 911. But I don't want to stay here alone," Tyler whimpered.

"Just lock the doors." He slammed the door hard, yelled a muffled, "Lock it," at Tyler again, and took off running.

* * * * *

As the thunder of the shot reverberated around them, Holt skidded to a stop, nearly going down altogether when his back leg slid on some loose rocks.

"Stop!" Trip yelled, as Holt raised his hands in surrender. "I mean it."

Holt caught his breath. Trip had aimed high and to the right at the last minute, firing into the night sky. He wasn't aiming at him. Yet.

"Just talk to us, Trip. Okay?" Holt begged. "Just talk. I won't come any closer. But you've got to keep that gun down. Please. You don't want to shoot anyone by accident." Holt waited, and when Trip lowered the gun slightly, he continued. "Tell us what happened. None of this makes any sense to us."

"She saw," Trip said, and it was obvious he meant Emma. "She wanted to go get her phone, and I thought maybe I could find a way to finally get to her computer. I had to delete that photo. It was the only thing I did wrong. My only mistake." His eyes seemed distant, as if seeing, not the people in front of him, but something else far away. "She grabbed the phone from her room and said she wanted to use the bathroom real quick before we went back to the maze. I knew her password for the computer. I'd seen her use it at school." He cut his eyes at Emma. "I had tried to erase it straight from your phone," he started to explain. "That's why I took it that night in the alley. But your phone password wasn't the same as your computer password."

"You broke her arm?" Chloe interrupted, trying to make sense out of his disjointed story. "That night in the alley? It was you that attacked her?"

"I didn't mean to," he whined, and the devastation on his face suggested he truly meant it. "It was an accident. I just wanted the phone. My photos go right to the cloud and I figured hers did too. If I could delete it from there it would be gone everywhere. I didn't think she would chase me down."

"It's okay, Trip," Emma said softly. "I get it. I'm fine—"

"No!" Trip shouted, beginning to rock back and forth on his heels. "It's not fine."

"Trip," Holt interrupted soothingly, "finish telling us about tonight. Help us understand."

Trip nodded. "I opened the computer right to her photos and found it. That first photo Chloe took with our feet propped up. See, that night, when you," he nodded at Holt, "were there talking to her dad, I heard you. I heard you say they had concrete evidence, and I knew. Because I'd had to scrape it off my shoes. It had gotten all over the outside. I got it off the sides real good, but I was in a hurry and didn't bother with the bottoms and then I forgot about it once I got in the car and drove off. When you said it at the house, I checked, and it was still there, all caked in the treads.

"I panicked, went home, and scraped it off. After that I thought I was good, but then I saw the photo of the three of us in Starbucks on the night of the fire on Emma's Instagram, and remembered the bad photo with our feet in the air. I knew it probably showed the caked-on concrete. I was scared that eventually someone would see it and figure it out. I knew I had to delete the bad one."

"What happened tonight?" Holt pressed.

"I've been trying to get on that computer all week, but everybody's always been around. If I'd just…" he shook his head hard, as if chasing the thought away. "At the maze, when she said she needed to run home I thought, you know, maybe, maybe I can get on it if it's just us. And she did, she left me with it. She went in the bathroom and I found it, zoomed in on the photo real close, just to see how bad it was. It was so obvious. And I just froze, thinking what could've happened if Mr. McConnaughey had seen that. I should have just hit delete that second, but…I don't know. And then Emma was behind me, asking me what I was doing, looking over my shoulder at it, asking what that red stuff was on my shoes, and I freaked. 'Cause now she knew, and if she ever mentioned it to you or she ever heard any of you talking about red concrete," he said, tossing his head in Holt's direction, "it would come out and it would all be over. So I just took off. I didn't think she would follow me—could follow me—I was driving so fast." He glanced around at everyone, the weight of his confession seeming to sink in. "And now I'm trapped. I'm out of options."

"No," Holt disagreed, "you're not. You still have options."

Trip laughed, a desperate, mirthless laugh. "Really? What options?"

"Reasons matter, Trip. I'm an attorney. I know."

"You want a reason?" Trip roared, the placid confessor replaced by enraged crusader. "He was destroying my family! He blackmailed my mom! She and my dad had finally started to make it work. Before that, they were always fighting. About them. Me. Keeley's career. Mom was career obsessed. Dad ignored everybody but Keeley. Then

Keeley tanked. She started cutting. It woke them up. Everything changed. They worked it out. Suddenly we were almost a family again.

"Until Phillip Donner started blackmailing my mom. I heard her talking to some guy one night." His face turned down even more, revulsion creasing its edges. "She…I think she had an affair with someone…whoever she was talking to. It happened before she and my dad got better. But then she broke it off and everything improved and we all…" He paused, realizing he was drifting. "That night, she thought I was asleep, but I'd heard her yelling and it woke me up. I thought she and dad were having another fight, but it was something else. It was that guy on the phone. She was telling him that Donner had threatened to tell everyone, including Dad, about the affair, tell the news channels, tell anyone that would listen."

He stopped to breathe finally, something he hadn't done much of while expelling his story. It was rushing out, a deluge he had dammed up with fear and loyalty for far too long. "She told this guy that Donner had told her that unless she threw the Sims lawsuit, unless she intentionally let him win, she would lose everything. He was right too. If Donner had spread that around, that would have been it for my mom and dad. And Keeley would have lost it again. That's when I planned the bomb. I thought maybe I could scare him and his investors away. That maybe he would sell the project and move on and he wouldn't need my mom anymore. It wasn't hard. Instructions for that sort of thing are all over the internet. I found so many different kinds…" He was rambling. Disconnected.

"But that's not what happened," Holt pressed, trying to get him to focus.

Trip shook his head, wagging the gun in time with his movements. "It only made Donner more angry. He threatened my mom again. She was crying all the time…and now, I've made it worse. Now everyone will know the truth anyway and our family will fall apart and I'm to blame—"

"Why Kurt Sims, Trip?" Holt interjected, steering Trip away from his increasingly frantic realization, trying to diffuse things. "Why frame him? He's Jacob's dad."

"Exactly. Because he deserved it. Because—"

"Trip, don't." Jacob's voice was steady and firm as he stepped out from the shadows at the entrance to the clearing.

Trip paused for just a moment, eyeing his friend with a mix of sadness and determination. "He was terrible to Jacob." Trip let this hang in the air, the truth settling on everyone before continuing, his words ugly and sharp. "Mr. Sims made Jacob feel like he wasn't worth anything. He said…awful things. All the time. And he hit him. I've seen him punch Jacob twice when he didn't do well on the field—"

"Trip, please stop," Jacob urged, stepping closer to the group. "Dad doesn't…he doesn't mean to. He's just not right. Hasn't been since mom died. He doesn't want to hurt me—"

"Stop defending him! Don't you see? If you don't get away from him, he might end up really hurting you. Killing you or something. You wouldn't leave. So I was going to make him leave. He already had a history with Donner. The cops were going to suspect him anyway. The rest wasn't hard."

"You planted the bomb materials and the concrete residue at Jacob's house," Holt surmised.

Trip nodded.

"And that day at Jacob's when someone jumped out at us from the closet—that was you?"

Trip nodded again. "I had messed up. I'd had my ball cap on when I planted those concrete bits in Mr. Sims' treads and on the floor in there. I was so nervous and hot. I thought I was gonna pass out. I must've taken it off without realizing it. It was stupid. But I had to get it back before anybody realized it didn't belong to Mr. Sims."

"Trip," Holt started, his voice even more solemn, "what happened with Reese? At his house?"

Trip looked away, over the cliff's edge. His body started to quiver, and energy seemed to issue from the hand holding the gun, so much so that Holt took a small step back.

"Trip?" Holt inquired gently.

"That was an accident." His tone begged for understanding as he swiveled abruptly to face Emma. "I didn't mean it, Emma. I promise I didn't." Fresh droplets snaked down the existing tracks in his makeup.

"Trip," Chloe said soothingly. "We just want to understand. Just tell us what happened."

"Like I said, I hadn't been able to get into your phone," he said, looking at Emma, "but I knew the password for your computer. So I went to your house while all of you were at the carnival. I figured I could get in, delete it, and get out. But then he showed up. He must've heard me upstairs, looking for your laptop. I couldn't find it. I was headed downstairs to search when I met him at the top of the stairs. I had on a ski mask, so he didn't know it was me. He started swinging this golf club, we fought, and he fell." The tears were pouring now. "I didn't mean to hurt him. He wouldn't get up. He just laid there. I was terrified. There was so much blood from his head. But he had a pulse, so I thought he would be okay. I remembered that crazy box with the writing on the porch you told me about and thought I could use that, you know, make it look like something else, part of that or whatever. I thought he would just wake up and have a broken leg or whatever…"

Trip's voice drifted off, and for several moments everyone stood in silence, not saying the thing they were all thinking. That it hadn't been just a broken leg and that Trip had not called 911. He had just left Reese there on the floor. To whatever fate awaited him.

"You all think I'm a monster."

"No," Holt said. "No, we don't. We think you were scared and in way over your head."

"No!" Trip shook his head and raised the gun towards his own head. "I almost killed him."

"But you didn't, Trip, stop!" Holt bellowed, holding up his hands. "You're not a killer! You're not! You didn't mean to hurt Reese and you didn't plan on killing Donner either, did you? It was an accident, just like Emma's arm and Reese's fall. You just wanted to talk to him. To convince him to back off your mother. You wanted to scare him. And what happened? He jumped you instead?" Holt postulated, grabbing at theories. "Or maybe pulled a gun on you? Did one of his hired hands—"

"I didn't kill him," Trip asserted, pained disappointment and disbelief filling his eyes.

"I know you didn't *mean* to kill him. You just meant to scare him. You took Kurt's gun—"

"I took the gun, I even wore Kurt's stupid boots out there, but I didn't kill him!" Trip shouted, as slowly, like a creeping tide at dusk, a deeper melancholy enveloped him. "But you think I did, don't you?" He took a resolute step towards the cliff's edge. "You all think I did."

"It was self-defense, Trip. We can work this out," Chloe said, her tone begging him to listen.

Trip shook his head. "No. You think I killed him. And everyone else will, too." He spoke with finality, and in one sharp movement upward, drew the gun's muzzle to his temple.

SIXTY-SEVEN

Instead of following Chloe and Holt into the clearing, Jack stepped sideways into the woods surrounding it, out of sight of the teens who were standing much too close to the outcropping's edge. Circling around the left side of things, he judged that the cliff's edge dropped straight down twenty feet, into masses of sloping brush and tree-covered terrain that probably dropped another thirty feet to a final floor not visible from this vantage point. The best-case scenario if Trip jumped off was that the kid would end up with a nasty set of broken bones that might or might not change the way he walked. Worst case—that jump would be as effective as a shot from the gun the kid was barely holding onto.

Jack could hear Holt trying to carry on a conversation with the boy, urging Emma to step away. Jack didn't know if Holt could hear it in the kid's voice, but he had been around enough desperate men during his military career to recognize the sound of someone imploding when he heard it. The teen wasn't bluffing. He truly believed he was out of options. Not a mental place you wanted an armed, scared kid to be. No matter what Holt thought, no matter how long he stalled, there was little chance he was going to talk the kid out of doing what he came there to do.

Moving as quietly as he could with a leg that fought him every inch of the way, Jack picked through the heavy underbrush on the downward slope. The moonlight was just bright enough to illuminate a series of staggered, narrow clefts across the face of the drop. It was going to be a lot like scaling a cliff without rappelling gear, but if he could make it to within a yard or so of the top, he might have a chance.

Maybe.

*****

Trip swept the gun up to his head just as Jack propelled himself up and over the outcropping's edge. In a single, swift movement, Jack wrenched the gun from Trip's shaky grip, while simultaneously dropping the boy to the ground by sweeping his legs out from under him. One of Trip's lingering fingers, however, involuntarily depressed the trigger before he completely let loose, sending a booming crack out over the ledge.

Screams from everyone else echoed the crack reverberating in their ears as Trip lay on the ground, panting, slumped over, heaving sobs. Emma ripped herself from Chloe and ran to Trip, falling over him and whispering, "It's okay. It's okay."

Chloe moved to her sister, gripping Emma's shoulder. She looked over gratefully at Jack, bent over a few feet away, gulping in breaths, his hands bracing on his hips.

Thank you, Chloe mouthed, her own breathing still labored.

Holt plopped down beside Trip, rubbing his face and exhaling weakly. "Trip," he said, putting a hand on the boy's back, "whatever you do, do not say another word."

SIXTY-EIGHT

"Where's Tyler?" Chloe said, her gaze flicking up to Jacob from where she squatted on the ground, the meaning of his presence finally striking her.

"He's fine. He's in the car. Locked up," Jacob insisted.

She was already moving, quick steps crackling on loose gravel. "We told you not to leave him!"

"I left him with my cell," Jacob said, justifying himself as he ran after her.

"I'm calling 911," Jack said, keeping pace with her as he pulled his cell out.

"I already did—or at least, Tyler should have. I told him to call 911 when I heard the shot," Jacob said. "The cops'll be here any minute now."

"He's probably scared to death," Chloe seethed, bursting into the lot to find the back door of her car wide open.

"Tyler!" she yelled, darting to her car and ducking inside. But her words fell wasted into the deserted back seat, empty except for Jacob's abandoned cell phone.

* * * * *

"Tyler!" Chloe called again, turning in circles, looking in and around the other three cars as Jack did the same.

"Tyler!" Jack bellowed, as Holt, Trip, and Emma appeared at the edge of the lot. Holt walked alongside Trip, gripping his arm tightly, more out of an effort to hold the boy up rather than to keep him from absconding.

"What's wrong?" Emma asked. "Where's Tyler?"

Chloe threw her hands up. "I don't know! He's just gone…the back seat's empty."

"He was right here when I left," Jacob pleaded, guilt sharpening his features. "Maybe he just went looking for us—"

Chloe shot a look at him. "No, you left your cell with him, right? Well, it's on the back seat. He wouldn't have left it."

"Hold on. If he still has his phone on him, then I should be able to find him," Emma said shakily. "Just let me check my cell."

"I didn't think about him having one when I left him mine," Jacob mumbled to himself as Emma pulled her phone out, groaning as she tapped several buttons.

"The data out here is just 3G," she said, frustrated. "It'll take a minute." She fidgeted back and forth, one foot to the other, while waiting for her app to load. "He's got to be okay. He's got to," she muttered nervously to no one in particular.

"If somebody took him, they would've checked him for a cell phone. He won't still have it on him," Jacob lamented.

"Except that yours was left in the backseat," Jack corrected. "If someone did take him and found your phone on him, they might not have looked any further. They wouldn't expect him to have two."

"Or maybe nobody took him, and he just wandered off and left Jacob's cell because he had his own. He could've seen an owl or something and gone off chasing it," Holt suggested.

"It's up!" Emma shouted excitedly, as she pressed Tyler's name on the list of friends in her Pal-Pinpoint app. A spinning compass needle appeared, indicating the app was searching, looking for Tyler's current location. It went round and round in painful suspense.

"I don't understand. Why didn't Tyler say something about this app earlier when we were looking for you?" Chloe asked Emma.

"I haven't given it permission to share my location. I don't want people knowing where I am all the time," she explained.

Jack squeezed Chloe's shoulders as they waited for Emma's phone to finish locating Tyler. "Holt's right. It's possible he just wandered off."

"Yeah. Maybe." Chloe's tone made it clear she didn't believe that was true.

Seconds later, when the needle stopped spinning and Tyler's dot appeared on the map over five miles away, it was terrifyingly obvious she was right.

* * * * *

"He's there," Chloe cried, tapping the screen, "on—what does that say? 'Trailblazer Road.'"

"Wait a minute," Holt said, pulling the phone from her. He studied the map and the tiny dot representing Tyler, his face falling. "I know that road," he said ominously, his finger tapping the screen glass agitatedly. "It's part of Trailblazer Court. It's a trailer park southeast of here, in Harrison County." His clouded expression tightened even more.

"What is it?" Chloe asked.

"I think I know who may live there—who may have taken him," Holt said, his voice incredulous, as if he didn't believe his own conclusions. "I think it's my client's ex-husband." He looked at Chloe expectantly. "Dermot Crutchfield? You were there, at his hearing that day we went to court with Kurt, remember? It's a custody case. I represent the mother. He's the father—been AWOL forever. Owes thousands in child support. Hasn't shown up to anything, but—"

He cut himself off, pausing, as he lit up with understanding. "Oh, the box!" he exclaimed. "The box on Reese's porch! That happened the Friday before Crutchfield's hearing. I *told* you it was probably one of our domestic crazies," he said, zeroing in on Chloe. "Remember? I said it might have been one of our other cases. Crutchfield is angry because we're working with his wife to terminate his parental rights. He wants us to stop helping her. Reese keeps trying to take his kids away, so now he's taken Reese's son."

"Would he hurt him?" Jack asked.

Holt's eyes flicked soberly to Chloe and Emma, then back to Jack. "We need to get there. Now."

"Okay, come on. Let's go," Chloe urged, tugging on Jack's sleeve and stepping towards her car. "Emma, I need your cell," she demanded, holding her hand out. "So we can track Tyler if he moves."

Holt pulled his own cell out and handed it to Jacob. "Call 911 again and keep them on the line. I'll talk to them in a second," he instructed. As Jacob dialed, Holt turned back to Chloe. "You're a good fifteen minutes away from the trailer park, at least. I'll stay here with them," he said, gesturing at the teens with his free hand, "and deal with the police when they get here, which ought to be any minute if Tyler got a chance to call 911. We'll send help over there as soon as we can," he said, as Jack and Chloe slid inside her car. "And be careful," he cautioned, leaning down beside Chloe's open window. "Ten-to-one, Crutchfield will be armed."

Emma squeezed past Holt, bracing herself against the window frame. "Let me go with you! He's my brother, too."

"Emma, no," Chloe told her resolutely as Jack started to back the car up. "You stay here with Holt. And you," she said, pointing at Holt, "better take her keys. You've got enough to worry about without her leaving when your back is turned."

Holt held his hand out to Emma, who dropped her keys into his palm as Jack tore out of the lot, the hazy red glow of the taillights piercing the cloud of dust trailing behind.

SIXTY-NINE

Jack made it to Trailblazer Court in less than ten minutes, racing over miles of winding, unlit back roads into the depths of Harrison County, where there were more deer than people and a significant chance of slamming into one when flying at sixty miles an hour in the dark.

He went around the last bend so quickly that he had to slam on the brakes as they came up suddenly on a worn, depressing trailer park of only eight trailers, spread wide down the long, straight stretch of Trailblazer Road running right down the middle. At the entrance, a single utility post light illuminated two sections of mildewed, white fence that bordered either side of the road. The section on the left bore a sign that read "Trailblazer," while the sign on the right, hanging loosely from the only nail still holding it up, finished, "Court." Jack cut the headlights and turned in, rolling along at about ten miles an hour.

"Can't you go faster?" Chloe pressed.

"I don't want to warn him we're coming. I don't want to spook him. That's when people get hurt."

Chloe swallowed thickly. "He's got to be okay."

"He will be."

"What if Crutchfield's armed?"

"He needs to worry about whether I'm armed."

"Are you?"

"What do you think?" he asked.

This was not your family-friendly trailer park, with kids' bikes, balls, and bats left behind in the yard. There were no cheerful pots of flowers or well-manicured lawns like you found in many such communities. Instead it felt like the kind of place a cable station would use as the set for a show about meth dealers.

Each lot was about fifty yards wide, giving the trailer occupants a decent amount of privacy for whatever nefarious activities might be going on inside. The units all seemed to be in a similar state of disrepair—rusted patches marring the stained white or cream exteriors, boards missing from the rickety wooden steps leading up to small landings at the front doors, and broken windows scattered throughout. Only one yard had been mowed anytime recently. The rest were surrounded by ankle- to knee-high crabgrass and ragweed, with paths worn down by consistent treading to the front door.

Lights gleamed dimly through dingy curtains in several units. One or two trailers were completely blacked out, looking all but abandoned. Most had at least one vehicle parked in front, a couple of them with a second vehicle stereotypically up on concrete blocks.

Jack rolled the windows down as they neared the halfway point down the street, telling Chloe to listen closely for tell-tale sounds. But the puttering of the car engine was the only noise disturbing the unsettling silence of the place. Holt had texted to tell them that Crutchfield's place would be the last one on the right. It finally emerged from the darkness, sitting about thirty yards off the road, as forlorn as the others. A single window at the far-left end of the trailer gleamed through its covering, though no shadow moved against it. The dirt driveway led from the street right up to the front steps, where a gray Camry was parked. Jack came to a quiet stop one lot down from Crutchfield's property.

He turned to Chloe, his face like stone. "I'm going up there. Stay here, call 911." He handed her the keys and slipped his SIG Sauer from his waistband. "Tell them we found the place. Stay on the line till they get here. And keep your weapon out," he told her, eyeing the handgun she had unholstered and placed on her lap during the drive there, "but don't come out here. It's just for your protection, got it?"

Chloe wanted to argue, because every instinct told her she should get out and search for Tyler. But Jack knew what he was doing. So she nodded and he kissed her forehead quickly before slipping from the vehicle and closing the door silently.

Chloe held 911 on the line as she watched Jack crouch low and move across the lawns to the parked sedan. She described what was happening, unable to keep the quiver out of her voice as the operator repeatedly told her Jack should return to the car, lock the doors, and wait for the dispatched officers to arrive.

"We can't just sit here and wait," Chloe argued. "He's in there somewhere."

"I understand, ma'am, but…" The operator's voice faded into the background for Chloe as Jack made it to the sedan and crept up to the rear passenger window, keeping the car between himself and Crutchfield's trailer. She held her breath as he rose up just enough to look inside. He scooted forward to the passenger window, peered through it then turned back to Chloe, shaking his head. Tyler wasn't in there.

Chloe's heart dropped. *Where is he?* she wondered, her pulse pounding into her ears. *Inside the trailer? With Crutchfield? Or somewhere else?* She caught her breath, her eyes flashing to the Pal-Pinpoint screen again. Service was so bad out here that Tyler's dot had turned into a large circle encompassing a wide area around the trailer park and beyond. It was impossible to know exactly where he was now. If he had moved, they wouldn't know it until it was too late.

Jack made his way around the car to the trailer, headed for its one illuminated window. Moving stealthily, he pressed against the trailer, sliding along it in order to avoid detection from anyone inside that might be looking out. Because the trailer was on risers, the base of the window was at nose-level. Slowly Jack pushed up, just far enough so that his eyes rose above the bottom of the pane. Jack hovered for a moment where a minuscule slit separated the drawn curtains, then shrank back down. He held up one finger and shook his head again. *No Tyler.* He paused, held up a second finger and shook his head once more. *No Crutchfield, either.*

Had Holt been wrong? If they had raced off to the wrong location…

Jack tapped his chest and thumbed towards the far corner of the trailer. He was going around. Though he couldn't see her, she nodded her understanding, and watched as he disappeared around the side. There was no telling what he was walking into. For the hundredth time in the last hour, Chloe prayed that God would keep him safe. Would keep Tyler safe. Would show them where he was.

The seconds dragged by, the 911 operator doing her best to assure Chloe that help was on the way. She waited, pulling nervously on a stray curl as the blackness of the night seemed to close in on her, the light from the trailer window its only challenger.

And then, something cut through the vacuum of light and sound. Movement out of the corner of her eye. A flicker of something, illuminated by the moon. Movement…at the back of the car.

The trunk was opening.

SEVENTY

The trunk opened just a crack, and two tiny fingers groped outward, like some kind of bad horror movie where a doll trapped in a coffin tries to escape.

"Tyler!" she gasped and, forgetting Jack's instructions and the woman on the phone, Chloe darted quietly out her door and charged towards the sedan, holstering her weapon and hunching over as best she could while running at full speed.

She crossed the distance in less than five seconds. When she reached the trunk, she threw it open. Tyler lay inside, his mouth duct-taped shut, feet and hands bound with zip ties, his arms outstretched towards the opening.

"Tyler!" she cried softly, reaching in and grabbing him. She pulled hard, lifting him into a sitting position. "Are you okay?"

Tyler nodded. Other than the wet tear streaks across his face from when he had been lying down, he looked all right.

"We have to go, quickly. Come on," Chloe said, taking him beneath his arms and hoisting him up and out of the trunk. He landed, wobbling unsteadily on his bound feet. "Okay. It's okay," Chloe assured him, bending over to sweep him into a cradle position. "I'll carry you."

"No, you won't." The icy growl came from directly behind Chloe. She screamed, spinning around to find a hulking Goliath in a dingy plaid shirt and baggy jeans, menacingly standing just a breath away. A dark, heavy beard covered most of his face, with sideburns reaching up to black eyes that bore through her.

He shoved her aside so hard that she crashed to the ground while he picked Tyler up, dropped him back in the trunk, and, over Tyler's muffled screaming, slammed the lid shut. Before Chloe could scramble to her feet again, he was on her, and she was crab-walking backwards, trying to remain out of his reach.

"Stop! Stop!" Chloe screeched, kicking at his thick hands as they grabbed for her. She made contact with his shin and he roared. Diving down, he snatched her up by the shoulder and threw her against the trunk, where she spun to face him.

The barrel of his gun was so close to her face that Chloe could barely focus on it. He glared at her, the corner of his mouth turned up in a snarl. Chloe's eyes flashed fleetingly to the trailer and back.

"Looking for your friend?" he grunted ominously. "The one sneakin' around the backside of my house? He ain't comin'. He's taking a siesta, courtesy of yours truly. Now you're gonna listen and do what I tell you, or you'll be joinin' him. Got it?"

"Look," Chloe said, holding her hands up in surrender. "We just want Tyler back. Give us Tyler and drive away. The police are on their way. You can be gone. We won't stop—"

Crutchfield pressed the gun barrel into Chloe's forehead. "So you're *not* gonna listen?"

She caught her breath, the metal cold against her skin. "Yes, I mean…no, I am…I will…listen."

"You're gonna walk into the trailer, sit down, and shut up," he ordered. "You're gonna be still while I fix you up with zip-ties and that's it."

"What about Ty—"

"The boy's no concern of yours. Now, you do one stupid thing and I'll—"

A loud crack filled the air as a swift flash of a metal bat collided with Crutchfield's head, sending him stumbling to the right, falling one foot over the other. Crutchfield writhed on the ground, disoriented, as Jack snatched up his weapon and stepped a few feet back, the bat slung over one shoulder and Crutchfield's gun outstretched in the opposite hand. Though clearly in command, Jack wobbled a bit as he leaned heavily on his good leg, and something about his gaze seemed slightly unfocused.

Crutchfield moved to press himself up, and Jack tensed. "Stay down!" he yelled. "Do not test me on this."

Chloe turned, knocking on the trunk. "Tyler! Open it—open it! It's okay now!"

The lid cracked again, and Chloe ripped it open the rest of the way, nearly diving inside as she wrapped Tyler up in her arms.

SEVENTY-ONE

"Hey there," Chloe said, as Reese slipped through the backdoor onto the porch where she sat, watching Tyler and Jack toss a football around. The soft mid-afternoon light peeked through the tree line, casting a golden glow on the still-green fescue and the man and boy tromping through it. "You get a good nap?"

"Enough," Reese said, gently lowering himself into a chair at the patio table. "It feels like I've done nothing but sleep the last week and a half." He watched Tyler catch a long pass and smiled. "He looks better."

Chloe nodded. "No nightmares last night." Saturday night after finding Tyler, the boy had been unable to sleep well, wrestling with bad dreams until dawn. But last night, he had surprisingly slept like a rock.

"That's good. Really good. I'm glad we kept him out of school today, but maybe tomorrow he can start back? Get back to normal?"

"Probably a good idea."

"I've already set up something with a therapist. Emma too. Just to be sure."

"They'll be okay."

"I know, but still." He groaned softly, lifting his injured leg to incline it in the chair beside him. "How about you?"

"I'm fine. It's Jack you should be asking about. Crutchfield whacked him pretty hard with that bat."

"Not hard enough," Jack muttered, just loud enough for them to hear, before tossing the ball back to Tyler in a perfect spiral. "Should have done better than a side-swipe."

"He didn't know how hard-headed you are," Chloe called out, chuckling.

"His mistake. Along with taking my gun, but leaving the bat." Jack grinned at her, then jogged towards Tyler. Despite the twenty-four-hour headache and a full night of Chloe waking him every two hours to monitor the concussion, Jack's spirit seemed lighter than it had been in months. Even though he would never admit it, Chloe knew that stopping Trip and swooping in to handle Crutchfield was a big part of that. It was proof that Jack could still do the thing he loved doing the most—be a protector. The limp was still there—she could see it now as he chased after Tyler—but it wasn't derailing him. She smiled, thinking of how they had met like this, him playing football with a friend and 'accidentally' hitting her with the ball. Her heart warmed at the thought and, as she watched him, nervous flutters raced through her, as discombobulating as ever.

"Have you talked to Holt?" Reese asked, snapping her back to him.

"Um, yeah," she answered. "He stopped by while you were out."

"Any updates?"

"He said the D.A.'s office dropped the charges against Kurt this morning. He's out. But now, child services is investigating, so he'll probably be back in court soon. Jacob is set up to stay at his aunt's indefinitely. That was working really well already, so apparently the powers that be saw no reason to change it."

"How's Jacob holding up?"

"Emma's been with him a lot. She's over there now, actually. I told her she's got to go back to school tomorrow, but today it was good for her to be with him. She says he's all right, even seems maybe a little relieved that he's out of Kurt's house. But he's worried about his dad. He never planned on telling anyone what was going on with Kurt. I think he was just planning on getting out of there when he turned eighteen." Chloe shook her head sympathetically. "There's more, but Holt can tell you when he comes by later. He said he'll be busy sorting Trip out the rest of the afternoon, but he'll stop by after that."

Confusion flitted across Reese's face. "But we're conflicted out of Trip's situation after everything that's happened. What's his involvement?"

"He's not representing Trip. Cecilia Tucker hired some other lawyer for Trip, but apparently she wants Holt around, at least initially. She thinks he might be able to add something, have some sort of insight. He says she's crushed. Trip did what he did because of the affair. The guilt is killing her."

Reese nodded. "I can only imagine."

"He says they're charging him as a juvenile, so, hopefully that'll make things a little easier. Maybe he can start over eventually. It's really sad. They've got him on suicide watch."

"What are they charging him with?"

She shrugged, waving an uncertain hand. "I'm not sure. You'll have to ask Holt. But he's admitted to almost everything—the bomb, you on the stairs, the assault on Emma in the alley—so, I guess, whatever stems from all that. He's also been talking non-stop. Explaining a lot of things."

"Like what?"

"Like how he managed it all. Apparently he got the idea to actually frame Kurt when he found the stuff on his shoes. Before that he figured they would suspect Kurt, but with the concrete, he realized he could really seal the deal. The night Donner was shot, Trip hung out at Jacob's house till Kurt passed out. Kurt's been passing out most nights, so Trip was counting on it happening eventually. When he finally did, Trip used Kurt's cell to call Donner and convince him to meet at the overlook. He said Kurt didn't even budge when he used his thumb to unlock Kurt's phone."

"I've told Kurt a dozen times that his drinking was going to ruin him," Reese said sadly.

"Yeah, well, you weren't wrong. So, Trip called Donner, muffled his voice with some kind of harsh whisper and pretended to be Kurt. He told Donner that if he wanted to end the suit he needed to meet him at the overlook. It had to have sounded sketchy. I'm surprised Donner went. Still, he must've been pretty surprised when it was Trip that showed up."

"I'll bet."

"But Trip still claims he didn't kill him. He says he went out there meaning to. He even wore Kurt's boots and took Kurt's gun, planning to frame him, but he says he lost his nerve, dropped the gun, and ran. He says Donner pulled a gun on him, actually."

"What?"

"Yeah, it's confusing."

"When did Trip plant everything?"

"He says that after the overlook he went back to Jacob's and told him some story about wanting to spend the night. That things were too tense at home. While Jacob and Kurt were asleep he got up, hid the bomb supplies and put the boots back, and scattered the concrete bits he had saved in Kurt's closet. That's when he wedged some in the treads of the boots."

"Does the D.A. believe him? About not killing Donner?"

"Well they haven't charged Trip with Donner's murder yet, but Holt thinks it's just a matter of time. They found Kurt's missing gun in Trip's trunk when they searched his car. The gun he had at the overlook Saturday night was a different gun—one he took from his dad. Holt hasn't heard about the forensics yet, but he says that finding Kurt's gun hidden in Trip's trunk isn't good. He thinks that the way things are going, they'll probably add the murder charge by tomorrow at the latest."

"But there's still loose ends that don't make sense—the corpse in the drum and Holt getting beaten up—that wasn't Trip. Does he know how the D.A.'s office is treating it?"

Chloe shook her head. "They aren't saying. He thinks they're trying to be thorough, flesh it out before they charge Trip."

"What about Vettner-Drake and Banyon and all that? Is the D.A. looking at them?"

Chloe shrugged. "Holt told the police about our dealings with them, but beyond that it was all just conjecture. There's no proof that they were involved in anything. Just hints that suggested they could have been. And if they were involved, he says they're too careful to leave any useful trail behind. Holt doubts the police will get much further connecting those dots than he did."

"And if they don't clear up the corpse question?"

"Holt doesn't think it will keep them from charging Trip with Donner's murder. He says him having the murder weapon will trump the uncertainty. The prosecution will just argue the other unexplained incidents are unrelated. He says Trip's attorney can still argue that it's evidence that points to someone else being Donner's murderer, and try to generate some reasonable doubt, but that may be about it."

Somewhere not too far away, someone was burning leaves, the peaty aroma drifting into Reese's yard, reminding Chloe of campfires and roasted marshmallows. Their conversation halted momentarily as they watched Jack tackling Tyler as he tried to dodge him.

"Tyler liked going to church with you yesterday," Reese said, interrupting the silence. "Said it made him feel better."

"I get that. It makes me feel better too." She eyed Reese encouragingly. "Finding your place in the big scheme of things will do that."

Reese pursed his lips together. "It's not really my thing."

"It wasn't mine either."

Reese sniffed. "Well, maybe I'll take him next week, if he likes it so much. Can't hurt, right?"

"No," Chloe said, shaking her head. "Can't hurt. You should ask Emma too."

"Look, I know that on most scores I have no idea what a teenage girl is thinking, but on this one I'm pretty confident she won't be interested."

Chloe smiled. "Maybe. But ask anyway. You never know. And," she continued, raising her eyebrows knowingly, "the last thing you want to do is leave her out."

"True," Reese agreed. He leaned back in the chair and jerked his head at Chloe's laptop, open before her. "How's the article?"

"I'm wrapping it up now. It turned out pretty well, I think. My editor says—"

"Izzie? Your editor, right? And she's your best friend?"

Though the comments seemed a little like an eager student offering the teacher answers to a pop quiz, she appreciated the gesture. He wanted her to know he had been paying attention. That he cared.

"Yeah. She says it'll be in the March issue. Just in time for spring."

"Well that gives me time to tell everyone I know to be looking for my daughter's article."

She snorted good-naturedly. "Okay."

"You ready to get back to your life?"

"Yeah. It's time. Now that you're back and moving around…my poor dog is probably losing his mind."

"Bring him next time. Tyler would love it."

Next time. The thought was a good one. *Who would have ever thought there would be a next time?* But watching Jack and Tyler, and sitting here with Reese, drinking coffee as a troupe of bright orange leaves danced down onto the table, it felt right that there would be.

*****

By eight o'clock, Tyler was tucked in and snoring softly. The pizza boxes from dinner lay open on the coffee table, containing a single, lonely cheese slice abandoned and cold. Chloe had just come down from Tyler's room to sit on the couch beside Jack when the doorbell for the side porch rang.

Holt stood on the landing, his tie opened wide at the neck and hair rumpled from one too many passes through it.

"Hey."

"You look awful," she said as he dragged past her.

"I feel every bit of it. It's been a day," he said, making his way to the family room and dropping his briefcase beside him as he plopped down on the other couch facing Jack. Spying the pizza, he nodded inquiringly at the slice. Jack signaled he should take it, and he did, folding it in two and inhaling almost half in one bite.

"You want something more than that?" Chloe asked. "I can fix you something—I've got some chicken leftover from yesterday."

"Seriously? That would be great. I'm starved. Didn't get a chance to eat today."

"I thought you were grabbing something when you left here earlier?" Chloe called from the kitchen as she rummaged through the refrigerator.

"Planned on it," Holt replied, sinking back into the couch. "Stuff came up." He eyed Jack. "I'm sorry to barge in, really, but I wanted to update you guys in person."

"No problem. Not barging. According to Tyler, you're part of the family," Jack said.

Holt chuckled. "Gotta love that kid."

"So what's the word on Crutchfield?" Chloe asked from the kitchen.

"That's as good as done. The guy is too stupid and too mad to keep his mouth shut. He owned up to everything."

"Which was what exactly?" asked Jack, leaning forward.

Holt swallowed another bite. "Apparently his grand plan was to take Tyler to punish Reese, then go grab his own kids from his ex-wife. After that he was headed out to Oklahoma or some such place where he has a cousin. He says he was planning on dropping Tyler off in a Walmart parking lot somewhere along the way, but who knows if that's true."

"How did you find all that out?"

"The investigators brought me up to speed once they had a handle on what was going on. And he copped to the hospital note and thing with Emma at the antique mall."

"Were you right about the box on the porch?" Chloe asked, bringing a warmed plate of chicken and rice over to Holt.

Holt nodded, taking the plate out of her hands. "Oh, man, this smells good." He shoveled in a bite and kept talking. "It was a Coalsworth Chewing Tobacco packing box. Crutchfield chews the stuff constantly. His wife complained about it nonstop during the divorce proceedings. He figured one of us would remember and know he was sending us a message to back off, without being able to actually prove anything against him. Only we didn't notice because he ended up turning the box so the logo was on the bottom. Neither one of us ever saw it."

"He sounds like an idiot," Jack said.

"An idiot with a plan, though. Apparently he had been following the kids around for a couple weeks—driving to their schools, parking down the street and watching the house—looking for the right moment. He was following you, too," Holt said, nodding at Chloe. "Did you ever notice anyone following you?"

Chloe thought of the car running her off the road. "Yeah. I might've, now that I think about it." She shifted in her seat. "Did you see Trip?"

"Yeah, well, that's the thing I wanted to talk to you about."

"Did the forensics come back on the gun?" she asked.

"It's not that." He wiped his hands on his pants and set the plate on the coffee table. "So when I got home today, there was something waiting for me."

"What do you mean?"

He reached into the outer pocket of his leather briefcase and pulled out a generic, recordable DVD. "Somebody left this leaning against my door."

"Did you watch it?"

"Yeah. And that sent me right back to the investigators for another three hours. I just left there."

Jack leaned forward on his knees. "So what's on the DVD?"

Holt stood, moved towards the media console, and slipped the disc into the Blu-ray player. "I think it's better if you see it for yourself."

SEVENTY-TWO

It's night, the colors filling the screen with mostly muted versions of black, brown, and gray, though lit by a decent amount of what must be moonlight, amplified by the night mode of the camera of whatever cell phone was being used to record. The screen pans wide, resolving into a shaky view of what looks like a clearing, significantly obscured by heavy brush and tree trunks between the clearing and the person holding the camera. Two figures stand in the clearing. Furthest away, on the far side of the clearing but facing the camera, is someone who appears to be dressed in something dark. About ten feet closer to the camera is a second person, who has their back to the camera. The two people appear to be in some sort of standoff.

The person filming seems to be doing it from a hidden location, far enough away so that the conversation between the two in the clearing is indistinct, muffled. The camera wobbles, as the person recording inches forward, presumably to get a clearer shot. The lens finds a path through the branches and the picture resolves with new clarity.

It's the trailhead at Wilton Hollow Overlook.

Trip is the one dressed in black, his arm outstretched with a gun pointed towards the person opposite him, Phillip Donner. Though Donner's back is to the camera, something about his stance makes it clear he isn't scared. His hands rest on his hips, like a father angry with a petulant child, as Trip waves the gun in his direction, yelling something that sounds like, "You should have left her alone!"

This goes on for another half a minute, Trip's body language growing increasingly tense until finally he fires a shot in Donner's direction. The picture juggles chaotically as the person filming reacts suddenly, dropping to the ground. For a second or two, heavy breathing overtakes the audio. The deep browns and rust of the nearby ground cover fill the screen, the camera pointed down after the holder's knee-jerk reaction to the gunshot. Then the view swings upward again. Donner is still standing, and Trip is still pointing the gun at him. The shot must have gone wide. And now Trip is shaking violently, and Donner is bowed up, yelling at him to drop the gun. Donner reaches into his waistband and withdraws his own gun, pointing it at Trip, who drops his and takes off, charging into the brush in the direction of the main road.

Donner turns toward the overlook's edge, and the camera catches a side view of his face. First, he's smirking, then he's laughing, apparently amused by the turn of events. His laughter fades, and he pauses for several moments, looking over the cliff's edge, as if mulling something over. He tucks the weapon back in his waistband and turns to go.

His face fills with shock and the camera pans right quickly.

Claire Donner is standing in the center of the clearing. Trip's gun is no longer on the ground. It's in her hand. Donner's hands fly up, holding her off as he bellows, "Claire! Claire—don't!"

She fires, the first shot catching him in the side. He stumbles towards her, and she shoots again. This time it strikes him in the chest and Donner goes down.

She waits several feet away as he struggles to breathe. Finally she ventures towards him, until she is hovering over him. He has stopped moving. She raises the gun once more. She fires one last shot into his chest, then walks away. The camera follows her as she exits down the path leading to the parking lot.

The person filming doesn't check on Donner. Instead, the camera remains trained on Donner's body, lying in the dirt. The screen zooms in. Donner's face isn't visible, but the blood spreading and soaking the earth is. Donner is still. Very, very, still.

All goes black.

* * * * *

"Yeah," Holt said, leaning back into the couch again as both Jack and Chloe swiveled their gazes onto him. "Trip was telling the truth."

"And it was just left at your door?" Chloe asked, bewilderment flushing her face.

Holt nodded. "No note. No nothing. I watched it, made a copy, and took the original straight to the investigators. That's why no dinner," he said, smiling weakly. "The good news is that now Trip won't be charged with the murder, obviously."

"But, Claire Donner…I mean," Chloe pitched forward, "I thought you said you didn't find anything on her. Your private eye guy was looking at her, right?"

"Yeah, but, he had just started, really. Something could've easily been missed."

"Or not," Jack said, piping in. "Maybe there wasn't anything to find. What was her motive?"

Holt shrugged. "They picked her up about an hour ago. And that's all I know. For now, anyway."

"But the gun, in Trip's car?" Chloe pressed.

Holt held out his hands wide. "I don't know. But she could've easily planted it. She's had lots of time. Obviously she was there at the overlook. My guess is that she stumbled onto an opportunity and she took it. She would've known she could frame Trip if she needed to, and probably planted the weapon in preparation for that. Frankly, if this DVD hadn't landed in my lap, it probably would have worked."

"Which begs the bigger question," Jack said, voicing what they were all thinking. "Who recorded that?" he asked, pointing to the screen. "And why did they keep it quiet until now?"

SEVENTY-THREE

"Mr. Adams. We speak finally." Elise Banyon held the phone to her ear as she swiveled to face the panoramic glass window that made up one wall of her office.

"Mmm. Although it's not like we haven't communicated. I'm sure you know I got your message. Though I was surprised it wasn't delivered by a better class of thug. Plaid shirt didn't exactly scream college graduate."

"Sorry?"

"I doubt you are. But it isn't why I called."

"Do tell," she replied.

"I got a DVD a few days ago."

"Netflix?"

Holt snorted. "Not exactly. But it was a pretty good show."

"I wouldn't know."

"Now see, I just don't believe you," Holt said.

"Mr. Adams, why are you calling me?"

"The DVD was of Phillip Donner's killing. It just showed up on my doorstep, like a pretty little present. Any idea how it got there?"

"Like I told the Franklin police when they contacted me yesterday, I have no idea. Thank you for that, by the way. I thought you had come to the belief that my office and my client were not involved in the unfortunate events surrounding Mr. Donner."

"Well, that DVD came from somewhere, and they thought it would be a good idea to talk to the people I've had contact with during our investigation. And so your name popped up. They were especially interested in your compulsory car ride with Chloe."

"That's not how I remember it," Banyon told him.

"I'm sure it's not. So the DVD—it's quite a show. I mean, the only way I figure somebody would have been able to be at the right place at the right time like that is if they were already following Donner and just happened to think something was going down, and just happened to be recording when Claire Donner shot him."

"If you say so."

"I was kinda hoping *you'd* say so."

Banyon chuckled mirthlessly. "I doubt anyone who played any part in that would own up to it."

"Yeah, probably not. And I think you and I both know there won't be any tracing that DVD back to whoever left it."

"Probably not," she agreed.

"But what I can't figure out is, why? I mean, why would whoever filmed that video choose to reveal it now?"

"Maybe whoever left it didn't want a seventeen-year-old boy to be charged with a murder they knew he didn't commit."

"Naaahh," Holt sang. "Cause I'm pretty convinced that whoever it was, they don't really care who is charged, as long as it's not them."

"Well, they must have had their reasons," she said.

"I'm thinking they were business reasons. Of a sort. See, I think they needed Claire Donner to go down for the murder she committed."

"Needed?"

"Claire Donner's been talking ever since they picked her up, probably hoping to cut a deal that avoids her ending up with a needle in the arm. Turns out she and Donner's company accountant, Jernigan, were having an affair. She was a trophy wife, tired of Donner's multiple affairs, with a prenup hanging around her neck like a millstone. Jernigan had access to the money. They think he had been submitting fake bills to the company for over two years, then paying them, then socking the money away for a sunny day on a Jamaican beach with Claire Donner. Apparently she followed Donner that night, thinking she would catch him in yet another affair and finally have what she needed to invalidate the prenup. Instead she got rid of him in another, less-contested way."

"You are certainly privy to a lot of inside information on this investigation."

"It's not all that inside. She's cutting a deal and the whole story will be in the press by tomorrow. But that isn't really what I wanted to talk about."

"And what did you really want to talk about?" she asked, her tone making it clear that she, in point of fact, was not interested in knowing.

"The thing is—Claire and Jernigan's little retirement program caused a significant loss of cash flow that helped drive Donner's company into the ground. Her little retirement plan was part of what destroyed her husband's company. And even though Claire Donner managed to squirrel away a huge chunk of cash by most standards, lo and behold, she has no idea where it is. Apparently, the money disappeared with Jernigan, who apparently got nervous and had already high-tailed it out of Dodge before her arrest. So now, Claire Donner has nothing, Donner's company defaults on all its debts, and the lenders, well, they'll never see a penny now."

"That must be terribly frustrating for the people Donner owed money to."

"I would imagine. I would also imagine that those people, if they had caught onto what was happening in time, would not have wanted to see Claire Donner skate off into the sunset with their millions and her new beau, and live happily ever after. Although, let's be honest—you've probably seen Jernigan. I don't think anybody believes that relationship would've lasted past him carrying her bags out of the St. Kitts airport."

"It's a nice little theory, Mr. Adams. Want to hear mine?"

"That is why I called."

"My theory is that if your theory is correct, whoever left that DVD would not care to be trading theories."

Holt snorted.

"So are we done here, Mr. Adams?"

"Yeah. We're done."

"No. I mean *are we done here?*"

"If you're asking whether you'll be hearing from me again—you and I both know that I know something pretty screwy is going on here, even if I can't prove it, and frankly, don't even truly know what it is. But I do know it's not related to my client and, as it turns out, it's apparently not related to Donner's murder. So as long as I, and none of the people I care about, get any more visits from your associates, yeah, we're done here. I called because I didn't want there to be any confusion about future repercussions, as in, how quickly the police will come knocking on your door, should there be any further shenanigans."

"Well, I assure you that your concerns are entirely misplaced. I don't know anything about any shenanigans, and I feel certain that, you being the smart officer of the court that you are, your future will be entirely shenanigan-free. I wish you good luck with your theories, and best wishes for a speedy recovery from your recent…injuries. Goodbye, Mr. Adams."

*****

"So you're sure Adams is not a threat?" The father in New Jersey had taken her call himself, no longer forcing Banyon to deal with his idiot son. She was grateful.

"I'm sure. For all his posturing, I think the real reason he called was to make sure I knew that he wouldn't be digging in our business anymore, and to call the hounds off."

"You believe him?" he asked.

"Yes. He has no reason to push anymore. At this point, it's up to law enforcement to do the digging. And we both know they won't find any connections. The best they will do is find out the same information Adams found out, which leads to nothing. Nothing provable anyway."

"I'm still concerned about Bellamy."

"Bellamy hasn't worked for you in years. They asked you their questions last week and you satisfied them. They've dropped it. He's been working down here in his own agency for some time now, and Vettner-Drake has paid him off the books. In cash. There is no trail to find. They won't connect him to you even if they look. All they'll find is the evidence we've planted in his office suggesting that he was enforcing collection on some huge gambling debts Donner had racked up. I'm telling you—it's fine," she insisted.

"Donner was an idiot to take him out. He had to know we would eventually come after him—if his wife hadn't gotten to him first."

"I suspect he panicked, with that last real estate repurchase payment being so overdue. He knew the rules—either you repay in cash, or you pay the price another way. My guess is that when Drake had Bellamy go meet Donner to collect, they got into it. Either Donner couldn't or wouldn't pay. Bellamy probably tried to offer a bit of physical incentive, and somehow Donner got the better of him. Pretty smart, actually, sending Bellamy's cell phone on a trip to Florida like he did. Probably stuck it on a semi and let it go. Gave some credence to his story that he paid Bellamy our money and that Bellamy must have taken off with the cash if he didn't deliver it to us. It bought Donner a little bit of time, anyway."

"Update me on Claire Donner," he said.

"My people tell me that from what we can find, it looks like she didn't have a clue that Donner had been creatively financing his project with you or that there was anybody out there that would be looking for the cash. The accountant did, obviously, but he apparently never shared that information with her. It took us longer than I would've liked to uncover what she and the accountant were doing, but, once we did, he had already taken off. We confronted her, led her to believe Donner's debts were gambling debts, and gave her one day to pay us back with what they had taken. Instead, she bought an airline ticket.

"So," she continued, "that forced our hand. We made good on our threats and turned the video over to Adams. The accountant did make it to Jacksonville before we caught up to him. He had what we believe was most, if not all, of the money—three million in an offshore account. We had him make an electronic transfer before we, well…handled him."

"Yeah. I saw the numbers. It's not everything Donner owed."

"Well, you're not going to get it all back. It was a bad investment," she told him candidly.

"And you're sure Claire Donner won't talk?"

"We got a message to her right before they picked her up that she better keep her mouth shut if she didn't want something worse than prison to happen."

"And they can't trace the video back to us?"

"No. It was sheer luck that we got it at all. We were only following Donner because at the time we had started to wonder if he was conspiring with Bellamy."

He sniffed loudly. "My son thinks you've left us exposed by getting her arrested instead of permanently eliminating the threat. Plus, she made a conscious decision to ignore the debt and keep the money for herself. We don't normally tolerate that. I'm not sure I like the precedent it sets for our other clients."

"First, as I explained to your son, she isn't a threat. Like I said, she doesn't know anything that would point the authorities to us. And, think about how would it have looked if she *and* the accountant had both disappeared? Without her around to take the blame for shooting Donner and provide an explanation as to why, the police would have had two unexplained murders and two unexplained disappearances on their hands. The intensity of their investigation would have skyrocketed exponentially. I would not want you to have to weather that kind of scrutiny. I have a lot of faith in our precautions, but nothing is one hundred percent secure. Better not to test it."

Banyon continued, hardly taking a breath. "Right now, the chance of them connecting Bellamy to you on this is slim to none. With the gambling angle, they won't have a reason to think the story goes beyond that. But, if we had imposed a more severe sanction for her choice to run off with your money, that would have increased your risk of exposure to unacceptable levels in my opinion. Hence the DVD. It keeps you out of the line of fire, yet still sends a clear message to your clients that you do not tolerate failures to repay. The people that do business with you will know what happened. They won't be able to prove anything, but they will know. Your reputation for strict enforcement of your clients' obligations will remain intact."

"I still think she got off easy."

"You know," Banyon started ominously, "people die every day in prison. It is an unfortunate reality in our penal system. And so often it is impossible to determine who was the culprit or why they acted. It just…happens. It's rarely ever traced back to anyone, or any reason, outside those walls. At least that's been my experience."

"So," he said, clearly mulling over the import of her comment, "it's possible that Mrs. Donner might end up paying the standard price for her theft from us after all."

"Yes," she answered menacingly. "I would say that outcome is a *distinct* possibility."

SEVENTY-FOUR

The chilled air rippled Chloe's hair as she stood in Reese's front yard, Emma hugging her neck. A cold snap had passed through overnight, signaling the season's further dip into late autumn. Chloe had failed to slip a jacket on before walking out of the house, and now a shiver ran down her spine as she pulled away from the teen.

"I wish you didn't have to go," Emma bemoaned. "I liked not being outnumbered. And now who am I going to talk to?"

"You can call me anytime. I mean it," Chloe added, squeezing Emma's shoulder. "Or try your dad, even. You might be surprised."

"We'll see," Emma hedged. But Chloe had spotted her allowing Reese to hug her over pancakes at breakfast this morning and thought the girl's frostiness towards her dad might finally be melting. It was a good sign.

"Aww, don't leave," Tyler whined, grabbing Jack around the waist. "Dad's broken and now nobody's gonna throw the ball with me."

"I am not broken!" Reese declared scathingly. "I can still handle you," he said, playfully pulling Tyler off Jack and tickling him as Tyler squirmed away.

"How about," Jack said, reaching for Tyler and pulling him back, "you take it easy with your dad for just a little bit longer. He's not broken, but he's not one hundred percent yet."

Reese nodded in grateful agreement behind Tyler's back.

"And I'll still take you on, Tyler," Holt chimed in, as he leaned casually against the hood of Chloe's car, his suit pressed and wingtips shined. The sharp morning sun glinted off his Rolex as he ran a hand through his perfect, slicked back hair. Other than the dark bruises beginning to yellow around his eye and cheekbone, all evidence of the harried Holt of the last few days was gone.

"Yeah!" Tyler shouted as he darted past Holt, who high-fived him as he continued on around the car, jumping into the driver's seat and pretending to steer.

"So we'll see you at Thanksgiving, right?" Reese asked, stepping up to Chloe.

"Thanksgiving," Chloe said, hugging him. "I'll bring the sweet potato pie."

"Just bring you." Reese locked eyes with Chloe, a faint wetness shimmering in the corners of his.

Moved by his genuine affection, she smiled and squeezed his arm before moving towards the car.

"Time to go buddy," Jack told Tyler, who was still inside the car pressing buttons.

As Jack scooted Tyler out of the car, Holt pushed off the hood, coming around to the passenger side as Chloe reached the door. When she opened it, he grabbed the door at its top, pulling it the rest of the way and holding it for her. "So…it's been a pretty wild ride," he said.

Chloe chuckled, nodding. "Yeah, you could say that. Not what I was expecting out of this little family reunion."

"You made a difference here, you know," he said, his voice soft, his gaze flashing to Reese and the kids. "They're different because you came."

"Me too," she replied, smiling. Leaning in, she hugged him with one arm. "We'll see you at Thanksgiving?"

"Wouldn't miss it," he answered as she ducked inside. He shut the door after her, then leaned down, extending his hand through the window to Jack, who shook it.

"Thanks for everything you did, looking out for her," Jack said.

Holt tipped his head. "Thanks for not punching me in the throat."

Jack laughed amicably, nodding his head as he slowly backed down the drive and into the road. Tyler jogged to keep up, stopping at the street but continuing to wave as the car rolled to the stop sign, paused, then turned, heading for Atlanta as Holt and Chloe's family disappeared from view.

*****

"How you doin' over there?"

Jack reached over to squeeze Chloe's hand as they cruised along I-24 at seventy miles an hour, about two hours still to go before they reached Atlanta. "You've been awfully quiet."

"I guess I'm a little lost in my thoughts," she replied as she stared out her window. In the distance, crisp blue skies with puffy clouds hovered over the hills surrounding Chattanooga. "I didn't even know those people two weeks ago. And now," she sighed, "I'm really gonna miss them. I forgot what it's like…having a family."

"Well, you've got forever to get used to it again," he said, patting her leg.

"Yeah," she agreed warmly, taking the last swig of coffee from the travel mug Reese had lent her. "Uh-oh, I'm out," she announced, shaking it tellingly. "Hey, I think a sign back there said there's a Starbucks at the next exit. Could we make a quick stop and grab another? Last night's pizza and zombie-shooting fest with the kids is really kicking my butt."

Jack laughed. "Told you you should have gone to bed."

"Yeah, yeah. Jack always knows best."

"Just so long as you've figured that out."

She flicked him on the shoulder as he took the off-ramp. The Starbucks was about a hundred yards down on the right.

"Popular place," he noted as he pulled into the drive-thru lane, the last of a dozen waiting cars.

"I'll just run inside instead," she said, hopping out. "Park over there," she said tilting her head toward several open spots, "and I'll be right back."

As she walked into the building, Jack navigated into one of the spots and parked. Looking in the rearview mirror, he could see her through the glass, patiently waiting behind another customer for her turn at the register.

He reached into his pocket and extracted a small blue velvet box. His nerves rattled just holding it, and he took a deep breath to calm his restless stomach. "Point a gun at me and I'm all ice and steel," he muttered to himself, "but ask a girl to marry me…"

He opened the lid to reveal a startlingly brilliant white solitaire in an antique platinum setting. Scrolls of the precious metal surrounded the stone like ivy on a trellis. The clerk in the antique jewelry shop on Main Street where he had bought it yesterday said it was from the 1930s. A perfect ring for someone like Chloe, who relished eclectic, vintage pieces.

He had been looking for something like it for months. And then, yesterday, there it was. He went to the shop on a whim, just in case, thinking how special it would be to her if the ring came from that place, where so many wrong things were finally righted. He had taken finding the ring as a sign. He had been waiting for the right moment for so long it seemed. Much too long.

"Just hold on till tomorrow night," he told himself, thinking of the grand plan he had concocted and already set in motion. He grinned at the thought of her reaction, the joy on her face, jumping into his arms—

Bam, bam, bam!

Shock coursed through him as he jerked up to see Chloe standing behind the car, banging on the trunk, laughing. In one smooth motion he snapped the box shut and slid it back into his pocket as she came around.

"You jumped, like, ten feet," she said, grinning as she slid in and latched her seatbelt.

"Yeah, you're hilarious," he said, his heart thumping wildly in his chest. He took another deep breath. "Keep laughing, kiddo. Payback's coming."

"Not a chance," she said, leaning over to kiss him. "I know all your moves."

"We'll see," he said, grinning as he threw the car in reverse. "We'll see."

FRANKLIN, TENNESSEE

As you could probably tell from the book, I LOVE this place. I grew up in this town before it was hip; before it was a "must-see" destination. In my day it was a little Civil War town on the outskirts of Nashville, and we had to drive about twenty-five minutes just to get to a working theater. It was a great place for a childhood, and though I ended up settling elsewhere, my heart still belongs to Franklin. So what better place to set my second novel than this charming little piece of Americana?

Many of the places and businesses in the book are figments of my imagination. Among other things, some of the courts, judges, attorneys, studios, Harrison County, the trailer park, and the Tri-County officials and departments are completely made up and not based on anyone or anything that actually exists. I have also taken liberties with some of the geography, historical sites, distances, directions and hours (docket times and operating hours, etc.).

However, some of the named establishments in the book are very real and you should definitely take a trip to Franklin and visit them when you do. Support them. Shop local. I promise the town is even lovelier than described.

The festivals I mentioned are real. My favorite is Dickens of a Christmas. It is well worth the effort to go—you have never seen anything like an entire street full of costumed people reenacting the song and dance number from *A Christmas Carol* while you sip hot cider and snack on roasted chestnuts.

Eat at Puckett's, shop at The Factory, take the ghost tour, check out the plethora of antique stores, get coffee at Merridee's, and browse Landmark Booksellers. Visit Carnton Plantation. Although the nearby Halloween hay bale maze was just wishful hoping on my part, the plantation tours (though I took some liberty with the date and times of the Halloween tours—you'll need to check beforehand) and stories are genuine, and well worth your time. And definitely, *definitely,* visit Philanthropy—a real live, beautiful shop on Main Street that supports charitable business endeavors all over the world. While you're there, pen a prayer onto one of their tags and hang it on the prayer wall. Then take a prayer from the wall, commit yourself to lifting it up, and bless someone else's life.

TO THE READERS

I hope you enjoyed this latest installment in the Unintended Series. If you did, please consider leaving a positive review for UNINTENDED WITNESS on Amazon.com, Goodreads.com, Bookbub.com and the like. Good reviews are essential to getting a book out there and I would be very grateful for yours. If you want to read more CleanCaptivatingFiction by D.L. Wood, please take a moment to leave a review. I thank you in advance for taking the time to submit it.

Please also consider:

--Visiting my webpage and subscribing to my newsletter at www.dlwoodonline.com. When you subscribe, you'll receive a FREE download of my award-winning short story, *Blood from a Turnip*.

--Liking and sharing my Facebook page at @dlwoodonline.

--Following my twitter account at @dlwoodonline.

If you haven't read the first book in the series, UNINTENDED TARGET, I highly recommend that you go back and read the story that led to UNINTENDED WITNESS. It's a thrilling tale of suspense as an unsuspecting Chloe is hunted by a murderous conspiracy after her computer-hacking brother makes her the only link to stolen information the killers are desperate to recover. You'll also learn why she is so close to Jack, and why that wasn't always the case…Available now on Amazon.

COMING SOON FROM D.L. WOOD

Want to know what the next thrilling release from D.L. Wood will be? Get the announcement when it happens by subscribing to her newsletter at www.dlwoodonline.com. We promise not to spam you or share your information and you can unsubscribe at any time.

BOOK CLUBS AND EVENTS

If you are interested in having D.L. Wood at your book club or event, please contact her for scheduling information at dlwood@dlwoodonline.com.

If you like Christian thrillers, you might also like . . .

The Titus Ray Thriller Series

by Luana Ehrlich

I'd like to recommend another author who writes Christian fiction in the mystery/suspense/thriller genre. Her name is Luana Ehrlich, and she writes the Titus Ray Thriller Series, which features CIA covert operative Titus Ray who is brought to faith in Christ by a group of Iranian Christians after a botched mission in Tehran, Iran.

Luana is an award-winning author, minister's wife, and former missionary with a passion for spy thrillers and mystery novels. You can read more about Luana on her website LuanaEhrlich.com.

You can find Titus Ray Thrillers on Amazon, including *One Step Back*, the prequel to the series.

Also, if you enjoy contemporary Christian music. . . .

The David Freeman that visited Tucker Studios in the book is a talented contemporary Christian music artist and worship leader. You can check out his music on iTunes, Spotify and the like, or click the link for his website.

IT'S HARD TO FORGIVE

In Unintended Witness, Chloe struggles with the issue of forgiveness. It is something we all struggle with from time to time and can be especially hard when we have been terribly hurt by the person at issue. Chloe wrestles with the contrast between God's instruction to Christians to forgive and the human desire to refuse to do so because it feels wrong to us to "let the other person off the hook." It is something she is learning how to do as a new Christian, but frankly, it can be difficult no matter how long you have been following Christ. In the end, when we choose to forgive, is it the forgiver that finds peace. As for me, peace is something I crave. Fortunately it is something God promises.

Peace of the heart is something Jesus Christ offers to those who surrender their hearts and lives to him. It is the knowledge of Him and what eternity holds for me that gives me peace and hope when nothing else can.

If you are searching for peace and hope, please consider that God himself extends an invitation to you to know both by knowing Him through his son, Jesus Christ. For more information, please visit my website at dlwoodonline.com and click on the section entitled "FIND HOPE."

God Bless.

ABOUT THE AUTHOR

D.L. Wood is an award-winning author, attorney and worship leader who writes CleanCaptivatingFiction™ that entertains and uplifts. She loves the art of storytelling, particularly any story involving suspense or the epic struggle of good versus evil. In her faith-laced suspense novels, Wood tries to give readers the same thing she wants in the novels she reads: a "can't-put-it-down-stay-up-till-3am-story" that stays clean without sacrificing an iota of quality, believability or adrenaline.

If she isn't writing, you'll either catch her practicing behind the keys or curled up with a cup of tea and her Westies, bingeing on the latest Sherlock series. Speaking of which, if you have a BBC mystery/detective series to recommend, please email her because she has nearly exhausted the ones she knows about. She loves to hear from readers and you can reach her at dlwood@dlwoodonline.com. D.L. lives in North Alabama with her husband, twin daughters, and Westies, Frodo and Dobby.

11435301R00214

Made in the USA
Lexington, KY
11 October 2018